Coppice & Brake

A Dark Fiction Anthology

edited by Rachel A. Brune

CRONE
GIRLS
press

Seaside, California

Published in the USA by Crone Girls Press
Visit our website at: www.cronegirlspress.com.

Coppice & Brake © 2020 Crone Girls Press

ISBN: 978-1-952388-00-2
ISBN (eBook): 978-1-952388-01-9

Cover design by James, GoOnWrite.com
Interior Design and Typesetting by eSpec Publishing Services

Interior accent images - www.fotolia.com
Vector raven or crow in grunge style and Vector silhouettes of ravens, crows, other birds © LHF Graphics

For Dad, who told me to go for the gold
but probably didn't mean start an indie horror publishing press...

 # More From
Crone Girls Press

Anthologies
Stories We Tell After Midnight, Vol. 1
Coppice & Brake

Want to get the latest news about our newest releases?

Sign up for our newsletter at http://eepurl.com/gPT5s1, join our Facebook group at https://www.facebook.com/groups/cronegirls, or follow us on Twitter at https://twitter.com/CroneGirlsPress!

And now … thank you, fiends. We so hope you enjoyed your stay with us. If the sights you have seen and the dreams you have escaped stay with you after losing these pages, wouldn't you do us the favor of warning other of what they might encounter, should they happen to open these covers?

Share your thoughts, whether they be the careful, measured words of the diligent reader, or the sobbing cry from the asylum, on Goodreads or Amazon.

And, thank you … *we'll be seeing you soon.*

 TABLE OF CONTENTS

DOG'S BLOOD TRAIL

Gabrielle Bleu

I T HAD BEEN AN ACCIDENT. HE WOULD SAY THAT IT HAD BEEN AN accident. The father stood alone in his kitchen, trembling with what he had done, the walls of his white stucco house closing in around him. The screaming and crying had gone on for hours, and the man had only wanted some quiet. He had shaken his baby. His boy had quieted then, gone blue about the face. He was still wrapped in his blue-checked blanket, arms and legs and lungs still.

The man, with his wife arriving home soon, panicked. He could not let her know what he had done, let her see the way the boy lay still in his arms. The man hurried out of the white stucco house, to the alley behind. Gently, like he was laying him down in his crib, he lowered his son into the plastic bin. To stall. A stopgap. He would come back for his boy and think of a better plan. Police were called, a break-in, a disappearance. Mother and father forgot to bring the dog in from the rain outside amidst the flashing red and blue lights. The dog was left alone, as the wife went weeping to her room, and the man stayed sitting in his kitchen, staring at his hands. The squad cars left, and the dog slipped his chain.

The dog got into the trash.
The dog found the body.
The dog swallowed up the boy.
The boy and the dog were the dogandtheboy.
The two entities had tangled into one, and barking, crying, sobbing, crept back towards the house to get out of the rain. It was slow going, dragging too many pairs of limbs, tiny fingers catching in claws, a

wailing mouth unused to the teeth biting its own tongues. The baby's weak body and blurry vision stretched and warped around the dog's tendons and eyes. Both brains remembered the warmth of the white stucco house, and both dimly hoped it would hurt less inside.

When the chimerical face of his dog and his boy pushed through the dog door into the kitchen, the man shrieked, a jagged sound welling up from beneath his ribs. The boy and the dog surged towards him, to press a wet nose and warped flesh to the man's leg. He recoiled, jerking back in his chair. His wife continued to weep in the other room, too distraught to notice the noises he made, his scream so much like her cries. The low gurgling of the baby and the dog was barely loud enough for the man to hear.

There was no sensibility, like there had been with the Minotaur, a sturdy head upon sturdy shoulders; limbs organized in a human way. The son and dog were a jumbled mass of flesh. Beneath the dog's head, the baby's face had erupted out of the furred torso, pushing past the rib cage. Kicking infant's legs had cracked and broken their way through the dog's hipbones, and pin-wheeled madly above the dog's back. The baby and the dog moaned and growled and whined, and the father shivered out of reach.

They would not believe it had been an accident, the man knew, if they saw what stood on his clean linoleum floors.

Without a better plan, always without a better plan, the father led his beast into the hollow beneath the white stucco house. It was little more than an unfinished basement, dirt and crawl space and stairs going up. What mattered was that it had a door, and one that could be locked. The father kept the key and continued to tell his wife a story, a lie, while listening to the sounds that came up from underneath. He had loved his boy. But he also loved his wife. He loved his white stucco house. He loved his life within it.

The mother tried to live around her grief, and the father lived always aware of the rustling in the floorboards. In this limbo, his wife above, the dogchild beneath, he kept vigil. They had more children, twins. They were quieter, staring and silent. The father wondered if they knew about their sibling trapped beneath the earth. Knew what noise had cost him. Years went past with nothing more than a wet snuffling underground. The father said that it was only nightmares the children were having. Nothing was underneath their beds, no monsters lurking as they slept.

His wife was sometimes unsuccessful in avoiding grief, and in those moments, she stared out windows and through open doorways. Recently, she had started staring at the floors, and the father had started to worry. His children asked for a puppy.

The rustling beneath the floors became great groanings and sighs. Too loud, as the child chimera languished in the basement. The father worried that his staring wife and silent children would discover what trembled and whined beneath their house. The stucco walls should have been a home for his son, his first-born. Instead the man had abandoned his child to the foundations.

The noise at last was too much to bear.

So, he waited, until the mother and twins had gone out. He took his straight razor and went into the basement, where the chimera had grown large. The twisted mound of its belly dragged along the ground as its double spines pressed against the base of the foundations above. The father hoped his son could not see the gleaming blade in the dark.

It was much different work than shaving, this surgery. As soon as he began the first incision, the dog squirmed, and the boy squalled. The father continued to cut, the dirt beneath him turning to mud with the dog's blood, with his son's blood. At last he cut his boy free, and the father took him up in his arms. The father howled.

In succeeding in separating the boy from the dog, he had also failed. The boy had come away without skin, the form freed, but with a price. The bloody mess of a child continued to shriek. The dog, trailing great, loose flaps of skin from its body, wheezed and spasmed at the father's feet. It died in silence. A good dog.

The father cradled his still bleeding, still crying boy in his arms, and bore him from the hole beneath the house.

In the yard behind the house, where the monstrosity had first taken form, there was a shed. The father kept his tools there, wedding presents he had never used. Among them there was a hand axe. The man took it in one hand, while cradling his child in the other. He left the yard and the house behind.

The white stucco house sat on the edge of a forest, and the forest crept down to the ocean. The father ran with his boy to the tree line and laid his bloody charge down among the roots of an ancient oak. Then the man took his axe and began to work. Tree after tree the father felled, and lashed their trunks together, a fearsome shamble of a raft. He took his screaming son, who bled still, years and years of two bodies' worth of stale blood, and set out to sea.

He thought there, on the open water, the two of them would be safe. The boy's cries would draw no attention out in the ocean; no one would find the sound or its source. No one around to look upon his bloody form, to know the father's crimes.

His dog-freed boy would not stop bleeding, and his blood overran the ramshackle raft, leaking into the saltwater that carried them. The man feared someone would see the trail leading to his crime. Schooners, fishing boats, yachts without worry, would see the red of the water, and find him, converge on him and his boy. No one saw, and no one came, but the blood would not stop. It threatened to capsize the vessel, so the father set the son down and bailed. He cradled the blood in his cracked and shaking hands to throw it overboard.

The ship did not sink, but the bloody trail was followed. Not by boats, nor police, nor the wails of his wife. Instead the beasts that churned the waters beneath his boat began to surface, drawn by the cries and the blood. Huge oarfish threw their heads and long bodies on the deck. Eels squirmed up between the planking. Sharks nudged the boat with their great, blunt heads. Scores of fish threw themselves on to the ship to die as they tried to reach the source of the chimera blood. The father beat them back with the crude oars, with the splintering mast, with his own bare fists. He howled all the while, louder than even his suffering, bloody son. The sound of the beasts throwing themselves against the ship grew louder and louder.

He fed his darling bloody boy to the sharks. Soon after, himself.

During the daylight hours Gabrielle Bleu lifts mammoth tusks and whale ribs for a living. At night, she moonlights as a writer, and also as a werewolf. Her work has appeared in the Story Seed Vault and the Arcanist. Follow her on twitter @BeteMonstrueuse for her thoughts about monsters, and find more of her work at gabriellebleu.com.

RAFF AND THE SCISSOR-FINGER

R.K. Duncan

RAFF LUTHIER WASN'T LAZY, NOT REALLY, BUT HE LOVED WANDERING into the woods and finding new trees and secret places more than he liked working in his father's workshop that always smelled of wax and sawdust. He was no good at making instruments, not like his father. John Luthier's work was known wide, and players sent to Father from as far south as the capital at Norcrest for his lutes and fiddles.

Raff had been trying to shape the wood for the soundbox of a new fiddle; not an order, just a practice piece for himself, but each time he tried to carve a gentle curve, his chisel slipped through and scarred the wood and ruined it. He was so clumsy, with his useless fingers that would not do as he ordered them. Whenever he picked up a chisel or a plane, it felt like his hands belonged to someone else, a stupider, slower boy who shamed himself and his family. His father had let him begin to work without guiding his hands three months ago, and still Raff was no better.

Today, he had thrown down tools and ruined wood after a third failure, and Father had come to see what was the matter, and he had told Raff not to mind it, that the trick of it would come with practice, but Raff had marked how his father was so careful to speak slow and calm and pleasantly, and known how angry he was at the waste, at the noise disturbing his important work, at Raff's own uselessness.

So Raff had run out into the woods instead of staying there and weeping and throwing a tantrum like he was still a baby. It was cool under the trees, but the wind was blunted, and very soon he found a path that he had never found before, winding deep into the forest on a clear track under an arched roof of leaves that turned the sunlight green as his imagination of the sea.

Raff walked slowly, pausing to look at how the light revealed a maze of dazzling complexity in the bark of one wizened tree and then going on a few paces to see some new marvel. The path he walked was so smooth and clear of undergrowth, and its sides so thick with briar and fern and twisted roots, that it felt half like the old holloway that father said had been a road since the old Gallian empire, and Raff could imagine that he was on a secret road into fairyland.

He became so lost in the pretty little things that littered the trunks and the brush around him that he did not notice the darkness until the light turned grey and grew so dim he could barely see beyond a single rank of trees at either side. When he looked up, the leaves were lost in black, more like night than cloud, but that was nonsense. He hadn't been in woods that long.

He heard a scraping sound somewhere behind him, like his father drawing a chisel blade across a whetstone. The path there seemed darker and more twisted than he remembered. He went on. The sun would come out in another moment, and then he would know the way and cut through the underbrush for home.

The trees were strange in this part of the forest, black and twisted, with barely any leaves, as if it were winter, or they had all been burned and split by thunderbolts. Even without the canopy above, it was still dark, with only a directionless grey light to guide him. He tried to imagine that he was a fairy finder, walking boldly into the dark forest to rescue a stolen child and send the monsters back into the shadows of the West.

The path twisted tighter, so that he could see less and less ahead, and then suddenly he came to a dead end. In front of him, the trees were a wall, twisted together and gnarled and dead from each one strangling the others with root and branch and fighting for sun in the shade of their dead leaves. He heard the sharpening slide again, close behind him now, and he very much wanted to scream, but there was no one who would help him there to hear, and he was sure whatever was there would only come quicker and be hungrier if he did that.

Raff turned. There was something in the road. It was tall, maybe taller than a tall man if it had stood straight instead of being hunched and gnarled like the dead trees. In its face were set eyes deep as drill holes and a mouth like a ragged saw-cut and barely a nose. It was black, and its arms and legs were thin, with bulging joints like the growths on gnarled trunks. It hid its hands behind itself. Raff thought it might be smiling.

It — the fairy, what else could it be? — breathed in like a whisper of wind through leaves and over sharp edges, and its voice was deep and grinding and gleeful.

"Do you want to go home, Little Boy?"

Raff felt very small, but he had to answer. He did not think that a fairy could hurt him very badly if he made no mistakes but in stories, they were always tricking people into saying the wrong thing, so that they would be in the fairy's power. He knew he had to say something; being rude to a fairy was terribly dangerous in all the tales.

"I do, yes."

He would tell the truth, but not give the fairy his name or talk too much and say something that would give it the power to hurt him, or trap him in the forest for a year, or take him away to fairyland forever.

"Shake my hand, Little Boy, and I can set you on the path back to your home."

Raff's heart was in his throat hearing the offer and then fearing what the fairy really meant. He knew a fairy would not go back on a promise, but that had not really been a promise, had it? The fairy only said it could send him home, not that it would, and he did not think he wanted to shake its hand. Why was it hiding its arms behind its back?

"Do you promise to take me home?"

The fairy drew itself up tall and nodded its head up and down, slow and exaggerated. "I swear that after you shake my hand, I will set you down in sight of your home at once."

Raff put his hands out in front of him.

"Let me see your hands first. That's fair."

The fairy frowned with that saw-cut mouth like a black slash into deep night, but then it laughed like dead leaves in a windstorm.

"Alright, Boy. Take a look!"

The laugh rose to a cackle as the fairy thrust its hands out. At the end of its black arms like twisted branches, each finger was a silver scissor blade. It laughed and laughed until it must choke soon.

Raff snapped his hands back behind himself and shouted.

"No! No, I won't!"

He had no space left to think of being mannerly, his head was so filled up with fear of the sharp silver scissors.

The scissor-finger shouted back in a voice as big as the forest.

"If you won't be my friend and shake my hand, I made no oath to take you home. You can stay here and learn to be a nicer boy."

It stretched its arms out and stood up taller than a tall man, and cut and cut at the dead trees all around with a snick and a slither of metal on wood. Branches and trunks fell down with a boom and a rattle, and Raff was trapped tight in a wooden cage, too heavy to move, too tight to stand up in, with no hole bigger than his fist to slip through.

"I'll come back again later, Little Boy, and we'll see if you're ready to be better friends."

It was gone into shadow and bare branches, and the sound of scissors sliding against each other faded slowly.

Raff examined every branch and beam of his cage. There was nothing else to look at. The cuts were so smooth. Those silver scissors must be sharper than his father's best knives and chisels.

He was thirsty. He wondered how long he had been in the woods, and whether he still was, or if he was already away in the West, and if he was, whether drinking anything would trap him there forever.

He couldn't tell how much time was passing in the dark. He might have fallen asleep, but the sound of scissors slid in from the woods just often enough to keep him sweating coldly and working to breathe slower.

The fairy came back once to look at him, but Raff lay still with his eyes shut and pretended to sleep, and it went away after a little while.

Raff was hungry. He had gone over every inch of the cage more than enough to know he couldn't move it or squeeze through. Maybe he should say yes when the scissor-finger came again. His fingers weren't worth much, after all, not against the fear that would keep Father from work. He always hated it when Raff was gone without a word, and said he got no work done while he was worrying. What else could Raff do, except starve here and leave Father wondering forever? Did he have anything to offer the fairy that was worth less than his hands? How much was a hand worth anyway, when it was too clumsy to do the work his father made so easy, when it would never bring a smile of honest praise to his father's face?

The next time the scissor-finger came back, Raff sat up and looked at it, though his eyes still flinched away from those bright silver finger-blades.

"We have to make another deal before I can shake hands with you."

The scissor-finger bent its knife-gash face close, like a dog nosing after food.

"I am my father's only help at his work," Raff said, "his only prentice. You have to promise that I'll be able to help him with his work after you take me home, or that he'll get other help if I can't. You must promise that nothing you do to me will hurt him or make it so he can't work and make his instruments."

The scissor-finger rested its chin on its awful fingers and thought, then pointed one blade at Raff accusingly.

"That is too much to ask for nothing offered, Boy. If you want my promise, you must make one. You must swear this is not a trick, and pledge that you will never leave my wood or try to before you have shaken my hand."

"And if I do, you'll promise what I asked?"

"Yes, Boy, if you swear not to even try to make your way out of the wood without shaking my hand, I'll promise that your father will never be without…assistance in his work."

Maybe now Raff's hands would be good for something at last. If the fairy made him good enough, or brought a better prentice to his father, it would be more than Raff could ever do alone.

"Alright. I promise I won't try to leave the wood without shaking your hand."

"Then it is sealed, our first bargain and our second."

The scissor-finger held both hands out to Raff, all ten blades splayed for him to see. They were so sharp, so bright in the dark wood, like little pieces of the moon.

Raff stared.

He tried move his hand. He had sworn. He had to do it.

He couldn't make himself reach and touch the silver blade.

The scissor-finger must have read the struggle in his face. It laughed.

"You'll work yourself up sometime, Boy. You've nothing else to do."

It was still laughing like a storm of dead leaves long after it had vanished back into the twisted woods.

Raff waited in the dark and wondered why he was so useless, even once he was resolved what he should do. He was no longer hungry. He barely felt alive. He looked at his hands and tried to memorize the whorls of his finger-pads, the wrinkles of each knuckle, in case this was his last time looking at them. Again and again he swore to himself that he would do it, he would reach out and be done when next the scissor-finger came. He was not sure if that would make it easier to reach his hands out through the bars when the time came.

Something tapped at his cage. Raff sat up to look out. There was a woman there, kneeling to look him in the eye. She had iron-grey hair, and her face was lined. She wore a patchwork cloak of every color and kind of cloth, and she had an iron ring on every finger. A finder! Just like in stories. His father had called a finder to save him. Maybe this was even Grey-Haired Maddie, whose stories he had heard, but how had she come there so soon? Was it only luck that brought her, or a sight of the future that told her where she would be needed, or had he been trapped in this fairy wood for years while the scissor-finger laughed at him?

"Are you…How did you?" he asked, breathless.

She slid her hand through the bars and over his mouth before he could say more.

"Shh. Shhh. You must be quiet, Raff, and you must tell me about the fairy who trapped you here, and the bargain you made with it, as quick as you can."

Once he started, it was like something had broken inside, and all his fear spilled over at once and rushed out of his mouth like a stream of water.

"It's a tree thing with scissor-fingers and it said it would take me home if we shook hands but I made it show me its hands and I said I wouldn't and it said I could stay here until I'd be its friend."

The finder patted his shoulder and pressed a finger to his lips. He didn't try to tell her about the second promise. He felt ashamed of it now, of trying to deal with a fairy to make himself a better luthier, or stop fearing his father's shame.

"That's good, Raff, quiet now."

The scissor-finger was behind her, between her and the way back. She smiled at Raff, and stood up and turned around, with her hands hidden under her patched cloak.

It laughed at her.

"You cannot take the boy, Finder, or go free out of my wood without my leave. What will you pay for that?"

The finder did not sound frightened when she answered it. Raff saw her fingers moving through the cloth.

"I will make the same bargain you made with the boy; and let me stand for both of us. We will show our hands, and shake them, and then I and he will both be free to go."

"Agreed, Finder, but you must swear to shake at once, as soon as we have seen each other's hands, not make me wait with the same trick the boy has."

"Done. Show me your hand."

Raff almost thought the finder was straining not to laugh.

The scissor-finger put its awful blades a whisper from her face.

"Do you like them, Finder? Think of how smoothly they'll cut through you, flesh and bone and shriveled skin."

The finder shrugged and held her left hand up, and it was bare. The scissor-finger frowned.

"That is the wrong hand for shaking with. Show me the other."

The finder shook her head.

"We agreed to show and then shake hands. Come, I will use my right."

The scissor-finger's right hand pushed forward, slow and trembling, as if it were straining not to and still was forced. The finder reached out her right hand and clasped it, and the silver scissors cracked and twisted and wept black blood like oil on her five iron rings. The fairy crumbled to the ground and cradled its ruined hand, blubbering and muttering softly, like the scratch of twigs on a windowpane.

"You were clever, Raff," she said, "to be so careful with the bargains you made, and to remember them to tell me. Now come home with me. Your father has been worried."

The cage around him was only a few thin fallen branches now, and Raff pushed them off easily, and he took the finder's hand and walked, but he could not go past the scissor-finger. After three steps, his feet fixed to the ground and he could not lift them. The woods ahead still twisted dark and pathless, and even as it cried, he thought he heard the scissor-finger's laugh.

The finder turned to look at him, and her dark eyes were stern.

"What other bargain did you make, Boy? What binds you here?"

Raff looked at the ground. This confession did not spill out easily.

"I...I promised I would not try to leave without shaking its hand."

"And what did it offer you for that?"

"I made it say that I wouldn't be too hurt to help Father, or that someone else would, and that it wouldn't hurt him so he couldn't work, whatever it did to me."

"Shake then. We must be going."

She pointed to the scissor-finger crumpled on the ground, and there was no smile left in her lined face.

Under her eyes, he could do it. He walked forward with little steps, feeling himself shake if he tried longer ones. Raff did not look at the knife-gash face, only the broken silver hand. He reached out and held one twisted finger lightly, clenching his teeth against the pain so hard he felt cords knot and fray and pop in his jaw and down his neck. Three gentle pumps up and down and he let go. Even twisted, even broken, it was so sharp. The cuts ached to his bones.

The finder bandaged his hand and led him out of the dark woods, back to his father's house.

Ever after, Raff felt the pain of those cuts in his right hand, and the scars never faded. His hand trembled, limp and useless, save when he held a chisel, blade, or saw, or any tool his father taught him how to use. Then he was steady, and his work soon gained a reputation almost the equal of his father's, though different musicians bought from father and from son. All of them, whether they sought it out or avoided it, said that Raff's instruments gave a strange sound, like the wind whistling over dry leaves and bare branches, and sometimes a tap on the frame would echo with a sound like silver scissors sliding one over the other.

R. K. Duncan is a queer polyamorous wizard and author of fantasy, horror, and occasional sci-fi. He writes from a few rooms of a venerable West Philadelphia row home, where he dreams of travel and the demise of capitalism. In the shocking absence of any cats, he lavishes spare attention on cast iron cookware and his long-suffering and supportive partner. Before settling on writing, he studied linguistics and philosophy at Haverford college. He attended Viable Paradise 23 in 2019. His occasional musings and links to other work can be found at rk-duncan-author.com

Terracotta
Daughter

JZ Ting

I F I CONFESS, DAUGHTER, WILL YOU FORGIVE ME? CAN YOU STAY YOUR Snow Wind Sword, your lightning feet and thunderous fists long enough to let me speak? Or have I hurt you too deeply, cutting to the bone just as I did your precious Qiufeng?

Ah, I've pushed too far. But look, there's a breath of air between your blade and my neck. You cannot hurt your mother. I birthed you, raised you and yes, killed for you. You stand before me strong and free because of what I did. Even if you can't forgive me, you owe me your respect.

You will listen to what I say.

Do you remember the day the Imperial decree arrived? Dragons had been sighted in auspicious clouds, your brother was at his lessons while you painted Qiufeng dancing in the garden. She was your only companion, for despite your fame as the most beautiful girl in Jiangzhou, you were meek as a rabbit and painfully shy. Your father thought it virtuous; I disagreed. When I was sixteen, my hands were red assisting my mother in the birthing room. You were too timid to haggle for dumplings.

I often wondered how I birthed such a daughter.

But the decree. You know it claimed you for the Emperor's harem, but did you know my first instinct was disfigurement? A gash across your cheek, perhaps, or a burn along your shoulder. Some damage easily healed so that you'd only be rejected, not crippled.

I did neither. You were—at least then—a disappointment, but you are my daughter, my flesh and my beauty, then and now and always. In any case, sending damaged goods to court would disgrace your father. Not for nothing was his name synonymous with Jiangzhou's finest teas, exported to noble mansions and immortal caves alike. Certainly your brother, Baosheng, could have inherited a wealthy business in a kinder life.

You didn't know. Last month, during the uprising. Their deaths are part of the story, if you let me tell it.

Your father's reputation was built on more than tea. For years, Innkeeper Zhao would tell how when his wife was ill and he in debt, your father called on him saying, "If a donkey is overloaded, neither donkey nor master will reach home. Here is my wife to help you. We will revisit the debt when all is well." Zhao kowtowed with gratitude streaming from his eyes, for your father even refused to charge interest. Three weeks later, when his wife was again making her sage's beard noodles, Zhao repaid the debt in full.

Mrs. Zhao's ailment? Since when have you been interested in the medicinal arts? Well, I counted the brown spots on her face and prescribed a mixture of mugwort and white fungus to cool her qi, so it must have been her liver. The rot took her eventually, but she had three more years because of me.

Zhao was one of many. Magistrates with aching mothers, noble daughters needing beauty creams, craftsmen with sonless wives, your father made me see them all. In return, he gathered favours like a dog does fleas and preened to hear his name praised over every pot of phoenix tea. "How generous of Merchant Wu to send his wife to help!" the men of Jiangzhou said, or, "My domestic harmony is restored thanks to Honourable Merchant Wu!" I was not told if they praised me.

Don't misunderstand. Children matter more than fame and your father kept me in silks and sculpted villas. But like most men he was ignorant, well-meaning but incapable of seeing the world in any light not his own. To him, my arts were merely a useful pastime to be indulged while your selection as an Imperial concubine was Heaven's reward for his good work. The cruelties that awaited you were beyond his imagination.

I did not imagine. Although my Imperial physician parents sought to shield me, as a child in the palace I saw enough: treachery, poison smiles, the jealousies robed in brilliant brocades and corpses hung in mourning white. In the Emperor's golden scroll, I saw your fate and wept. How could you, a raw girl who wilted under my kindest beating, stand up against an army of concubines? A Consort? What of the Empress herself, a woman rightly feared for raising her husband to the dragon throne? No, the palace would devour you like a tiger, and I wouldn't even be sent your bones. I decided there and then that just as my mother sent me to Jiangzhou far from the palace, so I would find a way to save you.

Your hand trembles. Holding a sword so long must be tiring. Why don't you sit and drink some tea?

It was Qiufeng who inspired me. Unintentionally of course, as it was not your maid's place to speak with me; however that does not mean I never listened. Unlike you, Qiufeng always had something to say.

I remember the moment as clearly as I see you. Your father, rounder than usual on celebratory wine and roasted duck, had bade me massage his shoulders while he nattered about how you would surely win the Emperor's favour, the prestige he would enjoy, and his dreams of claiming royal relations. You were silently bent over your paint brushes hoping to avoid my attention as always, Qiufeng watching by your side. And as usual when told to sleep, your brother was playing pretend.

He was an emperor that night. As my maid vainly sought to catch him, he strode the painted halls with my nine-pearl comb atop his head, brandishing a wooden sword while making grand pronouncements like eating only sweet buns for breakfast or that his twelfth birthday be celebrated with a week of fireworks. "Let him be," your father slurred when I tried to scold. "Boys can do as they like and it's good that he's a fighter. Who knows, with his sister in the Emperor's bed, he could become a general!"

I held my tongue. A wife rarely wins direct challenge with her husband, and my fingers were already manipulating him to sleep. Then Baosheng strutted over to you. "Hey, concubine!" he said haughtily. "Get up and dance for me!"

"Now, Young Master," my old maid coaxed. "Miss Yuchen is your elder sister which makes her a royal princess, not a concubine."

"No, she's a concubine, the decree says so!" Baosheng whipped his sword at your head. "Concubine! Stand up and dance!"

I heard you beg Baosheng to leave you alone, which only made him worse. So Qiufeng intervened. "Your Majesty," she said, skirts rustling as she bent in kowtow. "Let this humble one take care of you."

Baosheng's tone instantly changed. "Ah, Noble Lady! Yes, leave that crybaby and play with me!"

"I'll gladly do so. But His Majesty should know that if I dance, I'll have no breath left for stories."

Storytelling was Qiufeng's skill, as you well know. Even as a child she could stop your crying with tales of gods and heroes, leaving me free to rest or work. A worthy return on her purchase price. "Stories?" Baosheng asked excitedly. "Do you have something fun? An adventure?"

"Hm." Qiufeng placed a finger against her cheek. "Shall I tell of how your grandfather healed a travelling monk only to discover that it was an injured tiger spirit in disguise?"

"I know this! The tiger spirit was so grateful for Grandfather's help, it gave him safe passage instead of eating him on the spot!"

"Aiyah, I'd better tell something else! What about your grandmother, did you know she once journeyed far into the mountains to fetch a lotus from Lord Laozi's temple?"

"To make a soup giving the Empress Dowager another five years of life! Is that right, Xiaxue?"

"It is, Young Master!" my old maid said. "Your mother has told these stories many times."

"Then how about a heroic story?" Qiufeng asked. "Do you know how Nezha carved up his own flesh and bones as sacrifice, only to return to life and defeat the Dragon King?"

"No—tell me!"

And Qiufeng did. There's no need to repeat it. All that matters is that as she spoke, I thought of your frightened face among a thousand women, each a beauty vying to warm the Emperor's bed. I thought of how if you weren't bullied or beaten by a rival of higher rank you'd be forgotten, a caged, lonely bird never to leave the palace except as ashes.

I grieved. I wanted to rage and demand Heaven to give you another fate. Then Qiufeng described Nezha's resurrection.

"It was done by Taiyi Zhenren," she said, dramatic as a stage performer. "The pure immortal had Nezha's spirit brought to his magic cave where, using Taoist arts, he merged it with a beautiful new body carved from lotus roots. Poof! Nezha lived again! Dancing in joy, Nezha took up his magic weapons and flew to battle..."

In my mind, Qiufeng's words became a lotus. Jointed tubers sprouted hands and feet that danced in a golden light, water trailing like silken sleeves beneath a petal crown. Suddenly I remembered my dowry chest, the brocades and books my mother packed and at the bottom, a little lacquer box.

Your father was snoring. Standing, I left you all and strode to my private workroom where I retrieved the box from its hiding place and opened it like a nightingale's egg. There on a silk cushion was a single pill, no larger than a thumbnail and red as cinnabar. *For your daughter, when you have her,* my mother said when I was sent away. *You'll be demanded to produce a son, of course, but a daughter is yours to mould. Teach her our arts so she continues them, and if ill winds threaten, this may alter fate.*

A Life-Giving Pill. And right away, I began to plan.

I see your face. It's the one you wore whenever I made you memorise meridians or slapped you for forgetting which herb did what. You're wondering how such a precious pill came to be.

I was told that it was created by He Xiangu, the maiden of the Eight Immortals who taught your great-grandmother the Taoist medicinal arts. My mother heard there were originally three pills. One was used in a previous generation to save our family. The other, she said, was lost for love.

You would have heard these stories if you followed in my footsteps.

The next morning, I dressed in plain robes, had Xiaxue carry my medicine box, and ordered a rickshaw to take us to the ceramics district. Given his business, your father had many connections with artisans there, bolstered by my visits to their womenfolk. This gave me the perfect excuse to go from kiln to kiln where I was welcomed in to see new wives, check pregnancies, or whisper advice on menstrual pains. As I worked, I admired each kiln's wares. Most offered pots and tea-sets, but others displayed colourful guardian gods commissioned for temples or servants destined for wealthy tombs. These I examined closely.

The best work was by Old Li. A master artisan, he was also an infamous patron of Jiangzhou's brothels, both before and after he bought a wife. Respectable women never let their shadow fall against his door, but my chaperone and medicine box gave immunity from Jiangzhou gossip. Even a lecher's wife deserves care.

"Madame Wu." Old Li leered at me from his door with hands stained grey from clay. "You look more beautiful every day."

I bowed. "Master Li. My husband asked me to come to the neighbourhood to see friends and I happened to hear your wife was ill. I thought I could be of assistance."

"Ill? Since when? Baiyun!" This he shouted into his house. "Get out here! What's this about?"

A girl of sixteen appeared behind him. Although lovely and neatly dressed in peach linens, she had the furtive eyes of a hunted rabbit. "I'm here, husband," she said timidly. I thought of you.

"Why so slow! Don't you see that we have a guest?"

Old Li smacked her head, so I bowed again. "Madame Li," I said warmly. "Forgive my presumption, however I heard about your condition and thought I would offer my service. I see that I am just in time."

She blinked. I met her gaze steadily, counting the faded bruises on her cheeks until she read my face. "I am unwell, yes," she said, eyes darting to her husband. "I feel cold and my blood sluggish."

Old Li paled. He hurried us indoors where he ordered Baiyun to sit and showered me with questions. I gently chased him out to his workshop and snuck a glance at what he wrought there. Elegant clay beauties smiled vapidly into space, some seated with instruments, others posed in dance. Many were life-sized. My pulse quickened.

Li Baiyun was unwell. Not from illness, but general low vitality from stagnant qi. I prescribed a mixture of red dates and ginseng root to heat her blood, and if she pocketed another mixture that cooled libido, it was our secret. Satisfied, I left her cooking with Xiaxue and went to see Old Li.

I found him calculating funeral costs. Like any man confronted with women's issues, he'd jumped to conclusions. I gave him only minimal reassurance, emphasising the need for ongoing treatment, which of course I would provide. Old Li asked my price. No need for coarse matters, I said, before mentioning that I wanted something made. He caught my meaning immediately.

"What do you need?"

I told him. Old Li looked thoughtful then smiled wide and wicked. "An interesting project. Although I wonder why it needs to be so... anatomically correct."

"If I'm to teach another, I must have means for a student to practice. Better a clay model to suffer the inevitable mistakes than a live patient."

"But why does a model need to look like your daughter?"

"That's none of your business."

"Hm." He tugged his wispy beard, his leer returning. "Do I get to see her?"

"Unnecessary. I'll provide detailed instructions and you can look on my face imagining it twenty years younger."

"Because that's all children are, right? Copies of their parents?" Old Li snorted. "My father taught me to work clay. He also gave me his fists, his temper and his dissolute nature. I've never known anything else, but I do know better than to pass those on — forget filial piety, just give me my work and a pretty girl who cooks and fucks!"

I held my tongue and head high. Old Li laughed an ugly laugh. "Don't worry, Madame Wu, I'll do it. After all, I'd be lying if I said I've never fantasised about the beauty of Jiangzhou."

We agreed on seven days. I'd asked for three, but Old Li said that was impossible and just as he deferred to me on his wife's health, so I reluctantly deferred to him on this. It left no time for error — and I only had one pill.

I studied. When your father threw out your paint brushes, replacing them with dance lessons, I buried myself in my mother's books. When he had you reciting ways to please the Emperor, I memorised accounts of those who'd gone before. Lord Laozi and his wooden temptress. The lacquer man that sang for the court of Zhao. The monks who drove tigers from their temple with a warrior of sun-baked mud. All these and more I meticulously dissected, pulling fact from theory until I found their veins, warm and fragile, pulsing towards the heart.

Every day, I returned to Old Li's kiln. I brought medicine for the wife, instructions for the husband, and checked the progress of both.

Every night, I prayed fervently to He Xiangu for success. I reassured myself that it could be done. That it had been done. But doubt gnawed.

Two nights before your departure, Old Li paid a late visit to our house. His donkey cart squeaked and hawed, but the herbal congee I'd made for dinner kept you all asleep, and he wheeled his delivery into my workroom without incident. Old Li himself made crude jokes about secret trysts but was discreet enough, especially when I thanked him with a fatal mandrake tonic he thought was for sexual prowess. Leaving Xiaxue to see him out, I unwrapped the sackcloth with eager hands.

I saw your face. The sculpted eyes were your eyes, the nose your nose, and the delicate lips smiled the soft smile you never wore for me. Even the hair, which Old Li had shaped into butterfly-wing coils, was textured to give the black glaze the appearance of countless strands. Most astonishing was the skin, which was smooth and pale, yet warm. A porcelain slip poured over a hollow red clay core, Old Li had said. Touching the cheek, I was surprised to find it cold.

Your body followed. Here Old Li's intimate knowledge of the female form was on proud display. Your neck. Your slim waist. The graceful lines of your arms and legs, and the alluring curves of your breasts and hips. Old Li had even placed the firing holes in your mouth, ears, nostrils, buttocks, and between your thighs. The whole work was impossible not to view with a man's eyes and I had a foolish, blushing urge to replace the sackcloth. At the same time, my breath quickened.

She was perfect. You were perfect.

The Life-Giving Pill was waiting. My fingers trembled as I placed it upon my tongue to taste my breath, my desire, my sharp and desperate need. Then I pressed my lips to your statue's clay ones and passed the pill between. Nothing happened.

Shaking the pill out from between the statue's legs, I again put it in my mouth, this time with a whispered prayer to He Xiangu for aid. Again, I frantically breathed the pill into the statue's mouth. Again, nothing.

Why? Medicine is founded on the flow of qi, the energy that breathes through each and every living thing. I knew pressure points to direct it, which herbs heated and cooled it, and a thousand ways to make it stop. I even held a spark in the form of an immortal's gift. Where had I gone wrong?

It seems so clear with hindsight. With so little time left, there was only ever one choice. I summoned Xiaxue without hesitation. "Fetch Qiufeng," I ordered, knowing my maid would be as silent as her name. Then I covered the statue, took out my knives, and made a pot of fragrant tea.

I see your fingers curling on your sword-hilt. You were never stupid, only innocent. That, of course, is long past.

Qiufeng arrived. Despite being roused from bed, she had put on a dress of bamboo green and pinned her hair into a simple bun. "Madame," she said, bowing deeply. "How may this one serve you?"

Her voice was low and careful. I gave a gentle smile. "Sit with me," I said, gesturing to the tea I'd laid out. "Yuchen's imminent departure weighs too heavily for me to sleep and I yearn for company."

Obedient, Qiufeng sat on the embroidered cushion, arranging her skirts and glancing about with unmistakable curiosity. "You've never been in my workroom before, have you," I observed.

"No, Madame, you've forbidden it. Only Elder Sister Xiaxue is permitted in here to clean."

"Very true. For every ingredient here that heals, there is also one that harms. Many can do both."

"Like ginkgo." Qiufeng smiled. "Ginkgo seeds are commonly used to soothe respiratory problems and improve circulation, but will be poisonous if eaten in large amounts."

I stared. "How do you know that?"

"Madame of course remembers that I follow Miss Yuchen to all her lessons. Although I do so to fetch and carry, I cannot help but hear and learn."

In all the years I had tried teaching you, never had I imagined there was another student, and a willing one at that. Her face, however, was plain as rice. "You've served my family for a long time now, yes?" I asked, pouring tea.

"Ten years, Madame. Since I was eight."

"How time flies." I smiled as I handed Qiufeng a steaming cup. "I hope that we've been kind to you?"

"Very much, Madame. Master Wu is straightforward and honourable, and Miss Yuchen is a sweet, sensitive girl. Young Master Baosheng is exuberant as all boys should be and although Madame is strict, I am awed by your skill and wisdom. The angelica root soup you made for my stomach pains after I stuffed myself on lychees is a memory I treasure."

I had no memory of that. "You care for my daughter," I said, swirling my tea thoughtfully as Qiufeng drank. "It's therefore only natural that I care for you. How is she?"

"Very tired, Madame. Every day she studies feminine conduct and trains in dance and music. Every night she weeps knowing each morning brings her closer to leaving. I try to comfort her by reminding that I will also go."

"Go?"

"To the palace. Miss Yuchen is more than beautiful, she is kind and noble and will surely be blessed with the Emperor's attention. If raised to rank she will need a maid, and if raised higher she will be targeted. I wish to protect her. With everything I've learned from you, I can do that."

Bile bloomed behind my tongue. A liver imbalance which, if you remember your lessons, is often caused by intense anger or jealousy. Somehow, I swallowed it. "You would do anything for my daughter?" I asked.

"Yes. We've grown up together and have engraved our names on each other's hearts. There are no secrets between us."

"Is that so." I studied Qiufeng's face, her strong jaw and the slowing vein beneath. "What does she say about me?"

Qiufeng was starting to blink heavily. "You're her mother, Madame. She respects you as any filial daughter should."

"But? Don't flatter, speak!"

She struggled. Too late, her dark eyes widened white and wild, realisation fighting to become defiance. "But you're cruel, Madame. You care not for other people and the generous physician you show the world hides an ugly arrogance. You want Yuchen to be more like you but she can't, she won't, no matter how much you judge and punish. Yuchen says that whatever hardships the Emperor's palace holds, at least it won't have you."

"Not have me? Ignorant, ungrateful girl—" Blazing, I leaped to my feet. "The palace will have a hundred of me. A thousand. All will judge, all will deceive and when they hurt her, it will not be from love or kindness. Not like me!"

Qiufeng slumped, hands drooping limp as leaves, spilling nightshade tea across the floor. For one wild moment I regretted, but then I saw butterfly pins of carved jade in her black hair. My gift to you on your fourteenth birthday. You'd given them away.

I shut my eyes. Harnessed my breath over and over until it was forced to calm. Then I called Xiaxue and had Qiufeng's body dragged to my work table.

How much do you want to know? Shall I describe Qiufeng's soft skin, how easily it was cut, or the stink of blood mixed with pungent herbs? Shall I reassure you that Qiufeng never woke, that she couldn't feel her ribs shatter, nor hear Xiaxue sob and vomit? Or is this too much, too painful on your broken heart?

Let me tell you instead of magic. The arms, legs, hands and neck of the statue were all moveable, even removeable, for Old Li had made them fit with the torso like a lid into a teapot. In this way I could squeeze Qiufeng's Five Organs inside and string them up with silken threads. The remaining space was stuffed with rice-paper scrolls inscribed with a concubine's talents. Dancing. Music. Literary classics, court rituals, the three obediences and four virtues. Her blood stained the paper as thoroughly as my hands.

I didn't care. I breathed the Life-Giving Pill between your porcelain lips and into Qiufeng's stomach where I felt qi wake and warm and flow. And though I'd told myself it was only clay, when your double smiled and called me *mother*, I collapsed and wept.

I had Xiaxue say that Qiufeng had run away overnight. I still remember how you screamed. Afterwards, when you'd rejected every plate of food and command to leave your bed, I shut myself in my workroom and took my clay daughter into my arms. I fed her your favourite sweet rice cakes, told her of all the proud women who led to her creation, and when she named every herb upon my shelves I shared her delight, caressing her head against my shoulder, just as my mother had done with me.

Four soldiers and a eunuch accompanied the carriage from Chang'an. The eunuch had a golden dragon embroidered on his black brocade and he accepted your father's kowtow with a haughty expression Baosheng would later imitate. Then he demanded you.

Your father was embarrassed. No doubt he made excuses to conceal how you'd locked yourself in your rooms. Perhaps he prayed as well: for time, for your good behaviour, for me to produce you and save him face.

Could you see us? If you peered through your shutters, could you see yourself radiant in jades and silks smiling obediently by my side? Did you wonder how she could kowtow to me not with fear or resentment but gracefully, with gratitude? Or had Xiaxue already straightened your spine with false hope, given you a bag, and pointed you west?

I suppose it's not important. In the end, one daughter left in a carriage, the other fled on foot. Neither knew how desperately she was missed.

Two months later, a mutilated corpse was found in the rice paddies downriver. No one braved the decay to identify it, and Jiangzhou teahouses were soon filled with tales of hungry water demons. That night, Xiaxue threw herself off the bridge.

Years passed. Baosheng grew tall and troublesome and your father fat. I mixed medicines for patients but had nothing for my despair. Widow Li remarried. The country began to fail.

It wasn't obvious at first. News of flooding in distant provinces, or dead birds falling from eastern skies. No doubt the flying swordmasters you met and trained with saw more signs. Then in Jiangzhou, a locust plague devastated the tea fields. Your father tried to absorb the loss. Drought followed.

Whispers spread of divine punishment. Imperial virtue compromised, the mandate of Heaven passing. People said that instead of attending court, the Emperor preferred the company of a beautiful concubine who poisoned her rivals and enthralled him with endless tales. In return, the Emperor lavished her with favour. Gold. Pearls as white as her porcelain skin. Fresh lychees couriered from the south every week. A glittering pagoda worth two years of taxes. Soon the whispers rose to rebellious shouts until every tongue within the four seas cursed her name. Wu. Noble Consort Wu, the beauty of Jiangzhou. Because of her, the country was in turmoil.

Your father hung himself from shame.

In disgrace, I fled to this shack. Some find me: desperate widows, famine orphans, mothers terrified of birthing another starving mouth. Beyond that I am shunned, left to waste in rotting silks and cursed by all Jiangzhou for bringing Noble Consort Wu into this world.

Baosheng couldn't stand it. He ran off to join the rebel army as it marched on the capital and was killed in the last charge. But his death was not in vain. As blood flowed through Chang'an's paved streets, the Empress led the court in demanding that Noble Consort Wu be put to death, giving the Emperor no choice but to agree. Reluctant, he sent soldiers to her pagoda. They brought a white scarf. Before they could use it, Noble Consort Wu defiantly threw herself off the highest roof. The shatter of pottery echoed across the city, I'm told. But you knew that already.

You fought there as well.

There isn't much left now. Only you and me.

I see your face. It's older, yes, and hardened, but noble too so I believe. There are clear skies within your eyes and strange journeys on your skin. Yet despite your growth, you flinch beneath my gaze. You're still my daughter. My only daughter.

Did you think of me these past few years? Did you miss me, curse me, perhaps thank me for your existence? Or did you only think of Qiufeng, bold and clever Qiufeng, wondering where she'd gone with your name upon her heart?

It doesn't matter. You're here. You stand tall lifting your sword above my head and although you weep, you're so strong, so beautiful, and I am so, so proud. I have no regret.

I did it all for you.

JZ Ting is an Asian-Australian emerging writer of escapist imaginings. Her writing has previously appeared in Australian literary magazines, and she finds inspiration from years of geekdom in movies, novels, anime/manga, and computer games. She has lived on four continents, speaks bad French, Mandarin and Japanese, but stays for Sydney's beaches where she pretends to be a mermaid.

THE HOMELESS SPECIAL

Andrew Jensen

I HATE HALLOWEEN," STEVE, THE BOSS, GRUMBLED. "STUPID PRANK orders. Listen, Rey, if this turns out to be a joke, feel free to eat the pizza."

"What's on it?" Reynard asked carefully. As the newest delivery driver, this was his first Halloween at International Pizza.

"Double cheese with triple anchovies and pineapple. That's why I'm suspicious. I have to take these orders seriously, but we always get a couple of no-shows, or bogus deliveries."

"So if I'm going out on a bogus delivery, do I still get paid?" Rey asked.

"You're getting a free pizza, aren't ya?" Steve looked at the expression on Rey's face. "Just joking. Sure, you get paid. I might even pay you extra to eat the pizza, so no one else sees it."

"I'll pass," Reynard said, stuffing the box into the stay-hot delivery bag. Like everything else at International Pizza, it was a cheap knock-off. Rey could guarantee on-time delivery, but not a hot pizza.

Rey slid into his customized Civic. He'd tricked it out personally, and he liked to brag that you always knew when your pizza was arriving. Between the glossy black paint, the purple ground-effects lights, the orange rims, and the dance music blasting from the high-end sound system, the whole block knew.

That car was his pride and joy. Who cared if it had over 250K on the odometer? It had almost no rust, and it was perfect. Besides, the ladies loved it. Well, a couple of the girls in the church youth group had admired it. He hoped they'd like to ride in it someday.

He spent a mint on those little air-freshener clip-ons. The smell of pizza tended to linger. He might have to clip on an extra one or two to wipe out the anchovies. You never knew when you might have company.

Rey stuck his phone onto the dash-mount, with the International Pizza Delivery App running. It would give him a quick route to his address. It was cheap, probably a free download that Steve had re-branded. Sometimes it tried to send him down streets that had been closed for months. Today, it refused to give him the address. It just gave him GPS coordinates. Rey shrugged. He'd better hurry.

Rey took pride in his work. Jobs were hard to find in Katzenham, even after-school jobs, and he had no plans to lose his. He'd worked for Tim's before he was old enough to drive, and everyone said he could go up in the organization if he stayed on. But this was better. This was a legit reason to have a car.

Good thing, too. He'd had to live in it for a couple of weeks after his mom's new boyfriend threw him out. Then a family at the church had said he could live in their basement for a really cheap rent.

Rey didn't like to think about that. It had only been six months ago. He suspected it was because his own dad had been black, and the new boyfriend was a racist jerk. Too bad the guy didn't say it out loud. That might be the straw that got his mom mad enough to actually stand up to the guy, instead of letting him turf Rey. Maybe. Anyway, the car was the main thing he had to remember how life used to be.

No! The App was leading him onto Concession 4! Rey hated country roads. Bad for the paint job, and flying death to his lights. He slowed down, to avoid kicking up too much gravel.

The App announced that he'd arrived. What? He was in the middle of nowhere! There was just this little bridge, obviously new, but just barely wide enough for two cars to pass.

Stupid Halloween prank. No way he was going to eat this pizza. Maybe he'd throw it into the dredge-cut ditch below the bridge. The fish could eat the anchovies. Tough luck about the pineapple.

First, though, he called Steve and told him what he'd found.

"Is there a rock on the rail of the bridge?" Steve asked.

Rey peered ahead. His custom halogen headlights lit up the dark bridge like a kind of eerie daylight. Yes! There, at the far end, was a rock, with a paper flapping underneath. He drove forward.

"I got an extra text after you left. It said the money would be in an envelope under a rock." Steve paused. "I wasn't sure it was worth telling you, but maybe this is for real."

Rey got out of the car and swapped the pizza box for the envelope. There was money there, including a bit extra.

"Hello?" Rey called. "Is someone there?"

Silence.

"Shall I put the change in the envelope?" Rey tried in his best customer service voice.

"Keep the change," came a deep, damp-sounding voice from under the bridge.

"Thanks," Rey squeaked. He jumped in his car, drove until he found a lane where he could turn around, and then drove back. The pizza was gone.

Rey got back in record time. He didn't even mind the paint scratches.

"Probably a bum who got his hands on a cell phone," was Steve's opinion. "As long as he pays, who cares?"

Steve was creating his next special pizza. He was going to call it "The Kosher Collision." It would feature Montreal Smoked Meat and some ingredients normally only found in Chinese food.

"Did you know that Jews eat Chinese food at Christmas?" he enthused. "It's a kind of tradition. I found out online. And making it my November special will let me test to see if I should keep it through Christmas. My grandfather was Jewish."

"Did he eat Chinese food at Christmas?" Rey asked.

"I dunno. Never met him. He died before I was born."

"Um, I don't think it's kosher to mix meat and cheese, Steve," Rey said. He remembered that from Sunday School.

"Shut up. This is my culture, not yours. You can't culturally oppress me with your White Patriarchy!"

"What? I'm black! Where did that 'White Patriarchy' crap come from?"

"Good, eh? I've been continuing my education online. That's the way they're talking at all the colleges these days." Steve went off, chuckling.

Schmuck. Ray would've said it out loud, except he didn't think Steve would get it. Instead, he followed him into the kitchen.

"You're white. You can't claim white oppression against yourself."

"My one grandmother came from Hong Kong. And don't forget my Jewish grandfather."

"I'm pretty sure your Jewish grandfather was white," Rey pointed out.

"Tell that to the skinheads who've moved in downtown."

He had a point, Rey thought. Katzenham used to be pretty calm about race; it had been at the Canadian end of the Underground Railroad, and was regularly visited by black folks from Detroit looking for trouble-free fun. That was changing these days. Small racist insults were getting bigger, and louder. Now there were even skinheads.

The youth pastor taught them to look for the best in everyone, no matter how they looked on the surface. Rey was prepared to make an exception for racists.

The phone rang. A minute later, Steve hung up, grinning. "Your friend under the bridge called again. Same order. He specifically asked for you to deliver it. Electronically pre-paid this time, with a decent tip."

"Same order?" Rey asked. "Really?"

"All the cheap booze probably pickled his taste buds. Hey, maybe I should put it on the menu: *The Homeless Special.*"

Rey shifted uncomfortably. "Don't you think that's kind of tasteless?" There were lots of reasons someone could be homeless. Why be mean to them?

"Totally tasteless, but the customer wants it anyway. Maybe others will too!"

"No, I meant..." Rey started. Steve had turned his back to open a jar of anchovies. "...just don't write it on the bill," he finished, lamely.

There are lots of ways to end up homeless, Rey thought again a couple of months later as he drove to the bridge. *Maybe this customer isn't so bad.* This would be his fifth delivery to the guy, and he hadn't seen him yet. Most of them had been in the dark, and often near the end of the month. For some reason, this one was off schedule.

It was daylight, but wouldn't be for long. It was early enough that the rush of orders wouldn't happen for a while, so maybe he'd have the chance to connect with this man. *You know, look for the best in him.*

Besides, it was early February, and anyone who lived under a bridge in that much cold was kind of impressive.

The stone was in the same place as always, with a bit of snow dusting it this time. Rey put the pizza box under it before calling out: "International Pizza, your order's here!"

"Thanks," came the familiar deep, moist voice from under the bridge. A hand in a tattered knit glove followed by a filthy coat arm reached up quickly and grabbed the box.

"You stickin' around? 'Cause I ain't sharing." The voice was still unpleasant. And now Rey could smell something unpleasant too. Something fishy. More than just anchovies.

"Do you mind if I ask you a question?" Rey asked, cautiously.

"It's a free country." The sentence ended with the sound of vigorous chewing.

"Why do you always ask for me, specifically, to deliver your pizza?"

"I like your car. Those purple lights shine into a spectrum you people can't usually see. It makes everything look pretty."

So, the bum was a racist. "You people." There's no good way to say that. No good way to hear it. Rey had been wasting his sympathy on a racist. Probably the jerk deserved to be homeless. He sure had no social skills.

"Listen man—" Rey began.

"Don't call me 'man,'" interrupted the bum. "It reminds me of the 70s. Everyone was called 'man,' even the women. It's not respectful to ignore what someone really is."

Ah. Maybe not a racist then. The Social Studies teacher had talked about trans people, and the need to respect them. The Youth Pastor had talked about them too. To the Youth Pastor, all LGBTQ people were monsters, not people, so you didn't have to try to see the best in them. Rey wasn't worried. So far, all he really knew was that this was a customer who tipped pretty well. As long as he wasn't a racist, Rey didn't mind.

"Sorry, dude..." he tried.

"No 'dude' either. Call me Jan." He (she?) pronounced the first letter somewhere between a J and a Y.

That clinched it. Not a skinhead. You couldn't be both trans and a skinhead too, could you? Well, could you? Maybe he could ask the teacher.

"Okay, Jan," he said. "I'm Rey."

"Pleased to meetcha. Pardon me if I don't shake." Jan heard some slurping.

"How come you live out here under this bridge?" Rey asked, almost before realizing that it was rude.

"It's a nice bridge. New. Clean. And the dredge-cut down there is so deep that there are fish in it. I like fish."

"I noticed. But don't the farmer's fields run off into it? Isn't it polluted?"

"That which doesn't kill you makes you stronger." The voice quoted, deep and rumbly.

"Other homeless people live under the bridges downtown. They get more handouts there."

"I'm not homeless. The bridge is my home. I have what I need."

Rey was silent.

"You're wondering about the phone, aren't you?"

"Yeah. Not that I'm complaining. You're a good customer. But this isn't like the States. You need an address to get a phone. I don't think bridges count. Sure wouldn't for welfare."

The voice laughed. "I could tell you the truth, but then I'd have to kill you."

Great. A sick sense of humor too. Time to leave. "Well, I'd better be going."

"It was a joke, Rey. I found the phone on Halloween. My first pizza order was the first time I've ever used one of these. I've gotten a lot better since then. Seems I've got a natural talent. Anyway, the owner hasn't come looking for it. Someone named Vince. I can't get into his bank accounts, but he has a lot of Paypal money with the password stored. So I celebrate once in a while. Today's my birthday."

"Happy Birthday." Rey's own phone started ringing in the car. Saved by the bell! "That's the boss. I'd better get going if I want to keep my job."

"Okay. Nice to talk, Rey. Catch you later."

Later that night, Rey told Steve about the bum's phone story.

"Vince?" Steve asked. "Like Big Vince the biker? They pulled his body out of the river a few months ago. Said it was a rival gang. The news said he was brutally cut up."

"I must have missed that," Rey mumbled. He never followed any newsfeeds.

"And that other stuff you said? About how you thought he was a skinhead, and then you realized he's a trans bum?" Steve's voice dropped to a whisper. "Truth is, he's a trans-skinhead-biker-killer-wino-homeless-guy. Watch your back!"

Steve burst into loud laughter. "The look on your face! Totally worth it! Rey, he's just a tramp who found a phone. He's buying pizza. That makes him a customer. We don't spy on our customers."

Rey left, betrayed and furious. Jerk! He'd shared his concerns, and Steve had mocked him! He wanted to help the homeless guy. He was really concerned. At church they said you have to love the sinner and hate the sin. How can you love someone if you don't take the time to get to know them?

He drove for a while, not caring where. It was late, and his mind was going even faster than his car.

Rey slowed down as he realized something. *He* felt betrayed, but wasn't he really the betrayer? He'd told Jan's secrets to Steve. Steve, of all people! Half the city would know by tomorrow, if Steve went and tweeted about it.

He'd betrayed Jan's confidence. He was as bad as Judas in the bible! Homeless people are vulnerable, right? First, he'd treated Jan like some scary monster, and then like a reject. Had he ever treated him decently, like a normal human? He owed Jan an apology.

Rey looked around, registering his surroundings for the first time. He was halfway down Concession 4 already. Some part of him must have known he'd end up back here. His conscience was driving him. Literally.

Rey stopped on the bridge. He shut off the engine, but left the lights on. Between the lights and the snow, the bridge was a bright mix of white with weird purple highlights. Rey got out of the car, and called out: "Jan? Jan, are you here?"

Jan's voice came from under the bridge. "Rey? How come you're back so soon? Didja bring me a free birthday pizza? I'm hungry again."

"No, Jan. I'm here to tell you something. I'm really sorry..." and then he was blurting it all out: his fears, his stupid assumptions, what he was taught at church and school, and worst of all, his betrayal of Jan's secrets to that jerk, Steve. By the time he was halfway through, he was weeping with shame. By the end he was feeling better. Maybe confession really was good for the soul.

"A trans-skinhead-biker-killer-wino-homeless-guy?" Jan was roaring with laughter. It echoed under the bridge. It made the bridge sound like a cavern.

"Rey, that's the funniest thing I've heard in years! What a great birthday present! Thanks. Hey, is this Steve guy the same person who makes the pizzas?"

Rey was confused, but relieved that Jan seemed to be so forgiving. "Yeah. Steve is the owner of the pizza shop."

"I'll stop by to see him later. Too bad. I liked those pizzas."

"Pardon?"

"I'll tell you the truth now, Rey. You didn't reveal any secrets, 'cause you had me all wrong. I'm not a racist. I'm not a 'man' or a 'dude' either. I'm a troll."

Jan leapt onto the bridge. The halogen headlights of the Civic showed every detail of the troll's seven-foot height, the grey, damp skin, the needle-sharp teeth, grinning nastily, and the long claws that flexed on both hands and feet. Rey couldn't help but notice that the purple ground-effect lights glinted off of Jan's eyes. They were beautiful. And so very cold.

Jan walked forward, leaning in close enough for Rey to smell anchovies and other fish, mingling on the troll's breath. "I don't worry much about good and evil," Jan remarked. "I just do what's best for me." Rey leaned back, but he couldn't get away. He was trapped against his beloved car. "And my sexual identity?" the troll whispered, gently sliding a clawed hand up either side of Rey's face, "is none of your business."

Rey felt the troll's grip on his head get tighter.

"Right now, you're hoping there's good somewhere deep inside of me, aren't you?" The troll grinned.

Rey tried unsuccessfully to nod. He couldn't even blink his wide, terrified eyes.

"There will be in a minute," Jan said.

Darkness was all Rey could see through the troll's gaping jaws.

Andrew Jensen lives in Braeside, Ontario. He is the minister at Knox United Church, Nepean.

His speculative short stories have been published in over a dozen magazines and anthologies: most recently two issues of Mad Scientist Journal, and the cover story in Dreamforge issue 2.

Andrew is also the author of a book of Church humour called God: The Greatest User of Capital Letters, published by Wood Lake Books.

When not writing or ministering, Andrew plays trumpet, impersonates Kermit the Frog, and performs in musical theatre. You should have seen him as Henry Higgins...

THE PLAY DATE

James Van Pelt

L IAM SHAPED THE LIFE CLAY IN HIS HEAD, HAPPY TO BE HANDLING IT. It was squishy and tingly and squealed a little when he twisted it. What would he make today? He focused his attention on Arthur's tabletop, then did the trick that made the thought-clay whole and animate. A miniature tiger, three inches long, appeared on the table. It looked at him and roared, a tiny, cute roar that made Liam laugh. He moved his fingers slowly toward it. Sometimes the tigers panicked and ran away. It might die if it fell to the floor. But this one batted its paw at Liam's finger, then grabbed and bit and wrestled with it. Liam laughed. Its claws and teeth were too small to hurt.

In fourth grade, he'd learned how to materialize blocks and balls, and, when he grew better, more complicated objects like ladders and wheelbarrows. All small, of course. Only an adult could construct something big. To demonstrate for the class, Mrs. Henderson made a desk for herself with a marble top and polished wood legs.

But now he was in fifth grade, in the gifted and talented program with Arthur and three other fifth graders. Only he and Arthur could make tiny living things. Mrs. Henderson gave them both gold stars. His mom and Arthur's mom arranged play dates, so, as Mom said, "You can reinforce each other. We're so proud of the two of you."

Arthur's playroom was much nicer than Liam's. Arthur had a little trampoline and fish tanks. He had his own refrigerator filled with sugary drinks Liam's mother wouldn't let him have, and he had a stash of candy. Arthur's mom had set up a card table for them to work on next to a couch. She'd put two folding chairs up for them to sit on.

The tiger let go, rolled on its back. Liam petted its tiny tummy. He could feel it breathing beneath his finger. He'd started making tigers last week. The first ones weren't very good. Either they didn't look like tigers, or they were dead or died soon, but he thought he'd figured them out pretty well by now. They were easier than lions. He could picture them better in his head, which made shaping them possible. Unless he really knew what a thing looked like, he couldn't shape it.

Arthur sat down beside Liam, who hadn't heard him come in. "A tiger's cool. What do you feed him?"

Arthur's mom kept his hair very short, and he had a high forehead that caught the ceiling light. Liam giggled when he remembered his mom wondering if he waxed it. He was taller than Liam, and broader in the shoulders, a junior version of his father, a bruisingly large man Liam stayed away from when he was in the room.

"Feed them? I dissolve them when I'm done playing. What would you feed them?"

"Watch," Arthur said. He closed his eyes. Liam watched the table; soon a spot of air the size of a marble swirled into motion, and a second later, a tiny sheep stood on hooves the size of pencil points.

Liam laughed and clapped his hands. "That's awesome. He's so cute." The sheep's head turned up at the sound of his voice and twitched its tail.

Liam leaned forward to get a closer look, so he didn't see the tiger start its charge. The tiger gripped the smaller animal in its jaws and shook until the sheep dangled, a coat of red darkening its chest and forelegs.

"Oh, no," Liam said, his eyes tearing. "That's awful. Erase it. Make it go away."

Arthur shrugged. "Tigers eat. Sheep get eaten. What's the big deal?" But the sheep shimmered into a rainbow of colors before winking out of existence. A few seconds later, Liam wove the special thoughts together, and the tiger rainbowed away, too.

"You boys behaving?" boomed a voice from the door. Liam turned. Arthur's dad filled the space from frame to frame, blocking the light behind him.

"Yes, sir," Arthur said, stiffening in his seat. His hand moved up to a faint bruise on the side of his face.

"We don't want any bad reports from our guest, do we, son?"

"No, sir. Of course not."

Arthur's dad laughed, a loud, false, threatening sound that made Liam want to crawl under the table. "Dinner in an hour. Your little friend will be gone by then." He caught Liam's eye and winked.

Then he left, and the room felt lighter.

Arthur's head was down, looking at his lap. Liam didn't know what to say to him. If they'd been at his house, his mother would have brought cold milk and a plate of cookies. His dad would sit down with them and ask what they were working on.

"Do you know how to make a snow globe?" Liam asked. The suggestion sounded lame. He tried not to think about the poor sheep. "The first couple of times I tried, I got water all over the place."

Arthur put his hands on the table. "I can make something really cool. Cooler than a snow globe. Cooler than a tiger. Do you want to see?"

Liam nodded. Arthur didn't sound excited. He sounded mad.

"Watch close. It's complicated."

Arthur leaned forward over the table. The back legs of his chair came off the floor, and the knuckles in his hands grew white with pressing against the table. The whirly spot appeared in the air in front of him, but nothing came of it for seconds after seconds after seconds. It just whirled, whistling slightly. Liam had never seen anyone take so long to make a materialization. Even Mrs. Henderson's desk popped into being almost instantly. The class had oohed and ahhed appreciatively. Of course, she was an adult. She could make big things.

The whirling air darkened, took form. Abruptly, on the table, facing away from them, stood a little naked man, two inches tall. It moved its head, took a step forward, and Liam knew it wasn't a toy.

Liam's voice shook. "We're not supposed to make people, Arthur. It's the first standard, the most important one. Mrs. Henderson gave us the rules."

The little man turned toward them when Liam spoke.

"It's not a person, Liam. It's just a materialization. It came out of my head."

The little man studied Liam first, then turned toward Arthur. Liam thought he looked familiar. He reminded him of someone.

"Hello, Dad." Arthur brought his fist down hard, smashing the figure into the table. Bones crunched. Blood splashed. Arthur wiped his hand on his pants. He concentrated again, dematerializing the evidence. Even the stain on his pants vanished.

"Goodbye, Dad," he said. He faced Liam. "I told you it would be cool."

"That's bad," Liam said. "Mrs. Henderson..."

"What does she know? If she wants to give me a gold star, she should do it for this." He pushed away from the table, and as he did, a dozen whirly globes popped into existence. Arthur didn't even watch as he dug into a closet filled with athletic equipment. "You can never find a baseball bat when you need one."

The first little man knelt where he appeared. Another and another formed on the table. They looked around, looked at each other, bemused at being born. A platoon of Arthur's dad. How much did they know about themselves? Were they his dad mentally too?

Arthur came out of the closet triumphantly, holding a baseball bat. "I like to call this game 'whack-a-dad.' Pitch one of them in here, why don't you?" He put the bat on his shoulder. The little men moved away from him, crowding toward Liam.

"You can't, Arthur. It's mean. They're alive."

"Only as long as I want them to be," he said, raising the bat over his head. "Watch this."

"Run!" Liam yelled. He tipped the table, spilling the men onto the couch.

Some jumped to the floor and fled under the couch. Arthur squashed the ones on the cushions with a flurry of blows. The little man closest to Liam raised his arms over his head at the last second, but the bat smashed him anyways. Arthur grunted with the swing, his eyes sparkling and alive. He dropped to his knees, poking the bat under the couch. Two men sprinted to the left, along the baseboard, before running behind a recliner. Arthur clacked the bat hard against the wall, stretching to reach it. "Got you!" he announced.

A minute later, he sat on the floor, the bloody bat in hand, breathing hard. "Did I goosh them all?" He laughed. "I told you it would be cool." He gazed at the bat. The blood vanished, and when he got up to check the couch, the broken men disappeared there too. "I wasn't paying attention to how many I made. Did I get them all?"

Liam didn't look at the recliner. "I think so. I don't like this, Arthur. I don't want to play this game."

"You want to make snow globes instead?" Arthur snorted. "You got to come up with something better than that."

"Why kill them? You can just dematerialize them. They're scared." Liam flashed on the little man with his arms over his head. He didn't want to be killed. He tried to save himself.

Arthur braced the bat across his knees, looking satisfied. "My dad says, 'Make 'em, break 'em, erase 'em.' I'm just listening to my dad."

Mom's voice came from the front of the house. She'd come to pick him up.

Liam didn't talk on the drive home. His mom said, "Did you have a good time, honey?"

Houses and trees streamed past the car window. Liam leaned his head against the glass, feeling the wheels buzzing against the concrete. He thought about the two little men under the recliner. As long as Arthur couldn't see them, they were safe. He had to see them to dissolve them. He couldn't smash them or dematerialize them, but what were they doing right now? Were they cold? What would they eat? Did Arthur have a cat? Did they know they were Arthur's dad? Did they know how much he hated them?

"Mrs. Henderson called," Mom said as the car merged onto the highway. "She says there's a school-to-school competition next month she'd like to enter her best students in. She said you and Arthur would be the team captains. You'll need to practice together more if you want to win. Tomorrow's Saturday, so Arthur's parents said you could go over in the morning."

Liam pushed his food around on his plate during dinner, eating little. He went to bed, but couldn't sleep. When he closed his eyes, he imagined the little men in Arthur's house, waiting to be smashed. He imagined himself, hiding in the springs underneath the recliner, peeking out when the lights were off, planning an escape, but where would they go? This wasn't a world for two-inch men. They should have been dematerialized. Mrs. Henderson said, "You create from the universe's raw essence, and you return what you've made to the essence. It's a balance."

He lay in the darkness of his bedroom. He concentrated until a firefly appeared in the middle of the room. Its silent light blinked on and off as it flew from the dresser to the top of a picture frame hanging on the wall. Soon, he'd filled the room with fireflies, all blinking gently. Fireflies don't flit, like houseflies. They float: fairies, glowing on their own for no reason, a pale, clear light that cast no shadows. It was beautiful, but one landed on his face, creeping him out. He returned them to the universe's essence and waited for the dawn.

Arthur's father opened the front door to let Liam in. Liam glanced back at his mom, but she was already pulling from the driveway. "You have two hours," the dad said, directing Liam toward the playroom by his shoulder. The man's fingers were hard and dug in. Liam bit his lip so he wouldn't yelp. "Maybe Arthur can teach you something."

The toy room had been rearranged, but Liam checked the recliner first, which hadn't been moved. Would the little men have stayed there all night? Bookshelves, a toy box, a dresser, and two more heavy chairs could also serve as hiding places. Maybe they'd left the room in the night.

The table from yesterday was gone. In front of the couch on the floor was a large pillow. Ten feet away was another. Arthur said, "Mrs. Henderson sent Dad suggestions for today. There's a 'mirror' contest where the judges show you an object for five seconds, and then you try to make it." Arthur thumbed through a sheaf of papers with instructions. Beside him was a box. Liam saw a paperback book, a pencil sharpener, and a small lamp with a frilly lampshade. "Totally stupid, of course. Who would want two lamps like this? I have a better idea." He took a roll of colored tape from the box, then made a two-foot by two-foot square on the carpet. "That's the arena. I make something and you make something, and we see which one wins."

Last year, Liam remembered that Arthur had brought a large jar with a garden spider in it, a lovely green and white spider with long, delicate legs, but what Arthur liked about it was dropping other insects in with it to see who would win. The bee and the spider ignored each other, as did the wasp and spider. A compact, muscular-looking jumping spider, though, immediately was consumed. Arthur and the other children crouched around the jar and squealed in delight. Liam didn't want to watch, but the garden spider's methodical draining of the jumping spider unfairly fascinated him.

The second day, Arthur found a praying mantis to feed to the garden spider. He waited until he had an audience before dropping the insect in. The garden spider didn't have a chance. Praying mantises fight like ninja assassins.

The show ended, though, when Arthur stole the class anole, a small lizard, from the terrarium. They'd had a contest to name the lizard during the first week. "Mr. Happy" received the most votes. The kids sucked in a collective breath when Arthur held it by its tail above the jar before dropping it in. The lizard and mantis didn't seem to see each other. The lizard pressed itself against the glass. After a few minutes nothing happened, so the kids wandered away. Arthur said to no one in particular, "A lizard is an animal. The mantis is just a bug. The lizard should win." He sounded disappointed. Later, Mrs. Latch came in to start class. They were a half hour into a reading lesson when she screeched from the back of the room. Liam turned in his seat. Mrs. Latch held the jar with the mantis in one hand and covered her mouth with the other. She said, "Mr. Happy's head is gone. It ate its head."

Liam thought Arthur was just continuing last year's game. Arthur sat cross-legged on a pillow. "I hope you've got more than a tiger."

Liam shook his head. "I don't like killing things."

Arthur said, "I thought you might not want to play, so I raised the stakes. Turns out that I didn't get all the dads yesterday." He pulled a shoebox from behind them, then tipped enough for Liam to see the little man inside, scrambling for footing in the box. He put the box down. "I thought it would be fair if we materialized something at the same time, but let's do it this way. I'll materialize, and then you match it. Otherwise I'll set mini-Dad's box on fire."

There was only one mini-dad in the box. Liam worried that Arthur had killed the other one, or maybe he had it in anther box (or maybe he got away!).

Liam sat. "Okay. What do you have?"

Arthur grinned. "Here you go." The tiny, spherical whirlwind spun into life in the middle of the arena. When it finished, a three-inch tall Tyrannosaurus rex stood on the carpet. Arthur said, "I watched *Jurassic Park* five times to get him right."

Liam got down on this hands and knees to see the dinosaur up close. It cocked its head and looked back at him. The detail was impressive.

So, how to win without killing anything? Liam settled into the pillow, thought for a minute, then focused. Out of the whirling marble, a three-inch long porcupine coalesced into existence. It waddled toward the T. rex, unconcerned and lazy.

"Hey, not fair. A tyrannosaurus is way bigger than a porcupine."

"You didn't say that was a rule." Liam felt like clapping his hands. He'd always loved animals. His bookshelf at home had several picture book encyclopedias of the natural world.

The T. rex circled the porcupine, roaring, a barely discernable noise from such a small throat. It closed on the shorter animal, tried to bite, then backed away, a spear-like spine clinging to the side of its face.

"It's a draw," Liam said. "Send the little man back. He doesn't belong here."

Arthur shook the box. Liam couldn't see, but he heard the thump of the little man bouncing off the sides. "You have to win. No draws. Try this."

The T. rex, still pawing at its face, shimmered before disappearing in a multi-colored flash. A swirling materialization globe replaced it. When it cleared, a shiny black scorpion emerged, stalking the porcupine.

Liam matched it with a three-inch long pill bug with a hundred legs and sliding armor scales. When the scorpion struck, the pill bug rolled into a tight ball. The scorpion's stinger clicked when it hit, but didn't penetrate.

"That's still a draw, you cheater!" Arthur reached for the baseball bat.

"No!" Liam wanted to grab the box and run with him, but Arthur was larger and faster. He'd never be able to beat him. "I've got another."

The pill bug rainbowed away, and in its place a Nile crocodile fell into existence. Blood pulsed painfully in Liam's forehead. He'd never materialized different things this close together, and the creations were hard! To make them right, he not only had to keep their shape in his head, but there were also moves he didn't consciously control, the ones that gave the creature animate life, that made it behave like the animal Liam was thinking of when he brought it into being.

"Ah, now you're playing the game," Arthur said. "Can you imagine when we're older and can make big things? I could materialize a velociraptor in the mall. I could put a mountain lion in a roller coaster. They'd be screaming for real then."

Everything Arthur said sounded wrong to Liam. He didn't know what to do. Mrs. Henderson wouldn't approve. And it occurred to him that Arthur was a danger. It wasn't just what he made or what he did with them, but Arthur himself, who didn't worry that he killed things, or that his creations were scared and suffered and died in pain. Arthur was more monstrous than a T. rex. He was the scorpion in the room.

In the arena, the scorpion spotted the crocodile and moved in, its tail high in the air. The crocodile opened its jaws and hissed. When the stinging tail flashed down, the crocodile clamped down on the scorpion's leg. The two tumbled together, stabbing and biting. A thick skin seemed to protect the crocodile, but it could only bite at the scorpion's legs. One snapped off, but the scorpion wasn't handicapped. It retreated while the crocodile didn't seem to realize that the leg in its mouth wasn't attached to its opponent. The crocodile gnawed on the leg while the scorpion circled it, its stinger high in the air, glistening.

Liam wished he could direct the crocodile, make it obey his commands, but once he materialized it, it was on its own. The best Liam could hope for was to come up with a stronger opponent for the scorpion. For its size, nothing seemed appropriate. An elephant or rhinoceros couldn't defeat a scorpion if they weighed the same. If they were in an aquarium, a shark might work, but here, he had nothing. Maybe an eagle, or a pterodactyl? He could do something mythical, like a dragon.

Before he could make the replacement, though, the scorpion struck, landing its stinger at the base of the crocodile's skull. Did it know that that was a vulnerable spot? In the real world, a scorpion never met a crocodile on even footing, so either the scorpion was lucky, or he carried with him an instinctive knack for finding his prey's weakest point. The crocodile arched backwards in agony, rolled onto its side and died before Liam could vanish it back to the painless void.

"I won," Arthur said. "Crocodile wasn't bad, but it didn't save mini-Dad." He picked up the box, shook it again. "I've thought a lot about this. I could toss him down the garbage disposal."

Arthur set the box down. The little man faced him, his hands on his hips. "Do you understand me?" Arthur asked. "Do you know what I'm going to do to you? What do you think? Maybe a taste of the belt? How about a hand on the stove? That would be nice, right? After all, I'm the big one now."

"He's just a little man," Liam said. "He's never done anything to you."

Arthur sneered. "I made him. He's mine. I can break him if I want. I've already done it a hundred times."

Liam felt sick and wished he was home in his room where he could make fireflies or flowers, or just lay quietly in bed reading a book.

"Nope, a simple squashing will do the trick. The world's a tough place, Dad. It's time you learned that." He rocked forward, his hand out, palm down, descending on the little man.

Arthur lurched, off balance. "Shit! Ow!" He fell to his side, grabbing at his thigh. The other little man, a duplicate of the dad in the box, stood on the floor, looking determined, holding a thumbtack awkwardly in his arms. He dropped it as he sprinted to the box.

A rescue mission! thought Liam.

Arthur waved his hand in the air. "I'm bleeding."

Liam shut his eyes, focusing on the thought clay. The little men needed help, a distraction. Six creation spheres spun to life in the air between him and Arthur, who was scrambling for his bat. The little man reached the box, jumped for the edge. Hung on. Inside the box, the other one realized what was going on, then threw himself against the same side. The box began to tip over.

"Not so fast," Arthur said, bat in hand, as he put his foot on the box's other side, pinning it down.

The first hazy sphere resolved itself into a hornet three inches long, wings buzzing like a tiny saw. It flew in a widening circle, joined by the others. Liam moved back. They were twice the size of natural hornets, black and yellow, huge jaw-like pinchers on their faces, a sting sharper than a hypodermic. One flew close by Arthur's face. He swung the bat awkwardly from his sitting position, taking it out with a messy splat, but the others swarmed around the room.

"Bastard," Arthur snarled. He swung at another one, but missed.

"I can make them faster than you can kill them," Liam said.

"They don't matter. We'll see what I can make for you in a minute." Arthur brought the bat down hard on the shoebox, missing both men while crushing the box on one side.

"Arthur!" The voice boomed in the room. Arthur's father stood at the door, his face purple.

Neither boy moved. Arthur held the bat over his head, poised for the killing blow. The wasps buzzed in the air for a few seconds before Liam unmade them in bright rainbow flashes.

Arthur's dad strode into the room, larger than life and angry. He picked up the shoebox, looked at the little men closely.

"It was a game..." Arthur said.

"These are me. You were going to kill me?" His voice rose at the last. "These are me!" He set the box on the ground gently. It was the gentleness that scared Liam. Arthur's father contained the anger. Only a tremble in his hand when he released the box showed emotion.

"Your mother and I have talked about you, Arthur," the dad said, straightening. "We have been concerned that you are not going to be what we hoped."

"I didn't mean to, Dad." Arthur looked at Liam desperately. "We were playing."

"Make, break, erase," Dad said.

Liam wished he could be anywhere else, but neither of them seemed to remember that he was there.

"Your mother will be so disappointed," Dad said. "Such a waste of time."

"No, Dad. I can be better... I can..."

The rainbow of unmaking shimmered around Arthur, swallowing him up, and then the spot was empty, as if Arthur had never been.

Dumbfounded, Liam squeaked, "You can't make people. Mrs. Henderson said."

"Children can't," Dad said. He stepped on the shoebox, crushing both little men like mice. "When you get older, you'll understand." He glanced around the room. "We'll turn this into a nursery again." He rubbed his chin. "Maybe a little girl this time. Yes, that might be better."

Sometime later, Liam sat on the bench by Arthur's front door, waiting for his mother to pick him up. A rabbit peeked at him from under a bush at the edge of the yard. Liam wondered if it was a materialization. How could he tell? Did the little men know what they were?

Arthur's dad opened the door just as Mom arrived. She smiled at Liam from behind the wheel.

"Be good to your parents," Arthur's dad said. "Treat them right."

Liam looked at his mother bleakly. All it takes is a thought. A thought and what is made is unmade. Was he real? What if even asking was a disappointing question? Mom smiled again. She waved for him to come on.

The first step was the hardest one he'd ever taken.

James Van Pelt is a full-time writer in western Colorado. His work has appeared in many science fiction and fantasy magazines and anthologies. He's been a finalist for a Nebula Award and been reprinted in several year's best collections. His first Young Adult novel, Pandora's Gun, was released from Fairwood Press in August of 2015. His latest collection, The Experience Arcade and Other Stories was released at the World Fantasy Convention in 2017. James blogs at http://www.james-vanpelt.com, and he can be found on Facebook.

COLD DREAD AND HOT SLICES

Spencer Koelle

THIS WAS NOT HOW LALANA WANTED TO SPEND HER TWENTY-SEVENTH birthday, but she couldn't ask for time off on her second working day. She read over the list of backups again. She could do this.

Cold air rolled over Lalana as she dragged the metal door open. Green trays of dough balls and grey tubs flanked the entrance, while yellowish vats and steel trays of toppings obscured the wall further in. The room smelled of pizza sauce, yeast, and, for some reason, peppermint. She tugged the cart in, and the door gently swung shut. Lalana crouched on the greasy floor and pulled out the list.

Lalana fumbled with the grey lid of the shredded mozzarella tub through the cheap, oversized plastic gloves. She didn't see a scoop. Charles had said she wasn't fast enough with the dough stretching, and she still kept screwing up on the line. She couldn't come back and ask her manager for help again.

She bit her lip and stuffed handfuls of cheese into the silver tray. After she returned, she could ask if there was a better way to do this. Somebody had scratched homophobic slurs on the metal wall behind the cheese, along with a weird symbol that looked like three 'Y's at angles to each other, joined at the tail.

Once the tray was full, Lalana straightened up and tried to rub some warmth into her arms. The restaurant provided the black apron that barely fit, but she'd had to pay for the stupid little hat. Then, the train pass to get here had used up the last of a modest furry cyborg smut commission. She still needed to find a trans-friendly roommate before her ex-boyfriend kicked her off his moldy couch.

The cheese looked greenish, but her shirt looked green too. It was probably just the lighting. She opened the tub of sauce. At least this had a scoop. It was slow, awkward work.

Movement caught Lalana's attention. She struggled to resolve the colors and shapes into something her brain could interpret. Did somebody leave a pile of sausages next to the mushroom tub? No, it was too pink. It was waving, like something underwater. Long, thin cones reached out from the bottom of a tube, each split halfway down. Four branched out from the bottom, then three further up, then two, until the top ended in a split point. The whole thing was a lurid, steaming pink.

The bizarre growth stopped moving. Fear replaced confusion. It leaned towards Lalana. The peppermint smell grew thicker, and she could feel its attention pressing on her. She backed away faster. Her skin crawled with its awareness.

Cold steel slapped her back. She fumbled with the door. It didn't open. She pushed harder. She could still feel that horrible polyp scrutinizing her, harsher than the chill of the air. She pounded until the metal rang.

The door swung inward.

"You alright?" the warm-faced Venezuelan prep cook asked her.

Lalana jumped over the threshold and squeezed the middle-aged woman tightly. She couldn't form words. She dared a glance behind her.

The walk-in fridge held her cart and lots of tubs and vats. There was no magenta thing straining towards her.

Lalana released the woman, jerked back, and looked down. "Sorry," she stammered, clearing her throat. "I forgot which way the door opened. Sorry."

The woman gave her a concerned look and patted her arm. "It is okay."

"Thank you," Lalana said. She reached in with one arm, shifted the cart over the threshold, and headed back towards the warmth of the front. Somebody else could get the other backup ingredients.

The cook had turned back to prepping onions. Lalana gave the fridge one last look, then swung the door shut, gently. Maybe she could go to that free mental health seminar at the library. Maybe she should try harder to meditate.

She still felt cold.

"Lalana, where is the dough?" Charles demanded.

Lalana looked stupidly at the cart with only three stretched discs left.

"Go back to stretching dough," the manager said brusquely. "I'll handle the line."

Lalana nodded meekly. The cart would be full by now if he hadn't taken her away from the stretcher to handle the cheese and protein stations.

The two rolling-pin-like parts of the dough stretcher spun to a halt, the dough stuck halfway down behind the plastic screen. It was her second week, and she still kept screwing this up.

A cluster of college students pushed past the door. The first one ordered a plain cheese pizza. It took seconds to complete. Sweat glued flour to her fingers, soaked her side rolls, and funneled down her back.

When Lalana restarted the machine, the dough dropped out in a misshapen pile. She set it aside and struggled to guide a new dough ball into the machine. She didn't look to see if the tray was empty, she just slammed the next stretched crust onto the table for the line worker to pick up.

Normally she found this work soothing, but she was still sweating and tight with tension. She sniffed the air. Among the hints of burnt crust and seasoned sauces, she caught a trace of peppermint.

She glanced around. Three boys and a girl sat together near the front of the store. The old-timey lightbulbs flickered on the end of quirky pipe fixtures. Yvonne was getting a drink from the artisanal soda fountain. (Drinks were free for employees, but they still had to pay for pizzas, although at a thirty-three percent discount). A splash of bright pink caught her eye, but it was just a pair of earbuds nothing squirmed, or waved, or intruded on her notion of what was possible in the living world.

She returned to the dough, pulling off the ball and clearing the spot it left with a scraper. Mumford and Sons wailed in the speaker system, just audible above the rumble of the stretcher and the roar of the oven. Mumford and Sons was always playing overhead.

What had really happened in the walk-in fridge last week? She hadn't experienced any other episodes at work or at home. She'd smelled peppermint a few times at work without any apparent source, but maybe that was just the cleaning fluid they used or somebody's body wash. It was just stress.

Finally, Lalana reached the end of the dough tray. The peppermint smell was stronger. Did the naked yellow bulbs seem a little yellow-green? She wasn't sweating anymore, despite the heat of the oven.

She gave the green plastic tray another scraping, tipped it over the trash can, and shook out the scraps. The next dough tray was empty. Who had stacked an empty dough tray under the full ones?

"I'll get more dough," Yvonne volunteered, setting down her pink drink. Lalana flashed her a grateful smile. Nothing else strange had happened here, but she still wasn't ready to go back to the walk-in fridge.

At least she had tips to look forward to today. They weren't technically servers, but they had a tip jar. It might be small, but any cash in hand helped. Her stomach growled. Her SNAP benefits wouldn't refill for two weeks, and she'd run out of foods she could take to work in reused Tupperware. It was also incredibly hard to work around pizza all day and not crave pizza.

The air smelled more like candy canes than pizza. She shuddered. Yvonne wheeled in the second cart stacked with six trays of dough.

"Thanks," Lalana murmured. She still felt cold. She still smelled something sharp and minty.

She turned to Yvonne, who had started folding pizza boxes. "Did you ever see anything weird in there?" It took a lot of courage to force the words out, and they were barely audible over the background noise.

Yvonne sipped her drink and stared at her. "What?"

"I mean, in the walk-in fridge," Lalana stammered. "Anything weird there?"

Yvonne frowned at her. She returned to the boxes without answering.

"Never mind," Lalana muttered.

"Try to go faster," Charles said over his shoulder, in what he thought was an encouraging tone of voice.

She hated feeling like an idiot when she screwed up an order, or had to ask the boss for help with some simple task. If she couldn't even do *this* right, then what use was she?

Lalana had almost filled up the cart when Charles shouted, "We're running low on San Marzano tomato sauce!"

She tried to remember where the sauce was. There was sauce in the walk-in fridge, and some backup in the reach-in, but the closest was in that pull-out drawer under the cutting board. Everyone else was on the line, dealing with a lunch-time rush.

Lalana pulled the drawer out. This time she did scream.

The pink polyp waved, graceful and slow, nestled between two tubs of red sauce. It bunched up and then stretched out, like a time-lapse flower. The split tip at its top pointed to her. The other appendages followed.

There was a knife on the board for cutting beef sausages and green apples. She grabbed it. The thing tilted, facelessly studying her.

Lalana thrust the knife at it. The pink substance parted like a waterfall. One of the limbs hovered in mid-air. When she pulled the knife out, it was whole again.

She tried a second swing, but her heel skidded on a wet patch of tile. In the corner of her eye, the polyp glowed purple and faded from sight. Steel sang out as she bounced against the oven.

Charles and Yvonne helped her to her feet. Her head throbbed but her vision was clear, and she counted the fingers Charles held up. She nodded solemnly as he reminded her not to scare the customers, and to be careful because the sink leaked a lot.

Before returning to the dough stretcher, Lalana pulled out the drawer again. There was a patch of clear gel, right where the polyp had been.

"Hey, Lalana, we need you on the line!" Charles shouted. She struggled to force a pair of static-clingy gloves over her fingers.

The line stretched out past the front door. Lalana scrambled to remember what sauce a Savory and Slow pizza had.

She remembered to check the drawer at the end of her shift, but by then the substance was gone. She had a lot of questions, but no answers and no plan.

Lalana inspected the condiments stack. It was one of those things you did when there wasn't much to do but you still had to look busy.

The busy days were hectic, stressful, overwhelming, humiliating, and panic-inducing. On the plus side, they did seem to go faster, and they didn't give her too much time to think.

Nothing weird had actually happened since her strange experience with the polyp in the sliding drawer last Tuesday. She had drained her plastic flask in three gulps right at the train station, twelve meters from the pizzeria, after clocking out that day. She'd recited every prayer she could remember on the train home instead of reading Metro and Philly Gay News, getting dirty looks from other passengers.

When Lalana had reached her ex's house that afternoon, she'd tried to look up that squirming pink apparition on the web, but had just found lots of marine biology and imaginative porn. She'd looked up aliens, American nature spirits, and demonology, and found nothing that resembled her encounter, nor any practical advice for protection that could apply to her situation. She couldn't afford any silver or jade things, and she couldn't very well draw unbroken lines in white and black ash around the pizzeria. She'd given away her last can of vegan coconut soup as alms at the nearest temple, even though it was Tibetan and she'd been raised Therevada, for what that was worth. She couldn't bring herself to ask about that grotesque pink entity in person.

Lalana looked over the shelves of the dry storage room. She didn't smell peppermint or feel cold, but there were many dark containers that could hide something deeply pink and writhing. She whispered a prayer. She grabbed one of the saltshakers, shook some grains into her hand, and tossed them over her shoulder.

Lalana inspected the big box of parmesan. It was just cheese. She twisted off the crusty metal top and awkwardly scooped cheese into the container. Lalana couldn't bring herself to *talk* about the apparition to anyone, not even her online friends. It was strangely shameful, as private as it was horrible. She still didn't even know if anyone else could even *see* it.

The sound of children greeted her when she returned to the front, along with a hint that might have been peppermint. She grabbed one of the saltshakers as she replaced the parmesan, filled her fist, and flicked it over her left shoulder as nonchalantly as she could.

"Lalana, you need to get on the line!" Charles said.

She hurried up, muttering prayers, but stopped when an old white lady in the family glared at her.

"Welcome to FRESH Custom Organic Pizza! Is this your first time here?" The script rolled off her tongue. She tried to ignore the faint peppermint smell. There were lots of dark, roomy containers in here.

"No, it's not," a middle-aged woman in sea-green said, smiling a little.

"Then welcome back!" Lalana said. "What kind of crust would you like, whole wheat or gluten-free?"

This began a complicated negotiation between the parties. It transpired that the oldest woman wanted a gluten-free crust, but that it was a preference rather than an allergy. Lalana was ashamed to feel relieved at that. She was glad there were options now for people with celiac disease, but she didn't know how to prepare pizza off the line, and she didn't feel ready for that responsibility. She was about to grab a cola when a young man in slacks and a dark gray T-shirt sauntered in.

"Hi. Welcome to FRESH Custom Organic Pizza, is this your first time here?" Lalana began.

"Just a cheese pizza," he said.

Lalana started, trying to remember the right way to tilt the spoon, how far down the grip to hold it, and ensuring an even distribution of sauce. She'd gotten a lot of conflicting feedback on that from more senior staff.

"Is it true about the guy who died here?" the man asked in a casual tone.

"What?" Lalana said. She sprinkled on the cheese.

"Some crazy Swedish inventor. He got himself killed a few years ago. You know, this place was boarded up until they sold it?"

"I don't know," Lalana said. "I'm not from around here."

"Okay. What's the wifi password?"

Lalana glanced at the sign on the wall and told him.

"Wipe down your station," Charles whispered in her ear. She flinched and grabbed a rag from a sanitizer bucket.

When she'd finished, she went to grab a soda. Sam was in front of her.

"Do you know about the guy who died here?" she asked

Sam stared at her. "No idea."

She shrugged and got a cane sugar cola. Lalana could smell the peppermint again.

On the pretense of cleaning and checking stock, with one hand on the matches in her pocket, she checked the reach-in fridge, the cooler drawers, and behind the dough-stretcher. None of them hid a swaying pink interloper.

When Charles checked up on her, she asked if he knew anything about the dead European inventor.

"Naw, I started here two years ago. But hey, you work hard, and you could become assistant manager in no time!"

"Thanks," Lalana said. She didn't want to become assistant manager here. She didn't want to memorize the ingredients and optimize her dough-stretching and dish-washing and box-folding. She wanted to work somewhere with lunch breaks longer than fifteen minutes that wouldn't get forgotten if things were busy. She wanted to be able to sit down now and then. She wanted to use her Associates Degree and get a living wage, or at least something closer to a living wage. She wanted not to think about how easy it would be to draw the knife across her thigh in the bathroom. She'd already started hitting her head against hard things when she was alone to punish herself, but she hadn't resumed the cutting, yet.

Most of all, she wanted to walk into work without clammy dread, tense and braced for some quivering pink horror that defied explanation.

"Hm?" Charles had asked her something.

"I said, do you have a boyfriend?" Charles repeated. There was no hunger in his voice, just friendly openness.

"No," she admitted.

"What about a girlfriend?" he asked, folding boxes without even looking at them.

"No," she said. She turned her attention to the dough scraper.

"Aw, why not?" he said, still smiling.

"Broke up," she answered, still looking away.

"Ooh, that's too bad. Was the sex good while it lasted?" His tone remained upbeat and conversational.

"That's... kind of personal," she said, trying to control her breathing. An irrational voice insisted that he must *know*, that he saw something *wrong* with her and was just asking for the look of the thing.

"I guess so," he said with a shrug. "Why don't I take over that, and you can start cleaning the fixtures?"

Lalana nodded and tried to relax a little. She grabbed the sanitizer, a spare stool, and the rag. She was tall enough to reach most of the fixtures without grabbing a stool, but whenever she reached for something high, her cheap white shirt rode up.

Lalana breathed in, ran over the noble truths in her mind, and set her stool in place. She wasn't supposed to hate the music or the owner or her boss. She wasn't supposed to desire a more stable job, or a better living situation, but she was still really excited that she'd found a friendly, agender Latinx roommate in West Philly with a bedroom to spare. If she did the math right, her first paycheck might be just enough to put down a deposit. If it wasn't, well, she could at least buy a tent with it, or if not a tent, then a sleeping bag.

Lalana wrung out her rag and applied it to the dusty, swinging lamps. It didn't seem to make much difference, more just shifting the grime around, but that might be part of the vintage look the owner was going for. She sniffed the air. The peppermint smell was faint, but she could still catch it.

Lalana stayed close to the light sources. She peered into the dim corners for any recess where the polyp could hide. She saw only cobwebs on the ceiling, napkins and stray vegetables on the floor.

Her stool started to tremble when she reached over to the big, rusty tools. She could recognize part of an old water-pump, and the huge gear. What about this thing in the middle, though? It had a net of gleaming steel threads, digging into the wall, and concentric rings that looked like lead, rusty iron, and polished bronze. It was odd to see so much rust on the second ring, because the rest of it was spotless. There was one tiny, moving part in the center, a magnet on the end of a turning handle, with the words "Haraldur Magnus Gudmudsson" engraved on it. It might have been a quotation, or it might have been a name.

Lalana drew a deep sigh of relief when she passed the family on her way to clean the front glass. One of the children was nibbling on a pile of sticky red-and-white candies.

She picked up the squeegee and brushed away some stray mark on the glass. It looked a bit like a 'Y', with 'V's at the top of its tips and one upside-down at its bottom.

Lalana barely tasted the pineapple, goat cheese, and chili oil on the pizza she felt guilty about spending money on, even with the discount. She'd already checked her online dating profile twice, and there was only one message that wasn't a straight cis man asking for "discreet encounters".

Her left leg hammered against the cold floor almost as hard as her heart. She tried to drag some speck of her attention away from the minty hint in the stale air and the many, many shadows in the cluttered storage room.

Lalana closed her eyes, took several deep, deep, breaths, recited a sutra, and then took a sip of her soda.

Movement caught her eyes. She looked into the dark corner and saw nothing. She rubbed her nose on the too-short sleeve.

"Charles wants you on the line," Davis said. Lalana almost knocked her drink over. She still had six minutes left on her break, technically.

"I'll be right up," she said, biting her lip and staring into the shadows. She knew he was staring at her ass, but she could ignore that as long as he didn't try anything physical or take creepshots.

After Davis left, Lalana pulled her apron on and crammed the last slice of the personal-size pizza into her mouth in one fluid motion. She squeezed the small bag of dried basil, iron chain, and salt packets in her right pocket while she stepped behind stacks of crates and investigated every dank corner. The minty smell didn't grow noticeably weaker or stronger.

She hadn't found anything unearthly yesterday when the lights turned greenish and the air smelled of candy canes in the dishroom around closing time, or earlier today when she was learning how to mix mozzarella and caught a hint of mint. Maybe one of the scavenged items was keeping her safe from writhing magenta nightmares.

Fear of the paranormal receded into mundane fears of shouting and failure. She strode past the cooler and the dry storage, into the warm lights of the service area. The line of customers already snaked around a row of tables. She squeezed past them, with difficulty, murmuring "excuse me" and ignoring the dirty looks she got for daring to take up so much space. She hovered between the protein and veggie stations, uncertain.

"Get on station three," Charles murmured into her ear, sounding more disappointed than angry. "I can't keep babysitting you."

Ronald slid the pizza up, with barbeque sauce instead of red sauce under the cheese. "Barbeque chicken," he confirmed.

Lalana sighed inwardly and kept up her smile. She had to change gloves every time she did the chicken. She separated the tougher chunks as finely as she could, then passed it on to the next station, whispering "barbeque chicken" to Tammy.

The sauce-stained gloves were a struggle to take off. Her hands were slick with sweat, but also curiously sticky. She took some precious seconds to get flour on her hands so the fresh pair of gloves would slide on easier. Then began the long struggle to make the flimsy, bag-like things to open.

Lalana smelled barbeque sauce and sausages. She saw the old wooden wall and quirky light fixtures. She smelled baking dough and melting cheese. She heard the roar of the industrial oven and the rumble of the automatic dough-stretcher. She smelled peppermint.

She stared at the silent reach-in fridge, the unopened drawers, the stacks of dough trays and pizza boxes. There were two different groups of noisy children, but none of them had any red and white candies. Nobody appeared to be chewing gum or sucking on breath mints. *Take it easy, Lalana,* she thought. *Nothing happened last time.*

The lights over her buzzed and flickered. The next person had a Farmer's Market pizza. She darted over the different meats, confused. Then she remembered that specialty pizza didn't have meat. A short, black kid with Tardis earrings asked her for a Savory and Slow. That took almost all the meats, and she just stopped herself from accidentally adding chicken to the mix.

Lalana became intensely aware of the sweat on her forehead, the flickering lights, and the minty aroma around her. A cute girl in a purple hijab asked her if there was any non-pork meat. She couldn't remember if there were animal-handling standards within halal dietary restrictions, but maybe this was a more relaxed individual?

"The sweet Italian sausage is all-beef, and the meatballs are veal," Lalana said hopefully. Since she'd gotten this far, her rules must be lax enough that she didn't have to prepare it off the line. "One second," she said, ducking back to change her gloves just to be on the safe side. Nothing was under the trays waiting for her.

"I'll go with the sausage and the chicken then," the girl said.

"Sure thing." Lalana smiled at her, grabbing some sausage with her left hand and trying to crumble the chicken with her right hand only. She tried to quell the un-Buddhist flare of resentment at the choice. The line was already reaching out through the front door. A lightning glance at the clock revealed that it wasn't even six yet. At least she had that date at the park with Alex to look forward to tomorrow.

"I'd like pepperoni, bacon, sausage, and the veal meatball," said the next customer. Lalana's hands moved without thinking. She stared to make sure she was actually putting the right things on.

"Let's move it people," Charles said, with an encouraging clap before he returned to the slicing and finishing station.

Lalana got through the next seven or ten pizzas without incident, and the hour hand crawled past the six. She was about to turn around so she could finally wipe her brow in her apron, but a whole family came up to her with four kid-sized pizzas that each needed a different topping. The smallest boy almost burst into tears when she put sausage on his instead of pepperoni, so she set it aside and started over.

Charles switched her over to the cheese station. This meant almost every request was the same shredded mozzarella, but it meant she didn't get many breaks where she could just wave the customer on to the next station. The lights flickered as she pulled on her gloves.

"Plain cheese," the customer said. A sauced-up gluten-free crust came before her. Lalana smiled at the customer and sprinkled it on. A second later she couldn't remember a single detail about him.

The mint smell was still there, overwhelming the different cheese scents. She tried to convince herself that the cheese looked off-white, and not faintly green.

"What cheese is that?"

Lalana struggled to remember. "That's our aged gorgonzola," she said. "Do you want it?"

"Does it cost extra?" the old woman in the teal jacket probed.

"You can get any cheese, sauce, and toppings you want, and it all costs the same here at FRESH custom pizza," she recited.

"I think I'll stick with the normal shredded cheese, but could I also have some of the fresh mozzarella chunks?" she asked.

Lalana blinked away sweat. She really wanted to wipe her face, but she couldn't do that with a glove on and the too-short sleeves, especially not with a customer watching. She crumbled up the chunked mozzarella. She bit back a gasp as something hot and damp curled around her ankle.

She passed on the pizza, but before she could look down another customer came up. "I'd like the gorgonzola, the feta, and do you do parmesean?" he asked apologetically. The pressure against her leg felt strange, like a vibrating toothbrush or something with lots of stiff, not-quite-sharp hairs. She shifted her legs and tried to stomp without making noise, but it didn't seem to make a difference.

"You can get parmesan at the finishing touches stage," Lalana explained. She blinked again.

"Just the gorgonzola and the feta then," the man said.

Lalana took a half-second to remind herself what feta looked like, and then applied the cheeses. She passed the pizza on. The next customer asked for mozzarella, and she started sprinkling on shredded mozzarella before the customer clarified that he wanted the fresh chunk mozzarella. She hastily apologized while the buzzing, metal-bench-on-a-sunny-day hot touch crawled over her. She asked the tall, thin-faced white woman to repeat her order. She tried to remember what went on a Kenneth Circle pizza, then had to waste time picking up a fallen-over menu card to examine it. She threw the chunks on, barely taking time to split them.

The next person wanted a cheese pizza with extra cheese. The mint burned in her nostrils, the lights buzzed and stuttered. Hot appendages curled around her legs like the tails of many cats. She couldn't look away from the cheese and the customers. Part of her didn't want to.

Sweat stung Lalana's eyes. Charles stopped her from putting the wrong type of cheese on a seasonal Sliced Pear special. Her throat dried up. Her smile stiffened. Nobody else looked down in her direction. Why would they? She didn't look down. She already knew that the bristling mass at her feet would be slowly moving and painfully pink.

The clock passed seven. Five or fifteen or fifty pizzas later, the clock passed eight. The line was still reaching outside the door. There was no time to grab a drink, or wipe her face, or look down.

Her hand moved to the cheese. She stared at empty space. She turned her head. Wood walls and steel piping met her. The line had ended.

She looked at the clock. *Just one more half hour.* Something bright purple flashed in the corner of her eye.

Lalana peered down, but now there was nothing squeezing her shins together. She became more aware of several pains that had been calling for her attention.

Charles was in the back. She'd already taken her break, but she was still allowed to use the bathroom, if they weren't busy. She staggered over to the single-occupant women's restroom, knocked, and dove in.

She locked the door behind her. She recognized the itch in her throat, the ache in her bladder, and the hollow pang in her stomach, but her legs were aching the most of all. After relieving herself, she sat down, then pulled up her legs and wrapped her arms around them. She bit her lip and cried, quietly, for a minute or two. That goal achieved, she stood to wash her hands.

Her ankle throbbed. She checked to see if she had sprained it somehow, but no. It was fine. Long patterns of angry red skin decorated her shins and right ankle, peeling like a sunburn.

This was probably bad. The polyp hadn't hurt her before. She tried to think about it, to plan, to adapt somehow. Her brain stalled.

Lalana dumped the reclaimed iron chain, basil, and salt into the wastebasket. Then she washed her hands and hurried back to wipe down the line.

Lalana tried to relax. She took a deep breath and drew the squeegee along the glass of the front door. She'd started today in a relatively good mood. She had a few things to be happy about.

She'd finally landed the room in a row house one block from the trolley line, and it came complete with a bed. She'd had a job interview with Starbucks last week, had sent out three applications to downtown admin jobs, and the coffee date with Alex had gone well. Her SNAP had refilled, and she'd treated herself to a microwavable curry. It was six days since she'd cut herself, two weeks since she'd seen her writhing little friend, and she hadn't made a mistake all day. Even her dysphoria had been pretty mild.

She finished up the door and started on the biggest window's front. Maybe that was why she couldn't relax.

"Lalana! I need you at the register."

Or maybe it was just prescience.

"I haven't used a register before," she said, scurrying over with the squeegee still in hand.

"It's not hard at all," Charles said with a genuine smile. Lalana shuddered inwardly. They had very different ideas about what was easy or obvious.

He ran over the instructions very quickly as he rung up a Savory and Slow pizza for the middle-aged dark woman with pearls. She asked him to repeat the bit about receipts. The information flew in and out of her head. Thankfully, Trent took over the receipt instead of her, and Charles reassigned her to the cheese station.

The first two people wanted Margherita pizzas, which she could do in her sleep. Maybe she was finally getting the hang of this.

During a brief break between customers, Lalana noticed the cheese was getting a little low. She sniffed the air for any hint of peppermint, then pulled open the drawers where the extra cheese was usually kept.

There was no shredded mozzarella. The clock said 11:53 a.m. A chill ran down her spine that had nothing to do with unearthly horrors.

Lalana darted to the reach-in fridge, squeezing past co-workers with hasty apologies and making sure Wallace didn't get a chance to pinch her ass. She inhaled again, smelled nothing beyond the smoke and sauce and melted cheese. She pulled open the steel door, rummaged around olives and sauces and milk boxes. There was no shredded mozzarella in the reach-in fridge either. Sweat ran down her sides and her knees trembled.

"Is something wrong?" the short, black new girl, whose name she couldn't remember, asked.

"Could you get some shredded mozz' from the walk-in?" Lalana pleaded.

"Sure!"

"Thank you," Lalana said. She hurried back to the cheese station.

She hesitated. Lalana didn't smell anything exactly, but the background noise sounded a little off. She blinked twice. The familiar scene around her still had a greenish hue.

The creepy, skinny, white guy with the Doctor Who jacket sidled in. He would linger for hours, just watching her and pretending to read a worn-out paperback with a raised silver title. Sometimes he ordered a second pizza after finishing his first. Sometimes he just went through eight or nine free soda refills. She'd checked with some co-workers, and he didn't linger the same way when she wasn't on the shift.

Lalana prepped his Farmer's Market pizza with minimal fear. There was no room on his person to conceal a firearm. If he ever turned ugly, she was pretty confident she could break his arm with one hand.

After she finished his pizza, she sneezed and had to go back and wash her hands again. She glanced around to see if anyone was chewing gum or eating mints.

All those thoughts fled from her mind when the new girl came back with the bad news. There was no shredded mozzarella left.

None at all.

The next dozen or hundred customers passed in a blur. All she could remember was repeating the mantra, apologizing for the lack of the most common pizza cheese and offering substitutes, like torn up chunked fresh mozzarella. Most people settled for that, some turned away. Nothing popped out at her or wrapped around her legs.

It wasn't until things started to calm down that she noticed what was under the table, in the farthest corner. A family was sitting together, two young men, a small child, and a white-haired grandmother.

The pink polyp brooded there, among shriveled olives and used napkins. The napkins stirred as if in a breeze when it poked them, but the olives remained unmoved. It stretched one half of a limb towards the old woman's black stocking, then reached out with the other half and two more. It didn't seem able to move from the spot, and her legs were pulled in, just out of range.

"Charles, could I do some sweeping?" she said, while dusting an herbed butter pizza with gorgonzola and shredded provolone.

"Of course not." Charles chuckled. "We need you on the line."

"Could you just check up on that family of four at the back-corner table?" she said, almost keeping the panic out of her voice.

Charles laughed again and turned away without answering her.

The child started crying. It couldn't be more than a toddler. It seemed to be pointing in the direction of the pink thing. None of the adults glanced under the table.

The more handsome of the two men tried to comfort the child. The pink horror did not reach towards his legs, even though he was only inches from it. The old woman muttered something, pushed her chair back, and shuffled over to the restroom.

The next customer chose shredded provolone instead of fresh chunk mozzarella. Finally, Charles asked the family how they were doing. He could have seen the pink aberration clearly if he'd looked down, but his eyes hovered, and he never seemed to catch it in his peripheral vision. It was like he was avoiding eye contact with somebody hiding in shadow.

Lalana prayed under her breath as she served up a Savory and Slow with feta cheese. The hot pink thing still swayed and shivered, like a slow-motion explosion of bubble gum. She tensed up again when the grandmother came out of the restroom and sat down.

Her legs were spread wide. Lalana wanted to say something, anything, to get her to pull back her heels. She couldn't think of anything to say.

The pink being closed four of its limbs through the tight black stocking on her right leg. She didn't show any reaction. After six endless seconds, it withdrew its tendrils.

Lalana exhaled. She asked the tight-lipped customer to repeat himself. She got to work spreading provolone evenly on his garlic sauce base.

With a silent flicker of purple light, the polyp vanished.

Lalana began to relax in earnest. The endless line of customers shrank to something that fit inside the restaurant. The wave of assault slowly reduced to a trickle. The creepy white guy finally left, pausing to ogle her one more time.

The family asked for a box and put three remaining slices into it. The grandmother rose from her seat and started towards the door.

She collapsed after the third step. Her head bounced on the floor and her arm twisted. She flailed and shuddered as her eyes rolled back. People screamed.

Matthew ran to the phone to dial 911. Lalana dove into the office alcove, snatched the first aid kit, and sprang out.

Lalana talked to her with slow, soothing words, putting a cold pack on the woman's head and a bandage on the tiny cut that had opened, which was still bleeding with great enthusiasm. She thought she heard one of the men say, "Not again!"

The ambulance arrived later, and although she said she could walk, they took her on a stretcher. Lalana didn't know any of their names, so she never found out what happened to the old woman.

Another train screamed into the station, scattering the dark pigeons and small brown birds. Lalana emptied a hot sauce packet into her soft taco.

She tried to think of the positives. She had managed the rent for her second month. The third date with Alex had gone smoothly. She had refrained from cutting herself for five whole days. She'd put in ten job applications today, and two of them were to places she was qualified for in her field. These were all good reasons not to hop onto the rails and welcome the Elmwood Line's cold steel kiss.

Lalana threw a pinch of the taco to a beautiful coal-dark pigeon. It hesitated, then pounced upon it, wings flashing emerald and indigo. She hadn't been caught drinking on the job, confining her nips to a few mouthfuls in the bathroom or dry storage, and even then only near the end of her shift. One of the housemates had let her borrow a black tourmaline crystal and a stone with a natural hole in it. Time would tell if they were any use dealing with her problem.

She'd run over every list of trans-friendly businesses she could find. Most weren't hiring at her experience level. It was hard to be patient when she'd spent the last seven months looking for work as her savings and donations from online friends withered away. Any day now, she could get a position somewhere, anywhere, as long as it kept her off the streets and didn't involve a throbbing pink phantom. At least it couldn't bother her outside the building, right?

She tried to take back the thought. She prayed. She clutched the stones.

Her train was delayed by five minutes. Some of the other people waiting gave her funny looks. She couldn't believe it. It couldn't be true. Her nose caught that sharp, fresh odor, between stale smoke and fast food.

If it was out here, ready to come for her, anywhere, well then, she didn't need to wait for another train. If she felt that heat on her leg, or saw it reaching out towards her, she would queue her goodbye post and solve everything at once.

An old black man shuffled forward, selling peppermint sticks for one dollar each. Lalana relaxed her grip before she ground the stones to powder. Maybe these ones did work.

A text message popped up. Alex hoped she had a nice day and that her dysphoria wouldn't act up. She breathed.

If things didn't work out, she could always accept the train track's invitation for the ride home. She finished her taco, read her newspaper, and tried to brace herself for another long, bitter day.

Spencer Koelle is a distressed bisexual pagan living in the City of Brotherly Love. He strives to create the change he wants to see in horror fiction, from better minority representation to a less Christocentric perspective, and subverting the status quo. He loves red wine, 80s horror on VHS, vegetarian cuisine, shy cats and friendly spiders. More information is available at his website www.spencerkoelle.com and his Twitter handle @KoelleSpencer.

 # CATCH OF THE DAY

Karter Mycroft

T HE FISH AT THE MARKET WERE HOVERING AGAIN. SYLVIA PACED between troughs of fresh-caught tuna, looking for the best, meatiest specimen to bring back to the restaurant. She was alone, having come early for the best selection. She examined each fish with great care, amused at the way they floated above the ice.

"Hello there." She came to face a big, sleek yellowfin, its toothy jaw hanging open as it hung in midair. Bulbous and silvery, with a stately fin and fierce triangle spikes, it was big enough to feed their customers all day long. There was something in its eye, too. Her dad always said the best fish had a shine to their eyes, a little spark of life behind their dead faces. It showed they had been strong while they lived. This fish undoubtedly had the spark. She slipped it weightlessly into a plastic bag and made her way out of the cooler, dragging it through the air like a balloon.

When she approached the counter it sank down in the bag, assuming its usual weight. She thought of asking the monger if he had any idea why dead fish seemed to float in the air these days, but he wouldn't know what she was talking about. They only floated for her, when no one else was around, and she figured that was the sort of thing she'd best keep to herself. She paid for the fish and said thanks and left the market.

When she got to her car, the big tuna was floating again. She strapped it in with the seatbelt like it was a person in the passenger seat. It used to be her dad sitting there on these trips. He always loved the fish market. These days he stayed in his room above the restaurant because he had trouble getting in and out of the car. So in an odd way it was nice having the fish float next to her. It was a great fish, too.

She pulled onto the street, swerving around a pile of roadkill that would have hit her windshield. It wasn't only fish that floated. There were birds, possums, raccoons, rabbits. Sometimes her knees brushed against dead bugs when she walked. The worst had been the time she had seen some poor dog belly-up in the air, entrails hanging down into a pool of dried blood. Nowadays, she tried her best to keep her eyes on the road.

The sun was creeping over the harbor when she pulled into the restaurant. The tuna grew weighty as she entered to find her brother chopping potatoes in the kitchen.

"Hey. Where's Dad?"

"Still asleep."

"I gotta show him this fish."

Her brother squinted over the counter. "That is a nice fish." He tossed something into the garbage. "Let him sleep, though. He needs it."

"If he's still out I won't bother him. But he'll appreciate this."

On the stairs up to their apartment, the fish hovered again.

She slipped across the hallway and cracked the bedroom door. "Psst. You up?" She peeked in. Her dad was a lump under the covers, sound asleep.

She would have to try later. Hopefully he would wake before they fileted the tuna.

Just as she was shutting the door, the blankets rustled. She smiled and slid inside.

To her surprise, the fish kept floating. Her heart fluttered. It never happened around anyone else. Did this mean her dad would see it too?

"Hey. Dad. Look at this."

He didn't answer. She approached the bed. His body lifted under the sheet.

"Dad?"

He rose until he floated a foot above the mattress.

Sylvia dropped the bag and screamed. The bag slipped off the fish and the bedsheet slipped off her dad and they floated together. His skin was pale, and his lips were blue; his eyes glazed over with an eerie shine. Heart pounding, she pulled out her phone and called 9-1-1, then sprang forward and pressed with all her strength onto his cold chest, over and over, tears welling as she fought to get his blood flowing and to keep him out of the air.

She was still crying when the ambulance doors slammed shut. The siren blared as it peeled out over the gravel and down the street.

When she opened her eyes, a firefighter was looking down at her.

"You're the one who found him?"

She nodded.

"It's a miracle you called when you did. We managed to get him breathing just now."

"Really?"

"Yeah. If he'd been out any longer he'd have permanent brain damage. Or worse."

She sniffled. She'd almost left him there. "So he might be okay?"

The firefighter sighed. "I can't tell you that. But he's awake. He's lucky to have you around." He stepped back. "He'll be at St. Mary's. You know where it is?"

She wiped her eyes. "Yeah."

"Okay. Hang in there."

When the firemen left, Sylvia stood, took a deep breath, and went inside.

Her brother wanted to go ahead and open the restaurant. He said they would need the money more than ever now that they had hospital bills coming. But Sylvia told him no. They should both go and stay at Dad's side until they were sure he was alright.

"We gotta ice your tuna, then."

"Sure."

Upstairs, the bedroom smelled like old man and there were big gray boot prints on the ground from the EMTs. Sylvia felt a chill when she entered. The fish was floating still by the bed, its teeth sharp behind its slack jaw, its wide eyes facing the doorway, shimmering.

Karter Mycroft is an author, editor, musician, and fisheries scientist who lives in Los Angeles. Their short fiction has been published or is forthcoming in The Colored Lens, Black Hare Press, Trembling With Fear, Lovecraftiana, and Made in L.A. Volume 3.

TRUMPET VOLUNTARY

Edmund Schluessel

T HE ORCHESTRA SWELLED AND STUNG AROUND THE STAIRCASE WITH ITS vacant elevated platform. The Mahlerine Symphony requires classical instrumentation — not a synthesizer or even an electric guitar to be found. In principle, every note could have been played by an orchestra from Brahms' time — apart, of course, from that final one of the Special Trumpet.

Each moment of life in the modern world is so much fine-filigreed art, procedurally crafted for all of us to fill the space available. When was the last time anyone heard a song on the radio they even remembered, much less enjoyed? Or watched a flitcom on the way to work that, while pleasing, wasn't disposable? It washes over us all like so much noise.

Ortolan's Symphony number 3, "For Gustav," is the only special work left ever since the advertising firms mined out Mozart. I was a boy falling in love with Bach when the JohannesAI turned the master's myriad compositions into a set of rules. Until the age of twelve I gorged on mock-Bach, until I grew sick on the glut.

My own boy was lucky: he was only eleven when he was selected to play the Mahlerine. It's better when they're younger. They can fully commit to the piece.

The audience drew their ravenous breaths as the conductor raised his arms. I saw the outline of my boy Robert as he took the raised stage, the black bell of his carbon-fiber trumpet. At the limit of my sight I think I saw the row of green LEDs down his cheeks saying his cybernetics were ready.

The conductor swept his right hand slowly and raised the winds, forlorn. I heard a rattle from the left as a bass player dropped his bow. The conductor called the contrabasses in on time; the errant player was not missed. Ortolan's Third quotes Beethoven's Ninth, not note for note but in spirit as the long thick strings of the double basses' quest for meaning.

I'd hoped my son's birth would bring meaning to my own life. My wife left me anyway when he was one — no joy in the relationship, she said. But I was a dutiful father, that much I'm sure of, and when Robert took a liking to the trumpet, I had a modest dream he would someday lead my trombone as part of a brass section.

He had no real talent, but he had enthusiasm, and something only the young today enjoy — passion more precious than life itself.

The first clarinet solo grated as it began, and as my eyes found the woman in the dazzling evening gown with the black stick between her lips, I saw the same trace of LEDs as Robert's cheeks bore. They call them "enhancers" but they're really controllers. We choose the note and the microsensors determine our intent and carry out our will more perfectly than we possibly could. The clarinetist's output might as well have come from a synthesizer. Her eyes roved the empty ceiling.

I curled my lip in annoyance. My son deserved more respect.

The lead trumpeter in the orchestra pit though, he was natural, and nervous. His cheeks, and all down his neck, were stippled with scars which he scratched at as he wobbled from foot to foot waiting for his cue. The lead trumpet in Ortolan's Third is a herald in the wilderness, John the Baptist singing the four-note motif of the Special Trumpet but never resolving it with the critical fifth note.

And this young man will never resolve that note. The scars show the places the Special Trumpet's enhancers, necessary to play the part, once were. He must have backed out. Sometimes they do.

As he played the motif the first time I agreed with his decision. This young man, Jerzy, he has natural talent. I go to hear him sometimes in the clubs in the Undercity, though I never take the procedural blockers most of the crowd down there seem to be on to screen out the visual artwork suffusing the world's surfaces. Once after his set I bought him a barley, and we reminisced about Robert (Jerzy knew him as "Rob"). Jerzy has Coltrane's bug: he wants to know every chord and every scale and all the ways they can fit together. I explained to him how Ortolan's work made all that jazz obsolete and he got up from the table and he's never talked to me since. I catch him looking me in the eye sometimes, when he plays those staccato midrange notes that feel like kitchen knives.

In the orchestra he didn't stab. He poured his soul out for my boy.

The Third's last passage ends in a whirlwind of desperation. The basses beg with outstretched trusses as the woodwinds mortify the flesh of the meditators and the trumpet pleads "not me, but who? Not me, but who? Not me, but who, but who?"

"But I."

The lights wash over Robert as he plays his first notes and I see his costume, custom made as it always is for the Special Trumpet in the Third, the only time it will be worn. The designer has failed to make herself invisible in the work: the costume is too functional for its own good, covering in paper-thin green fabric the lines of enhancer lights down the length of Robert's arms and thighs and concealing the cables connecting him to the orchestra's electrical generator. But beneath those strips of fabric, he is naked. He'd always been a chubby boy but if he'd been just a few years older his chest would have been golden-haired and broad. If he'd backed out from playing the Mahlerine, he'd have made a fine Dionysius.

Robert's answer to the orchestra's summons is perfect in pitch but flat in passion. The enhancers are doing their job. In an interlocking duet, the Special Trumpet accepts the crown from the Lead Trumpet and the Lead, his work finished, is heard no more. One by one the winds and brass surrender their dissent and at last the heavenly strings unleash themselves in a cleansing rain. The key ascends in whole steps from D flat to G and the whole orchestra joins together in an elaborate modulation that reads far more mundane on the score: by fourths from G to F. For every question the orchestra asks, the Special Trumpet, like Buddha beneath his tree, has his single note answer.

Hanging on F7, extending the chord so lushly Chick Corea would blush, the whole orchestra asks the Special Trumpet: what must we do to pierce the noise of art all around us? What must we, musicians, do to share the passions of our souls with other people?

I raised Robert not to understand death. When my own father passed, I told Robert he'd moved to a place far away without social media but that we'd see him again someday, if we were good. How else but freed of that mortal fear could he have the confidence for the Mahlerine?

Thus, the Special Trumpet sounds an unadorned B-flat, singing the natural note of the instrument, no valves stopped. A column of vibrating air connects our ears to the innermost reaches of my boy's lungs.

Every lie I told Robert's mother to let him be here is redeemed. She will be angry, of course. She never appreciated music as art.

Ortolan's score reads *"jusqu'au point de consommation,"* "until the point of consumption," as his only instruction to the Special Trumpet; the rest was left to a long, psychopathic footnote. The lights dim to gloaming around my boy as the light-emitting diodes covering his skin, the tips of the wires plunging throughout his body, change from verdant to the xanthophyll yellow of autumn.

At the age of forty-five I, a man of good health, can hold a note for about forty-five seconds. Robert's smaller lungs could, on their own, play for maybe twenty. The enhancers, here at the end of Ortolan's Third, take on their intended role: Robert can play what no unadorned human could.

The first wisps of smoke rose from the trumpet's bell, scattering the yellow light of the LED rig. Robert had sounded his last note for twenty-five seconds.

Somewhere in the audience below me I hear someone whispering. Looking down I see a clean-faced man with a smirk on his face in a black tuxedo whose fabric pastiches shifting Gauguin chatting to a woman in a satin dress projecting riffs on Picasso. She turns to him only to shush him, and he retreats and sits quietly. Good.

Robert's last meal will have been intravenous, to ensure he's clean inside as well as out. Like when my great-grandfather used to feed snails cornmeal for a day before broiling them in garlic butter. The scent of ammonia and the sting of smog diffuses through the orchestra hall as I watch Robert's gut shrink, fueling his ultimate note.

Blue flame dances along the bell of the trumpet, too. Fats to methane, proteins to nitrous gasses.

This is what he volunteered for. This is his will. I confabulate to myself as I watch Robert begin to be consumed from the inside out. For two minutes he has sounded his note, and I haven't blinked. I think of Robert's round, ruddy face when he was born, and how small he was in those first days. As he consumes himself now, he shortens, and the smoke from his trumpet turns white: burning skeletal phosphorus, and the acrid aroma like a dentist's drill gone mad makes some of the audience cough. Robert's legs thin from the inside out and his feet lift off the ground. His arms, too, shorten and his hands, limp, fall away from the instrument still held to his lips by the tendrils of the enhancers themselves.

I inhale deeply and my heart warms. Robert's whole body is the instrument now. No musician could ask for better. Wisps of his body and his soul are entering our ears and noses and mouths.

He's smaller than he was as a baby, his head still full-size but his body a collapsing double-fist of matter. In his eyes, I see perfect focus, a furrowed brow, a pinnacle of will.

As his eyes meet mine, he falls from that pinnacle. The enhancers anesthetize players of the Mahlerine six ways from Sunday, but I imagine myself with my own body converted to pure art, and I understand how terrifying it must be for one's own heartbeat to no longer sound inside one's chest.

Yet the note sounds on. Robert is begging, reaching to his father for help, his jaw working to break away.

He is the instrument, but the machine is the musician, playing Robert to destruction for the sake of Ortolan's hallucinations of demon flutes.

The bell of Robert's trumpet glows cherry red, and his last note surges. His eyes stare nowhere as his head falls in on itself and at last, he is gone from the stage and lives on in the fading echoes of the clarion.

"When a caterpillar becomes a butterfly, it consumes its own brain and makes a new one," Ortolan said when the shocked world first read his score. Don't mourn sacrifice in the name of beauty.

The silence of the orchestra hall breaks as someone far away retches. Far off to my right, to cover the unpleasant disruption, the muffled slap of evening gloves begins and turns into a ripple of applause. I'm not offended by the spectacle. Passion takes many forms.

For my own part, I take stock as I clap my hands and rise from my seat. My heart is racing, threatening to tear itself apart. My legs tell me to leap and my arms want to punch. I taste anger rising at the back of my throat: anger like none I have felt since I was eight or nine years old, back in the days before abundance. My father had just told me we couldn't afford a puppy. It was like my whole world fell down.

I pound the palm of my hand against the brass rail in front of me, again and again, hard enough to bruise. I can feel the rail shake and ring all along its length. The audience full of yokels mistakes it for applause. They begin to clap and cheer.

I can't breathe through my now-congested nose, but I gulp air. I can still taste the burnt, greasy crematory stink—and slumping into my seat again, I find I long for more. I blow my nose and dry my eyes and inhale. Robert is in me, and in all these hundreds of others. He's done what I never could.

The applause roils, then simmers, and the spell of silence breaks as concertgoers begin to speak to their companions. I make my way to the lobby, throwing my cloak around my shoulders and imagining only escape into the street.

Through the tall glass doors, I can see the advertising-plastered buildings of the Overcity but before I reach them, I'm intercepted. It's Eckström, the timpanist, a boor and a philistine, but as soon as he reaches out his hand, I can feel normal life resume.

"Nykvist!" he thunders, his fat hand enveloping mine. "Your Robert was superb!"

"He was," I agree. "I will..." What will I do? Will I miss Robert with an unhealing ache in the pit of my heart? Will I come to relish that ache? Will I feast on his death? "I will treasure his performance always," I finish.

"Well, Nykvist, you must come again next month," he replies, beefy mitt still encasing mine. "My Sophie has the Special Trumpet! I'm just meeting her now for dinner. Join us! You must!"

The words echo and resonate down to the darkest reaches of the pit within me. I must.

Pointing the way, Eckström pulls me through the crowd. My nostrils flare as I suck in the frigid outdoor air and together, bathed in the pervasive urban mist, we lope ahead to meet Eckström's daughter, and dine.

Edmund Schluessel is an author and mathematics teacher. His first book, *Infinite Metropolis* with Mikko Rauhala, comes out in January 2020. He's also known for giving "the nerdiest con talk ever" at Worldcon 77 as part of his ongoing series of popular mathematics and popular science lectures. He holds a PhD in gravitational waves. An avid socialist activist, he helped organize Finland's largest demonstration against Donald Trump and Vladimir Putin in his adopted home city of Helsinki, Finland.

THE RED SHOES

Holly Lyn Walrath

T HE OLD WOMAN HEARD CRYING IN THE FOREST. WEEPING AS FAINT AS the sigh of falling sand in the witch's hourglass. She'd given up the art of witchcraft long ago. Curses and promises and gingerbread houses. If other sorceresses still lived, she might have asked them if they grew tired of the taste of small children or the squeezed look on their faces before they went. She cringed to think how a part of her now wanted to hold them, to pull them up into her old arms and cuddle their soft cheeks to her own. But no children walked her woods these days. The children learned long ago to stay away. And no other crones to consult either, only her, alone in the rickety house by the creek in the gloomy woods. The cat died long ago, too. Or slithered off to become a part of the night.

She grew tired of the starlight, not that she could see a damn bit anymore. But her ears were as good as ever, and the cry in the woods was not the wind. *Not a child*, she prayed. *Or if it is, please, let it be a boy.* She might turn a boy into a puppy and not feel the ache in the gut, the pulling like bark sloughing off, her evil parts falling away and leaving her raw and naked.

The old woman consulted her hourglass. The damn thing had jammed, sure enough. The sand no longer trickled beneath its bulb. She cracked her big knuckles on the glass. A single grain fell. She scoffed and pulled out the pocket watch—stolen from the town clockmaker's son, ages ago, a romping blush of a child. Midnight. Twelve-oh-three to be exact. What other time for strange things to occur? And the moon, bold in the sky, billowed yellow against the starry night in the smeared window.

The cry sounded again, sweet and melodic through the trees. The old woman gave up on sleep and unfolded herself from the straw mattress, her bones crunching under her as she hoisted up her unyielding body. There—the cloak fastened at her neck. (She wanted a red cloak, longed to have a reason to go into town and buy one. But she sewed her own clothes these days and never found a child in the woods with a red cloak, or she would *not* swallow them whole, decidedly *not* cloak and all.) With its black folds enveloping her, she took up the knotted pine staff and opened the door into the night. It greeted her with a howl, as usual.

Oh, shut up, you old grouch, she thought to it.

She followed the sound through the trees, across the wood bridge with no trolls underneath because she ran them out as a young witch. The fight they'd put up! She halfway hoped they might return some day, the strange darling things. She missed the riddles they sang to her across the water at twilight.

By all rights she should have died years ago. A clever child should have come and burnt her up to a crisp, the right way to go, the decent way. But no such child ever came. Or at least if they did, it was her that did the burning. A woodsman should have done it—yes, with a big shining axe like thunder, snapping her neck. Or a knight on a horse as pale as moon rings, banishing her away to the farthest depths of the kingdom. Instead, the depths of the kingdom crept up on *her* in the night. And the magic remained a comfort but only as far as she could use it. She wove illusions—farces—chimeras shining for a few days, but then diminishing.

She picked her way through the trees, following the sound. It sounded real now. Yes, a real child, crying in the night. The old woman sighed to herself—her own breath reminded her of farting. The child started and hiccupped. A lovely redheaded thing curled in the litter of the forest floor like a fairy in bracken. Its white limbs were speckled like a wren's egg. Yes, it had to be a girl-child.

The start it gave when it saw her! She cackled a bit at it. It stared back at the old woman with a face as round as a looking glass, tears illuminating its cheeks in the moonlight.

For a moment the old woman leaned on her stick, her mind swimming with the memory of a thousand dead children—a thousand little faces never growing old in her mind's eye. She did not remember them as children, but as adults, happy and married, making new little children of their own. What a joy! New babies with that smell like flour behind their ears, and the parents sent the children off to play in the woods. For a moment the possibility of bringing back the dead children seemed real—so real she imagined herself capable of it—the greatest feat of sorcery ever accomplished. Who could boast of such a triumph? And this child would be the last one sacrificed, for the good of the others. As good a price as any. For the price of a red spell, a tuppence. Her eyes watered.

"I'm lost!" the little girl cried.

"Yes, Deary, you are far off the path," the old woman replied. "And it is so dark and dangerous in the woods. The wolves might come any moment." If only wolves still roamed the woods! Or werewolves—now they were a sight to see. At least from the waist down.

"I miss my mommy," the little girl said and dissolved into tears again.

"Deary, now, don't cry. Grandma is here. Grandma will take you to a warm soft bed, and there will be tea and cakes and crumpets." The old woman reached down and picked up the girl in her bony old arms. Her back crackled like firecrackers going off on a string, but the little thing felt as light as a bunny carried by its scruff.

Back to the hut. She weaved a panoply of illusion—the fire made up and stuffed animals and hot tea on the kettle, and the charm of it fooled even the old witch. The little girl ate all the crumpets, and the witch ate all the cakes. She felt so sleepy with the day rising on the horizon, warming the hut with its morning sun. *Witches sleep during the day because we might burn away in the light,* she reminded herself. The little girl tucked the witch into her straw bed and curled up on the rug beneath her like a cat. The witch could have sworn she heard her purr.

In her old age with no one to see her with a child asleep at her bedside. What would the others think? But the knitting circle of old witches had died, and she should have too.

The little girl chattered. She danced from tree to tree pointing at the birds and the flowers. What is this, and what is that? Walking in the woods down to the village, the old woman wondered if she would ever shut up. Did her parents live in the village? No, the little girl said, they traveled here and there. *Long gone by now, roaming drifters* — the old woman mused. Mayhap they abandoned her on purpose because of all the damn prattle she put up. The little girl said they had named her Anna. An uninventive name. The witch had half a heart to rename her, but she didn't. Best not to get too attached.

The path to the village fell apart under their feet. Deer still used it by the smell of it, but no human had stepped foot on it in ages. The light glared in her eyes, but at least she could make out the houses below with plumes of smoke curling around their chimneys. She had put on her best going-out hat and given herself the illusion of a doddery grandmother. It only required a pinch of clarity, of nicety.

"Let's see, where shall we go, Deary?" she said when they reached the skirts of the village. The walk was shorter in the old days, and the village sleepier. The tiny township now swarmed with hustle and bustle, store fronts closing for the day, and fat villagers running here and there with brown parcels wrapped in twine. A holiday, with all the stores decorated in orange and red. The houses boasted a hint of frost on their thatched heads, and the leaves whisked down the lanes with laughing sounds.

The old woman inspected Anna. Mass of red curls, skinny white arms poking out of an ill-fitting blue dress, smudged face like a painting. No shoes. No shoes! How could that be? The old woman clicked the heels of her own serviceable boots, complete with shining buckle, and scoffed at the sheer impossibility of it.

And then — on the corner — the wooden carved sign of a cobbler's shop. And in the window, the most beautiful shining red shoes in all creation. Little red bows — bright witty heels that might click just so — and the congenial rosy face of the cobbler behind the window. The tinkle of the chime over the door like fairy bells, and in an instant Anna perched upon a stool and the little red shoes fit on her feet like magic. How she cooed over them! Her girlish voice ratcheted up to a new octave.

Just the thing, the witch thought. Yes, they were just the thing for an orphan who needed cheering up and a spell to be under — the grandest spell — a turning of the earth backwards, years and years erased under the click of red slippers — taking the old witch back to the beginning so many years ago. She had wandered lost in the woods herself, a little girl, and by chance a fairy found her — or was she a queen? Or mayhap a sorceress like herself — yes, that was closer to the truth — a beautiful sorceress soaring through the trees, floating on air — and the sorceress gave her words to say, to promise — and the child who became the old witch watched a star fall from the sky — or had it been a starling? She tried to go back to the village, but they choked her — no, a priest held her up to the light, and the light buried itself in her heart — deep in her chest for no one to see the light tried to burn her *alive* — dead kittens and all — dead parents — dead children. Years and years of them, white-faced, brown-faced, sweet and mean, short and stout, boy and girl. She escaped into the woods, to hide what she had become. But all would resolve now, with the red shoes — two rubicund pieces of joy.

They walked around the town, Anna dancing with ecstasy. She leaned on the arm of the old woman, teetered on the edge of the fountain, and the villagers did not cast suspicious glances but smiled at them. They *smiled* at the old witch! How little they knew! She wondered how many of their children she'd killed, how many brothers or sisters, how many she had known as children. Surely, she knew some of their faces — but no. She left no survivors, she knew it in her heart. She hadn't let a one go.

The illusion felt so sweet she carried it on another day. She took Anna to the village and this time, they sat in the church itself, with all the villagers worshiping, no less! The same church where the priest walked the aisles with a burning rope — swinging sickness left and right, sweet incense. The old witch cackled to herself as she sat in the pew with Anna in her red shoes. How the villagers whispered and hissed! How it scandalized them, a little girl with red shoes in church! Aye, the fun of it was almost worth the chatter of the child.

Another day, another amusement. They took the red shoes to confession. The priest's face burned purple, and he sputtered over the prayers. The witch stared him down through the ivy wood of the partition, but he didn't recognize her. When she saw him again outside the booth, she realized the old priest must have died years and years ago. This one looked like a young boy, hardly old enough to be a man.

Sunlight aged the witch, and she took to sleeping through the day. Anna curled at her feet across the bedspread, her red hair shining like rivulets of patent leather. The witch's bones felt thin, hollow. *Perhaps I am dying,* she pondered. The final spell hung unfinished.

She bought Anna a red dress to match the shoes, and a red cloak with a silver clasp shaped like a dove. And the girl grew like a weed — a white daisy with a sun shining face. *That's what she is,* the old witch thought. A daisy draped in red. Bee's pollen. At night, Anna read to her. Fairy tales — that's what little girls like. But the old woman liked them too. She tried not to laugh in all the wrong places, like when the wolf devoured the protagonist whole.

No wolves in the woods to come hunting after *her* little girl. Her years of sorcery kept them both safe. They kept Anna beautiful. They could not keep her young. The old woman knew that herself. She tried it once — but youth is irrepressible, uncatchable, not like a firefly trapped in a glass. If you wished for youth, you merely got long life. And that just meant you remained old for a very, very long time.

Then one day, Anna asked to go to a dance.

"Alone?" the old woman said. "You would leave your dear old granny?"

"But Granny, you're too old to go to a dance!" Her voice echoed like bells in the trees, bells tied on leaves and sycamore boughs. The old woman felt weary of the sound, as beautiful as it was. Anna grew taller each day, her hair shone under the red cloak like fresh-picked strawberries. She wanted to spend more days in the village. At times, she seemed scornful of the witch. *Adolescence*, the witch surmised.

"The shoes — leave the red shoes. I'd like to look upon them. Wear some other pair."

"Granny, you know I can't go anywhere without my red shoes." She scurried away from the old woman's hands, soft pretty thing. The witch grasped at memory. Something about the dance and the shoes and the spell. Had she placed a spell on the girl? But she couldn't kill her — not this one — she was different. She was *special*. Anna would bring back all the other girls, all the other children. The red spell. But she never completed it! Her memory flared — she'd been distracted by the joy of Anna, her sacrificial beauty. The spell needed boiling, it needed words, had she grown so old as to forget all that?

"Go then. I'll make some tea for when you return." The old woman placed the big black kettle on the stove.

Anna kissed her gray cheek and dashed away, a robin in the woods.

The witch boiled water. Tea leaves — yes, for the mint and the smell. Then the heart strings. The lizards' tails. The frogs' feet. The black mud from the creek underneath the bridge where the trolls used to live. A lock of red hair. A silver bell. Apple drop candy. The blue eyes of a snow-white kitten. Dove feathers, crow feathers. Dust, ash, a broken hourglass. Wind from the woods. Memories of the lambs. All the little clippings and souvenirs through the years, fingers and toes and ribbons and bows.

It all boiled up, thumping against the lid of the pot. It steamed and simmered, and the old woman stirred and murmured over it. It turned a shining gold—yes—a gold like liquid sun, and the old woman heard a knocking at the window. A parade of children peeking through the glass, their souls darting against it like butterfly wings. So many dead children lost in the woods. She stirred faster, moaning over the pot. But their faces turned sad and dark and evil and laughing, like clear ringing bells. She whirled away, knocking the pot awry. Black sludge seeped into the floorboards. The old woman stumbled out of the door. The wind howled into her face, biting cold. A winter snowstorm threatened in the sky; white broken flecks fell through the trees, and her boots slipped in the icy muck.

She ran to the village with the strength of a thousand children in her bones. The town hall sparkled—rows of carriages lined the streets, and the horses huffed at her. The windows shone with a rosy golden glow but voices inside cried out—screaming and trapped. The old woman crawled to the window and looked inside. Taffeta and tulle! The dresses all in the way, crowding away from the center of the room. Faces etched in open screams—yes, yes, but where was the girl? The villagers pounded on the doors.

In the middle of the room—yes, she could see her now—Anna—red shoes flying. She danced—spun—twirled like she'd never danced before—arms akimbo and her legs unwilling partners. The shoes danced her, and she was their slave. A strange dance—like the death fight of two birds in the sky. The red shoes chimed like bells ringing again and again, clicking their heels feverishly. The people pushed each other, climbing over bodies to reach the door.

"Help!" Anna cried out to the villagers. They screamed louder, covering her cries.

"Someone, help! Make it stop!" Her heels flashed and sparks flew, and the wood scorched with their fever. Soon it would smolder and flame.

Then—a woodsman—a muscled man with a flannel shirt and a beard down to here—stepped out of the crowd, a shining axe thrown over his shoulder.

He walked forward, his face set. He heaved the axe down—its bright blade sung in the air. The old witch watched as the blade split the shoes atwain from the girl. The red—glorious to see. The old witch's heart seized up inside of her. She felt tears on her wrinkled cheeks. Red spell gone wrong, all the wrong red on the wood floor, stupid villagers slipping in it.

The old woman's shoulders slumped. She unlatched the hall door and kneeled prostrate before the crowd. Their feet plowed over her, clipping her face here and an elbow there—her old bones crushed like sparks on a grinder's wheel. Nothing to bury, nothing to miss.

Anna married the woodsman. She returned to the cobbler, and he made her new feet of sturdy wood. She became pious and hobbled to church each Sunday. They never found her feet in the red shoes. The villagers whispered they danced away into the woods. They never saw the witch again, although they found her empty hut huddled in the snow. It no longer looked like a witch's hut—a beef stew spilled on the floor, and the curtains were common gingham. Wolves roamed the forest. At night, the villagers swore they heard the howls of werewolves. The ravens talked, and kittens went missing. Parents no longer sent little children out alone to pick berries or to journey to their grandmother's house. Rumors grew of trolls under the bridges and fairies in the trees that grabbed your hair as you walked by. The wind howled ever more.

Holly Lyn Walrath's poetry and short fiction has appeared in *Strange Horizons, Fireside Fiction, Daily Science Fiction, Luna Station Quarterly, Liminality,* and elsewhere. She is the author of the Elgin Award winning chapbook, *Glimmerglass Girl* (Finishing Line Press, 2018). She works as a freelance editor in Houston, Texas. Find her on Twitter @HollyLyn-Walrath, or at www.hlwalrath.com.

THE RAT ROOM

Rebecca Dale

"THERE ARE ONLY TWO RULES," THE LANDLORD SAYS, "LOCK THE DOOR AND don't linger in the Rat Room."

The Rat Room. I should ask. I'm the kind of person who asks about a name like that. At the very least, it is a name that demands a quizzical look. But then there's the view, and it is all-consuming. I hold my face in my hands just to keep myself steady. Beyond the broken window is everything I have ever wanted. My body brims full of caffeine and exultation and distraction. There is no room for Rat Rooms. There is not even room for my old bed in Dubbo, hundreds of kilometres away and behind me now, forever.

I laugh as I recall the Facebook post that brought me here. The ad calls this studio a *stunning glimpse of Sydney's heart and soul*, which apparently means the grimy side of Central station and a wilting 7-Eleven beneath. But it's Sydney. It's not Dubbo. I have arrived.

I take the keys from the landlord in a daze. When I unclench them in my hand, there's a line of small cuts dredged into my palm. I lose the next three days sketching from that window, capturing a thousand angles until my fingers shed charcoal, pastel, and wax. I paint the saccharin streets nested under skyscrapers. Over and over I trace gutters and broken pavement straight on the window glass, and when my fingers make contact with the paper, I feel the sunlight go into me, warm as coal and daydreams. Tuesday night comes and I *should* be at my student-teacher meet and greet, but instead I drag my mattress over to the sill and get down, craning my neck at just the right angle, and draw the whole skyline like a nest with ink and a razor. I draw Centrepoint tower out and upwards like a warped needle, ribboned in a Westpac red that I mix from my own blood and strawberry syrup. Cottee's strawberry syrup. I am the Australiana hipster I've always wanted.

"The garbage is full," I say, four days later, as if it were a revelation, looking over at the pots of flaking paint, empty bottles, and the string of broken Christmas lights. I am hungry. This, too, comes at some surprise.

"So take it to the Rat Room," she says with a shrug. A roommate. Right! This is our first conversation. Also an artist—I know her face from Instagram—a woman in her forties who sculpts wax and makes furniture that art galleries called 'wildy curatorial'. She sorts broken tiles on the floor. She does not look up.

"And where is the...the, uh, Rat Room?" The question is awkward and overdue. I don't even catch the intrigue of it until I taste the words. The questions arrive. I measure them again on the top of my mouth with my tongue. The Rat Room. Bitter. And sweet? And acrid. Suddenly the spell of the city skyline is broken, and the rest spills out of me. Why. Why? How? How many? When? Why? She doesn't answer a single one, except to gesticulate wildly at the door and point her finger downwards.

I pull all my scattered sketches together into a pile and drop them onto my mattress. I look around at the studio and pick up empty bottles and piles of paper towel, until my nose stings from the scent of cheap cider and turpentine. There is a pile of melted doll parts in a corner that I leave untouched. Another artist like me, pain-stricken and paint stricken, who has abandoned their life somewhere and given up everything to live on a mattress in a tiny makeshift studio, where the walls are thin blankets hooked up from the ceiling. You get a sense for that kind of desperation, once you know what it looks like.

It is at the bottom, just as her spindly finger had predicted.

It is, at first, a disappointment. A room of nothing really, with an automatic roller door, lined with garbage skips. My fingers can't find a switch in the dim. I pull out my phone and shine a light, catching the edge of a Woolworths mud cake container peeking out from a pile of white garbage bags. I toss my own brimming trash bags on top, and hear the clinking of the bottles, the rustling of the finest plastic on plastic.

And then; such shrieking! Bubbling up from the din. Black shadows pouring from the skip, spilling over and tumbling outwards, swarming the floor. I stumble backwards as warm feet patter my boots. "Rats!" I scream, as if the universe would be surprised, as if naming them would make them stop, make them slide away from me. How long I spent frozen there, watching them squirm over me as they bolted to the corners of the room in a steady rodential rivulet, I don't know. Once they touch a dark corner they disappear.

Rats for days. Rats for eons. A room of rats. A Rat Room.

It was the bite that spurred me into action, a single needle-like jab of pain in my left ankle. It was my turn to squeal and wriggle. I look down and it is the Queen of Rats, a burgeoning sausage that is rat. Her monstrous body skids across the floor and away from me. I run. I don't look back.

I get lost, because I am not looking forward either. I clamber up stairway after stairway until nothing and everything looks familiar. Each grotty corridor is a mirror of the other. It is only when I pas a walkway splattered with red paint that I get a sense of my bearings. I lean on the railing and snatch up my breath, staring across the cavernous juncture below, where the walls are layered in posters and paste-ups.

No rats. Not a single rat below. Silence. Stillness. Just me and my own stupidity.

I laugh, letting it echo out. The sensation turns, and now I am giddy with inspiration. This is the right place, in the centre of the right universe. This place is called the Hibernian. It is old and rotting from the inside out. It has an old fancy name. It has history and religion. It has discarded its faith long ago for more eclectic tastes. I take in the winding corridors and peeling handrails, the graffiti-laden walls that tumble earnestly and endlessly. This is a place of secret printing presses, up-market hair salons and artists, like me, practically licking the concrete for that spark, the spark. I choose this. A little roughhousing from the long-tailed locals make it mine.

Still, when I make it back up to the studio, I lock the door with trembling fingers. I bury my head into the pillow with the keys clutched into a fist. A little talisman. The rules are the wrong way around, I think, as sleep pours into my head. Lock the door first. Lock the door first.

I locked it. I need you to know that.

I have dreams that night that are filled with shattered steps and bubbles of warped laughter. A hand reaches out. When I take it, there was no hand at all. I am holding a rat's tail. It convulses and drives itself into my skin.

Does it hurt?

There's a skill to avoiding your mother, but I've never had it. The phone buzzes, and I let it ring out. Once. Twice. Mothers know. Mothers persist.

"I'm worried about you," she says. A KitchenAid hums through the receiver. I taste pavlova at the back of my throat; crisp meringue and cream and the gritty seeds of the kiwifruit.

"I'm sorry," I begin, which is how I always begin. "I shouldn't have asked for money. I freaked out and I thought it was infected. Just don't tell Dad, okay?"

"But what happened, Sweetness? Are you taking care of yourself?"

I laugh. It's breathy and not very convincing. "It's just a bite, mum."

"You have to be more careful," she chides. There's parchment paper on her baking tray, crisping with every sweep of the spatula. "This is such a huge opportunity for you. And I just don't know about this studio accommodation. Two hundred and fifty dollars a week! And the shower is outside! No wonder you're not feeling well."

"It's perfect," I say. "My art can breathe here. I'm onto something life-changing. I sent you some pictures, remember?"

She clucks and puts something in the oven. Metal on metal. "But I don't know about these arty things. They seem rather dark to me. I don't like all of those eyes." She inhales, and thus I wait for the inevitable. "So when are you going back to art school?" She never says school. Always art school. She says it slowly, like she cannot understand their meaning.

"I'm feeling much better now. I have proper painkillers. Give it a few days and everything will be alright. I promise."

"That's good to hear." Again, she inhales. "Your father and I believe in you, so we're giving this a chance. But I need you to know you can come home. It's just money, Sweetness. There's no shame in coming home. You know that, don't you?"

When I get off the phone, I feel even worse. I take the gauze off my ankle and trace the skin there. It is raised and sore and not getting better. The colour is wrong, I think. Too vibrant. The wound glimmers. Or does it? I need a drink. The only place I've been to in the last week other than the studio is the medical centre.

I go to leave the studio, and my flatmate looks up from a pile of doll parts. "The garbage is full again. Take it down, will you?"

I don't even know her name. It's the last thing I want to do but my hand is gripping the handle and I'm walking and the garbage bag sags against my leg. I smell rotting meat. I could have said no. I don't know why I didn't.

We are having a conversation, like humans do. The recognition crashes over me. This is not some stranger who likes my art. It clicks when he says the word 'compelling' and raises his shoulders like a puppet. I am talking to one of my teachers. He teaches ceramics. I choke on the wine.

He pats me on the back and asks me if I'm surprised, to hear him speak about my work that way. And I laugh and laugh because I was but I am afraid if we talk about it a moment more it will erode away from time itself. I want him to say it again. I want to write that word on my soul. Compelling is what gets people into galleries. Compelling wins prizes. The studio throbs with people behind him. There is a thrum in the room, as if it is a plane high in the air and that air, compelled by physics and sheer human will, is pressing on my eardrums. He is wearing the finest suit jacket I've ever seen.

There's a kind of poise here that's missing in your previous work, he continues. I am the audience as then the ritual begins, the litany of names and movements. My artistic lineage. These gem-studded colours and neons! It's Vexta, he says. Do you remember that graffiti exhibition on Cockatoo Island, in the tunnels? I didn't. No matter. And here, he says, the anatomical precision of Fiona Hall, and her alienness. The allusion to Monet, all these strokes yielding out of focus and into the whole.

I nod and drink and commit it all to memory. My portfolio will espouse exactly these words come the morrow. I pour another drink, it's wine I think, while he stares at the canvas, brows narrowed, taking a step back and taking a step forward. The dance of critics.

Are they supposed to be eyes? I feel like it's all looking back at me. Is that intentional?

I shrug.

It's been a hard time for you, he muses. Your friends have been worried about you. Being so far from home, without any support. But this is promising. Hope to see you back in classes soon. Hope that limp gets better soon.

He doesn't, and it doesn't.

The text I've been expecting appears on the screen.

It's very important that you go to art school, Sweetness. We have an agreement. They're worried about your attendance.

Tomorrow, I promise, and dab Vaseline to the growing rash on my shin. Then I forget about it and paint until there's dawn creeping over the horizon.

The smell wakes me. In the dream I have my head curled up against the giant root of a tree, so tall I cannot tell where it ends. The branches reach forever and disappear into mist. I breathe in the wet earth, the sweet scent of decaying plant matter. At first it soothes.

The tastes on my palate congeal. Rainwater transmutes to rancid oils and paint thinner. When I reach out and touch the root it dissolves into dust. I have that faint feeling clinging to my head, you know, when you spray a fixative indoors. Even though they tell you over and over again to never, *never,* do that.

My feet hurt. I open my eyes and the flesh macerates like cherries. There are a thousand eyes. They want me to know.

Then a hand, clutching my throat, pressing down with the thumbs on either side of my voice box so I can't scream. I can't scream, I—

"What the hell are you taking that leaves marks like that?" She shakes me awake. The flatmate. This is not my mattress. She leans over me on all fours in the heart of the Rat Room. She is a black silhouette shaped like a flatmate. There is a plastic bag next to her filled with melted sequins and nail polish. Two ruined brushes jut out from the opening.

Flatmates are strong. She carries me all the way back to the studio and lays me down on her own sinking double mattress. It is softer than mine. It also has sheets. She makes me drink two large glasses of water.

She asks me again what I took. I shake my head and promise there's nothing.

"And you have to take care of a wound like that. Wash it every day, you know?" She laughs. "I remember when I was learning all that stuff at your age. How to take care of myself. How to go to uni every day. I heard you got into the National Art School. Don't waste your life by partying too much and forgetting to brush your teeth, and dress your damn wounds. You will regret that, I promise."

I don't say anything. My throat hurts too much.

"Did you get into a fight or what? Did something bite you?"

"Lock...lock the door," I croak. The keys are still in my hand.

"Give me the keys," the landlord says.

"One more chance." There's only begging left to do, so I do it.

"Mate, it's not my issue that you spent all your money on drugs and art supplies instead of rent. I gave you a warning. Now do I need to call the sheriff and have you forcibly evicted?"

Tears stream down my face. They are warm and taste like the ocean. I'd forgotten what warm feels like.

"You are clearly very unwell," he says, "That foot is nasty. You need to go to a doctor. Look, your parents are waiting for you downstairs. You have help. You should let them come up and help you. Help is good."

I shake my head fitfully. They don't get to have this place. It is mine.

The phone in my pocket buzzes. I already know it's some text about heading out to Dubbo before the sun goes down. If we head out now there would be time for some British Bake-Off before we all go to bed.

Getting out is the best feeling in the world.

Getting snatched right back is the worst.

"Your pieces are really something," says the flatmate. "This is just a minor setback. Keep working on it." She offers to take my bag. Somehow her sad eyes are worse than the stony gaze of the landlord. I shake my head—all I do is shake, these days, all the little parts of me. I lug the duffel bag over my shoulder. It has to be on the opposite side of my bad leg, or I topple over. Brushes and dried rounds of watercolour spill out of the unzipped opening.

"See someone about that leg!" she says as the door shuts.

I promise, I say.

I promise, I lied.

One last visit to the Rat Room, for inspiration's sake. That's what I tell myself. In honour to all the questions I should have asked and all the things I should have done.

I linger in the doorway, just like I'm not supposed to. My leg throbs and burns. If I close my eyes, I will see the forest from my dreams. The dreams don't stay put. I'm sweating. It's just a fever. I see that moment, just before I kneel down at the foot of the rotten tree, where I notice the bubbling of running water, the sound encroaching so softly that it melds to the silence. But here, in this place, I hear it so truly. If I reach out the river will be there.

I hear the tiny shrieks of a thousand bodies, pouring over each other and becoming one. Each is a single organ apart, cascading over each other, becoming a thing of fur and immeasurable small feet.

When did I fall asleep? The whispers that had always coaxed me to this place rise to the surface. Bubbles on my brain, popping, unravelling, wrapping themselves around me and pulling the threads tight.

There is a slip of a moment, the snap of attention when you realise you are on the precipice of the waterfall that you have heard for so long. It is a waking up, and my mind is clear. My flatmate was right. I failed here, but I won't fail forever. I can try again. I am on hands and knees. I pull myself up. I will go.

But I turn around. I dare to look. Just one last time.

And it smiles, that thing of a thousand eyes and muscles squirming. It is far worse than I could ever have painted. The eyes shine like tarnished coins.

It lurches and I recoil. We dance in such a way. The critic's dance. The bag scatters. It is consumed by rolling lines of teeth.

I am she of the weeping waltz, and I dance for roller door, the only exit left. There is no switch that my frantic fingers can find. There is no light. My fists batter the sheet metal. It gives way, like paper, and my hand goes right through, slicing itself up against the eroded edges. A pocket of the night sky pours in. When did it get so late? How long have I been here?

How many others were there, before me?

Their bites pucker my skin, right through my clothes. Small nips at first, but not for long. The smell claws into my lungs, just as surely as the little teeth embed themselves into my sinew. I open my mouth to scream. A ropey tail slides into the small gap between my lips. There's a liquid dripping through my fingers, thick and red like the raspberry jam my mother makes. Mouths rise up to suckle it.

Rebecca Dale is an Australian writer and librarian, obsessed with all things Australiana and gothic, preferably together. This is her fourth published story. She lives in Sydney with two beautiful partners and a grumpy rabbit.

Keys Without Locks

C. Patrick Neagle

A LBERT COLLECTED KEYS. HE STARTED DOING SO WHEN HE WAS JUST a child, perhaps because of his last name, which was Keye. With the self-centered ego of a child, he was thrilled to discover a thing in the world that had been named after him.

When he was somewhat older, yet at a time when his parents still kindled hope that he might become something other than a cubicle dweller, they jokingly told him he should become a locksmith, since he loved keys so much.

"Perfect job for you, son," his father said more than once. "You already know everything there is to know about keys: the teeth, the wards and so forth."

"They're called 'bittings', Dad, not 'teeth,'" young Albert responded, sighing heavily in the manner of a put-upon pre-teen. "And 'wards' are in locks, not on keys."

"See, son, you know everything there is to know." Albert realized only much later, looking back on the memory, that his father often said this last with a glint of humor in his eyes.

With more than some irony, despite the focal point of his hobby, Albert had no interest in locks, except in that keys existed because of them. In fact, Albert eventually found he preferred collecting keys without matching locks. The keyways these had once fit into had all been lost, destroyed, or, Albert sometimes suspected, never existed at all, the keys crafted, perhaps, by someone like himself who saw the beauty in the form and the mystery, not in the function.

Therefore, Albert was as surprised as anyone, had anyone else known, when he became obsessed by the keyhole that appeared one night in his wife's forehead.

Normally, Albert was one to sleep all through the night once he had closed his eyes. His days of cubicle life were tiring. But one night something, perhaps the weight of moonlight on his neck, woke him.

Kathy was turned toward him in her sleep, as he was toward her. The moonlight, where it snuck past him and shone on her, illuminated her lovely face. Albert sighed.

He knew he had married above himself — above his position, above his looks, and above his intelligence. Why Kathy loved him, he had no idea, though he loved her for her beauty, her wit, and the fire she sometimes let burn when angry.

He thought these things, and smiled, and then he saw the keyhole.

At first, he reasoned that it was a shadow, a trick of moonlight.

But, no, definitely a keyhole, perfectly shaped to allow for the insertion of a standard flat key. Albert extended a finger, but he didn't touch the indentation in his wife's forehead, not then.

No, this lock needed a key — one that wouldn't fit anywhere else.

That first night, he didn't go down to the basement to search his collection, but the next night he did, as well as the night after, and the night after that. He had a lot of keys, each hanging on its own tiny hook behind his worktable, and many more in boxes and small bags littered around the workshop.

Some nights, he would fit one into the lock in his wife's brow and jiggle it, knowing it wouldn't fit. This would be a key he'd never found a lock for, but which he thought likely to have been made for a safety deposit box, or a locker at a train station.

Other nights, certain he had the right key in hand, and knowing this particular key had no absolute provenance, he twisted the bow beneath his fingertips, expecting to feel a satisfying give as pins slipped over the notches and protrusions of the bittings.

What always came instead was just the regular resistance. On these nights, Albert would sigh and settle back to sleep, tucking the failed key away so Kathy wouldn't wonder why her husband had started taking his hobby to bed with him.

In the mornings, the keyhole wasn't there. It existed only at night, when his wife slept and he didn't.

"You seem more tired than usual," she told him eventually, but without any suspicion that Albert could detect. Albert quirked his lip and offered a half shrug, saying something about how work was busier than usual. Kathy shook her head and ruffled his hair as she passed. He thought about stopping. But that night, he returned to his quest. And the next. And the next.

Then he found it.

The key was not unusual in any way: just a basic house key, gold colored. The bow had the usual hole for slipping it onto a key ring. There were the usual markings key makers used.

The only thing off about it was that Albert had never been able to track down what the markings on this key signified. They weren't in any of the usual books, not even on any of the not-so-usual websites.

With no assurance, however, that this one would elicit a reaction different from the others, Albert slipped the key into his wife's forehead and twisted.

There was no resistance as well-oiled pins gave way beneath the pressure.

Albert's breath clicked in his chest as he tried to inhale at the same time he'd been about to exhale.

He turned the key the rest of the way.

There was an *opening*.

Cold winds howled somewhere behind Albert's eyes. He had the impression of dark forests where snow lay on high, black branches and in the shadows of steep slopes. He felt caves and the dark spaces beyond, where fearsome things growled and clawed. He had the sense of a moon high in the night sky, washing the landscape with steely light.

His wife opened her eyes and stared into his staring into hers.

"Oh, Albert," she said. A tear formed and dropped away down her cheek. "I wish you hadn't." She sighed. "But I knew you would. You and your keys. It's just that, well, I loved you so much because of them. Such an unusual thing to collect. Keys without locks."

"Not all of them," Albert said, his voice cracking. The hollow wind blowing out from inside his wife's head still screamed through his own.

"No, not all of them," Kathy agreed. Then she opened herself wide and drew Albert through her door.

C. Patrick lives and writes in the Pacific Northwest, where he is also the host-and-gamemaster of the humor-and-horror actual-play podcast The Gothic Podcast. He has been previously published in The Rag Literary Magazine and Typhon: A Monster Anthology, and writes the Lady Starr, Space Ranger audio drama. He doesn't have any pets, but he lives with two dogs, three cats, three humans, and uncountable newts that have taken over the pool in advance of the coming of the Great Newt God.

WHITE-TAIL LIES

Friedrich Sarah E. Thompson

THE FIRST LIE I EVER TOLD CAME CRAWLING OUT OF MY MOUTH WHEN I was four. With its hairy legs tickling my throat and jabbing against my cheeks, I had no idea what to do. I remember looking up at my father, tears in my eyes and eight twitching limbs poking from my mouth, wondering if I was going to die. He turned aside in disgust, called for my mother, and left me on the kitchen tile with hands cupped, ready to catch whatever had emerged from within me.

It was enormous, at least to me. The first time is always the worst.

My mother found me crouched on the floor, staring at my hands under the fluorescent lights. The pearly-white spider I'd coughed up scuttled along my fingers, gentler than I had feared, though that was little comfort. I couldn't see my mother's face with my eyes fixed to the lie, but from the flat tone of her voice, there probably wasn't much to see.

"I told you," she said. "Good girls don't lie."

To this day I wonder if I imagined it, the flicker of movement when I lifted my head, like something scuttling from her mouth.

"Keep quiet about this," she told me.

The spider roamed further up my arm, raising goosebumps with every step.

"This isn't something to be spoken of in polite company."

She didn't need to tell me that, in this case, all company was polite company.

I did my best to keep honest after that. I rarely spoke at all. And when I wondered at the truth of what I did say, my stomach clenched and roiled, a voice in the back of my mind whispering that it was more than just fear that twitched in my gut.

Maybe someone smarter than me would have figured out how to dance around words, avoiding definitive statements, but me? I just shut up. Easier that way. By now, people have learned not to expect verbal replies from me. My tongue feels like a stranger in my mouth and silence comes by default. I'm a creature of nods and shrugs.

I'm grateful for that now, as I stumble through the city with a group of girls whose birthdays I don't know, celebrating a milestone I'm afraid of.

One foot in front of the other. I haven't drunk too much yet, but I've never had anything more than a glass of champagne at a cousin's wedding before. Maybe I'm not built to handle alcohol. I'm not sure if that has anything to do with the lies, but who knows? They're as much a part of me as the rest of my body.

After the first tarantula, I didn't lie again until I got to school. My kindergarten teacher came to my little table, knelt by my pink plastic chair, and asked if I'd finished the reader I picked out. I told her that I had and spat a pearlescent huntsman onto the table.

I didn't meet the principal's eyes as he told me that was a very cruel trick to play on my teacher, that I shouldn't touch spiders at all, let alone put one in my mouth. I nodded along with him, trying to tell myself that the tears came only from embarrassment, that the sharp and brutal sting I'd felt as the huntsman was crushed under the teacher's shoe was coincidence.

I can't blame everyone for avoiding me after that. It hurt, but I couldn't expect them to put up with me. They were real people, who knew themselves and could expect to grow into real adults with jobs and husbands and futures. I was a vending machine for filth.

As I grew, though, sometimes thoughts would catch me when I wasn't looking. They'd ask me what else was growing inside me, what the tightness of my throat was trying to keep contained. I swallowed those thoughts whole, but I never could get the hang of swallowing the lies. They seemed to appear inside my mouth, without having crawled from anywhere. I had more questions about them than I could articulate, but it wasn't as if there was anyone I could ask.

Sometimes I watched my mother, precise in everything from her criticisms to how she combed her hair, and wondered how much she knew. Not just where they came from, but why they could be any size, any species. I would hover in her doorway, questions ready to go, only to meet her gaze in the mirror and feel them die in my throat.

High school was… different. Easier, perhaps, having the reputation of never speaking instead of being the kid who ate bugs. More acceptable, at least. But just as lonely.

Things only changed when I stumbled into someone else's life by accident. Katie. Popular in that mild way, with iced-coffee coloured hair and nothing important to say but always a smile to say it with. She was on crutches for a while — I could never figure out how to ask why — and one Tuesday, she and I were the last people left in the geography classroom. I carried her bag for her down to English. She thanked me.

Actually, what she said was, "Aw, thanks Georgie! You're a star," which is different to just thanking me. She said my name and made no comment when I only smiled in reply. That was the most I'd gotten in years.

I helped her go from geography to English for the rest of the month. She got her cast off, but I hung around. One day at the train station after school, I was the one who handed over a fiver to get a bucket of hot chips for her friends, and I was in.

They invited me out, to Annie Chau's fifteenth birthday. I hadn't liked it, not the noise or the boys, but knowing that they had invited me was a high I would never tire of.

In the years that followed, I often wondered what would happen if I told them. They wouldn't have believed me, but what if I'd showed them? I almost did, several times. Strangely still seconds where I found myself ready, a lie and a spider at the tip of my tongue. Like that time after we'd been working on our group film for drama. We were working with Annie Chau again — everybody's friend and nobody's — when Katie had to leave early. It was just me and Annie then, sitting on her floor covered in loose school papers. Annie leant back with a smile, as if she really was happy to see me. I nearly said it then. Nearly blurted out,

"When I lie, spiders come out of my mouth."

But I knew what would happen next. Questions. Hundreds of them, with no answers to be given. So I kept as quiet as usual that day. At least until I got home, where I closed my door and shoved a towel beneath it, crawled under my bed, and lied to myself.

I wanted to learn the mechanics of it, where the spiders came from, but they eluded me in the strangest way, somehow appearing in the folds of my tongue as I spoke. As if I were sculpting them with the movements of my mouth. As for what happened to them after they emerged, I wasn't sure. They were still spiders, intimidated by my size, and scuttled off into the shadows almost as soon as they were born. I never saw one again. I knew they were real, corporeal, though. The big ones crowded my mouth too much for me to doubt that.

Throughout, I took notes. What lies birthed what spiders, their breeds, their sizes, whether they were lies of omission or magnitude, and what I lied about. And each time I filled a page, I ripped the paper to shreds and popped it in my mouth. Even though it was clear no spiders actually lived inside me, I still imagined them in my stomach, feeding on the notes I fed them.

But my brain couldn't stay focused on the spiders alone. I couldn't forget that look on Annie Chau's face, how completely at ease she was at having me in her home. I told myself not to read into it. She was just being nice, the way she was nice to everyone.

And yet, I couldn't help myself.

"Annie Chau is my friend."

Nothing happened.

"Katie Parrish is my friend."

Still nothing.

I rubbed the heel of my palm against my eyes, head full of insults. What was I doing? I wasn't a Magic 8-Ball. But though I tried to keep the rest of the experiments bland and mundane, I couldn't help but feel I had somehow profaned my classmates by exposing their names to my spiders.

Not that it came to anything. I remained as ignorant as to the nature of my lies as I had been that morning, if not more so. I googled it, because I was heartsick and horrified, not stupid, but that only gave me advice on how to deal with cats coughing up spiders they'd caught. After a while, I found myself just staring at the blank screen of my sleeping phone, my mind just as empty.

The next day I went back to school and said nothing, as usual. Katie sat two seats down from me in geography, passing her phone to show me pictures of her dog. I smiled. She didn't ask for more input than that, and somewhere, down beneath my relief, I felt the bite of regret. Did she ever wonder about my silences, what I thought?

Would I even know what to say if she asked?

That was a worry I could keep in the back of my mind, however, buried among the dust and the empty spaces where I was supposed to keep hobbies. Katie kept me around through high school, and that fear never had to be anything more than a constant pinch in the background.

But high school is over now.

"Bloody hell, Georgie! You alright?"

I don't know whose shoes I've vomited on. All I can see is a swirl of colour, and I know I'm looking at pavement, but I can't seem to see it.

"Sorry."

Sorry is a good word. It's never a lie, it's never dangerous. 'I'm sorry' is too close to a statement, but 'sorry' is just right.

"I hated these shoes anyway," she says, whoever I've vomited on. I blink, and there's the sound of them being thrown into a bin on the street.

The street. Outside The Armistice, one of those pubs that never looks too hard at IDs. I'm drunk. Walking with Katie and her friends. Our friends.

"Are you sure you're okay?"

"Just tipsy," I say. Something tickles out from my mouth. "Let's keep going."

I keep my eyes to the ground as we stumble on, but it seems less than a second to my drunken mind before bare feet appear in my vision and a hand takes mine.

"Do you wanna go sit down?" It's Annie Chau. I hadn't even remembered that she'd been invited. She probably felt the same way about me.

"Your shoes," I say. I don't think I've been this drunk before, my voice runs off by itself. "Sorry."

"Hey, I don't care about the damn shoes, do I?" I can tell from her voice that she's smiling, but I can't look up from the ground. "Shit," she murmurs as I sway. "You need some water and a big thing of chips, yeah?"

I don't know why she keeps speaking in questions. Part of me wonders if she's mocking me, but I know that this has nothing to do with me, not really. Annie Chau is just nice to everyone.

"Me 'n' Georgie are gonna grab something to eat, we'll meet you up on Macquarie, alright?" she calls ahead.

One of the boyfriends shouts in assent. The group all have different boyfriends to the ones they'd had last year. Different names, same bland faces. I'd never had a boyfriend. Didn't know how to tell if I wanted one.

Annie takes me to a chip shop — the type with too-yellow lights and mirrored walls to make the cramped space look larger — and dumps a halal snack pack in front of me. I barely register that she's handed me a fork before she starts tearing into it.

"You're nice to me."

I didn't mean to say it aloud, but I'm too drunk for regret. It's a statement, and one that doesn't produce a spider, but I'm not sure if it could ever be a lie. I still don't know how ignorance affects my condition; it seems to change on a case-by-case basis. Or perhaps I'm just not as ignorant as I want to be.

"Can't very well leave you to fend for yourself, now can I?" Annie asks, laughing through the chicken.

"I meant always. At school and stuff."

Being misinterpreted has nothing to do with the spider thing, but it still feels wrong. Dangerous, somehow.

Annie quietens, looking down at the mess of chicken and chips. She won't want to speak to me after this. People don't talk *about* being friends or caring about each other or how they interact. They just do it. Like Katie and her friends, the ones who have probably already forgotten about us in the noise of Macquarie Street. None of them ever told me I was nice.

"Well," Annie says eventually, "isn't that how it works? You're nice to me and I'm nice to you — is it really that surprising?"

The uptilt at the end of her statements grates at me. Questions. She knows, somehow. She saw that lie crawl out when I said I was only tipsy. Or something else, a moment at the train station, in class. Anywhere. It doesn't matter. High school has ended, and with it, this false security.

"Stop it." The force of it feels strange in my mouth.

Annie jolts. "What?" she asks. "Do I sound insincere?"

My grip around the fork tightens, and I know it'll crease my palm.

"Stop making everything a question so you can catch me. I know you know, so just... say it, and be done with me."

At last, I look up to meet her eyes for what could have been the first time of the night. I must be really drunk, because all I see is my fear in her eyes.

"What's this about?" She's leaning forward as if she truly wants to know.

And I hate it. I hate that she could lie so honestly, having mastered this skill I never dared approach. How she used it against me and expected me to not even notice. There's a heat in my throat that had nothing to do with the chilli sauce, and I'm folding inward, becoming something small and scuttling that belongs only to the dark spaces.

"Nothing," I spit.

The lie hits the table hard, but steadies itself. Bird-eating spider. Huge. My throat is raw, and tears are rushing to sweep the world away, but I can't close my eyes yet. I have to watch the spider, listen to the screams. I have to lose Annie Chau, the only girl who was like me, who didn't have a proper best friend, who knew her place on the periphery. Annie Chau who could have been my best friend, had I noticed any of this before tonight. Annie Chau, who I liked, maybe a lot.

She doesn't scream. It's the shock, I tell myself. I hear panting, but it's just me. Her clenched hands shake. I hope she doesn't faint. I wouldn't know what to do. She puts her fork down onto the lino tabletop, and her hand hovers, trembling.

Is she going to hit the spider or me?

But when her hand comes down, it's slow, palm upwards. The bird-eating spider, still in its wide-legged stance as it reels from the fall, turns to her, a weight to its legs that gives me pause. I haven't dealt with many this big. Is it a true spider, with the defence instincts to match those fangs? Or is it something else? One large, white leg finds purchase on Annie's fingers, and then another, and then it is sitting in the palm of her hand, curled close like a newborn kitten. For a moment all I hear is breathing, mine and Annie's, out of sync.

I feel her eyes move, from the spider to me. I could always tell when she was looking at me in class. At the time I thought she was trying to figure me out, and a second ago I would've said there was something sinister about it. Now I have no clue what that searing gaze means.

I meet it.

That look in her eyes pulls me tight; I'm raw, on display and open. And yet, she doesn't look away. Hope twitches to life inside me, a many-limbed thing.

"It's easier," Annie says, voice almost hidden in the sound of the street outside, "to only use questions. You can't lie if you never make any statements."

My mind is blank, washed out by shock.

Annie looks down at the spider in her hand and then back up to me, a smile drawing across her face.

"I've never seen anything like this," she whispers.

Her lie is beautiful. Where mine stumble, hers glides out, seemingly coming into being as it slides between her lips. Its white scales slip into shadows of rainbows as the blue-tongued lizard heaves its back legs to leap from her mouth to the table.

I don't hesitate. It's cool, firm in my hands, curling around my wrist in a strong but tender grip. It's beautiful, and yet it's Annie who I can't take my eyes off.

"Hey," she says, her breath still shaky. "Do you wanna go somewhere quiet? And—"

For the first time, I don't have to think before replying.

"Talk?"

Friedrich Sarah E. Thompson is a bigender author from Sydney, Australia. With an affinity for fantasy across all mediums from short fiction to RPGs, he enjoys playing with traditional tropes and unearthing the human emotions within even the most played out of narratives. She can be found on Twitter @fsethompson.

THE ANOMALY

David J. Thirteen

EVERY DAY OF OSWALD'S LIFE, HE BOXED. AS FAR BACK AS WAS WORTH remembering at any rate. While the years had gathered and snowballed from an innocent pebble to a boulder large enough to crush Atlas, it was a constant. In the undefined space between his living room and kitchen, the heavy bag hung. Bolted to one of the beams of the cramped bungalow, it formed the axis to his current existence.

He was mixing it up with some hooks and jabs, not really doing more than working up a sweat and listening to his fists smack the hide. Habit freed his mind to meander through the dark and twisted alleyways of the past until Sam got home.

"Look what I found, Poppa," the boy said. He struggled to keep hold of his prize while shutting the door and throwing off his backpack in a single whirlwind motion.

"What?" A glance would have told him, but his attention was on raw skin peeking out from the tape wrapping his hands. Traces of blood filled the cracks and crevices of his fingers. The workout had been light, and his calluses thick. He shouldn't be so chafed.

"Look," Sam said. Less an invitation this time and more an order. He held a sign made from flimsy tin. It bowed and buckled in the boy's outstretched hands. Its dull gray background reminded Oswald of the filing cabinets at Barrymore and Associates, where he'd been a clerk for so many years. An unrecognized logo was formed by chipped white paint. Below it, two columns of tightly packed numbers ran to the bottom. A calendar. The angle made it difficult to read. The distance from the bag to the door added to the challenge.

Oswald came closer and saw specks of rust foxing the edges, and the dates tracking the year 1956.

"That's old. Where'd you find it?"

"On the street, in a pile of stuff someone was throwing out."

Once it would have been garbage, plain and simple. But the newer generations were basking in the refuse of the past. It was the type of thing you'd see on a wall in a sports bar or hanging in a basement, what they call a man-cave. If it were for sale, the store would ask a stupid amount of money for what was nothing but trash.

Whoever had chucked it out had the right idea. People shouldn't be spending money on garbage. And a man shouldn't be hiding down in a cave. His home was his castle, as they used to say.

"But this is the best part." Sam twirled it in his hands revealing the back. No paint or writing marked the surface. No rust either. Just a gleaming silver. It held the reflection of Oswald's rail-thin body. Except in it, he appeared obese. The boy flexed the metal, and Oswald dropped a hundred pounds to look the weight he'd been three decades earlier.

"It's like a funhouse mirror. Cool, huh?"

With an odd fastidiousness, Sam propped it up in the gap between two tall bookcases. "Too bad it has an anomaly." His grandson pointed to a spot about halfway down the right side. Oswald bent to see, clenching his teeth against the strain on his knees.

Beyond the tip of Sam's small finger was a spot where the metal darkened to a brass tint. Curious if it was dirt or a defect, Oswald touched the dark ellipse. It was cold with a distinct oily feel, but his finger came away clean.

Sam's eyes watched him, waiting for something.

Was he expecting an explanation for the mark? No. It was the word: *Anomaly.*

He'd used it so casually Oswald missed the opening gambit of the game.

"Your mirror is tremendous," he said.

Sam frowned and began pulling poses in front of his new toy.

Oswald's reply hadn't been exotic or complex enough to keep the game going. The boy's father was better at coming up with words than he was, and Ricky could play with the boy when he got home. Which should be soon.

Dinner would have to be started. He unwound the tape from his hands.

Thursdays were the time for espressos and conversation. Why everyone gathered those afternoons, Oswald wasn't sure. But if he stopped by DeMille's any other time, the place would be deserted. The bakery was the closest he got to the banter at the gym—men jawing about the things that were important to them. Except here, the talk was less about girls and boxing and more about grocery sales and the latest medical misfortunes.

"Did you hear? Tony had to go under the knife. His prostate. The size of an apple," Ricardo said, shaking a veiny fist in front of his rapt audience as though displaying the source of Tony's misfortune.

Oswald sipped his coffee and listened to the gossip until it was time to get home to Sam. He'd have more time at DeMille's if he drove, but it was a point of pride to walk. Even though his knees hurt like a son-of-a-bitch.

He turned off Carlisle, and the stores and restaurants were replaced by rows of post-war houses. In the hush of the empty neighborhood, a voice full of swagger and threat came from behind him. "Well, looky here? Who's that?"

While he'd been saying goodbye outside the bakery, a bunch of teenagers had stomped into the bodega on the corner. The three boys were full of hyperkinetic energy and noise. They were big. Big enough to be football players, but they didn't look like athletes. It was the growth-hormones in the beef, they said so on TV. It was mutating people. Every generation was bigger than the last.

Were those boys following him?

Oswald didn't look.

"Hey, old man? You got a dollar?"

He walked, eyes forward, not wanting an acknowledgment to turn into a direct confrontation.

"How about a quarter? A dime? Look at that. See? He's too old to hear us. Hey, buddy. Hey, buddy. What's a matter? Stop for a sec and talk to us."

They taunted him, and Oswald walked faster than he had in ages. A cold oil of sweat covered his torso. His breath wheezed from his open mouth. His cheeks burned as much from the hot blood flooding them as they did from the sharp autumn wind.

In his prime, he might have taken them. Well, maybe if there were only one or two, he could have. Three against one was always unfair no matter how trained and seasoned the fighter.

But his prime was long ago, and these kids were fucking giants.

Would Sam grow up to be big like them? Or would he keep his delicate build and sweet personality?

Was it wrong, in this world, to hope he'd always be his little Sammy?

Oswald's tormentors kept their distance, although they could have outpaced him if they chose to. Any second, a hand could land on his shoulder and spin him around.

If it happened, he would fall into the momentum of the pull and deliver his best right hook, even though fighting would send him to the hospital. Leo Davenport, the best middleweight Oswald ever met, had to have both hips replaced last year because he fell on the ice. These brutes would be worse than ice.

Too young to care about consequences, they were capable of anything. Anything.

The first sliver of his lawn came into view. He kept on, one foot after the other, the brisk strides driving nails up his thighs.

The voice called out behind him, free of exertion. Closer now, it rang out with pure snideness, inviting the others to look at the pathetic geezer, questioning where Oswald thought he was going, asking why he was ignoring them.

Leaves crunched behind him as he crossed his yard. He'd be stationary and cornered if he tried to unlock the door. Home turf provided little safe haven.

A rake Sam had forgotten to put away leaned against the stoop. Oswald rushed to grab it. Once in his hands, he spun and brandished it like a poleax.

The three boys weren't there.

Beyond the tines of the rake stood one man. A singularly grotesque figure who had to be at least sixty.

"What's he going to do with that? Do you know what he's up to?" he asked to the air around him.

Heavy jowls distorted his face and basset hound rings hung below his eyes. Stringy black hair with streaks of gray started halfway up his scalp. The gray sweatshirt he wore was stained, and all that was left of the brand logo was the impression of white lines. It was tight over the flabby irregular pockets of fat hanging off him. On his feet were untied winter boots.

The guy was simple. That's what they used to call people like him. Ricky would have gotten mad at him if he used the word out loud. "What's a matter with you, Pops? Do you have any idea how ignorant you sound?" he would ask as though Oswald had exposed himself in public.

"Got any money?" the simpleton said, taking a step closer. Dried leaves caught on the rake brushed the front of his shirt. "Gimme some money."

"Get out of here." Oswald tried to sound menacing, but he had no strength to draw on. His muscles were empty except for a vinegar burn, and his joints had all the limberness of rusted iron. The siren's song of exhaustion was fogging the edges of his vision.

Turning his head to the front window, but never taking his eyes off the man, he yelled, "Hey, Robert, call the police."

Who the hell was Robert? It had just come out. It didn't matter who he pretended to talk to, but why not Ricky or Sam? Or his never forgotten Marilyn?

But for whatever reason, he'd invented this Robert as his ally, and he continued with the fiction. "Call the police to get this crazy bastard out of here. Do it now, Robert."

"What's he calling the police for?" The man cocked his head, in an animal pose of attempted understanding. "Frankie hasn't done anything wrong. Nothing wrong. He has rights like everyone else."

"This is my yard. Get out of here now." Oswald jabbed the rake forward, being careful not to touch him and compel an attack. It was a logic that applied more to wasps' nests than a man, but it appeared to work.

The simpleton took two slow steps backward and muttered, "He's leaving. He's leaving." He began to walk away, repeating the phrase, his voice getting louder until it echoed over the bare trees and quiet houses.

When Ricky got home, a broad smile and a cheerful greeting concealed the fatigue from his labors and the hour-long bus ride from the warehouse.

Sam dropped his infernal tablet on the couch and removed his earbuds. The bright, flashy game he'd been playing released squeaky carnival music. The tune pranced across Oswald's headache.

He lowered his head over the pan of spaghetti sauce simmering on the stove and massaged his brow. Steam coated his cheeks and hands in a clammy vapor.

The sauce had been one of Marilyn's staples. After her passing, he made a point to learn it. It was unthinkable to lose something so essential to the family's DNA. The recipe was simple and well-practiced. He'd barely had to pay attention while he opened the cans and diced the onions. It had allowed his mind to dwell on the afternoon's altercation.

He should have turned and faced the bastard earlier. Had he looked when the man first called out, it could have ended there. In the yard, he should have dropped the rake and raised his fists. Knocked the cretin on his ass, the way he once would have. Oswald never should have rushed home. Back on Carlisle Street, he ought to have stood his ground, and told the guy to go to hell. He should have clocked him with an uppercut to the jaw and laid him out in the yard for the neighbors to see.

"Hey, Pops, you're not looking too good. Everything okay?"

"A little tired. I might take a nap before dinner. Watch the sauce."

He shuffled off to the dark backroom. It had been his den before Ricky and Sam moved in. Not much had changed except a twin bed had replaced the sofa. He lay down. A light strobed across his closed eyelids in an aurora borealis of pain.

The taunts shouldn't have scared him. Even if it had been the teenagers, what would they have done? All bluster, those kids. And even if that bum had been a threat, there wasn't anything a solid uppercut wouldn't have fixed.

Oswald woke with no sense of having been asleep, except for the disorientation of no longer being sure of the time.

The door to the den opened.

His boys never entered the room. At most, they'd knock and speak through the door. They gave Oswald this one place to be his own. He appreciated it and was pained by it. This was their home now. They shouldn't think any part of it was closed off to them. The self-imposed restriction was a hesitation, an admission that this was a temporary situation.

Yet someone was coming in.

A silhouette blocked out most of the light from the hall. It was much too tall to be Sam and far too wide to be Ricky.

An idea pulled Oswald into a dark airless place. The man from the yard. He was here. In his room.

But, no. The deeper the figure moved into the den, the clearer his features became. He was perfectly bald, his skull sharp and distinct under a thin veil of skin. The ridges of bone were magnified by the deep shadows cast from behind. The only clothing visible was a long gray smock that billowed out around his knees.

He was huge. A giant, towering to the ceiling. His sheer bulk swallowed the room's empty space.

No sense of muscle movement could be detected as he neared. His progress resembled the motion of a clockwork manikin, the sort inhabiting haunted houses at the carnival.

Oswald's scream stayed locked in his lungs. The frantic scrambling of his arms and legs to get into a sitting position never became more than a thought, while a deep paralysis held him tight. The harder he tried to break free, the more blind panic took over.

The giant knelt by his bed. The flesh on his massive face was rubbery, lacking any lines or wrinkles that might lend it humanity. The impression was of a mask hiding something horrible beneath. It opened its wide maw, spreading its face into something impossible and vaguely fish-like. The monster locked its black eyes on his, staring at him with cold, alien regard as it lowered its head toward his stomach.

Its terrible face disappeared beyond the rise of Oswald's chest. Only the gleaming back of the giant's skull showed. He tried to see what the hulking thing was doing but couldn't budge. His view was fixed by the limit of his eye sockets.

The giant head thrashed from side to side. In absolute silence, it bobbed and whipped about like a dog worrying at a bone.

Oswald was completely numb. No sensations from the attack reached him, not even a sound. What the hell was happening? Where did it have its mouth? What was being done to him down there?

Oswald had to scream. His world shrank to that one primal need. The terror had to escape.

A noise broke the surface. It was nothing but a muffled "unn-unn" but it awoke hope.

The giant continued its strange and dreadful work. And even though he was plunged in a deep, woolen hush, Oswald imagined all sorts of tearing, slurping, wet noises to accompany the violent jerks taking place at the edge of his vision.

Oswald squealed, "Unn-unn."

He looked away to the pure darkness of the ceiling. Up among the shadows, the illusion of peace existed. He could pretend the lack of feeling meant a lack of danger. But something terrible was happening to him, and he needed to know what.

He lowered his eyes.

The head was no longer there. Oswald sprang out of bed. The creature was gone, the room empty.

Ricky approached his chair. "Pops, do you want me to heat up some of that spaghetti?" The slowness of his movements, and the quiet in his voice were the gestures of a caregiver, not a son. "You ready to eat something?" He watched Oswald's face as if he was expecting him to answer with twitches and blinks instead of words.

"No. Not hungry."

"You coming down with something?"

"I'm fine. Just tired."

When he had gotten up, he examined himself in the bathroom mirror with his shirt pulled up. No cuts or bite marks. No residual dampness had been left by a mouth pressed against his skin.

Nothing had attacked him. No one else had been in the house.

This was confirmed by Ricky and Sam's lack of alarm. The place was too small for people to hide or to sneak around without noticing. In the kitchen, his two boys were eating dinner and making each other laugh with their wordplay.

"This is a delectable dish of spaghetti."

"A flavorsome bowl of pasta."

"A scrumptious platter of noodles."

It had been a bad dream. Everything was fine.

Except he didn't feel fine. The pounding surf of a headache rolled in and out with a rhythmic, shuddering pain. Gray spots played an unending game of now-you-see-me, now-you-don't in his periphery. His knees wanted to curl up as though he'd taken a haymaker to the side of the head. He'd needed the wall for support to get to his leather armchair, where he collapsed and hadn't moved all evening.

The TV was on, the sound too loud, the picture too bright. They had a modern flat screen, but the shows rolled across it the way they used to with the old tube set when reception was poor.

The normal argument started up when Ricky told Sam it was time for bed. The boy didn't fight hard, knowing the inevitability of the outcome. But he exhibited his defiance by heading off to brush his teeth with creeping slowness. The pace must have been painful to maintain for a child who seemed to run everywhere he went.

"I think I'll turn in too," Oswald said.

"You need any help?" Ricky went to take his arm and steady him.

Oswald shook it away. "I'm fine, damn it."

Sam stopped, his mouth hung open.

He'd never raised his voice in front of his grandson before. Sam's shock awoke a shame within him, but the thumping in his head swatted it away. His son shouldn't have treated him like an invalid. He didn't need anyone's help.

Something in Oswald's face made Sam turn from him. Then, his eyes found the sign, and whatever tension the boy had sensed was forgotten. He smiled watching his body warp and bend in his funhouse mirror.

Oswald staggered to his room.

Sam said, "The anomaly is getting bigger."

For three days the anomaly grew. Oswald could no longer cover all of it with his splayed hand. As it expanded, it darkened, losing its brass tone and turning a yellowed bronze. It was the shade of a fallen leaf, the brightness faded to the muddy brown of rot.

And for three days, he'd had the same dream.

He'd imagine himself waking to the opening door, and the giant entering his room. It would glide to his bed on cogs and rails, where it would bend and feast on some part of Oswald he could never see.

The only thing that changed with each repetition was the intensity of the dread.

A connection seemed obvious, except the visitations were nothing but a nightmare, and the sign was only a piece of trash. The two things couldn't be linked.

Above the metallic splotch, tired eyes reflected back at Oswald. In the imperfect mirror, his face looked thin and goat-like. An old goat.

Below his throat, the stain covered a large section of his chest. It didn't cast back any of the colors of his shirt. It was a gaping hole.

He turned the sign around so 1956 faced him and slammed it against the wall.

Sam didn't notice its placement when he got home. Or if he had, in his rush to get back to his latest video game, he didn't say anything.

Oswald went to have a nap. His fatigue dragged down his body and mind. He hadn't worked the heavy bag in days. It was no longer his old friend but an obstacle that forced him to expend leaden steps to avoid it on his way to the den.

He had no rest. The dream came again and robbed him of any of the restorative balm of sleep.

Or was it the giant who stole it from him?

The monster feasted on his blood, soft organs, muscle, cartilage, marrow, right down to the gristle. It left his body light, aching, and weak. He wasn't being eaten piece by piece but layer by layer. If it kept up, Oswald would fade away.

He shook the crazy notion from his head. It had only been a nightmare.

When he returned to the living room, the sign had fallen away from the wall. The mirror side faced the ceiling. And the spot had spread again.

The backdoor's opening might have gone unnoticed, except Oswald had been sitting for hours with nothing but the hum of the fridge, and the monotonous tick of the kitchen clock disturbing the stillness.

Gravity held him fast, pressing him tight to the leather of his chair. The waning day painted the room in gray, matching the tone of his chilled skin. He should have gotten a blanket, but it was easier to suffer the cold than to walk to the closet.

Sleep called to him in the alluring voice of a lover, but he refused to succumb. The giant came every time he slept now. It was always hungry. Oswald held tight to consciousness, enduring the crushing fatigue.

The door was eased closed and furtive sounds of a jacket unzipping and shoes hitting the mat followed. These were false notes in the music of his routine. Sam should be storming through the front door, talking nonstop about his day, not sneaking in the back.

Oswald intended to call out a greeting but only managed a sigh. He'd say something when Sam came in looking for a snack.

But he didn't come through. He went straight to his room.

Now the tune of the day was lost entirely.

Oswald yelled his grandson's name. A rasp ending with a hum mocking the letter *m* came out instead. A second attempt yielded a whisper. The third time it rang out. "Sam."

How could that voice belong to him? It was so feeble. He persisted despite not wanting to hear himself again. "What's the matter? Come here, and talk to me."

Sam didn't respond.

It would have been easy to have left it. Oswald could go back to the numbing sounds of the house and the dimming light. He could sit in the quiet, a little longer.

A little longer.

The ticking clock told him to relax, calm down.

Sleep.

"Sammy, come out here. I need to talk to you. Now." His panicked words carried down the hall.

Reluctant steps padded toward him and stopped behind his chair. "What is it, Poppa?

"Come here, and let me see you." His voice was fading back to a rasp.

Moving with the same languid tempo as the afternoon, Sam shuffled into view.

At the sight of the boy, Oswald pulled himself up straight, spine rigid. It were as though he'd been hit with a defibrillator. Electricity jolted through his muscles, driving away his exhaustion.

Recent tears made Sam's face red and puffy. A bruise alive in blues and yellows closed his left eye to a squint, and a cut splitting his lip had scabbed over.

He took his grandson's hands in his. "Who did this? What happened?"

Sam looked to the window to escape— to see something other than eyes which might contain judgment.

"Kyle," he said after a long pause.

"Isn't he one of your friends?"

"Not anymore." He didn't cry but his shoulders rose and fell in convulsions. His face was stoic even as his body sobbed.

Oswald was on his feet uncertain of what he would do or say. If that little shit Kyle was in front of him, he'd... he'd do something stupid, but it would release some of his rage. With no outlet, he was left grinding his teeth until his jaw hurt.

The fury stalled his brain, and he might have stood there glowering at the injustices of the universe all night if Ricky hadn't come home early.

"Hey...what's going on? Sam, what happened?"

"The boy's been in a fight."

"Is this true?" Ricky asked kneeling in front of Sam.

The answer leaked out of him through his nose. The dam burst, and his weeping oozed snot down his upper lip. Ricky snatched him up in his arms.

"It's time he learned to box," Oswald said.

"Not now, Pops. Not now, okay? Sam, tell me what happened?"

Oswald stepped over to his neglected friend, the heavy bag. How much frustration and pain had he poured into it over the years, one punch at a time. He placed a hand on it as though calming a horse. "He needs to know how to fight back. When I was his age, it was a matter of survival."

"Take it easy, will you?"

With a fluidity born from the memory of doing it a million times before, Oswald pivoted and rocketed his arm out, landing an easy smack on the bag. Unlike any of those previous punches, the bag didn't budge. It was Oswald who swayed with the impact. His feet stumbled under him. He crashed into the wall, sending picture frames rattling.

"Jesus." Ricky left Sam and held Oswald to keep him from crumpling to the ground. "You're not well. I'm going to get you to the hospital."

He would have shaken free of his son's grasp, but he wasn't confident he could stand on his own.

"No hospitals." If he went in, he may never come out. It had happened to friends. The doctors put them through a battery of tests, never finding anything definitive. All the while, they grew weaker, and their will to fight dwindled.

They wouldn't find anything was wrong with him except old age. But this wasn't age. At seventy-two, he had grown used to the increasing number of limitations and humiliations. This was something new. He was being drained.

The monster in his dreams was draining him.

"I'll be alright," he said. "I need to fight it."

But first, he had to figure out how to beat a creature that left him completely powerless. He needed to adapt to this new and terrible opponent.

Oswald woke from his sleep. The door opened, and the dim sound of the TV grew louder. He'd slept through dinner. The hand at his side stayed still like a marble statue, despite his attempt to make a fist. He couldn't move his legs either.

The giant was coming.

In sync with the thought, the monster made its entrance. It stared at Oswald with shark eyes. The ruthless black voids were empty of everything except hunger. The putty of the massive face rippled when its mouth opened. The thin pale lips were slick with drool.

It bent down and began feeding, sucking, slurping — whatever the hell the damned thing did outside of Oswald's view.

This time he didn't try and scream.

One of the first lessons taught to a boxer was some hits can't be avoided. Sometimes you had to take them. You absorbed the pain. Kept on your feet if you could, crashed to the mat if you had to. But you took it. Owned it. Got up again and hit back.

The cold punched him in the belly and sucked the air from his lungs. The winter coat that had fit him last season drooped from his shoulders and ballooned around his waist. The wind slapped at his face trying to drive him back inside. Grass solid with frost crunched beneath his feet. His vision caused the backyard to tilt and wobble with each step, but he kept on toward the shed.

The oily stain on the back of the calendar had kept growing. As it expanded, it gained definition. It was still a blob, but if you knew what to look for, the human shape with a big, bald head could be seen. When both Sam and Ricky had left for the day, Oswald prepared himself for a bout unlike any he'd ever fought. One with the highest purse he'd ever played for. One where he couldn't take a single swing.

He was adapting.

The key in his trembling hands was slow to find the opening in the padlock. Twice he had to wipe his eyes to clear them and bring things back into focus. By the time he got it unlocked and yanked the door free, he was ready to go back to bed. No, worse: he was going to fall asleep where he stood.

Oswald pulled smelling salts out of his pocket and broke them, taking a long whiff. The burn reached into his sinuses and brought him back to the times when he'd be winking out in-between rounds, his corner man screaming, "Keep those eyes open. Stay on those feet. Put those fists up."

Past the lawn mower and the shovels, tools covered a weathered table. Most of them had been bought in sets when he and Marilyn were first married. He'd done everything in their little place on Kipling Road from straightening the crooked doors to replacing the plumbing. The wear on them spoke of the family they built. But he had other tools from before his life with Marilyn. From before he'd even been born.

He crouched down in front of the wooden box beside the table. Winter seeped into the creaking knee pressed to the floorboards. When the lid opened, the chest released the scent of grease and oil along with the mustiness of rotting wood.

He dug through a collection of saws, hammers, and pipe wrenches. These were his father's, passed down to Oswald when he had died. Sacred heirlooms. Relics. Handling them, Oswald could sense their power. Not only had they been built to last, they'd been used every day by the strongest son-of-a-bitch he'd ever known.

At the bottom was a torch with a solid brass base, wooden handle, and a faucet wheel behind its spout. He blew the dust off and placed it on the table.

Gripping the edge, he hauled himself up. An oil lamp sat on one of the shelves as it had since the last blackout. He pulled it apart to get at the fuel. The chimney slipped and smashed on the floor by his feet. Oswald kicked the larger shards out of his way so he wouldn't step on them and poured the kerosene into the blowtorch. Half of it spilled across the table but enough of it got in.

He put the cap back on and pumped the plunger three times to prime the torch. Then, he scanned the table looking for one more thing: his tin snips. These he slipped into his back pocket, then left the shed.

The door was left to flap in the wind. If he succeeded, he could come back and set things right. If he didn't, it wouldn't matter.

The whine of the hinges and clack of the door banging against the jam followed him to the house. His lurching movement reminded him of the zombie movies Ricky used to watch as a teenager. He panted plumes of hot vapor into the late fall air. Not a hint of sun broke the cloud cover. At the patio, his legs gave out and he landed hard on his hands and knees. The torch rolled away across the paving stones.

"Damn it to hell," he said loud enough for the neighbors to hear.

His body rose a few inches and collapsed again. It wanted to stay down, to rest, to find peace.

"Not yet. Give me ten more minutes," he whispered into the ground. It was a bargain. With whom, he wasn't sure. God? Death? Himself? It didn't matter. He just needed ten more minutes, and it would be over.

"Stand up, you bastard."

He bit his cheek until his mouth filled with the tang of blood. It was good. Between the sour taste and the sheen of sweat on his face, it brought him back to the struggle of the ring. All that was missing was the stench of the canvas, and he'd be right there, rallying his strength, refusing to stay down for the count.

Oswald snatched up the torch and threw himself at the back door.

After being in the frigid air, the house was uncomfortably hot, but he didn't bother taking the coat or boots off. He crashed down the hall to the kitchen. The calendar lay on the counter with the light burning bright overhead. Except for the tools from the shed, everything was laid out for him as if he were about to perform surgery.

The lights flickered, allowing the deep drab of the morning to infiltrate the room for an abrupt moment. The stain in the metal rippled and flexed.

The giant had grown strong. It reached out into the waking world. Oswald's eyelids grew heavy. He could barely keep them open.

The end was right in front of him. Sleep, then death. If any justice existed, Marilyn would be waiting for him. He just had to stop resisting.

But how could he rest knowing the creature still existed?

Once it sucked him dry, it would start in on his boys until it no longer needed to hide in the reflective surface of a piece of trash. Then what?

"Ten more minutes," he whispered, and pulled the tin snips from his pocket.

When Sam came in, Oswald was dozing in his chair.

"Poppa. Poppa," he called. "You won't believe what happened today—"

Sam stopped. His face tilted with curiosity at the strange object under his grandfather's feet. "What's that?"

Oswald followed the gaze and looked down at his outstretched legs. "Is that my mirror?"

"I'm sorry, Sammy. You know how tired I've been. I needed something to prop my feet up. I'll get you another mirror. A real mirror. This is now my impromptu ottoman." He smiled, inviting the boy to match his uncommon words.

His feet rested on an eight-inch hollow cube with the dates of 1956 spread over it. Icy cold seeped through it into Oswald's socks. His heels felt a thumping like a frantic knocking or the beating of an anxious heart.

David J. Thirteen is a horror author based out of Toronto. Returning to writing in 2012, he garnered over a million reads posting serial novels on the Wattpad platform. This led to him joining the Wattpad Stars program and having his first novel, Mr. 8, published. His most recent work is the found-footage, haunted house novella, The Garrison Project. David is a member of the Horror Writers Association's Ontario chapter. His real surname is a chaotic convolution of vowels and consonants. Certain mispronunciations may summon beings from beyond the void.

In the Forests of the Night

Joanna Michal Hoyt

So Chon and I — that's Asunción Rivera, the woman I'm going to marry if we get through this day without getting arrested or permanently losing touch with reality, and if she forgives me for last night — were on an Amtrak train, more than halfway through the twenty-four-hour ride to the Protect Real Americans rally that we thought — hoped — we could interrupt and transform. We were both pretty keyed up, so Chon was brainstorming worst-case scenarios and ways of dealing with them, and I was imagining bits of *Les Misérables*.

"If you keep imagining like that, you'll wear us both out," Chon said. "Save the image-projection for tomorrow, Thea. You need to sleep now."

"I need to be alert when we get there."

"I'll wake you at six. Sleep now. Shut off that heroic stuff in your mind..."

"I can't."

"...and breathe with me." She bunched her jacket against the window and leaned her head on it. I bunched my jacket against her shoulder and leaned on her. We held hands, and I matched the rhythm of my breath to hers. Nineteenth-century France fell away around me, and then twenty-first-century America fell away too, and the dark bore me up like a warm sea.

I woke abruptly, feeling Chon upright and rigid at my side. It was still dark outside the windows, but the train lights were coming on.

"It can't be six yet."

"It's midnight. I can feel the pattern shifting."

"Shifting how?"

"I don't know."

I accepted that. Chon's gift was energy-reading not imaging. "The train's stopped. Where are we?"

"We're not at a station," she said. "Engine problems, maybe. Or maybe *la migra*."

"Immigration? Here?"

"We're within a hundred miles of a border," she said very quietly and in Spanish. "They can board."

"The Canadian border!"

"The law doesn't say it has to be the southern border."

"*Ay Dios!*" someone said behind us. Chon craned her neck, then whispered, "Two rows back. Both sides of the aisle."

I looked back between the headrests. Two rows back on the other side of the train, a dark-haired woman in a faded coat sat in the seat by the aisle, her body still, her eyes darting. I would have thought the window seat next to hers was empty if I hadn't heard the little boy say, "Mami?" and heard her shush him. Across the aisle from the woman, a man sat with his hands folded in his lap, whispering to the tall dark girl beside him.

"You think they don't have papers?" I whispered in clumsy Spanish.

"Shh," Chon answered. "They must be thinking about him—their energy's all flowing that way." She gestured with her head toward the little boy. Then she sucked in her breath as two men with guns and uniforms entered our carriage.

"There has to be something we can do!" I protested—in English. I was too upset to translate.

"Like what?"

"Make them go away...la migra, I mean. If all of us stood up to them..."

"All of us? Thea, the Anglos on this train won't care."

"They have to!" I protested. We looked at each other, squeezed each other's hands, breathed together again.

A jumble of disconnected images rattled through my mind. I didn't have time to sort them out before the officers stood over us—they'd made their way down the compartment very quickly.

"Are you a U.S. citizen?" the shorter one asked.

"I refuse to answer," I said.

"I'm not asking you, ma'am," he told me. Well, if they weren't questioning blondes, that explained how they'd come down the car so fast.

"Then you shouldn't be asking her," I said. "Racial profiling is unconstitutional."

"I am a citizen," Chon answered.

"I need to see your ID," he said.

"Why?" I asked again.

"Here," Chon said, handing it over. "Asunción Guadalupe Rivera Cruz. Naturalized citizen." He held it up to the light, nodded.

"See, that was easy," he said, handing it back. "Thank you, ma'am."

He passed the blond couple behind us, stopped by the people Chon had pointed out to me.

"Are you citizens?"

No answer. He said something fast in Spanish, of which I only caught, *"Papeles."* Papers.

A pause, then the taller officer said, "Come with me." He repeated it in Spanish.

"¿Por que?" the man asked.

"We did not do anything," the girl protested in slow and accented English.

"Come on," the short officer said, his voice a little sharper this time. The tall officer bent over the woman, took her by the arm.

The fear-pictures flowed quick and sharp through my mind. That was one of the double-edged gifts Chon had brought me: when we were together, with her energy-bending and my image-gift, I could see what other people saw inside their minds. Not explanations, mind you, just pictures. A child in filthy clothes screaming inside a chain-link fence, ignored by armed and uniformed men outside. Also, a dusty yard in which men with guns and without uniforms leaned menacingly over the picture-maker...

Something distracted me. Another current of pictures, of feeling, from someone else nearby. A little blonde girl smiling, safe inside a white picket fence. Ominous dark figures who had leaned over the fence being pulled away. Safe, safe, all safe. Such a relief...

My hand hurt, either because Chon was squeezing so hard or because I was squeezing so hard. Fury boiled up between us. Behind my eyes I saw the first of the images we'd prepared to send out—oh yes, after miserable months of receiving the ugly images the PRA rallies put into people's heads, we'd decided to try turning the flow and sending our own pictures out—at the rally in the morning. Uniformed men with guns led a family away. The family had yellow stars on their coats, and the gunmen's uniforms had swastika patches on the shoulders. Their language... I didn't speak their language. I needed my laptop, I needed Google Translate so I could get the German words right...

But how could I think about the words when the music was there, scattering everything else?

I needed to not listen to the music. I needed, I needed my...

My what?

My rucksack, of course, packed with soap, chocolate, a Bible, a warm jacket, some aspirins, a pack of cigarettes to trade—even in the KZs you could trade, they said. But I didn't have it with me. The rucksack was at home and they picked me up off the street, with—with her. The one next to me. The one I loved. Why couldn't I remember her name?

I turned to her. To Channah.

"You're losing control," she hissed. "You're taking this too far."

"*I'm* taking this? *They* grabbed us, *they're* taking us." I didn't point out that she had a yellow star on her coat, and I didn't, that they wouldn't have taken me if I hadn't been the woman who loved her.

"Grabbed us? What do you mean?"

"Why do you think we're here?" I asked, gesturing at the rough wooden planking that came up to her chin and my shoulder, the crisscross of barbed wire above it.

"Thea, what in hell are you doing?"

"I'm not doing anything!" Something stirred sluggishly in the back of my mind, unable to break through the music. Perhaps just a reminder that she was the last person I should quarrel with. "I love you, Channah," I said.

"Don't you even know my name?" Channah asked, her voice ragged.

Couldn't she hear me? What had gone wrong? I listened to the voices around me. Weeping. Praying. Whispering. Planning? Out of focus, like the forbidden radio we hid in the attic, so much static you could hardly follow the words.

"Where do you think they're taking us?" I whispered.

"Nobody's taking *us* anywhere. It's the family behind us. You started this to help them, but this isn't helping. You've got to stop it before somebody gets hurt."

"I didn't start anything! I can't stop anything! Channah, if I could help I would."

"You... *Mein Gott...*" Her voice was turning rough with static too. She jerked her hand away. She disappeared.

I stared stupidly out into moon-shot mist. Had she climbed up and crawled out through the barbed wire? How could she have done that without my seeing her? Would she have done that, leaving me behind?

It's true what they say, I thought, *the Jews are magicians, she's done something out of the Kabbalah.... Like the students in Elie Wiesel's memoir...No, they couldn't do anything to stop Hitler that way, they just thought they could, and some of his friends went mad trying... No, who's Wiesel?*

How can I wonder who he is? He wrote that memoir about the Shoah...

What? When?

The music swelled almost loud enough to drown my thoughts. A klezmer lament. I'd heard it on YouTube.

On what?

Channah was back. "You're dreaming," she hissed in my ear. She grabbed my arm hard enough to leave a bruise. "Sit down. Take my hands. Breathe with me."

"I can't sit," I said.

"I can," she observed, settling herself comfortably onto empty air. "I'm not trapped, and you don't have to be." She let go her painful grip on my arm, took my left hand in her right, and reached her left hand through the solid planking of the wall.

I gasped. Choked. Reality itself was falling apart. I groped for something to hold onto.

The music. Cello music. Classical. It didn't cover the harsh voices calling out in Serbian behind us. The voices of the ones who'd stopped the train here where nothing should stop. I looked, dismayed, at the one next to me, the one I loved.

"Asja," I whispered. I shouldn't have said that name. That wasn't a safe name, not now. Not when they'd stopped the train to take the Muslims off it. I'd seen the bodies... "Teodora," I said loudly to her.

"No, that's not my name! Neither of those!"

"Say your name," I whispered.

"Chon," she said loudly and firmly. "Asunción."

The train faded again. Came back into focus. So did her face, lovelier than ever without the hair that used to hide her high forehead. They'd shaved her so they'd know her if she ever tried to cross back into *el Norte*. Ike didn't want any more wetbacks, that's what the men who raided the farm said when they grabbed Chon for her Spanish name and me because I wouldn't leave her. They grabbed a lot of others too. Each of the cloth-covered benches on either side of the aisle held three or four people. The aisle was full of people too. The man who'd shaved our hair had commented on the numbers. There were hundreds of thousands on buses like ours, he said. If it wasn't for Eisenhower protecting America, the aliens would have sucked the country dry.

Dry... We'd heard about the last deportation train dropping people in the middle of the Mexicali desert. Eighty people died of heatstroke, or of thirst. Where would they leave us? Someone behind me sang *Salvo Rociera*, a funeral song before the deaths began.

But how had Chon stuck her hand through the solid wall?

"It doesn't seem real," I muttered.

"What you're seeing now isn't real," Chon said. "Come with me. Breathe with me."

I did. Our surroundings flickered, solidified. Chon's face stayed the same, dark and intent, but her long hair was back. Her coat was new, shiny. I stood in the aisle of the Amtrak, my laptop dropped onto the plushy blue aisle seat I'd left. Chon reclined in her seat by the window, her right hand stretched out to me, her left hand sticking out the open emergency exit window.

"Chon?" I said. "What happened to me?"

"Same thing that's still happening to them." She gestured round the carriage.

People stood, staring at terrible things I couldn't see. People cowered on the seats, hiding their heads.

"We have to wake them up," I gasped. "Most of them. If we could keep la migra distracted..."

"No need, now," she said. "I got the family they were detaining out. Through the emergency exit."

"Won't they run into more agents?"

"They'll have a chance. They're not stupid. I walked them past the end of the train. I didn't see any more agents. Maybe the other agents —

if there are others — are stuck like them." She pointed at the seats where the mother and son had been. The immigration agents sat stiffly side by side, staring straight ahead. Each man had hands close together as though cuffed, neck pressed back against the backrest, eyes fixed on some invisible menace. One of them also had a faint purple shadow on his jaw which might, given time, deepen into a bruise.

"What...?"

"God knows where they think they are," Chon said. "I can guess what someone else thought — why they hit them. I didn't try to wake them. That family was the only one I woke, and I only managed that by hauling the boy out the window. The rest came after us, and once they got outside, away from you, they started to listen when I explained I wasn't with the paramilitaries or the FARC and they weren't in Colombia any longer, and with any luck they weren't going to get sent back now. Thea, what the hell did you do to everyone?"

"I don't know," I said. "I was so angry. It started with one of our images, the Nazis taking Jews away, but it went somewhere else. Those weren't my pictures, not most of them. It got away from me. With the music playing—"

"You got away from me, too," she said.

"You couldn't see what I was seeing?"

"I could, at first. But I couldn't make you stop seeing it, or even make you remember it wasn't real. The way the energy was twisting, it made me sick. I had to pull out. I thought if I did, it would break the bond and you'd come back from wherever you'd been, and that bending in the air would stop." She took a jagged breath. "And I pulled away and you... you just kept on going, and the air kept seething."

"And you left me."

"And I got the family out, and then I came back and got you out. But who were you bonded with? What in hell were you doing?"

"I told you, I wasn't doing it. I just couldn't think, with the music."

"There's no music."

I listened. There wasn't. "But there was, before."

"I never heard any. Where was it coming from?"

"It was everywhere."

She frowned. "The bending in the air was everywhere. Thea, can you let yourself go back enough to hear what they're hearing, but not to believe it?"

"I might be able to," I said. Considered briefly. "Pigs might fly."

"Okay, we don't want you getting sucked back in. Better let me navigate. I can feel something back there," she said, gesturing down the aisle. "Come on."

The aisle was choked with sleep-standers. One of them staggered as I pushed by her, clutched my arm and called me by a name that wasn't mine. The music sawed at my mind again. Somebody sang about a snake that bit and killed a woman who'd tried to rescue it, then said it was her fault for taking it in.

I whipped around, hearing the serpent hiss at my shoulder. That one beside me had a woman's body. But her eyes... her eyes had the vertical pupils of a snake. And even apart from her eyes, she wasn't an American. Not a real one. Not with that dark skin, those foreign features, that loose outfit that could be hiding anything. Drugs. A gun.

A gun. She was easing something out of the folds of her skirt. She knew I'd spotted her. She was going to shoot me. Her serpent eyes caught mine, clung. She hissed again. No time to run. I grabbed her wrist and twisted.

The shock and pain that poured into my mind had nothing to do with snakes. It came from closer, from someone I'd hurt, someone I—

Someone I—

I took a step forward. Stared as the music faded.

The stranger standing in the aisle had let go of my arm. Chon stood facing me, her right wrist nursed in her left hand, her face slack with shock.

"Thea!"

"Did I hurt you?"

She didn't answer. She didn't have to.

"I'm sorry, I thought you were... I mean, I thought it was a snake that was going to shoot me—it was the music—" I reached out to her. She flinched. I decided not to point out that if I had known it was her, Chon, and I'd wanted to incapacitate her, I would have grabbed her left wrist.

Further down the train somebody screamed, a high thin tearing sound that went on and on and on.

"*Dios*," Chon gasped. "Thea! We have to stop this." I set a hand on her shoulder as she hurried down the aisle, and she didn't shake it off.

Chon stopped abruptly, staring at the occupants of two seats on the left. The man in the aisle seat had a well-pressed suit and a pale face set in lines of horror. The woman in the window seat was curled into a ball, half-hidden under her long red hair. Her hands twitched. I tried to push our bond the other way, to see what Chon saw, and for an instant I glimpsed the knotted threads of purple shadow passing around and through the man and the woman... and also through the tablet that lay on her tray.

Chon woke the tablet. The text of a speech was open on the screen. She scrolled so fast I had to scan, not read. Brutal murders of white girls by dark-skinned immigrant gangsters. (Purple highlighting around some revolting details.) Illegals running deadly drugs. (Purple highlights around a vivid description of what it looks and sounds and smells like when someone ODs on fentanyl.) Illegals getting taxpayer help while citizen veterans go homeless and hungry. (Purple-bordered picture of a terribly disfigured blond man with a medal pinned to his filthy coat, a cardboard sign saying HOMELESS VET, PLEASE HELP propped against the leg he still had, and an empty cup near his stump.)

"The kind of stuff the rally speakers might say tomorrow."

"One of the speeches they're going to make today," Chon said. "And you see what the purple-edged parts are."

"Vile," I said. "Images," I said more slowly. "Nightmares. Things to project. You think they can do what we thought we could do? Can make people see things—I mean, not convincing them, just putting the pictures right into their heads?"

Chon nodded. Kept scrolling down.

I sort of choked out loud. Chon looked at what I'd seen, and then at me.

The lyrics to the snake song were there. So was the dark-skinned snake-eyed figure. The structure of his face, the color of his skin, were really rather like Chon's.

"That's what you saw when you looked at me? That's what you believed? That's why you wrenched my wrist?"

"It wasn't me, it was this dream—"

She grabbed my wrist as I spoke. I thought maybe she was going to twist it, to show me what it felt like, and I wasn't going to stop her. But she just held on and stared me in the eye, and I remembered, I couldn't help remembering, some things I had thought about Chon. Things I would never, never have said to her. Things I was angry at myself for thinking.

"I'm sorry!" I said.

The girl whose phone Chon had held began to gasp for air.

"All right," Chon said. "Be sorry. Be as sorry as you can. Spread it."

I grabbed her hand—not the one I'd hurt—grateful that she let me.

But I couldn't stop it now, they'd broken out, they were wild. The women with the snaky hair, their eyes weeping blood, wanting blood for blood for blood. The air was full of hissing.

The snake-haired women leaned over that one I loved. She looked half dead with fear, with exhaustion. Like. Like.

Like the man in the play. Like Orestes, who'd done murder to avenge murder, who ran away from the bloody-eyed Furies who haunted him for his crime until—

Until he stopped running. He turned and faced them. He stood his trial before them. And they changed.

"Stand," Chon's voice said faintly through the hissing. "Stand."

I stood, though all I wanted to do was run from those horror-figures who were turning their terrible bloody eyes to stare at me. I held Chon's hand tight and I made myself look back.

"I'm sorry," I said. "I didn't mean this. I just wanted to keep people safe."

Ssssafe, the snakes hissed, flickering their forked tongues at me.

"Really, that's all I wanted! Somebody has to stop the rallies. Somebody had to help that family." I remembered again the images that had passed through the family's mind as the agents tried to lead them away. The foul US holding cell, the...well, I guessed the men in the dirt yard must be whoever they had gotten away from down south—

Other images came back into my mind. The dark-skinned, snake-eyed figures. The blonde girl inside the picket fence—no more than five or six, laughing in a shaft of sunlight. Precious and fragile. Loved. Threatened by the dark figures—take them away, take them away...

I felt Chon pulling her hand away from mine. "No," I told her, pushing the words through the thrumming air. "I don't believe those pictures. But I see. They wanted to protect the ones they loved. But they were wrong about the danger...and they were doing so much harm...we had to stop them...they deserved..."

Yesss, the snakes hissed. *Yesss, ssissster, we mussst ssstop them. We mussst punish them.*

"No! Not 'we!' Not 'sister!' You're monsters!"

Monsssters, the snakes hissed. *We are all monsssters.*

Chon's voice. To me, "Orestes confessed." To the snakes, "We are. We didn't mean to be, but we are."

I knew what should follow. The acquittal. The change coming over the Furies' faces: their eyes streaming clear water not blood; the writhing snakes taking on a gentler curve, becoming branches held up to shelter suppliants in the holy grove. Not Furies any longer. Mercies.

I could imagine those images, but I couldn't make them real. All I could do was stare into the snakes' eyes and say, over and over, "I am so sorry..." and try not to notice my voice hissing on the sibilants. I wept; tears, not blood.

There was a terrible sound that cut through the hissing. And then there was nothing. Nothing.

I lay on my back with my left arm under me. Someone had hold of my right arm. *La migra knows what we did*, I thought. *What we tried to do. They've knocked me down.* I gasped out "Where's..." and then thought that maybe they hadn't grabbed Chon and I shouldn't say her name.

"Open your eyes," Chon's voice said above me. I did. For a moment I saw the snake's eyes, gasped and turned my head away. I blinked, looked back at Chon, her face closing, her hands releasing mine.

"What did you do to her?" a tense voice asked somewhere above me. I tried to sit up, winced at the throbbing in my head. "Nobody hurt me," I muttered.

"She was frightening you." That was a man's voice. A man's face over Chon's shoulder. The man in the suit, the man with the woman with the phone with the speech.

Chon took my hands again. "She's had another of her seizures," Chon said. "She'll be all right. I can take care of her — I've done this before."

"'s right," I mumbled. "Chon. Helping. Always...Thanks."

"Seizures? What has she been taking?"

"Nothing," Chon and I said indignantly.

"Ma'am?" A uniformed man bent over me. Not Immigration. Conductor. "Are you the one who was screaming?"

"I don't...think so. Sorry, I... it's just my...epilepsy. Chon's helping me. Chon, did I scream?"

"No." Chon helped me up. "That was someone further back. Sorry, sir, we'll get out of your way." I leaned on her, shuffled back to our seats, keeping my eyes down.

"Thank you," I whispered.

She set me in the window seat, took the aisle seat herself, pulled out two legal pads and two pencils.

Don't talk out loud, she wrote. *People can hear us. Some of them might know Spanish as well as you do. Not that that's saying much.*

Okay. I saw the immigration officers heading down the aisle after the conductor, looking confused and profoundly unhappy, passengers flinching away from them as they passed. *Do you think they remember what happened?*

I don't know. The air isn't seething now but there's still a sort of tingling. I can't make sense of the pattern. What do you remember?

Everything. I think. Chon, I'm sorry I hurt you, truly I am. That wasn't really me. It was...it must have been that couple with the phone. You know that, you said it: they're —

They can do what we could do.

Could? Chon, don't you think we still — I stopped there. *You don't trust me? You won't —* I didn't know how to finish that sentence. *I was just trying...*

You said that before you passed out. We were just trying to keep people safe. They were just trying to keep people safe. We're lucky no one died.

I still don't understand what happened. How did the PRAers grab my mind?

I think you grabbed theirs. Okay, we grabbed theirs. But you went all the way down into the nightmare, and I didn't. The nightmare spread fast. Faster, maybe, because so many people were still asleep, drifting. The music you heard? Bet it was just fear. Everyone's fear. You tapped that.

But while I was still in it, everyone saw my kind of pictures. I mean, they added different details, but the basic idea was mine. When I pulled out the other lot took over the imaging... If they send out their images at the rally, and there's nobody there with a different idea...We did pull them out of it at the end.

The end? Look at me, Thea.

I did. For just a second I saw the snake, flinched. Then I saw Chon's face, the face I loved, and I reached for her — and she flinched.

Chon, what's happened to us? Will it go away?

I don't know. We don't know anything.

What are we going to do now?

You can decide what you're going to do, she wrote. Then she laid down the pencil. Tore out the pages she'd written on. Tore them up. Sat there, close-lipped. I put a hand on her arm. Tried to match her breathing. She shook my arm off. I stared out the window across flat white frozen fields glowing faintly in the light of a sickle moon stuck in a flat gray sky. I imagined the migrant family trudging across that cold emptiness. If they froze, if they died, and it was my fault...

"No," Chon whispered. So she was still listening to my mind, after all. "We weren't two minutes out of a town when the train stopped. They'll be able to get warm."

"So we did some good."

"And some harm."

I opened my mouth. Shut it. Tried to feel for Chon's mind again, but she was holding it shut. I sat there in the loneliness and unknowing with Chon, together and apart, until we reached our stop.

Chon didn't look at me as we collected our bags and left the train. Didn't speak to me as we lined up to enter the rally. Took the end seat in a row full of people so I couldn't sit with her. Which left me time to write the whole thing down in case...

Fifteen minutes until the keynote begins. I don't know what I can do. I don't know what I should do. I just know Chon is here, and I'm not leaving.

Joanna Michal Hoyt lives with her family on a farm/intentional community/nonprofit in upstate New York where she spends her days tending gardens, goats, and guests, and her evenings reading and writing odd stories. She enjoys stories where all the characters are fully human and flawed, stories that honestly show our brokenness and also the hope that persists amidst that brokenness. Her short fiction has appeared in periodicals including Mysterion, Mythic, Daily Science Fiction, and in various anthologies. Links are online at https://joannamichalhoyt.com/short-stories/

A Woman Unbecoming

CM Harris

"On your left," he snarls.

Though there's plenty of room on the trail, Alice swerves right, jerked from her reverie of watching asphalt blur beneath her knobby front tire.

The guy buzzes by on a mint-green Bianchi, wearing less-than-opaque white Lycra shorts. His ragged breath confirms he is riding for blood and glory.

A roadie announcing the obvious. *Great.* He's probably incredulous that she's riding her mountain bike on a paved trail on this perfect summer day. Probably thinking, *Ooo, how extreme!*

No. Calm down, or it will happen again.

Alice didn't require clairvoyance to know the trail would be crowded on a blue-skied Sunday. The Greenway had been so cluttered in Uptown she chose not to turn on her music and carefully wove through the walkers, rollerbladers, families puttering along. Once the pavement cleared out in the Minneapolis suburbs, the hot summer wind rumbling pleasantly past her earbuds, the occasional cricket, the siren call of a cardinal, Alice found she didn't really need the songs for inspiration.

She was content, felt good again. Even her new knee, though tender, felt strong. If she could keep feeling like this, she might even be able to get along with her co-workers at the agency, maybe not tank another performance review.

Alice exhales, pushing out old toxins. But it only serves to wake up the new ones.

Another roadie echoes, "On your left." This one's a bit more winded and takes longer to pass. He wears a purple T-shirt and, thankfully, black Lycra shorts. His paint-chipped Peugeot squeaks with every revolution.

And then it starts, though she tries to fight it.

The two guys are co-workers. Gary. And, David? No, Dan. They work for 3M Office Products. Drones out of the hive for the weekend. Letting loose. And it's imperative that they put a woman on a slower bike well behind them.

She can see it, hear it as if she were there: earlier that week at 3M Office Supplies Division, Gary explaining *Le Tour de France* to Dan, trying to coax him out for a ride, trying to establish dominance.

Then, just an hour ago at Gary's house, the two men stuffed their Taco Bell midsections into tights. As Gary mixed endurance drinks (they would be riding thirteen miles after all) he informed Dan where to get the best price on a steel Bianchi. It wouldn't be as tricked out as his own carbon fiber frame but a nice starter that could be upgraded.

Dan insisted he was just fine on his old Peugeot.

The other man sighed. "You at least need a real jersey."

Dan did not argue, though he did not agree. Sure, his baggy T increased his drag coefficient but it also made a convenient tent when his junk got all jumbled up in the bike shorts. He wasn't about to tell his manager that those white shorts were as transparent as negligee. That would mean admitting he'd seen the man's butt-crack in all its bushy glory. And you didn't embarrass this guy.

After everyone is clear on the fact that the road bikers have indeed passed in the left lane of an abundantly wide trail, they fall into line in front of Alice.

And then they slow down.

Alice triggers a short burst of the Jekyll's brakes, and the discs screech against the pads.

Gary points at the ground to his side, indicating a right turn, which unfortunately, is the same direction Alice is headed. All three exit the trail and speed toward an industrial park intersection. The roadies slow, bikes wobbling as they gape at road construction signs.

Alice knows where the detour is. She veers into the grass, then bunny hops off the curb, free of the roadies and their sloppy thoughts invading her head.

"Hey," Dan says, "she didn't call it."

"What?" Gary says as she speeds away. "She passed on the *right* and didn't call it?"

"Nope."

The other man growls.

Gooseflesh rises on Alice's arms. She understands that grunt from way down inside her. She blinks rapidly. If she closes her eyes for too long she'll absorb too much of their anger and then the ebony strands in her mind will get too sticky to untangle.

Should she slow and take their dressing down? Or turn and head home? This is the most remote part of the trail. Even on the weekend, the prairie by the interstate is often deserted.

Alice can't afford a run-in right now. She's too skittish. It's only been a few months since a surgeon replaced her knee ligament with the Achilles tendon of a cadaver. She's still trying to gather strength and courage before venturing back onto the sketchier dirt trails.

She could pull out her phone. Make a show of dialing 911. Film whatever shenanigans they're going to pull. She does have that multipurpose tool, the one with the serrated blade, in her Camelbak, but she'll look like an idiot fumbling around with it.

Okay, okay. Settle down. It's not going to go that far. Just let them have their say.

This new paranoid side is exactly what her boss had been complaining about. But there was something un-right planted inside her now. Forget the metal pins in her shin, never mind the sutures. You can't get away from a dead man's flesh, once it's threaded into you, your vascular network giving it new life. The surgeon had scoffed at her fears. We hit it with a good deal of radiation, he'd said, I doubt your body will reject it.

But what if it rejects me?

The roadies pull up behind Alice, their rear wheel hubs like a swarm of hornets.

She gives in, closes her eyes, and slides open her new invisible window into the mind.

Gary is trying to will her to look at him, staring at her with his melting glare.

Dan shakes his head. "Just leave it." He prefers to watch the pulse of her buttocks.

Gary snorts and speeds up. He pulls into the left lane and begins to pass, but then slows and turns to her.

"On your left!"

Alice opens her eyes and stares forward, nods to music that's not playing in her earbuds.

"I said, on your left!" Gary screams. "ON YOUR LEFT, YOU FUCKING CUNT!"

He passes laughing, as does Dan. They pedal off, shaking their heads, lesson taught.

Alice glowers. Why should she have announced passing when she wasn't even near them? It's not that she's opposed to politeness. She must have said "on your left" a dozen times in Uptown.

She does have to admit his statement has a certain cadence; like something a particularly foul-mouthed drum corps would chant as they marched onto the football field:

On your left, you fucking cunt! On your left, you fucking cunt!

And now she's chanting it too, panting it out.

The roadies aren't fast. She's reeling them in at a worrying pace. They are all over their bikes, torsos wagging, arms yanking the handlebars to get up the slightest incline. They rock and bounce on their saddles with every stroke, seat posts set too high.

She'll catch them soon. *Crap.* But, damn it, why is she supposed to cower? If she was a guy, they wouldn't have said a word.

At the far end of the loop, where the trail runs parallel to a retirement home, Alice focuses her energy. She can't pass them going full bore; she must take them at ninety percent. A racer once told her, *never pass if you can't stay ahead.* Pull up with the quads. Push out with the hamstrings and glutes. Round out every corner of the stroke with the calves, ankles and toes as if you're removing dogshit from your clipless shoes. Spin. Spin. Make like an eggbeater and spin!

Ahead, an elderly woman with long white hair hunches over a motorized scooter and putters toward them in the left lane.

Alice slows and nods a smile at her. *Stay human, girl, stay human.*

The crone leers back with crooked yellow teeth, her eyes dark and hollow. She raises a big-knuckled forefinger as she passes, her mouth agape—black inside.

Rip their legs off.

Bile rises in Alice's throat. She looks over her shoulder.

The old woman is gone. No scooter. Nothing.

Alice kicks it, a chill tickling at her back like fingertips. She passes the roadies and veers back into the lane a few bike lengths ahead.

"What the hell," Gary yelps. "Can you believe this shit?"

Dan chews his lip. There's no going back when Gary gets the scent. This is how the guy dogs 3M underlings, even a few lateral execs. It never ends well for anyone. He wishes he had begged off this stupid ride. But as ordered, he falls in behind Gary's rear wheel, drafting to conserve energy.

The three turn toward the city, west wind pressing their backs, and sail at thirty miles per hour on the downdraft. Great white clouds have piled up in the early evening sky. The moon hangs above the Minneapolis skyline, nearly as orange as the sun's own reflection off the glass-plated towers. Shadows lengthen along the Cedar Lake trail, sprigs of yarrow and mustard grass bend to the will of the breeze. The bogs are cooling down.

Alice and the roadies rage across the asphalt, which runs parallel to the Burlington Northern train tracks. Tires howl and mouths pant in a *ménage à trois* of anger and fear and glee like hounds on a rabbit. On a downhill sprint, the men catch her, Gary yelling again and again: *on your left on your left on your left.*

There are millions of guys like this. Why can't she just ignore the furious voice rising inside like other women do? Could she make it to the off-road section, where skinny tires fear to tread, and just remove herself from this mess?

Who cares! Your knee is fine.

The wet voice is that of the cadaver in the U of M holding tank. It slowly bobs, an eye donor with dark pits in its orbital sockets. But the pits go infinitely deep into an abyss, far into nothingness until stars twinkle into view.

So just fuck it. Fuck it all.

Alice. Oh, Alice?

Let's see what these maggots have got.

They race by the Vonartis building, a fortress of pharmaceutical laboratories, which pumps out a sickeningly sweet steam reminiscent of Franken Berry cereal. Thick power lines buzz above them, and Alice's left leg tingles in response. Deep inside the knee, something gives way, not with the firecracker pain of her original injury, but with a sloughing of materials no longer needed, materials repurposed.

Dancing on her pedals, she flies up the next hill and gloms onto Dan's rear wheel. She nudges his tire with the Jekyll's front knobby, creating a whirring hiss. He pumps harder, adding a couple inches of distance.

"Here she comes again!" Gary says with a rasp. "Goddamn."

Goddamn, indeed.

Alice glances down in shock. The new knee is working smooth as silk. In fact, the post-op quadriceps bulge and pump larger than those on her right leg. The skin on the left side of her torso stretches and stings hot, just as her forearms once did when bullies on the playground handed out those snakebite skin twisters. But this time, instead of wincing, she swoons, eyelids fluttering. *So nice.*

Alice hammers past Dan and then Gary. It would be so easy to veer over and push him into the fence, into the cattails or that pond—her balance on the Jekyll steadier than his stranglehold on his expensive thoroughbred—and so delicious to see that fabric torn to strips. She sweated out any semblance of meek miles back. The only reminder of the gentler sex is her hourglass figure that tricked at least two of them into assuming she might be managed.

Another mile ticks off without them catching her. Maybe they're right on her tail. She refuses to look. But she sees the sparkling green pain behind their eyes and feels their hearts flubbering in their chests. Both are beginning to devise ways out of this situation with egos intact.

On the prairie straightaway, Alice eases up.

TRAIL CLOSED FOR REPAIRS

It's over. No way are they going to follow her into gravel. They probably turned off the trail to their posh homes in the Cedar Lake neighborhood. Her lungs rake in hard gasps of dense, pollen-filled air. Rotten disappointment rises in her throat and her leg begins to twitch and twang like a strike to the funny bone. Sparks dance in her vision, as furiously as spermatozoa under a microscope.

The wind carries up a sharp gust of male pheromone. Alice's nostrils flare and her mouth begins to salivate. It smells wonderful, feral.

She passes the sign and sees that the trail construction is nearly finished. No rock, just an onyx ribbon of fresh asphalt for another hundred yards. Without the yellow stripes, it's anybody's road.

Gary pulls up beside her, pushing into her space, his snarling face inches from hers. His body odor activates something in her even deeper down than his first grunt.

Her stomach growls.

"I know you can hear me, *bitch*! ON YOUR L—"

His face lengthens and he falters.

For an endless moment as they roll along, she sees what he sees, the growing hugeness of her, the veins snaking black down her leg, up her arms and forking across her neck.

He shakes off his hesitation. "On your—"

Her right hand secure on her own handlebar, Alice's left hand shoots out and grabs the man's helmet strap and mirrored sunglasses. She yanks down hard and swerves into the grass to avoid his flailing arms.

Dan catches Gary's pedal in his front spokes and they both go down in a twisted, skidding heap.

Alice taps her brakes and coasts, arms quivering, legs spinning backwards. Everything is green. So green. And black, but not. Black like nothingness. The nothing hungers for something.

Gary cries after her through furious tears. "You goddamn bitch!"

She slows, glances back, her left cheek drawn over her teeth in a sneer she hadn't planned. Half her face is numb, and drool runs down her chin. She rips off her glasses to force more light into the consuming green and black.

Dan groans but his weathered face, wild-eyed and hurting, falls silent when he meets her awe-filled gaze.

Alice turns her bike around. She can't leave the poor things like this. The hunger is too great.

She rolls up on them, dismounts, and lays the Jekyll down in a thatch of milkweed. Her metal cleats click the asphalt like talons. She limps toward them, a syncopation no longer from injury but from limb disproportion, like wearing stilettos with one broken heel. A mosquito, sated with her blood, takes flight from her arm and pops midair with a barely audible *snick*. Dark matter fizzes in the air.

Dan desperately tries to untangle his flesh from the bike.

Gary refuses to look at what she is becoming. "Bitch! You fu—"

Her post-op leg swings and smashes his nose up into his skull.

She cocks her head and peers at the comical way one of his eyes has rolled up further than the other. The brass cleats ripped off a good deal of his upper lip.

"Oh my god," Dan murmurs. "Are you cr—please, calm down. He's just an ass. You never called left, it's the rules." After wincing at her, he averts his eyes from her elongating limbs and fights the sagging weight of Gary and the Bianchi. One of his legs splays out from the wreck, an angry red swathe of road rash striping his thigh. His other leg twists backwards, the foot still clipped into a pedal.

Alice leans over Dan.

He trembles. "Please."

His genitals are bunched up sideways in the Lycra shorts. Though it's a classic target, Alice leaves them alone; he can't walk home on those. She chooses his ankle instead. When she stomps, it pops like turkey gristle on Thanksgiving.

His bellow becomes a wet gurgle as he clutches at his calf.

She feeds Dan her shoe with half the force she fed it to Gary.

He slumps back. All is silent.

Alice shakes her head, amazed. With every thump of her pounding heart, black veins stretch across her leg like worms. The skin on her left side is losing opacity, like the Visible Woman educational doll in the Christmas catalog that her parents refused to buy because one could see all the way through to the rectum.

This new knee is going to last forever. She'll have to start training her right leg alone to maintain balance. No, it will catch up. She feels like a new woman. So unbecoming for a woman. A woman un-becoming. She can't help but chuckle. There are others like her; she can hear their whispers, others who have been darkly blessed by the donor.

Alice searches the roadies' jersey pockets. She finds Gary's cell-phone and stomps it into black shards. She shrugs off her Camelbak and rummages around in the pouch. Though she's ravenous, she flings the banana PowerBar into the brush. Void flesh demands living flesh; it won't be assuaged with colorful packaging or sensible nutritional information. Ah, the multitool.

Gary stirs and dislodges himself from Dan. He whimpers and crawls toward the brush.

Alice allows him time to choose a more secluded spot amongst the chirping frogs and buzzing dragonflies. She picks through the attachments on the multi-tool until she finds the serrated blade.

The train tracks beyond begin to hiss. But there is no locomotive in sight. High above, a Delta flight drops its landing gear. Inside, three first time flyers clutch the armrests.

Alice crouches over Gary as he sputters blood. A bleached white incisor hangs by a thread of gums from the side of his oozing mouth.

Her elongating fingers pat her lips. "You have something there." Her voice is low and hollow, reverberating like a gong that can speak.

He reaches up to numbly smack a hand at the wrong side of his mouth.

"No, there," Alice says. "On your left."

CM Harris is the author of novels MAIDEN LEAP (Bink Books, July 2020) and THE CHILDREN OF MOTHER GLORY (Bella Books, 2009). Her short stories and essays appear in Oprah Winfrey's O Magazine, Escape Artists' Pseudopod podcast, Harrington Literary Quarterly, and QUEER VOICES: Poetry, Prose, and Pride (MN Historical Society Press, 2019). Her screenplay The Cost of Glory received Gold and Silver Awards from the 2018 Queen Palm Film Festival. CM Harris lives in Minneapolis with her wife and their twins. She is also the lead singer of the indie rock band Hothouse Weeds.

 # LIKE A CAT

Brian K. Lowe

THE FIRST THREE TIMES THEY KILLED ME, IT WAS THE ELECTRIC CHAIR. All three times. *Just my luck,* I thought, *to finish my run in a state where they still use the chair.*

I didn't know how good I had it.

They videotape everything nowadays. When I watched myself being led out of my cell, this cell, and down the last mile for the fourth time, my shoulders felt so tight I thought my arms were going to break. It's not that I can't watch somebody dying — that'd be a joke — but it's tough when the guy on the TV is you. And when it's the chair.

I knew the drill by now. I knew the door to the execution chamber, where they'd strap me down, put the wires on my chest and the straps around my ankles and wrists and head — like I was going somewhere? — and pull that switch and I'd jump and twitch and sparks would fly off me and if they hadn't done it right my hair and my skin would catch on fire and I'd start screaming and I'd jerk around some more and I'd be dead. Again.

But they hadn't gone there. They walked past that door and led me outside. I watched my own eyes go wide.

"What the fuck is going on?" my TV self and I asked. The difference was, here I was confused, but there I sounded scared.

The camera pulled back and I saw them tie me to a tall wooden post. When I stood in front of it the scar pattern in the wood formed an outline around my head. I figured out what that meant pretty fast, but not as fast as I did on the tape, because Number Four had already seen the firing squad.

The bastards didn't even offer me a blindfold.

"What the fuck is this?" I asked again. This time it was just me asking, because on the tape, I was dead. "I don't want to watch this shit anymore."

"You have to," Haskins said. "It's part of the sentence. On the anniversary of your sentencing, every year, we bring one of you out of the vat, and one of your victims' relatives gets to decide how you die." Haskins had been the ADA assigned to my case. I remembered him from the trial. Big, red-faced guy, he bullied the jury into convicting me of nine counts of first-degree murder. "And then they get to pull the switch."

Nine counts of murder one meant nine death sentences — four down, five to go, including today — and Haskins had been here for every one. I guess he didn't have any hobbies.

"Bullshit. You still can't make me watch. I've got rights, even in here."

"You see?" Haskins asked the two-way mirror, his puffy face getting all pink. "He says that every time." The big mirror was inset into one wall, coated with something that made it unbreakable, even when I hit it with my manacles. They'd put me in this holding cell for the last night of my life. It was just like my old cell, ten feet on a side, a cot, except they'd added the mirror. They'd also rolled in the video monitor, bolted to a heavy cart. The only thing missing was a toilet. I guess nobody thought the voyeurs on the other side of the mirror wanted to watch a dead man pissing.

Haskins turned back to me. "And every time, I get to tell you that you don't have no rights anymore. You're dead. You just saw it on TV, and if you see it on TV, it must be true." He smiled like a pig. If I could've reached him, they'd'd've had to tack on another death sentence. "And if you don't want to watch, I can have the guards pin your eyelids open in about thirty seconds." Nothin' between him and me but steel shackles and three guards. "But I won't have to, 'cause every time this happens eventually you quiet down and then we get on with it. That's why I love clones. You never change."

I spat in his face and closed my eyes tight and he laughed while the guards whipped me with billies a few times too many and strapped my head in a brace and pried my eyes open. They kept them open with little braces, just like in "Clockwork Orange." That was a funny movie —

funny until they did that shit to you, anyway. After that one of them had to spray something in my eyes every few seconds because I couldn't blink. It hurt like hell anyway.

Haskins kept on laughing and saying, "You never change," so that I didn't know if maybe he'd been lying to me all along—maybe I spat in his face every time and they had to restrain me, and he just kept repeating himself so he could have me beaten up in front of witnesses. I pulled against those straps until I heard my shoulder pop, and all they did was tighten them.

This thing about executing me a different way every time bothered me. No shit, it bothered me. I didn't mind dying so much, but I wanted to know what was coming so I could spit in the executioner's eye, too. But nobody was about to answer any of my questions—except Haskins. He could've told me. He *wanted* to tell me—he wanted me to ask so he could drag it out. I could see the excitement in his piggy little eyes. He was getting hard just imagining it. No way I was gonna give him the satisfaction.

My lawyer, he wasn't even there. I was already dead—four times over. I didn't see him on any of the videos, either, so I didn't know if he'd ever bothered.

From what Haskins said, it must have been five years since my trial. This was like his Christmas present; every year he got to unwrap a new clone and watch one of the vic's relatives off him. How many murder cases had he done, ya suppose? Did he come down here, like, every week? What a perv.

"I know who's gonna do you today," he whispered. He leaned in real close; either he didn't want the camera to pick up what he said, or he wanted to smell my sweat.

He knew who was gonna pull the switch, or the trigger, on me today. Somebody's husband, probably, or maybe a son. Some of those bitches could've been old enough to have a son. Maybe it had been a few years, maybe Junior had been waiting for this for a long time, maybe it was time to fry the bastard's ass who'd tied up his mama and tossed her off the pier.

None of those girls could swim worth a damn.

They hanged Number Five. He'd been right; my fifth victim's son turned eighteen the day before the execution, and his dad gave him my neck as a goddamned birthday present. It was even on fucking TV. I had to watch my own execution with a Channel Five logo in the corner. And I hadn't even stopped kicking before they went away for a fucking truck commercial.

Number Six just got gassed. It was the vic's mother that time, for Christ's sake; she could barely see straight enough to find the button. I don't know if she thought it'd be easy for her to do it, or if she thought gas was as close as they could get to drowning me, but it looked pretty quick on film. Better than the chair, anyway.

"I know how it's going down today," he had whispered to me before they came to take me, and I knew I was going to ask him before I did. He smiled. "You never change."

That one was on TV, too, but on cable. I guess pay-per-view paid better.

As I watched Number Seven die, I started thinking I should ask for a piece of the action—that'd get my lawyer interested in me again—but Haskins showed the video where Number Seven tried that. The judge practically laughed at him, and Haskins—who wouldn't miss it for the fucking world—*was* laughing. In the courtroom. Right into the camera. Right at me.

Number Eight, he got the chair again.

I'm Number Nine. Haskins is gonna have to get his rocks off somewhere else from now on. He said he's already got some new slob all lined up, a punk who shot three people in a convenience store. Only three, not nine like me, but hey, guys like me don't grow on trees.

I can hear Haskins coming; this is his last chance to say good-bye. He's gonna lean over me one last time and ask me if I want to know how I'm gonna die. I hope it isn't the chair again. But I don't care what the other clones did. I'm not going to ask him.

I'm not.

But only he knows if I will.

Brian K. Lowe lives on the edge of Los Angeles with his wife and many, many books. A graduate of UCLA and the Taos Toolbox workshop, he has published numerous stories, seven novels, and one non-fiction book on stock market fraud.

THE YOGURT SWIMMER

Richard Leis

A SNOUT BREAKS THE SURFACE OF GREEK YOGURT IN THE THIRTY-TWO-ounce container I have freshly opened and set on the counter. It sniffs cautiously, then sneezes and sprays yogurt everywhere. I yell. It pokes its entire head out and chirps. Mel is at daycare, Bill at his office. I'm between jobs and spend my days looking for work and being the stay-at-home dad, which includes grocery shopping and treating myself to some yogurt with a little honey.

I'm not eating this.

The tiny beast swims in easy circles like it's swimming through water. I watch it in disgust. When it launches itself into the air, I fall backward against the stove. It reminds me of Falkor, from *The NeverEnding Story*. Much better special effects here in my kitchen, though. I count four stubby limbs that end in round paws and short claws. The snout is long, and it has a mouth that smiles like a dog's does, no canines inside but a row of thin, squat teeth that might pinch. It shakes and reveals patches of white fur. It's sleeker than Falkor, though. Missing the floppy ears. It has two delicate membranous wings attached at its shoulders, two triangle fins on its back, and one whip-thin, ridiculously long tail that lashes back and forth behind it. And it's tiny, not enormous, about two inches long plus the tail. A living, breathing, complex organism and nothing like an enormous puppet in a movie at all. The dog-fairy-dragon thing backflips smoothly and returns to the yogurt with a splash. It's revolting. Yet breathtakingly beautiful.

If my husband Bill sees it, he'll be fascinated. My daughter Mel will absolutely adore the little beast.

I cannot let them find it.

I pick up the lid to cover the container. The creature stops swimming and diving and cocks its head at me. It lets out what sounds like an inquisitive chirp. But when I lower the lid, the damn thing hisses and snaps its jaws at me. It launches into the air and flaps toward me.

I drop the lid and scramble away, running like it's chasing me. In the kitchen, it splashes back down into the yogurt, but my upper back itches like it's right behind me, and I flee upstairs to the master bedroom. Lock the door. With those wings it could stalk the entire house. I listen but don't hear anything. I grab a pillow from the bed and push it against the gap under the door.

We've all heard about these visitations on the news. They've been going on for so long, they've mostly lost their novelty. Details from television and social media come to mind. Other little beasts, other homes of families with children. Should I expect a menagerie of these impossible creatures? A herd of tiny sheep on the hills of comforter on our unmade bed? Tiny monkeys swinging off our hanging clothes in the closet? I pull a tennis racquet out and lay it on the bed. In the master bathroom, I splash cold water on my unshaven face, look for crazy in my eyes in the mirror like I used to explore my face for gay. Tiny shark fins in the mouthwash?

In every report, in every interview, a parent describes the arrival of a miraculous little creature, something cute and charming. Descriptions vary. I don't remember hearing any of them described like the one in my yogurt. That's right, they always come out of something delicious or fun. A bag of candy. A tub of ice cream. A can of Play-Doh or a box of crayons. It's like someone is packing kid-friendly containers with an extra special gift. And Mel likes Greek yogurt swirled with honey from a bear-shaped plastic bottle as much as I do.

Here's the thing, though: those creatures appeared only in single-parent homes. Biological parent, adoptive parent, single grandparent, or guardian. Why? No one knows. No one knows what these creatures are, only that they bring comfort and joy when they arrive.

But ours isn't a single-parent home.

It isn't.

"Karl?"

Shit. I forget the tennis racket and hurry downstairs when I hear Bill call my name from the front foyer. He's home early. He passes through the living room and into the dining room where he drops his messenger bag on the table. I rush in after him. He greets me and there's gravel in his voice. Home early and wants to play before we have to pick up Mel.

Behind him, the swimmer leaps out of the yogurt container again.

I slide around Bill and put my body between him and the container so he can't see what's happening. I grab the lid I dropped on the counter and after the beast splashes back down into the yogurt, slam it down on top.

"What do you have there?" Bill asks from behind me. He rubs up against me. Yanks my shirt. Asks me where I want to apply the yogurt. I fake a laugh and pull away to carry the container to the refrigerator. The swimmer thumps against the inside and I nearly drop it. I growl in frustration when it chirps. Bill growls in return. I set the container inside, push it all the way to the back, behind the milk.

The monster wants Bill and Mel to see it.

Bill has a playful smile on his face, and he pulls off his own shirt. He has the most beautiful smile. I have to hold on to him. I grab his hand and pull him away from the kitchen. I lead him upstairs to our bedroom. I want Bill all over me, inside me, reaffirming our relationship and banishing figments of the imagination.

But sex isn't love.

And some doubts persist.

We go together to pick up Mel from daycare. After we get home, Bill sits down at the table in the dining room, his attention on whatever he's drawing with a stylus on his tablet. He's a graphic designer and always sketching new ideas. Mel comes downstairs from her room with her crayons and a big pad of colored paper and sits down next to him.

Clatter from inside the refrigerator. It wants their attention so badly.

I should have frozen it in the freezer.

"Let's watch a movie in the family room," I suggest. "I'll order pizza." I pull my phone out of my pocket and speed dial before Bill can respond. I speak loudly and order everything we need, including drinks, ranch dressing, paper plates, and extra napkins.

When I hang up, I pretend to be excited and silly. "Come on, come on!" I grab Bill's tablet. He's already closed what he was working on. I lead my family down into the basement where we keep the TV and video games, board games, and bins of Legos. I push Bill down on the couch. "Let's rent something!" I turn on the TV and use the remote to select a movie I think Mel will enjoy, but instead of starting it right away, I find cartoons for background noise, and then I sit down on Bill's lap. Mel giggles at us. Once upon a time, I'd been an aspiring artist. With Bill's stylus and tablet, I draw what I think is good enough to get the idea across.

"Cool," he says breezily, "but what is it?"

"You ever see anything like this before?"

"No."

"Anywhere in this house? Recently?"

"No. Is it one of those things from the news?"

I glance at Mel and the pad of paper she's brought with her. She's flipped to a new page. I hold the tablet in front of her and ask her the same thing. She says she's never seen the monster before, either.

So, it really is new to the house. Nothing they've seen already. One of them would've told me already if they'd seen it. Unless it's been here for a while already and they're lying to me. Maybe it dropped into the yogurt when I wasn't looking, while I was throwing away the seal I'd peeled off.

Bill looks at me quizzically, and I hate thinking anything negative about him or Mel. The monster is messing with my equilibrium. I don't bother explaining to him things I cannot explain.

The pizza arrives and I run upstairs and back down as quickly as possible. I serve Bill and Mel. After the movie starts, I drop down on the couch with them and make my plans. First, keep them away from the kitchen. Second, sneak downstairs when they're both asleep tonight and dispose of the monster.

Mel is curled up next to me. I have to protect my daughter from it, don't I? Maybe the media hasn't shared the whole story. Maybe some of these visiting monsters turn on their families and attack them. I couldn't live with myself if the monster hurt Mel. It's so small, but those claws, teeth, and tail can probably do damage.

I hug her close until she laughs and struggles. "You're silly, Daddy!" Bill is our daughter's "Dada." The biological father. I'm "Daddy." Love, marriage, and responsibility make that genetic enough. She's my one and only daughter, even if we used Bill's sperm and paid a surrogate for her egg and womb and those long months we waited.

Nothing's going to come between me and my family.

I reach out and cling to Bill, too.

Later, after we put Mel to bed and we're lying together in our own, I ask Bill if he still loves me.

My question sounds needy when spoken out loud.

Bill sighs. "You always ask me that, Karl. We're married and own a house." His finger moves across his tablet. He's always creating. "And I had a child with you."

Honestly, though, I want to hear him say that he loves me. A list of accomplishments isn't love. I miss when we were younger, when it was only the two of us, and our accomplishments weren't anything to list.

"We should have another one," he says. "Another little me running around."

Yep, your sperm again, I think. Your biology and not mine. I mean, it doesn't matter. I love Mel. It shouldn't matter. I didn't really want children, but we were in our thirties, financially stable and I had a job at the time I didn't think I would ever lose, so I had agreed to his plan. Since Bill was so excited about the prospect of us becoming parents, I thought it only natural he should be Dada. But Daddy is feeling a little left out now with this talk of another spawn of Bill and a monster downstairs that seems to think this is a single-parent home when all I want is some peace and quiet and a little goddamn Greek yogurt to forget I'm unemployed and not even biologically related to some kid I'm supposed to be supporting both financially and emotionally as much as Bill does.

I don't respond to him and the chill is unbearable, but Bill doesn't seem to notice and then he's snoring. I remember a woman on the local news being interviewed by a reporter about a tiny beast haunting her home. "Haunting?" she replied. She held her beaming toddler in her arms. "It's a miracle. A beautiful visitation." She gushed about how safe and loved she and her son felt. That's what all the single parents say about the creatures in interviews.

But I don't feel safe. I don't feel loved.

The hallway stretches long and dark between our end and Mel's bedroom on the other. I open her door a crack to peek in on her. She sleeps peacefully in the glow of her nightlight. I love her so much.

All I have to do is get the monster into the garbage disposal. Grind it up, let the evidence wash down the pipes. Bill and Mel might sleep through it if I'm quick enough. Maybe they won't. Once the monster's gone, what does it matter?

I set the tennis racket I've brought from our room on the table in the dining room. In the kitchen, I pull oven mitts out of a drawer and put them on. I listen in front of the refrigerator. Maybe it's already dead. Children crawl into refrigerators, get trapped, and suffocate. What about little dragons? On the other hand, maybe it doesn't need air. It arrived in a sealed container of Greek yogurt, after all.

I have a worse thought: what if it's grown? What if it's grown too large for the yogurt container since I put the leftover pizza away and it's burst out onto the rack where it paces back and forth like a cat waiting to be let out? If I don't do something about it soon, it might keep growing larger and larger until it presses so tightly against the refrigerator door that the door pops open. It might step down onto the floor, the size of a big dog, a tiger, licking the air, testing its massive wings, preparing for attack.

I would grapple with the monster anyway. Rip it apart if I had to — before it flies through the house and reveals itself to Bill and Mel. Before it puts them in danger.

But I find the lid is still on. I pull the container out and place it on the counter next to the sink. Nothing moves inside. I turn on the faucet. I hope it's already dead. Flip the disposal on. I place one oven mitt over the lid and tilt the container while picking it up from the bottom with the other. I have to be quick. I rip off the lid and slam the tub upside down over the drain at the same time.

I miss.

The yogurt plops out against the far side of the sink. And with it, the minuscule monster taking over my home.

The monster soars into flight with dizzying speed. I raise my mitts to squash it. It lands on my arm. Its claws pinch. I flail and swallow my scream. It flies back to the counter, squats down on the granite, hisses at me. It's a ferocious, dangerous monster. I feel for the handle of the iron pan on top of the stove behind me, then swing it over my head and smash it down onto the counter. Let go in pain, even through the oven mitt. The crash resounds throughout the house, but the monster flew out from underneath the pan before I made contact. It comes straight for my face. I drop to the floor and scoot back across the linoleum until my butt is on carpet. I cannot see where the monster has gone, but then I hear its chirps from the top of the cabinets, near the ceiling. The monster is just out of view.

I shake off the oven mitts and flex my pained hand. I stand up and retrieve the tennis racket from the table. I creep over to the sink, carefully open the cabinet doors underneath, and find a can of ant spray. Might not poison the damn thing, but I hope it will slow it down. It keeps chirping, like an alarm, loud enough that Bill and Mel will certainly wake up if they haven't already. It wants them to come downstairs, wants them to see what I'm doing to it.

I spray where I think the beast is hiding. It erupts through the cloud of bug spray. I swing at it with the racket. It banks to the right, swoops around me and out into the dining room, frantic to escape. I give chase. The bug spray seems to be working; its wings can barely keep it in the air. A pest, I'll tell Bill after I stab it and crush it under my feet into an unrecognizable pulp. Sorry for the racket. Do you really want another kid?

Noises from upstairs.

It darts left toward the living room, but I swipe at the air with the racket to cut it off. It swerves again, little wings beating hard, and climbs higher and higher, over the dining room table. I'll corral it in a corner, instruct Bill and Mel to stay out, then I'll destroy the monster...

It crashes into the far wall.

My triumphant snort dies in the back of my nose.

The beast doesn't hit and roll down the wall to lay broken on the carpet as I expect it to. It crashes and disintegrates across the wall in a splash of brilliant blue light. I jerk my head away and close my eyes against the flash. A tiny, mean, and fragile thing, but it has momentarily blinded me with its destruction. When I open my eyes again, I find it has left behind a large outline of itself on the wall, a rendering of fantastic detail far superior in design to anything Bill and I will ever be capable of creating together.

"It's beautiful," Bill breathes after he finds I'm okay. "Like the one you drew earlier." He admires its illusion of depth, the delicate precision of its lines, its glittery shades of blue and the way it seems to hover just above or within the wall, ready to flee at the slightest provocation.

I don't bother explaining things I cannot explain.

"Dada?" Mel pads into the dining room. She goes to Bill and he picks her up. He points at the creature on the wall. She gasps in delight.

That's when something invisible but physically solid pushes me away from them. I try to resist, try to call out. I'm still trying to catch my breath. My eyes still hurt from the afterimage of the bright blue light, like hundreds of tiny glowing beasts are flittering across my vision. I try to warn Bill we have to leave, but he and Mel are mesmerized by the yogurt swimmer's remains, a permanent stain, blueberry blue, on the verge of movement while they keep watch.

And then it does move.

My feet slide backward across the carpet. The unseen force pushes me out of the dining room. Neither Bill nor Mel look at me again. They watch the swimmer swim up from the depths of its demise. "Oh, Dada, look," Mel cries out in joy when the beast arrives to hover before them, transformed, blue now, not white, and as big as a small dog, a tiny dragon, an enormous figment of their shared imagination as it flaps its graceful wings. It chirps in greeting, and while I grasp for something to hold onto in the living room, and the front door opens slowly on its own to usher me out, the beast's brilliant blue aura wraps a single parent and his daughter in its promise of safety and unconditional love forever.

Richard Leis (he/him) lives in Tucson, Arizona where he writes poetry and fiction, attends and teaches writing workshops at The Writers Studio, and works in planetary science. His fiction has been published the House of Zolo's Journal of Speculative Literature. His essays about fairy tales and technology have been published online at Tiny Donkey and Fairy Tale Review's "Fairy-Tale Files." His poetry has been published multiple times in Impossible Archetype and has appeared in The Laurel Review, Manzano Mountain Review, HiRISE's MarsPoetica, and Star*Line. His website is richardleis.com.

TONES OF MEMORIES

Julie Novakova

Prague, August 1952

The street was quiet, sunlit and hot. Few people could be seen here on such a late Friday afternoon. That's why Joachim ventured out finally. He started walking nervously, reminding himself not to look around every other moment. He had no reason to fear. A mother walked slowly, pushing a stroller with a sleeping baby. A young couple was sitting on a bench, talking, laughing, eating ice cream. A man was reading newspapers on the next bench.

Joachim felt a chill go through his veins. He turned quickly, not to be caught looking at the man. He had glimpsed enough: The reader was a balding man around fifty, in a short-sleeved shirt and beige linen trousers. He could have been anyone. A clerk enjoying a free quiet afternoon, sitting in the warm sunlight.

No, it was too hot for that. He would have sat in the shade. There were two vacant benches shaded by the trees above.

Cold sweat ran on Joachim's forehead.

Could he be with the secret police? But they usually came in twos.

Joachim glanced at his vicinity quickly. He saw no other suspicious man. The couple, maybe? No; far too young for this job. They never looked young, even if some were.

And certainly not the mother with her child.

He calmed a little. No one was watching him. It was just his imagination playing tricks on him—as if the police usually spied on eighteen-year-olds! He wished he'd been back home already, listening to his beloved music, alone and safe.

I'm starting to be really paranoid, he thought grimly. *As if being plain crazy wasn't enough.*

Nevertheless, he hadn't seen any ghost in weeks. Maybe he was getting better. Maybe he was healing, from whatever it was that afflicted him before.

But he knew better than to believe this scenario.

It started with the Nazi occupation and the following war. Joachim spent most of the time in a hideout at a farmhouse in the country, belonging to friends of his parents. He scarcely remembered Mother's and Father's faces. His memories of them were few: Little Joachim sitting on Father's lap, observing his delicate work on a repaired violin. Mother softly smiling on them. The smile was the only feature of her face he could recall clearly. The rest of the memories were faint pleasant smells of wood, fine dust, and cocoa; beautiful subtle tones of Father playing the violin; Mother's similarly gentle voice.

At the age of six, he saw his parents for the last time. He remembered himself crying wildly, but his new guardians held him fast as the figures of his parents faded on the horizon. He saw his first ghost a few months later. Only after the war he learned that it was the day his parents died.

Joachim wasn't too scared by the apparition; more curious or confused. He didn't know what it meant, and he didn't see any other ghosts til the end of the war — til he ventured outside for the first time in years.

He never succeeded in getting rid of his fear of outside world and people. For most of his childhood, he kept company of books and music sheets; silent but for the sound of his own violin when his guardians hesitantly allowed him to play. It reminded him of Father. Joachim sometimes dreamed of being a music teacher and an instruments repairman like him.

He ended up a warehouseman. At least he didn't have to deal with people. The simple, solitary, and physically demanding work might have saved him from going truly insane.

After his guardians completed the task of keeping him alive through the war, they gave him some money, a small trunk with his few belongings, and a train ticket back to Prague.

He saw his first ghosts in years on the platforms of several stations. He thought his eyes were playing tricks on him and shut them tight. As he got off the train in Prague and started walking quickly to his old home, his terror rose.

So many of them, those strange misty shadows standing even in the brightest sunlight! Some of them tried to stretch their arms to him. He started running, screaming. Finally, he reached the house, ran through the gate and pounded on the door in panic.

A stern-looking woman opened it. "What are you doing here?!" she snapped.

He tried to explain. She frowned. "They haven't been living here for years! It's our house now, understood? Now get out!"

Joachim left, sobbing, too scared to look around in fear he might see another spirit. He didn't know where to go. Reluctantly, he headed to Vinohrady, where several of Father's previous pupils had lived. He hoped to find some of them at home and willing to help.

Turning to the next street, he almost went through a ghost. He'd never seen one so close. It rose above him, dark misty gray and with blurry contours from which Joachim's eyes ached. The boy screamed, unable to move. Finally, people ran to him to find out what scared him so much. A policeman was among them and asked Joachim what happened.

He was terribly frightened, tired, hungry and painfully alone but could somehow sense that if he told the truth, something terrible would happen to him.

"I'm trying to find my parents. Please, how can I find them?" he managed to say.

A few days later, he was stuck in an orphanage and might have counted himself lucky for not ending up in an asylum. He was even allowed to keep his violin, the only connection left to the paradise of his earliest childhood. It sustained him through the purgatory of hiding for years and would sustain him here too.

Joachim also discovered that playing it allowed him to keep the ghosts away if he wanted to—and much more. He learned to choose the right tones to chase them away, draw them nearer, or even make them talk. Soon he knew they weren't dangerous; they couldn't do anything in the physical world but linger helplessly until fading away. Sometimes, when he desperately needed someone to talk to, as he never confided anything to any living soul, he went outside in secret during nights, clutching his violin case, and if he saw a spirit, tried Sibelius or Bartók to allow them to communicate. Often, he had to stop them soon, as he heard only their pain and misery. Sometimes there wasn't even enough left to talk coherently. And sometimes he ran, terrified, even if no physical danger could come from them. Hearing was more than enough, though. He soon abandoned these foolish endeavors. For the fear of what it might bring to him, he even stopped playing the violin, turning to it just when his life without it seemed truly unbearable.

At his eighteenth birthday, the institution spat him out and stopped caring, much like his previous guardians. they had risked their lives for the frightened Jewish boy, though he could see they had considered him a burden. They did what they had, not for the love of him, but for the promise they gave his parents. They weren't loving, but at least they were just and honest.

Joachim learned later that after the Communist putsch in 1948, they were deprived of all their possessions and moved to some tiny flat in Kladno to work in a factory. He didn't remember any of his parents' prayers and couldn't learn any Christian ones either; any religion was considered undesirable under the new regime. But he felt that he needed to give them his thanks and wishes for everything to turn out better somehow, so he devised a sort of prayer of his own. He never used it again.

This was the kind of world the orphanage spat him out into. He spent his early childhood in the warmth and quiet of his father's workshop, the rest of it in a dark hideout surrounded by the sights, sounds, smells, and tastes of stories in his books, and his adolescence in the cold gray of the orphanage. At least it seemed now that something hadn't changed. This new world was certainly cold and gray to him, too.

Except when it got really chilly; when the secret police seemed to have taken an interest in him. Joachim didn't comprehend why; he wasn't important, he was a nobody. But maybe there was nothing logical about it. Maybe he was just deemed unfavorable: a Jew who survived; a boy whose first language had been German—in the country from which Germans were expelled violently immediately after the war; a young man with no apparent interest in joining the Communist Party; a weird ghost of a man who was scared of people and could fit nowhere.

Sometimes he wondered if life had anything in store for him—but what could that be?

How ridiculous, he thought. *I'm a nobody. But that's good. The less people notice me. I can walk through anywhere without a single glance.*

Maybe, someday, he'd turn into a ghost without anyone noticing.

He turned right on the crossroad and suddenly saw that the man with newspapers was gone.

The cold sweat was back, the suffocating pressure in his throat and chest, the dread rising.

He walked quicker and quicker, ignoring the pain in his side.

Maybe some people kept noticing him after all.

He finally had time to go to the local library to return a couple of books and borrow new ones. Joachim never went to the central library, for it was an old vast place full of memories — and sometimes even lingering souls — whereas this new, tiny two-room branch could hardly host such apparitions. The selection was limited here, but he always found something of interest: Flaubert's *Salammbo*, Stendhal's *Lucien Leuwen*, *Christmas Books* by Thackeray... Many contemporary authors were banned, and the ones favored by the regime Joachim consistently skipped. He could always turn to authors from the past whose voices no censor cared to silence. Thinking of the stories helped Joachim forget about the secret police for a moment — until he thought of this.

He left a minute before closing time and headed straight home. The streets were pleasantly deserted, and he could see no one following or watching him. Maybe he really was just paranoid; maybe, just maybe, the secret police lost interest in him after the first questioning and nobody would care to watch his insignificant life.

Joachim passed a now empty playground on his way. In the corner of his eye, he glimpsed a shadow behind one of the monkey bars where none was supposed to be.

He sped up a bit, not looking back. Bitter thoughts crept up his mind.

As he turned into his street, he thought he saw the shape again. But that wasn't possible; they never followed him for more than a few steps!

Eventually, Joachim broke into a run. His hand shook as he tried to unlock the door. As soon as he was inside, he leaned on the cold concrete wall and took a deep breath. Still, it took a while until he was able to calmly walk up the stairs into his simple, almost austere flat. He'd hung no pictures on the walls, brought no statues or vases people so often put on tables to make the place look more like home. The only things that could reveal anything about the personality of the young man inhabiting the flat were books on the shelf, music sheets in the drawers, an old gramophone and plates on the table under the window, and a violin case next to the armchair.

Joachim made himself a small dinner and sat in the chair to read like every other evening. He lost his sense of time, submerged in the book. But suddenly he became aware of a strange sensation. Coldness crept up his spine; a grayish shape occupied the space in the corner of his eye.

His hands froze on the hard cover. He didn't realize he was clutching it so strongly his knuckles went white. At last, he forced himself to turn around. A scream stuck in his throat.

His left hand fumbled for the case. Finally, he grasped it and took out his violin, still keeping an eye on the ghost across the room.

Strange; he felt frightened to death mere seconds ago, but the feel of his instrument calmed him instantly. His hands no longer trembling, he started to play.

He chose the wistful violin lead from Mendelssohn's *Violin Concerto in E minor*. The opening melody always evoked sorrow in him, and yet it was not without beautiful tones of hope. It usually drove the ghosts away.

Yet this one stood still in the corner of the small room, an unmoving blurred figure of gray mist and shadow.

Joachim was no longer afraid, perhaps for the touch of the ebony fingerboard and bow that filled his world along with the music. He managed to change into a new composition smoothly: Berlioz's *Reverie et Caprice*.

He almost gasped as the ghost's contours started sharpening.

It won't go away; then at least he should allow it to talk.

Jean Sibelius composed only one concerto in his whole life, the *Violin Concerto in D minor*. On its sad, dark background, bright tones unfolded into a rich gripping melody. Joachim focused on playing so much he nearly missed the moment when the figure's face began to be visible. When its lips parted and it spoke, he slowly stopped playing.

The ghost looked like a young woman. Despite her youth and still somewhat blurred contours, there were clear signs of suffering in her face.

Joachim gulped. "You...," he spoke but his throat was too dry. He tried again: "You followed me here. That... never happened before. And you didn't disappear after... when you heard... How is that possible?"

She produced a sad smile. "I don't know. But maybe it's because I'm not dead yet. However, I'm dying. Nothing can be done about that," she continued quietly. "I just... I came for help."

"But you just said..."

"Yes. Nothing can save me. My soul is here whereas my body lies in a State Security cell, still alive but without any chance of staying so for long. They don't know it yet but during the last questioning, they caused internal bleeding. I think I have a couple of dozen minutes left."

A new wave of dread went through Joachim as he heard the words *State Security*, the secret police. Now he finally collected himself enough to speak again: "Then what do you want from me? I cannot help you!"

"I need you to remember, firstly."

"Please, go away," he whispered. "Even if you tell me something... What would I do then? I'm a nobody. I can't do anything for you."

"I was frightened too," she carried on, paying no attention to his pleading. "It's gone now. I wonder what else would just diminish when I'm really dead. One moment, I was just gone from my body, drawn outside — to you, eventually. Then I understood what I needed to do. Sit down, please. Sit down and listen."

He obeyed, still holding the violin like a lifebuoy. A maelstrom of thoughts was revolving inside his mind. None of the previous ghosts ever wanted anything from him. They were dead, numb, barely capable of comprehensible speech. He always thought of his ability as a curse without any good for him as well as them. Was it possible that it had not been just a pointless burden after all?

The woman's voice sounded almost like the splendid tones his instrument could produce. He couldn't help himself but listen eagerly.

She began to tell him stories. Her own, for a start. A story of a young girl named Milena, about the same age as him. She wanted to study art and work in a museum. But the year she finished high school was 1948. For reasons she barely understood, she was not allowed to go to any university. Her parents were arrested shortly after. She started working as a waitress. Once, she wasn't careful enough, and talked with her colleague about her parents and their ideals. The colleague must have been an informer. So little sufficed to send her into endless rounds of questioning and accusations.

The man in the next cell was a dramatist. His plays criticized the regime openly.

Then there was an older woman, a mother of two teenagers, scared about them like nothing else could scare any mother. She signed the papers confirming her new status as an informer and was released. It was for the children, she kept telling herself.

In another cell, a former law professor was sitting on a hard mat, his face buried in his palms; unable to fall asleep. He stopped feeling the bruises long ago. The pain he felt came from knowing his fate that could not be avoided without giving up all the principles he ever stood by. He was not willing to pay this price, though it hurt.

They were all stories of the most horrible crimes; crimes that took place in broad daylight and yet no one lifted a finger against them. Joachim's thoughts inevitably traveled to his own parents. It seemed that one crime just followed another. Nobody could stop this dreadful cycle, it seemed. Or could one, after all?

Milena paused suddenly.

"I think I'm fading away now... I don't know how to make my-self stay. Please. Remember what you heard. And don't keep it to yourself."

"What am I able to do?" he breathed. But even as he spoke, pos-sibilities started to unravel in his mind.

Throughout his whole childhood, growing up in the cold stark orphanage, Joachim wanted to find his purpose. Now he did.

He might try to flee to country and either succeed — or die trying on the border. Abroad, he might start speaking to the journalists and TV reporters, tell them what's been happening here.

Or he might stay, write the stories down and publish them by *samizdat*. One by one, people would start retyping them and smuggling them further. One by one, they'd *know*.

The ebony fingerboard beneath his palm seemed warm and smooth. He looked at the violin.

He might create a composition encompassing each one of those stories, a piece bringing everyone hearing it to tears... He felt they'd learn the fates of those people even without hearing the actual words. It might not be enough; but he might do all of that. Everything he could. A memory found its way into his consciousness: Father, leaning above a broken instrument, carefully and patiently repairing it bit by bit. The smell of fine dust and wood. His world, gone.

Milena's ghost faded quicker than he managed to say goodbye. But he didn't need to. She would stay with him as a story — and all the others, too. Even his parents.

Joachim lifted his beloved violin again and started playing a new melody, almost unconsciously. His song would not be silenced.

Julie Novakova (*1991) is an award-winning Czech author of science fiction and detective stories. She published seven novels, one anthology and over thirty stories in Czech. She started publishing in English in 2013 and her work has appeared in Asimov's, Analog, Clarkesworld and other magazines and anthologies. Some of her works have been translated into Chinese, Romanian, Estonian, Filipino, German and Portuguese, and she edited an anthology of Czech speculative fiction in English, titled Dreams From Beyond, and co-edited an anthology of European SF in Filipino, titled Haka. She's also active in science outreach and education, nonfiction writing and translation.

 # GHOST STORY

Jeff Dosser

JOE SLAMMED THE DOOR BEHIND HIM AND STEPPED INTO THE FADING GLORY of a clear San Francisco dusk. Why was his mother such a bitch? A wave of guilt flooded him, and he banished the accusation as quickly as it came.

It was 5:30 on a Bayview Wednesday night, and the streets buzzed with life. A rap beat thumped from a Honda inching its way down the block, while the excited shouts of children and calls of parents ushering them to dinner swirled alongside the battered, fried, grilled, and spiced aroma of a hundred recipes whirling on the October breeze.

Snugging his Park Service jacket against the chill, Joe sauntered down the stairs to where a gate opened onto a shadowed alleyway running between his home and the next. Above the gate's rusted bars hung the only notice of his abuelita's home in back: a faded marquee with a hand-painted eye at the center. Beneath were scrawled the words: 'FORTUNE TELLER'.

At his grandmother's stoop, Joe tugged open the door and stepped inside. "Lita? I'm headed to work."

A table sat at the room's center and upon it a yellowed crystal ball. The only illumination came from a fringed lamp atop a corner table. The walls were crammed with floor-to-ceiling shelves, each loaded with plastic buckets of dried llama fetuses, stacks of bleached animal skulls, wooden boxes of exotic spices, or jars of opaque, unidentifiable liquid. They filled the space with a curious yellow aroma, evoking images of mystical places and faraway lands.

"Lita?"

Joe set down his heavy pack before stepping to a door on the far side of the room. He gave it a rap.

"Lita. You okay?"

From the far side of the scuffed door came a shuffle of movement followed by the sound of a toilet flush. The door swung open, and a tiny woman in a shawl scurried past. She paused at the edge of a patched green recliner before lowering herself in.

"I thought you was rapists," she said, "come ta take an' old woman's life."

Her eyes, as bright and dark as pebbles, looked up from a wrinkled face with skin that was fine as dried parchment. She wriggled into a chair and snugged her rainbow-colored shawl across her shoulders.

"Lita, no one's gonna bother you." Joe dragged over a chair and sat down.

No one dared breaking into Miss Lita's, as generations of children called her. Besides the bad luck of crossing a witch, there was the persistent rumor of the youth who'd broken in back in the '70s. The young man's demise beneath the wheels of a trolley the next day was enough to discourage even the boldest of thieves.

"Mmm, mmm, mmm. I always did like a man in uniform." A smile curled the old woman's lips as she cocked her head and considered him. "I'll bet you need all that weaponry ta fight off the ladies. Am I right?" She chuckled, more a half-wheezed cough than a laugh.

Joe glanced down at his crisp black slacks bloused over a pair of polished boots. His sidearm, radio-holster, and cuffs completed the ensemble. He had to admit a feeling of pride when he put on the uniform and pinned on his Park Service Police badge. He leaned over and planted a kiss atop of her graying head.

"Not as many as you'd think." He forced a smile.

The old woman leaned back bringing a finger to her lips. "Something's botherin' you tonight." Her eyes narrowed. "Your mother's been complaining again... about work." She paused, nodding thoughtfully. "And school? Yes, that's it. She wants you back in school."

Joe nodded.

"Phht, that woman never learned anything that wasn't taught in a classroom." Lita waved her thin hand dismissively. "Just like your father, God rest his soul." She made the sign of the cross and went on. "All those two ever thought about was money."

"Yeah, but money's a fine thing ta have." He looked back to the front door and the world beyond. Most of his friends had jobs or at least degrees. His best friend, Juan, was a staff sergeant in the Army. Juan had a wife and kids. What did *he* have?

Joe contemplated his stuffed pack and the supplies within. He had no idea if his plan would work, but he had to try.

"There's more ta life than money," Lita continued. She leveled a crooked finger and sighted along its length. "There's spiritual riches as well."

"Yeah... I know."

Joe leaned over, studying his boots. He'd been thinking his mother was right. That he'd been wasting his time and needed to finish his degree. Now, he wasn't so sure.

"Do you?"

Her sharp tone raised his eyes.

"There's few people who possess our gift, Joseph. Fewer still know how ta use it."

He straightened and met her stare.

"I've seen the way you look at the world. How you peer into shadows when the spirits are there. How you listen to their song when it's threaded on the wind." She leaned close, her breath both sour and sweet. "It was your great-grandfather who taught me about the gift, and his mother before him."

Joe consulted his watch, afraid of another of his grandmother's extended tales.

"You're late." She leaned across the table and laid her small, soft hand atop his.

"Just remember, you're never alone." She leaned back with a groan. "If you want a career, you can always take over the family business."

Joe rose from his seat and shouldered his pack.

"Working for Sandra?" He couldn't imagine a worse fate than slaving at the family motel beneath his tyrant sister's thumb.

"No, my child, here." Her lips creased into a smile. "At the family's original business. The business of spirit."

Joe rolled his eyes. "I'll see ya' in the morning, Lita." He paused at the door. "And close your windows, there's a fog coming in."

"And you be careful too," she said. "The spirit's power ebbs and flows, but tonight's a *full* moon. The curtain separating the spirit world is thin."

How did she know? Joe's eyes narrowed.

"You brought books," she said. "That's good. They like stories."

Joe's hand drifted to the pack's slick nylon and the squared corners beneath.

"Just follow your heart." She smiled. "And try that old one first."

On the bus ride to the pier, Joe mulled over what his grandmother said. It amazed him how she knew things it wasn't possible to know. Like the books.

With a rocking squeal of brakes, the bus eased to a halt, and he followed the thin line of riders down Front Street and onto the water-front. The westering sun lay shrouded in mist as he cut through the lines of tourists exiting the boat and found his way up the ramp.

Making his way to the bow, Joe watched as the lines were cast off and the engine's throaty rumble carried through his boots. Out ahead, Alcatraz lay silhouetted against a swelling bank of fog, with only the towers and swooping cables of the Golden Gate Bridge visible above its ghostly fringe.

As he stepped across the gangway and onto the island, a portly man in a Park Service green jacket hailed him from the edge of a crowd.

"Joseph, what's happ'nin'?"

Being the only passenger, as soon as Joe cleared the ramp, the chains holding back the mass of tourists were opened, and they streamed noisily past.

"I'm good, Mike." Joe joined the big man at the top of the stairs. "Busy day?"

Mike leaned against the railing watching the line of visitors crowd aboard.

"Not bad. A little light for this time of year." He cast an eye towards the mounting fog. "Gonna be a chilly one."

Mike dug into his pocket and produced a ring of keys. Most were normal sized, but three were the large brass keys of the original prison.

"We're all clear," a woman called from the ship's forward ladder.

Mike slapped Joe on the shoulder and strode down the ramp. "Take care, kid. We'll see ya in the morning."

By the time Joe dropped his pack inside the prison and retrieved his flashlight, fog wrapped Alcatraz in a damp, murky shroud. Relieved of his load, Joe left the prison to march the steep avenues of his patrol; past the gaunt, looming shadow of the water tower, along the guano-flecked path beside the power plant, the air sharp with the ammonia reek of bird droppings and the unseen cry of gulls, past the quay and its splash of cresting waves, and the rainbow-colored glow of San Francisco lost in the fog. As he glanced from the colorful rumor of the city to the hulking darkness of the island, a thread of uncertainty skittered along his spine. He was stalling and knew it. But what if he were wrong? What if they did mean him harm?

The first time he'd sensed them was in the wee hours that first week of work. An ebon, crystalline sparkle had formed around him like reverse fireflies glittering in the night. Joe could feel them darkling in the distance as he made his way through the long empty halls, past framed pictures of monsters once locked behind these hard iron bars.

On his first full moon, they'd driven him from the prison, their persistent glimmer rising and rising, until the terror sent him panting through the halls and rushing outside. Only on the boat ride home had Joe realized the emotions driving him into the night weren't anger or malice, but an anguished, frustrated cry. A cry for help?

With a grinding rasp, he turned the key and stepped inside once more. Joe hefted the cool metal of his flashlight knowing its light would drive away the specters should the terror submerge him. His gaze drifted to the dark corridors and what lay beyond.

He set the flashlight down.

Okay, you can do this. Joe's shoulders rose as he sucked in a long breath, then fell as he slowly let it out. He shouldered the pack and set off along the hollow aisles, past vacant cells and the whispered voices within, to the vast open space of the library.

Even through the fog, the brimming moon crashed through the library's double storied windows and filled the vast chamber with her alabaster glow. Joe stepped to the spiral staircase in the corner and found a spot on the steps. It had taken months to discover the library as the spot where he felt most attuned to their cries. In a way it made sense. Where else could the inmates escape the reality of their broken lives, but in the pages of a book?

He could see them now, the dark shadows pressing around in starved anticipation. He swallowed, feeling the hard, dry click at the back of his throat. Then one by one, he drew out the books, setting each aside as the moonlight narrowed.

His eyes darted to the hushed whisper of footsteps. Or was it the rustled scurry of rats? He sat paralyzed, like an actor who'd forgotten his lines; sweating beneath the spotlight as it riveted him to the stage.

At the pack's bottom, Joe felt the rough cloth cover of an ancient tome. Read the old one, isn't that what Lita said? A distant metallic clang echoed, echoed through the halls as he flipped open the cover and slowly began to read.

Joe sensed their self-loathing and the covetous rage of their misspent lives; felt their anguish break in waves of unshed tears and realized in their eternity of suffering, his stories provided an outlet, however brief.

"Call me Ishmael," he read, his voice rising as they settled in around him. "Some years ago — never mind how long precisely — having little or no money in my purse..."

Award-winning author Jeff Dosser is an ex-Tulsa cop and current software developer living in the wilds of central Oklahoma. Jeff's short stories can be found in magazines such as The Literary Hatchet, Tales to Terrify, Shotgun Honey, J.J Outre Review, and Mystery Weekly, to name a few.

His novels won the 2019 and 2018 Oklahoma Writers Federation Contest for best new horror, and his sci-fi shorts have garnered multiple L. Ron Hubbard's Writers of the Future Honorable Mentions.

When not writing, Jeff can be found prowling the woods behind his rural home communing with the denizens of the night.

 Shiny People

Elizabeth Donald

Shawn was pouring coffee into his giant thermos when he heard Rowen's voice muffled behind the door.

"Your daughter is up," he informed Debbie without turning around.

"Tonight, she's your daughter," Debbie said, her voice thick with sleep. Shawn turned around to look over his shoulder, across the small kitchen to the even-smaller living room. Debbie was on the couch, her mother's old purple afghan swaddled around her and thick fuzzy socks on her feet. She'd been fighting off a bad cold for days, and clearly the cold meds had kicked in.

A slash of hot pain struck Shawn's hand, and he jerked back, sloshing coffee. Sure enough, he'd poured the hot coffee over his own hand, and now there was coffee all over the counter.

"Shit," he muttered, running his hand under cold water while turning the other way to put the coffee pot back on the battered Mr. Coffee on the counter. This required some acrobatic twisting, but he got it done. Then he grabbed a handful of paper towels to sop up the puddle of coffee.

"That's coffee abuse," Debbie said in that soft, drifty voice.

"You're all heart, love," he said.

Rowen's voice came chirping through her bedroom door again. Shawn glanced at the clock: 11:23 p.m. He had to be on the dock in half an hour.

"Who is she talking to in there?" he asked, knowing there wasn't really an answer. Rowen talked a lot for a three-year-old.

Debbie didn't bother with a response. "Can you…"

"I'm on it," he said, leaning over the couch arm and kissing Debbie on the forehead.

Shawn walked down the short hallway of their duplex, tripping on a stuffed rabbit. Or maybe a unicorn. Sometimes it was kind of hard to tell, and Rowen's collection seemed to multiply when he wasn't looking. He didn't think it was possible for one little girl to own that many stuffed animals, but...

He paused right outside her bedroom door, which was decorated with a giant pink princess crown handprinted with Rowen's name. Debbie was an unstoppable crafter, though she'd slowed down a bit since Rowen was born. She was their first kid, and their friends with three or four kids said smug things like, "the first one doesn't even count, wait till you have four," but Rowen was energetic enough to keep them both hopping.

"You're funny!" Rowen declared on the other side of the door.

Shawn pushed open the door. Rowen's overhead light was off, but she was sitting up in the middle of her toddler bed, the cartoon-princess comforter puddled around her legs. Soft pink light came from the nightlight in the corner plug, and for a wonder her toys were mostly where they belonged, so he could walk a straight line to her side.

"You're supposed to be asleep, little princess," he chided.

"Sorry, Daddy," Rowen replied, smiling up at him with her mother's large brown eyes and his dimple. She was so small, so soft and adorable, sometimes Shawn couldn't believe he was supposed to be taking care of such a sweet thing. Nothing he'd done up to meeting Debbie had prepared him for this.

Sure enough, in half a second he was seated cross-legged beside her bed, and there was a little plastic crown on his head because Rowen was nuts for the princess thing, and she declared him King of the Forest and he was bowing before her as Princess Rowen and wasn't he supposed to be going to work soon?

"I've got to go to work, sweetie," he said regretfully, and her face fell.

"I don't like your work," she said, and in that moment Shawn didn't either. Usually he didn't mind the job—there was something satisfying about looking at the boxes he'd hauled and the trucks he'd loaded. It was tangible, solid proof that he was there, and he'd done something valuable.

But not if he couldn't be here with the princess.

Gently he pushed her onto the bed and tucked the blankets around her. "I'm sorry," he said. "I don't like to go, but we grownups have to do that sometime."

"Okay, Daddy." She rubbed her eyes, which was the universal signal for sleepy child, thank God. "The shiny people will keep me company."

"Shiny people?" That was a new one. "Who are the shiny people?"

Rowen's eyes were drifting shut even as she spoke. In her sleepiness, her voice sounded more like Debbie on the cold meds. "The shiny people in my room."

"Okay, you have fun with that," he said, smiling. He leaned over and kissed her on the forehead. "Dream pretty pictures."

He stood up, his knees popping a little more than he liked. He walked to the door and reached for the knob. Then he caught sight of himself in the large mirror over Rowen's dresser.

"Oops." He laughed quietly. He was still wearing the silly crown.

He stepped over in front of the dresser and removed the crown, wincing as its plastic curlicues caught in his hair and pulled a couple of strands free. I need to keep the hair I've got, thanks, he thought ruefully.

He laid the crown on the dresser. In the mirror, he caught movement behind him.

"Sleep, little lady," he ordered, turning around.

Rowen was asleep. She lay perfectly still in her toddler bed, the blankets he'd tucked around her undisturbed.

Shawn looked around, but saw nothing out of place. He frowned, then shook his head. I'm working too damn much.

He carefully closed her door and walked back to the living room, where Debbie was also drifting. "Princess is asleep, at least for now," he said.

"Thanks, babe," Debbie said. She seemed a little more awake than she'd been before, but he still put odds she'd drift off on the couch, and he'd have to move her to their bedroom when he got home.

"I'm off," he said, grabbing his lunch and thermos of coffee.

Shawn's scanner made a bleak electronic squawk instead of its usual pleasing chime. Kneeling on the metal floor, Shawn sighed and shook it. There were probably more specific technological tasks that would convince the balky system to behave itself and cooperate, but mostly Shawn got better results from smacking the damn thing.

Squawk. "My goddamn scanner's busted again," he called down to Kip, who was loading boxes on the conveyer belt to carry them up to the truck.

Kip mimed being unable to hear him. True, there was enough noise on the loading dock to deafen Beethoven, despite the foam plugs they were all supposed to wear as a tip of the hat to workplace safety rules, but then, workplace safety rules might have had something to say about making a man kneel on metal or concrete for eight hours a day, right?

Shawn stood up and mimed a cutting-throat gesture across his own neck. Kip took the hint and shut down the belt. "Scanner's busted again," he said.

"Shit." Kip sighed. "You smack it?"

"Damn thing's older than my car," Shawn said, reaching for the bar to clamber down from the truck bed. "I'll be a few."

Kip cocked a thumb toward the back door of the loading dock. "I'm gonna grab a smoke while you're unfucking that thing."

Shawn held up a hand. "Don't tell me, and whatever you do, don't give me one even when I ask you for it."

Kip quickly stuck the pack he'd been working out of his pocket back out of site. "Yeah, sorry. Hey, don't you mean if you ask for it?"

"Definitely when, and the answer is no," Shawn said.

Kip sketched a quick salute. "You're a stronger man than me, buddy."

Shawn held up the pistol-like scanner to his head and pretended to shoot himself in the head with it. Kip's laughter followed him out of the dock and down the hall to the relative quiet and sanity of the breakroom.

Of course, that was relative, because Chad Swinton was there. Swinton was the supervisor of Shawn's shift, which basically meant he sat at his supervisor station and did jack shit while Shawn and the rest of the night workers hauled boxes, except when he was on their asses about some idiocy or another. It was Swinton's idea that no one could have a cell phone in his pocket on the dock, not that any signal short of a nuclear explosion could have penetrated the warehouse's thick concrete walls. Shawn had been on the docks for six years, and he'd had good supervisors who treated them like human beings and assholes who treated them like subhuman robots. Swinton was a hell of a lot closer to the latter.

"Shawn, it's not your break time," Swinton reminded him in that punctilious voice that reminded Shawn why they sometimes called him Swine-ton.

Shawn lifted the device. "Scanner's busted. It's not reading anything."

Swinton sighed as though Shawn was greatly inconveniencing him by speaking to him. "Did you try the hard reboot?"

Shit. Shawn should have thought of that before trying to exchange it. "Yeah, it didn't work," he said, feeling the little flush in his face. It was a lie, and he'd never have let Rowen get away with such a lie, but he couldn't admit that he'd skipped the most basic step in computer device maintenance: turning it off and on again. He'd been taking day classes for a year in computer programming, hoping to get enough certifications to get off the loading dock and onto an I.T. desk somewhere, so this was really embarrassing.

Fortunately, Swinton didn't seem to clue in that Shawn was lying through his teeth. "Go trade the damn thing out and get back on the dock," he ordered. "We're behind schedule."

Shawn did not respond, "That's exactly what I intended to do if you hadn't stopped to interrogate me," because he intended to keep his job. Instead he sketched a mostly-not-sarcastic salute and walked through the break room to the tech counter, where a lineup of grubby scanner chargers lay empty.

"Shit," he muttered, looking about for one that wasn't in use. He went behind the counter and theatrically opened and closed several cabinets, while surreptitiously hitting the shutdown button on his own scanner.

"Found one?" Swinton asked without looking up from his magazine. It looked like a sports magazine from the cover, but it seemed to have an awful lot of pictures of girls in bikinis from where Shawn was standing.

"Working on it," he said absently, thumbing the ON button again. All the chargers were empty, and none were in the storage cabinet, either. If his scanner didn't reboot, he was going to have a serious problem on his hands. He pulled a new battery and slid it in place of the other one, which still showed a decent charge, but he had to do something like he was trying to fix the bloody thing.

The shiny people will help.

For a second he swore he could hear Rowen's voice, real enough that he looked around the dirty, smoke-stained break room looking for her. No one was allowed to smoke in the building anymore; it was the twenty-first century and such things were banished to an outdoor gulag where they could freeze their asses off in an Illinois winter where the air hurts your face. But there was a dim, impenetrable layer of grime that seemed to coat the ugly yellow walls and 1970s cabinetry that no cleaning supplies would ever penetrate, a thick almost-invisible coating that ensured Shawn would never have brought Rowen here, much less allowed her to hang out in the break room with the likes of Chad Swinton. Or even his friends on the dock, who were good enough fellas, but whose primary response the one time Debbie brought him a forgotten lunch was, "Hey, she's got great tits."

Of course Rowen was not here, and her voice had not mentioned the shiny people. That was the latest thing, and it had only been a few weeks. The shiny people apparently lived in her room, and she talked to them late at night and occasionally on a Sunday afternoon. At first Shawn was worried about it, afraid that maybe Rowen's incredibly detailed imagination was clouding the difference between make-believe and reality for her. But Debbie said all the parenting books said imaginary friends were absolutely normal. Usually the imaginary friend was a single human, not a group of people, and had a real name. Trust Rowen to be that special kid.

Beep. The scanner clicked on, green light glowing. "Looks like it just needed a fresh battery," Shawn lied again, sliding out from behind the tech counter.

Chad waved a dismissive hand. "Get back on the dock, break's over."

"You—" Shawn stopped. He was really going to have to talk to the shop steward about this one. Lie or not, defective equipment was not a break, and he shouldn't lose his precious fifteen minutes at 3 a.m. just because the damn scanner went on the blink.

But arguing about it with Swinton would not get him anywhere, not today. He stalked through the break room and didn't bother to close the door gently, letting it slam. They could also stand to fix that goddamn thing, he thought.

Kip was back on the dock, reeking of cigarette smoke and rubbing his hands together in the universal signal for goddamn it's cold. "Get a fresh scanner?"

"Nah, got this one working," Shawn said. He cocked his head back toward the breakroom. "Swine-ton said I lose my break over it, and I swear I'm taking this to the union. That's the last fucking straw."

Kip rubbed his hands together harder. "Man, I hate this place," he said. "Well, let's get back to it. Wouldn't want to fall behind schedule."

"Yeah, that'd be too fucking bad," Shawn said. He clambered up into the truck and knelt on the ice-cold metal floor, scanning the boxes.

Beep. Beep. Beep. A fucking robot could do this job, and if the news reports could be believed, robots were on their way to take them over. That was why Shawn was taking the classes, which cost money they didn't have and took endless hours away from Debbie and Rowen, but he knew someday he was going to come into this factory and find a pile of steel lifting the boxes and running a scanner that never needed a new battery, and what would they do then?

"Cooper!"

It was Swinton, who had actually emerged from the break room and was waving his arms at him from the door. He could barely be heard over the roar of the conveyers running the boxes up to the trucks, and several of the other dock workers stopped to crane their necks and try to hear him. Supervisors did not come out on the dock unless it was the end of shift or someone had screwed up.

From Swinton's face, it definitely looked like the latter. Shawn got back to his feet, his knees protesting mildly. "Yeah?"

Swinton waved an angry hand at him, and Shawn hopped down off the truck again. Kip gave him a questioning look, and Shawn shrugged: no clue, man.

He crossed the dock, well aware that all his coworkers were staring at him. He reached Swinton as quickly as was possible with some measure of grace. "What's up?"

"Phone call," Swinton snapped. "You're not supposed to get personal calls on the clock, and I wouldn't allow it except it's the police."

Shawn's heart staggered in his chest, and he fought down the unbidden panic. "What? What did they —"

"No idea, but that's two breaks, so hurry up and take your god-damn call," Swinton said.

Shawn manfully resisted the urge to punch the son of a bitch straight in the face and went for the break room door again. He didn't run, because panic doesn't work out well for anyone, but his mind was a hissing void. Debbie Rowen Debbie Rowen the house fire sick hurt dead no please no what's wrong?

The heavy phone receiver lay on the break room table next to the world's oldest coffeepot, the curled cord connecting it to the plastic brick on the wall like a geriatric snake. It wasn't a rotary dial, but one step short of it — another sign the twenty-first century really hadn't penetrated the factory yet.

Shawn picked it up, half expecting it to come to life like a snake and bite him. "This is Shawn Cooper, who is this?"

Before the officer could even speak, Shawn's traitorous mind was whispering to him. We're sorry to inform you that the house burned down and your family is dead.

Not true, shut up, stop panicking, whatever it is they need you to not panic.

"Mr. Cooper, this is Officer Dobbs," the voice said in a regulated, sane tone designed to maintain distance and calm at the same time. It was voice-by-rote, one step away from robotic. Cop-voice. "There's been an incident at your home and your wife—"

"Is Debbie all right? What about Rowen?" Shawn couldn't help interrupting. His traitor brain kept whispering Debbie Rowen Debbie Rowen hurt sick dead. Debbie had been sick, but he thought it was a cold, what if it was worse, what if she fell down and got hurt, Rowen wasn't even old enough to know how to dial 911—

"Your family is fine, Mr. Cooper," Officer Dobbs said in that calming voice. "Everyone is okay. Your wife asked us to call you and let you know what's going on, because she's talking to the detectives right now."

"What happened? What happened to my wife?" Shawn was interrupting again, but the flood of relief was now mixed up with new worries. What could possibly have happened bad enough to require multiple police officers at his home?

Officer Dobbs' voice became slightly more human and less cop-speak, perhaps sensing that Shawn was fighting off panic with a whip and a chair. "They're fine, sir. There was an attempted break-in at your house, but we have the suspect in custody and neither your wife nor your daughter were harmed. Mrs. Cooper is giving her statement to the detective right now, and wanted us to let you know in case you want to come home."

You're damn right I'm coming home. To hell with Chad Swine-ton.

Shawn was usually a pretty laid-back guy. He had his bursts of adrenaline, like the night he and Debbie were heading home from a New Year's Eve party and hit a bad patch of black ice. Their little compact car skidded halfway across the road and fetched up against a flimsy wooden guardrail standing between them and a steep embankment that was more like a cliff leading down to a rushing, ice-covered creek. For one heart-stopping moment, the back wheel left the roadway and he felt it spin in the air before the front wheels caught hold and the car lurched back onto the road. Up until that moment, everything had been starkly clear and details stood out perfectly in Shawn's vision, giving him a moment of thanks that he hadn't had so much as a sip of champagne at the party, in commiseration with Debbie, who was eight months pregnant with Rowen at the time.

But when the car came to a stop, and Shawn realized they were safe and still, he turned to Debbie, who was frozen in her own moment of terror with her one hand pressed against the dashboard and her other wrapped protectively around her swollen belly.

In that moment, the adrenaline rush dumped into him all at once as he looked at his wife, carrying his child, and he realized the full weight of what he could have lost in that moment. One extra inch. That's all it took. One extra inch, and the car would be in the river.

He felt that same sensation now as he pulled onto his street, at the moment he saw three police cars with rotating red and blue lights casting terrifying shadows on the facade of his house. A uniformed officer was taking pictures outside a window, pacing over the trampled-down snow along the side of the duplex that faced away from their neighbors. The other half of the duplex was silent and dark, so apparently the Yellers were not home tonight. Some of their neighbors were watching out of their windows, but none were gathered outside — it was too fucking cold for that, and it was something like four in the morning. Lunchtime for Shawn, sleep-time for normal humans.

He never felt less like eating in his life, and he might never sleep again. The sudden adrenaline dump, stomach sick and twisted and heart pounding, even though he knew it was okay, wanting to see them, touch them, know in his heart they were safe. Just like the moment in the car, he felt it now, like his whole body was a live wire and his mind barely functioning. He hardly remembered Swine-ton bitching at him as he clocked out, shouting something about a write-up and docked pay, until someone — Kip, maybe — told him to shut the fuck up or they'd report him to the goddamn union.

What did it matter? Shawn didn't care about anything until he saw Debbie and Rowen.

He approached the front door at a not-quite-run, and an officer blocked his path until he identified himself.

Then the mysterious Officer Dobbs appeared. "Mr. Cooper."

"Can I see my wife?" Shawn asked, still trying to stay calm, but if Dobbs tried to stop him, he really might lose it.

"Of course, she's in the living room," Dobbs replied. "Near as we can tell, the guy tried to get in through a window around the side of the house —"

"Jesus, that's my daughter's room," Shawn said.

Dobbs nodded. "She was asleep in her bed, according to Mrs. Cooper. He tried to climb in through the window—apparently the latch was closed but broken, so he was able to slide the window up and started to climb in."

Shawn was listening while Dobbs was talking, but he was losing control of the panic. They kept saying everyone was all right, but how could that be? Debbie asleep in the living room, Rowen asleep in her bed—

Dobbs was leading him up the path as he spoke. Through the open door, Shawn could see Debbie wrapped in her fluffy pink robe. She might be physically okay, but Shawn knew her well enough to know she was just on the panicky side of terrified.

"How did he—I mean, what happened?" Shawn asked.

Before Dobbs could continue, Debbie caught sight of Shawn and ran out the front door, launching herself into his arms. "Oh my God, Shawn, I… I'm sorry, I was asleep, I should have—"

Shawn hugged her close. "Babe, it's not your fault. That stupid latch, I should have checked it. I'm just glad you're okay."

She felt small and delicate in his arms, and that was probably just his head, probably realizing how very fragile life could be. Debbie and Rowen could have been taken from him while he was loading boxes into a truck, and what kind of a fucked-up world was it where those were the choices? Work or protect your family?

He looked over Debbie's head at Dobbs, who seemed to understand what was going on. Of course, he probably saw this kind of thing all the time. How many times did Dobbs stand on someone's front porch on the scariest nights of their lives—or the worst ones?

"How?" Shawn asked. "How did he—"

Dobbs hesitated, and for a moment, there was a crack in the smooth calm cop-facade. "We… aren't sure," he replied.

Debbie raised her head to Shawn. "I heard the screaming and—"

"Shit!" Shawn looked around. "What did he do to her?"

"Nothing," Debbie said. "Rowen wasn't the one screaming. It was him."

Shawn looked around. "The guy? The one who broke in?"

Dobbs nodded. "Near as we can tell, he got partway in the window and it… slammed shut on him. Broke his foot and both hands, glass shattered, cut him up pretty bad."

Shawn froze. "Rowen isn't big enough to slam a window like that."

Debbie looked up at him. "Rowen never woke up until I ran in the room," she said. "She was still fast asleep when I came in."

Shawn looked at Dobbs, who inclined his head toward her. "Mrs. Cooper retrieved your daughter and called 911. When we arrived, he was still... er, stuck in the window."

It should have been funny, but all Shawn could think about was little Rowen's sleepy face, and the crown, and the shadows in her quiet, dark room. Her little sanctuary. The shiny people will help.

"Please, Mr. Cooper, we need to finish getting Mrs. Cooper's statement," Dobbs gently reminded him.

Shawn left Debbie to finish telling her story again for the record, and went down the hall. The door to their bedroom was partly open, and a slant of light fell from the hallway across their bed. Rowen was curled up there, having fallen back asleep in the innocent bliss of childhood; the routine was disrupted, things were strange, but she was an adaptable child who had absolutely no idea how close she had come to true horrors that night.

A technician with a battered camera came out of Rowen's room and stepped around Shawn with a muttered "excuse me." Beyond him, Shawn could see the once mostly-neat little room, now a raucous mess, with her toy bin upended and the covers knocked off her little bed.

He went into the room, the overhead light overly bright compared to the soft glow of the nightlight when he left what seemed like days ago.

The window was a ghastly horror. It had not simply fallen down; it was smashed, with broken glass and streaks of blood along the walls. The wooden frame had splintered, crashing down with such force that it came partway out of its groove.

There was a patrolman in the room, crouching amid the broken glass. His gloved hands were sliding a crowbar into a long plastic bag. He looked up at Shawn. "I'll be just one more moment, sir. Then you can do whatever you need to in here."

"I'll have to board up that window," Shawn said robotically, one level of his mind focused on the cleanup and repairs and making everything normal again. Everything sane again.

The patrolman stood up with the crowbar. "You might get a contractor to rebuild the window frame entirely, sir. Replace it with something sturdier. It would be a shame for that window to fall again near the little girl."

Fall. It didn't fall; it looked like it had damn near imploded, but Shawn kept that to himself. "You're probably right," he said. "That crowbar... he brought it with him?"

The patrolman looked at it. "Guess he thought he'd have to smash his way in, but the window was unlocked," he said. "'Scuse me, sir, the detectives will be needing this."

When the officer was gone, Shawn stepped over toward the window and looked at the drying streaks of blood. Only a few smears had marked the inside walls, but on the outside, it looked awful. It's a wonder the asshole's alive, Shawn thought.

He turned away from the mess toward the voices. The flashing blue and red lights from the police cars outside cast strange dancing shadows through the shattered remains of the window onto Rowen's pink princess wall.

In the wide mirror over her dresser, Shawn saw movement again, fleeting and scant, and this time he did not look around for its source.

"Thank you," he said to the empty room. And as he moved to the door, he felt a gentle push against his back, shoving him out of the room where he did not belong.

Elizabeth Donald is a dark fiction writer fond of things that go chomp in the night. She is a three-time winner of the Darrell Award for speculative fiction and finalist for the Prism and Imadjinn awards, author of the *Nocturne* vampire mystery series and *Blackfire* dark fantasy series, as well as other novels, novellas and stories in the horror, science fiction and fantasy genres. She is the founder of the Literary Underworld small-press cooperative; an award-winning journalist and essayist with more than twenty years in journalism; a nature and art photographer; freelance editor and writing coach. She is currently completing her masters degree at Southern Illinois University Edwardville and teaches news writing at the university. She serves as president of the St. Louis Society of Professional Journalists and Eville Writers, and is a member of the national SPJ Ethics Commission, Missouri Writers Guild, AEJMC, ELLA and many other organizations for which she volunteers. She lives with her husband and son in a haunted house in Edwardsville, Illinois. In her spare time, she has no spare time.

ECCENTRIC ON THE GRANDEST OF SCALES

Voss Foster

MARTIN WOULD BE DIAGNOSED WITH LIVER CANCER AT 2:14 P.M. next Thursday. Only thirty-seven. Beth would propose to Lilly. Two years after the wedding, they'd adopt a little boy from a crackhead mother. Susanna, bless her blue-haired old heart, would trip over her cat when she came home from grocery shopping. Cat would die, Susanna would break her hip. No one would find her for several hours in spite of her screaming.

My hand lingered as I pushed the little cardboard cup of coffee over to her, the image of her toppling already fading from the reflections of the polished countertop. "Be careful out there." It was the most I could say. Couldn't spout off everything I caught a glimpse of. People would think I was nuts, I'd potentially lose my job. But still... Susanna was approaching ninety rapidly.

She smiled at me, teeth too straight to be natural gleaming under the fluorescent, industrial chic lights. "You're a sweet boy. But I'm always careful."

"Well, be extra careful for me." Her kids and grandkids should have been helping her out, but of course the good-for-nothing vermin who dared call themselves her family didn't care enough about that. Maybe they would when she fell. I couldn't say that for sure. The latte foam didn't show me that far.

"I'll try. But no promises." She winked a rheumy eye at me. "I'm still full of piss and vinegar."

I cringed watching her walk out. I wouldn't be seeing her for a while. Maybe not ever again, depending how bad things went.

I shook the thought off, flashed my over-practiced customer service smile to the next guy in line. He was cute. A redhead muscle-jock kind of dude in a tank top. Scruffy, too. My type.

I really hoped I wouldn't see *him* dying.

"What can I get started for you?"

"Triple shot coconut milk latte with a shot of hazelnut. Sugar free hazelnut." He glanced to the baked goods. "And... a slice of that cinnamon loaf. I'll do an extra ten minutes on the treadmill."

I plugged it into the register. "That'll be eight fifty-one." I took the ten and broke it out. "I'll get that going real quick."

He nodded and dropped all his change into the little tip jar.

I started in on the coffee. Couldn't help sneaking a few more peeks at him waiting at the counter. Nice arms. Nice chest. Nice butt. I *really* hoped I wouldn't see him dying. I kind of also hoped I'd see him in my apartment, but that seemed like a very slim chance.

I frothed the coconut milk and added it... and it was just bubbles. A bit of a surprise. Normally, the universe tossed visions at me as soon as it possibly could.

Still, there was something in that cinnamon loaf. It was fresh, uncut, and when I sliced off that first bit, my eyes focused on the reddish-brown swirl running through it. It undulated within the frame of the bread. I suppressed a sigh and watched the redhead's future play out in pastry.

He was gay. Or bi. Or into dudes. And he had a date at Barnaby's, that real chic bistro downtown. And it damn sure wasn't a date with me. If I was as good looking as his soon-to-be partner, I would have at least been able to scrounge up someone to do on a Saturday night.

I passed the coffee and cinnamon loaf across with a smile. "Here you go. You have a good day."

"You too." He waved, and I may have let my eyes linger on him a bit longer than the employee handbook allowed.

He held the door open for a woman I couldn't help staring at. She was... magnetically odd. Razor thin in a tailored suit. A men's suit. Gray, with a vibrant crimson pocket square. Every pleat in order. She wore mirrored, pince-nez sunglasses. Her hair was blindingly silver, a bob with the right side shaved clean to stubble. And four-inch stilettos that had no place out in the real world, yet there she stood in them, head almost brushing the top of the door frame.

Everyone looked at her, and it seemed as though she stopped a moment to let them. Her lips quirked up at the corners. Then she clacked to the counter and leaned low enough to look me in the eye over her shades. "I would like brewed coffee with two shots of vanilla syrup and whipped cream. The largest size you have." Her makeup was impeccable, eyeshadow in degrees of emerald, lips a peony pink. There was a husk to her voice, something roughed out and throaty.

"Anything else?" I sort of hoped not. Visions rarely appeared in whipped cream. Not never, but rarely.

She eyed the baked goods in the case. "Yes. Two slices of marble loaf." She handed over her card without looking.

I nodded and smiled, running the transaction. "Okay. That'll be twelve twenty-two." She gave no response, so I just accepted it and got to work. The coffee was done quickly—no visions there or in the whipped cream—and I sliced the loaf, waiting to see how strange this woman's escapades must be. Or how shockingly mundane. Marble loaf almost *always* gave me visions.

But when I turned it over, nothing came. I even squinted, just to make sure. Pushing fate, perhaps, but... marble loaf told the future more reliably than anything else in the shop. Every slice was a moving picture book of things yet to come.

But today, this woman was going to drink oddly sweet black coffee and eat two slices of cake that pretended to be bread. That was all the future I had for her. "Here you go."

She nodded. "Thank you..." Her eyes grazed over my nametag. "Cameron."

She spun in place and stalked back through the door. Leaving into an unknown future.

For once, unknown to me, too.

Susanna didn't return, like I knew she wouldn't. The redhead did. No cinnamon loaf this time, so the coconut milk did the talking. Nothing tragic, per se. Maybe a little sad. The date obviously hadn't gone well. He'd be sitting in his apartment that night, eating ice cream, and two other containers sat on the table in front of him. Never a good sign.

"Thanks." He took the coffee, and his smile wasn't nearly the same as it had been the day before. "You make a good latte."

"I do my best." There was nothing I could say to him that would make him feel better, of course. Nothing I could say period without coming off as totally insane. Or a stalker. Neither were good options.

Once again, he held the door for the silver-haired woman. She wore another men's suit, this one in rich navy blue with a golden hound-stooth tie. No sunglasses either. Simple eye makeup, but tangerine lipstick. And still, the same sort of heels making her just as tall as before.

"The same as yesterday, Cameron." She clicked long, French-tipped nails on the countertop. "Do you remember?"

"Large brewed coffee, two shots of vanilla, whipped cream, and two slices of marble loaf."

"Smart boy." She passed me her card again, and her eyes, iron gray, grated over my body. Head to foot and back again, just like my uncle had. But he was a cop and, if anything, this woman was... what, a fashionista? How much did that even pay?

"How long have you worked here, Cameron?"

"A few months." All full of countless visions. Something had gone screwy yesterday of course, but I *knew* I'd see something about her by the time I sliced open that marble loaf.

But... no. Just chocolate cake and vanilla cake. No miracle *Enquirer*-worthy children, no deaths in the family, no winning lottery numbers. Just... cake.

She took it with a nod. "I'll be back tomorrow, Cameron."

I just nodded. "I won't be here. Sunday's my day off."

She nodded. "Happy day off. Spend it as you wish."

"I... will." Why did I say that? Why did she say *any* of that? Why was the marble loaf refusing to talk about her? Why did it bug me so much to finally get a *break* from the constant bombardment of psychic bullshit?

Why did I have a feeling I'd be spending my day off at the damn coffee shop?

She was right on time, like some sort of strange machine cycled these people through the shop. Redhead came in; I pretended not to see his future playing out in the reflection of the espresso machine. Complete with a wife and a little baby girl, though he was already graying at the temples by that point. I hoped he was bi or pan and not just retreating into the closet in his old age.

He held the door open for the razor-thin woman. Decked out in scarlet pinstripe, with the sunglasses perched on her nose again. She stopped by the counter and placed what must have been her regular order. I stared at everything around her, almost *hoping* for some kind of vision to pop up. Something as simple as a trip to the grocery store, or turning the next corner after she left the coffee shop.

The blasted visions were a curse. Always knowing *something* about *everyone*. Sometimes — too often — a tragedy. A trauma. Nothing I could do about whatever was coming for them, either.

But damn it all, they were a *reliable* curse. Every person, every time, as long as I could remember. And the thought of them giving out and changing their pattern was... *unnerving*.

Dana behind the counter pushed out the marble loaf and the coffee. The razor-thin woman turned in place, somehow not toppling on her sky-high heels. But she didn't head to the door. She came straight for my table and leaned down, looking at me over the top of her shades again. "You came here for me, Cameron?"

Any words I might have had stuck in my throat. I just blinked and watched as she sat in the chair opposite me. This wasn't good. Maybe it wasn't stalking, but it wasn't *not* stalking, either. I knew where she'd be — but only because she told me — and I waited for her... so I could get close.

"I'm Adrianna. You call me Anna. Anyone who's in the least bit interesting does." She sipped at her coffee, somehow never getting a whiff of whipped cream on her lips. "You seem to have noticed me, and I *certainly* noticed you, Cameron."

"I'm gay." It just spilled out before I could stop it. Hell of a time for my word blockage to clear up.

"I was not implying I noticed you for sexual gratification. You're attractive, of course, but I hardly have need of another partner." She crossed one leg over the other and smiled beatifically. Her lips matched the brilliant red of her suit. "I noticed you because you notice *every-thing*."

"I don't think that's exactly right."

"Isn't it?" She clacked her nails against the tabletop. "You are hardly the first oddity I've encountered. I check on two dozen of you daily, more than that weekly, biweekly, monthly. Your *particular* difference may be unique, but your situation is not."

"You mean..." I leaned in closer. "You're talking about the visions?"

"Visions? Not entirely unique, then. Where do you see them?"

"In everything." I shook my head. "Wait, wait. Anna." The name didn't trip well off my tongue. Unfamiliar, not totally natural. As far as I could remember, the razor-thin woman was the first Anna I'd ever met. "I'm lost."

"Oh, most people are. The world probably works better that way." She sipped the coffee again, then slid a slice of marble loaf across the way to me. "I have an eye for these things. I always have."

"How can you have an eye for it?" Now the words flowed smoothly, evenly. Rapidly. "Do you mean there are more people like me? Where are they? Who are you?"

"I'll answer... two questions. Choose them strategically. And eat the delightful cake I bought for you."

"For me?"

"For whoever I'm speaking with on a given day. Today, that happens to be you. Two questions. More later, if I like you."

Two questions plucked out of the horde. I cycled through them. What did I need to know above all else? "Who are you? I mean, other than Anna."

"Well-worded." She sighed. "I am... I am an eccentric on the grandest of scales."

"What does that mean?"

"Is that your second question?"

I thought about it, rolled the possibilities around in my head a few times. This could be the only time she'd do more than deliver her order to me, and as intriguing as that whole statement was, understanding it wasn't the most important thing. "Why can't I see your future?"

"Better." Another sip, and a nibble at the marble loaf. "Most people have deterministic futures, Cameron. Humans, dogs, cats, insects, microscopic microbes. Some lucky few have no such nonsense to worry about as fate or destiny." She stood and nodded slowly, then slipped on her pince-nez again. "I imagine I'll see you again shortly. That is the way these things happen."

And off she went. A grand eccentric without fate. Whatever the hell that meant.

Anna sat at my table again, a puce satin suit with a long, slender black tie, and a matching houndstooth pocket square, though where she found puce and black houndstooth I couldn't even have tried to guess. "Two more questions." She passed me the second slice of marble bread. "Make them count. I won't correct you like I did yesterday."

I'd been thinking about them the whole day after talking to her, just in case I ran into her again, and she deigned to talk with me. "What do you mean you don't have fate or destiny?"

"I had it removed. Deterministic futures are cancer to freedom. Eat the bread, Cameron. It's yours."

I nodded and took a bite. Generic and bland and hardly important. Had her fate removed. How did that work? Was it a complicated process? It had to be, didn't it? A new gush of questions flowed through my head, but I couldn't be distracted. What I had to say was calculated out beforehand. "How did you actually know I was different?"

She chuckled, a musical, birdlike sound. "For one, I have never seen anyone stare so intently at baked goods before. So I knew, at the very least, you were strange. You also seemed taken aback when said baked goods did nothing of particular interest, which a normal person... well, frankly, a normal person would be more surprised if they *did* something of interest."

"But that means you just... stumbled into the coffee shop when I was there and took a guess."

She shrugged. "Yes, it does. As I said, I have no fate. I have no destiny. A whole, unseen world opens up when something so limiting and exacting is excised. Including the possibility to stumble upon something more incredible than yourself." She brushed her hair aside, reshaping the perfect half-bob of silver. "Now I have a question for you. How long have you had the visions?"

"As long as I can remember." It still felt odd to even acknowledge them to someone else. Leaden on my tongue. "Every day."

Anna nodded. "Well then, enjoy your cake."

She walked off and I sighed, watching images swim all around me. Wisps of steam playing out a complete hospital birthing scene. Twin girls. A fight that ended with a knife in a man's thigh. A drunk driving accident an inch from going lethally wrong.

These were all determined, according to Anna. No changing them. But then, was it already decided that I would meet her? If it was, how could she be entirely without a fate? Or was everything between us entirely outside the purview of any sort of destiny? Was I cracking the mold just by asking her two questions every morning? Or was whatever happened to her a crock, just a trick that made it seem like she was removed from it all while still keeping everything completely intact? Did they just make her fate... invisible somehow? If so, it was a trick with a very particular application: keeping clairvoyants from picking up on her. And how could I even say there was a "they" involved? Maybe she did it herself.

I munched on marble bread while I struggled to wrap my head through the knitting thoughts and threads. All without getting a massive headache.

I basically just had to hope Anna would show up again, and that I'd have time between making her coffee and slicing her bread to fire off some quick questions. If she was even willing to answer more.

Susanna wheeled herself into the coffee shop. I hadn't expected at all to see her, and definitely not by herself. She broke her hip. She killed her cat. Her family could have perked up at that. But instead, she rolled her wheelchair up and nodded to me. "Injured myself fighting off a band of terrorists. Does that earn me a discount?"

"Sorry. No patriotic savings."

"Well, darn." She sighed. "White chocolate mocha, small, with whip."

"Treating yourself?" I started in making the drink.

"I can get out of the house on my own, so I'm pleased."

The steam from the espresso machine wreathed her cup and showed a tiny version of Susanna in a hospital bed. Infected sores from staying stationary too long. Of course. "Do you at least have someone checking on you?"

"Oh, everyone has other things to do." She shook her head but wouldn't make eye contact. "I'm more than capable of handling things myself."

I knew that wasn't true. Otherwise she wouldn't end up with a nasty infection. "Well, just be careful. You need to focus on recovery so you can keep us safe from the terrorists." I handed her the coffee. "Godspeed, Susanna."

She chuckled, turned herself around, and left just as the cute redhead marched in. He seemed better, wearing aviators. In just a flash as he passed by, I caught a glimpse of him in an... *intimate* situation. With himself. The visions made no sense, but those sorts of things, when they popped up, made things all the more awkward.

He stopped at the counter. "White coffee double shot with caramel." He handed me the five before I could even ring it up. "So do they make you sit here when you're off, or do you just like the coffee that much?"

Guess he saw me over my days off. "I just like the coffee that much." I whipped together his drink as fast as I could, making sure to keep my eyes level on his. And nowhere else. I was already developing a crush on him, which was pointless. He had marriage and a family in his future. But there was no reasoning with my stupid brain.

"Thanks." *His* eyes lingered. "You make a good coffee... Cameron."

"I try."

He waved and wandered off, and Anna clacked in just on time. Did she just *wait* for him to leave before she came inside? Her suit was blinding white, with a black undershirt and a rose-pink tie. She came straight for me. "Same order, two questions."

I started her coffee. "If you don't have a fate anymore, how can you interact with people that do? That means your actions are determined."

"No. It means I'm interrupting the flow of destiny for everyone else. It's hardly my problem if they can't stand a few ripples in the pond. I am just a stone dropped into the water."

I steamed up her milk, letting that slip aside to be processed later. "Do people have any freedom, or is it all set in stone?" It was the kind of question I felt I needed to ask. If I had the chance to find out the nature of time and fate, I knew I had to.

"You're thinking now. That's good." She clucked her tongue and drummed her fingers on the countertop. "There is no freedom with fate. You have the illusion of free will and choice, but that's all. People will follow destiny like herded sheep and remain perfectly content. Which is not what you wanted to hear. It's not what anyone wants to hear."

I sliced into the bread for her. It wasn't anything I wanted, but I could hardly pretend to be surprised. I'd seen the future my entire life and watched it play out precisely the way I knew it would.

"I have another question for you, Cameron. A short one." She smiled peacefully at me. "The redhead. You want him?"

"What?"

"You want him, don't you? You lust after him?"

Way to be blunt. But if I wasn't honest with her, I was pretty sure she'd know, and I didn't want to cut off the flow of information. Anna was the *only* person I'd been able to talk to about the visions, and she was the only person I could remember meeting who seemed like she really knew anything.

"I think he's cute."

She chortled and took her coffee and bread. "Tomorrow. I won't be breaking my schedule just yet. But soon. Get to the point of your queries as quickly as you can, Cameron. I have other people to check on."

She turned and left me with that. Not an ultimatum, but some pointed advice I intended to follow.

"Two questions, coffee, marble cake."

I nodded. "How did you do it?"

"Trade secret. The only people who know are the people who do it. I am not one of those people."

I filled up her cup and started with the vanilla syrup. "Would I still have the visions if I didn't have fate?"

Anna didn't respond for quite a while. Long enough for me to finish cutting her bread. And when she *did* say something… "Do you want your visions gone, Cameron?"

"I… they don't do any good for me. I can't intervene in tragedies. I can't celebrate the good news." I shook my head. "I don't know what life would be like without them, but why not try?"

She nodded and took her order. "I don't know if you'd see them or not." More nodding. "It would be unique, I think. No other oddities have ever lost fate that I know of."

And she turned, and she left, and I knew nothing more than I had when she walked in. But I'd shaken the razor-thin woman in her tailored suit and her perfect, silver hair. I asked her something she couldn't fully answer, and I got the very distinct impression that hadn't happened to her in a long time.

"So, how long have you worked here?" The redhead leaned in close when he took his coffee. It was more calories than he normally ordered. Large white chocolate with whipped cream and caramel and two shots of hazelnut. Half-and-half, not coconut milk. And a cinnamon roll.

"A couple months." I pretended not to see the coming shot of his apartment, littered with ice cream tubs and take out containers and frozen food boxes. I acted like he wouldn't spend that night moping over low-budget rom-coms.

"You been in town very long?"

"A couple months." I'd seen too many tragedies back home, too many gravestones with names of people I knew. So far, Puyallup had been... less severe.

He nodded. "I'm Jeremy." He flashed white teeth, and blue eyes sparkled. "Umm, so, you don't have days off for a while, but when you do... how about you make a friend? I doubt you've had much time for that yet."

I knew what he meant. And I knew his future. He didn't have some mystically removed fate like Anna. He would get married and have kids and probably be happy. With not me. "I'll have to check and see what I've got going on." I couldn't make myself say no to Jeremy, apparently. Some stupid desire that still clung to me. Maybe by the time I talked to him again, I'd have the balls to fess up to the truth. "You'll be back, right?"

"It's on the way to and from the gym. So yeah. I'll be here again." He slapped his hands lightly on the counter, grabbed his order, and held the door open for Anna.

It was the first time I'd seen her in something approaching traditional. Simple black suit, white button-down black tie. She had the shades on, and the whole ensemble made her look like some sort of avant garde government secret agent.

She came to the counter and I already had her cup out, ready to start in. She touched my wrist. "You're leaving work."

"That's not going to happen."

"Your grandmother just..." She sobbed and wiped nothing from her eyes, and her voice rose into a wail. "Oh, God! If only I'd checked on her more often!"

Dale, the manager, waddled over. "Is there, something wrong."

"Oh, I'm so sorry." Anna sniffled, wiped more nothing from her eyes, and looked up at Dale. "It's a family matter. My mother passed away. Cameron's grandmother."

Dale's face turned dour. "I'm... so sorry for your loss."

She nodded and pulled a clean white handkerchief from her pocket. "I went to see her, and she was there on the floor." A tremble quivered up her body. "I know he's working, but this is a time for family to be together."

A little red rushed up Dale's cheeks, and a lot of red rushed up his ears. "Of course. You've got the day off, Cam."

"I can stay."

"You go be with your... with her. And my condolences." He shuffled a little in place. "Day off with pay, of course. For... bereavement."

I was pretty sure that didn't extend to grandmothers, particularly fictional ones, but Anna had a grip on my wrist and led me around the counter. "Thank you, sir. It's just so..." Another sob as she led me from the building. But of course, she righted immediately when we were out of sight and sighed. "There. You have somewhere to be, I believe."

"I have to be at work."

"Well you certainly can't go now. What would your manager think if you didn't spend at least a day or two grieving your poor, deceased grandmother?"

I just shook my head. "What is this about?"

"Well that's your first question. I suggest you save the other one. You'll need it." She took me around the corner to a shiny, vintage muscle car. Powder blue with white stripes. "You want your visions gone? You want freedom like everyone else does? I'm taking you to get it. I hope." She opened the passenger door. "So let's go."

"You mean... fate."

"Yes, I mean fate. The man who handles these things is in town today. This *is* what you want, isn't it? Real freedom? Real change? Real control? You want to be like me, a stone, instead of another meaningless, stupid fish in the pond."

I thought about it for a second. "If you can do this—"

"Perfect, get in."

We walked into the Sanford Motel. One floor, maybe twenty rooms. Anna led me to Room 14. She knocked once, then turned the handle. It actually opened. "I have him."

I followed her into sparse, dirty surroundings. Dim lighting from the table lamps cast the lone occupant in stark details. He was rotund, with a prosthetic leg. Maybe sixty years old. He wore a plain white T-shirt and blue jeans, and he sat on the very edge of the bed. Dark eyes peered from his face like two gleaming black widow spiders. I couldn't keep from shuddering at the image.

He stood with a groan and looked me up and down. "This one?"

Anna nodded. "I think so. I'll vouch for him."

"I don't like doing it to the young. Do they really need it?"

"He's been plagued by clairvoyance his entire life. Perhaps removing him from the flow of fate will end that particular curse for him. I can think of no cause you've undertaken that would be nobler than ending twenty-seven years of struggle."

I'd never told her my age, but I just let it go as the man moved around me, oddly smoothly for his condition. The spiders skittered their gaze up and down my body, just as Anna had done. Sizing me up.

"I'll do it because you say I should, Anna. Assuming he wants it."

A last chance to back out of... whatever. Before I could stop myself, a question slipped out. "Will it hurt?"

Anna shook her head. "It'll just feel... warm."

I sucked in a few deep breaths. This was a chance, and I knew it. It wasn't something I knew I wanted until it was mentioned, but now... "Let's go."

He immediately pressed his hand to my stomach, flat-palmed, fingers splayed. He held for just a moment, then pulled back. And the warmth hit, centered right at my belly button. I could feel that heat coming out of me.

And then I could see it. A glowing white ribbon studded with images. Not real, but clear as day, just like the visions. I saw myself in the coffee shop, clocking out later that day. Going home. Turning Jeremy down. Crying at Susanna's obituary. Moving into a bigger, better apartment with a bigger, better job. Getting a couple dogs. Losing one early to cancer. My hairline receded. I got wrinkles. I gained weight. I lost it. I married. We adopted. Twice. Our daughter graduated.

More and more spilled from my belly, from the core of my being, and the man looped it loosely over one arm until finally, I saw a car accident. I saw myself foresee it just as it happened, then nothing. The end of the white heat slipped free from me.

I shook as the warmth fled. I teared up looking at it all, laid bare in front of me. "That's my fate."

"Not anymore." Meticulously, he rolled it into a tight spool. It glowed like a little flashlight. And he stuffed it into a white-painted mason jar. "Now it's just a relic. You are free. You could die tomorrow. You could win the lottery. You could become a hopeless drug addict.

Or you could sail the ocean for twenty years, then disappear to an uncharted island." He nodded. "It's yours to decide."

I watched him pack the jar away, then turn to Anna. "Is it... is it supposed to be this hard?" There was a lot of good in that destiny. A lot more good than bad, from what I saw as it reeled out.

Anna's lips turned into a frown. She slipped out of her sunglasses. "You already asked two questions, Cameron. I'm afraid that's it."

I walked into work. A few people already sat and nothing appeared from their steam. No fate. No destiny. No future. For a brief flash, I felt that warmth in my belly again.

But only for a brief flash. Over the days grieving my falsified grandmother, it sank in what I'd actually given up... for this. A guaranteed happy life, for freedom that could get me killed. And I knew, in some deepest part of me, there was no going back to that man and getting my destiny returned. It was excised and packed into his cheap, glass canopic jar.

A slow day, but Susanna rolled in. She never looked wonderful, but today was bad. Dark rings under her eyes, a glazed look. "Morning, Cameron."

"Didn't sleep so well?"

"Oh, it's the hip." She waved it off, but still no eye contact. "Decaf black with cream and that cracked sugar syrup. And a bear claw."

It was a simple order, and I caught myself watching for her future, wanting to see what her family would do. And what they wouldn't do. But I couldn't. I didn't get to know those things anymore.

I handed her the cup and the pastry. "Susanna, listen. I get off in the afternoon. Why don't you give me your address and I'll help you take care of stuff. Until you're back in terrorist fighting shape."

"Oh, you don't want to do that."

"I do. I really do. I see you every day, and I want to see you up and *doing* every day, too."

She sat, stoic, for a few seconds, then smiled. "All right. If you're okay with it. I'm on the corner of Eleventh Street and Eleventh Avenue."

"Eleven-Eleven. Got it." I nodded at her. "See you later." In real life. As she wheeled out, I knew it was the right choice. If I couldn't watch her from her coffee steam, I'd watch her in person. And if her family wouldn't take care of her, then I'd do it for them... no, not for them. I'd do it for her.

Jeremy immediately walked in, grinning broad. "You check your calendar yet?"

I nodded. This one, I was doing for me. "Yeah. Turns out I'm free." I wasn't going to rob him of anything. I knew the relationship wouldn't last. But he was graying when he married. I could be a fond memory. Or a bad one.

But I could do it, in spite of fate. I could be... an eccentric, not an oddity.

Voss Foster lives in the Eastern Washington desert, where he writes sci-fi and fantasy from inside a single-wide trailer. He is the author of the Office of Preternatural Affairs series, and his short work has been featured by a variety of publications, including Vox.com and Alternative Truths. When not writing, he can be found singing, cooking, and playing trombone, though rarely all at the same time.

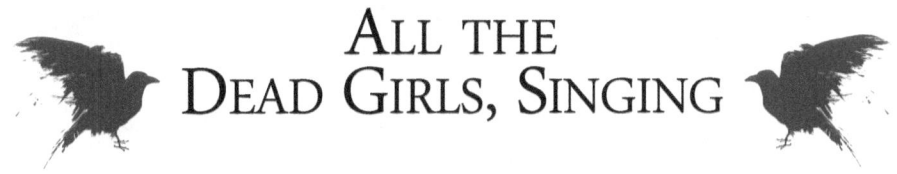

ALL THE
DEAD GIRLS, SINGING

Avra Margariti

S IX P.M., THE GOLDEN HOUR, AND THE TOWN OF FAIRVIEW IS MOURNING
its golden girl. Maya is not the first dead girl Fairview has produced, but she's by far its brightest, most virtuous child: school
valedictorian and straight-A student, purity ring glinting on her finger.
The only one not asking for trouble, going places instead of being up to
no good.

Collectively, the town decides it's a murder before the coroner can
complete his report.

In the three days since Maya Prokopiou was found dead on the
lakefront, water in her lungs and bloody gash on the back of her
head, the following things have been observed: mothers clutch their
daughters' hands tight enough to cut off blood circulation when they
walk down the street; fathers impose evening curfews on their girls,
claiming it's for their own good, as their sons roam free until the spindly
hours of dawn; families draw their curtains tight, then peek with
suspicion through the hairline gap at the quiet, foreign-looking
neighbors; the homeless guy under the overpass gets beaten up, and the
police only laugh and tell him to sleep his cracked ribs off; a sixteen-
year-old boy threatens to shoot his girlfriend, then tells her later he only
did it because he loves her so much he can't bear to lose her, to see her
turn into another Maya.

And now, it's the funeral: solemn black attire and maudlin eulogies
of pious tears. The sun dips below the horizon as Maya is lowered into
the ground. The church bell's knell follows her down.

Several miles from the town's only cemetery is the lake, its surface oily, rippling like a satin slip dress. The lake water has licked away any last traces of blood and hair from its slippery rocks, erasing all evidence of its crime.

This is where Fairview's no-good dead girls congregate. They pretend-smoke cigarettes they can no longer taste, though their mouths are always coated in tar and ash. They finger-comb each other's matted hair, count the stars popping in the sky one by one the way they used to count pimples or freckles on their faces. They pour incorporeal libation tears on the soft ground, their way of mourning their own.

Maya's spirit is nowhere to be found. This makes the dead girls restless. They hold hands, a daisy chain of trapped girl-ghosts. To-gether, they think about their last moments on the right side of the veil in an attempt to call Maya to their side. They relive their deaths. The men — always the men — who did this to them or made them do it to themselves.

In the distance, a rowboat sits like a curious water lily in the middle of the lake. The boat drifts away, setting a slow pace under the stars.

The dead girls fix their eyes on the boat and sing a melody, throaty from too many hours spent screaming at the world. A hymn the church choir director would have called angelic, were the girls alive.

The song peaks, a haunting crescendo. And still, no answer from Maya, Fairview's most golden of the dead girls.

On the opposite lakeshore, where sparse trees and empty log cabins dot the sprawling land, the cherry of a cigarette burns through the darkness. Thin, pink lips close around the damp filter. They belong to a girl. This girl is alive; there, but for the grace of God, the townspeople would say.

Four nights in a row, Alana has been coming to the lake after dark, feet braced against the caving bank, waiting in vain for the one she knows is gone. Maya was supposed to borrow a boat and come to their secret rendezvous spot three days ago, but she didn't make it that far. She was supposed to eat the food Alana had prepared for her, drink from their stolen wine bottle, and make love to Alana, her golden girl moaning in the silver moonlight.

She wasn't supposed to slip on the bank, crack her head open against the submerged rocks, and drown in shallow water.

Maya wasn't supposed to become Fairview's favorite martyr.

Alana hasn't given up. She licks the tear-salt away from her lips and breathes the smoke deep into her lungs. Through the pale mist cradling the water, a flimsy rowboat appears. Alana plants her lit cigarette in the silty ground, the wispy smoke curling upward. It's an offering to all the girls who, even in death, weren't good enough in the eyes of Fairview. Mouth curved into a smile, Alana wades through the shallow water while the boat seamlessly draws near. The figure sitting at the bench seat is familiar, even as the moonlight slices through her diaphanous form.

"You came," both girls whisper as one. They extend trembling fingers toward each other.

Alana drags the boat to the muddy shore. She's crying again, happy tears that ghost lips kiss away.

In the distance, across the lake, the last notes of a smoky, warbling song linger.

Avra Margariti is a queer Social Work undergrad from Greece. She enjoys storytelling in all its forms and writes about diverse identities and experiences. Her work has appeared or is forthcoming in Flash Fiction Online, The Forge Literary, SmokeLong Quarterly, The Journal of Compressed Creative Arts, Argot Magazine, and other venues. Avra won the 2019 Bacopa Literary Review prize for fiction. You can find her on twitter @avramargariti.

SWING A DEAD CAT

Shannon Scott

T HE DEAN'S EYES, REVIEWING ANNA'S RESUME, STRAYED AGAIN AND again to a Chipotle menu resting on his keyboard. After several sighs, he rubbed his nose and placed her resume on a thick stack of papers.

"You seem to know your stuff," the Dean said. "Ms.? Mrs.?"

Anna wanted to say, *Professor*, but instead she said, "Please call me Anna."

"Anna." He repeated her name with disappointment, and she wondered if she should have offered a better name. Maybe something more exotic or gender neutral?

"You certainly seem qualified," he said. "I'm only concerned that you may be too qualified." He waved his hand at the parking lot crammed with rusty beaters outside his window. "We're not exactly the Ivy Leagues here."

She was prepared, having worked as an English adjunct instructor at several private colleges, for this very comment. She had to assure him, without directly stating it, that every university was packed with dummies, especially the expensive ones.

"I've worked as an adjunct instructor at community colleges before," she said. "I don't see any difference in student ability. If anything, the students here are more motivated to succeed." She smiled confidently. The Dean picked up the menu from his keyboard.

While he openly considered his meal options, she stared at his desk, which was covered in files, smudged Post-it notes, burrito wrappers, several grimy Chapsticks, crumpled Kleenex, and a nail clipper. A horsey blonde woman scowled at her from a plastic-framed photo. In the photo, the Dean sported his greying ponytail and soul patch, his arm around the woman, likely his wife, as they stood in front of a mountain range.

"Are those the Rocky Mountains?" Anna said. Then added, maybe a little too urgently, "I hiked those right after college. It changed my whole perspective on life. I really connected, you know, with the earth." She had never hiked a mountain. She didn't, in fact, know exactly what state or states the Rockies were in.

The Dean looked up from the menu, where he had been scanning additions to a burrito bowl, and focused on her face for the first time during the interview. He must have made a decision, she thought, about her or the guacamole, she wasn't sure which.

"Frankly, Anna," he tilted his head at the nearly toppling pile of resumes, "there are so many English adjuncts, I could swing a dead cat and hit a dozen of you."

"He didn't really say that?" Betsy set down her Bloody Mary and gawped at Anna, who was still dressed in her interview clothes, less crisp now and stained at the cuff with coffee.

Anna drowned her hash browns in ketchup.

"Who even uses that expression? It's sick." Nikki signaled to the waiter for more coffee, and he obediently brought a pot straight to their booth, no small feat in a brunch hour rush, but that was Nikki. "I hope you told him to fuck off."

Anna had not told the Dean to fuck off. She was not Nikki. She did not smell of designer perfumes with names like *gold rush* and *white diamonds*. If Anna wore a scent, which she did not, it would be called *desperation* or *ramen again* or *wait, let me try another card*. In truth, she had sympathized with the Dean's plight. So many redundant Janeites and Brontëites to interview, all striving to stay relevant in an era where tweets and Facebook posts were graded as written assignments.

"I took it as a joke," Anna said. She kept her eyes down and shoveled in food.

"That was no joke," Nikki said. "That was an insult. What did you say to him?"

The hash browns went down hard, scraping her throat, and Anna took a big swig of ice water. In her mind, a dead cat was still being propelled above her head, over and over, held by its tail, whirled with a mad momentum by the Dean. "I told him he was right," Anna said. "That I was a dime a dozen."

"You did not!" Nikki's voice was sharp, quieting a nearby table of diners who suddenly handled their cutlery more gently in order to eavesdrop.

"He laughed," Anna said. "I showed him I can take a joke."

"No," Nikki blotted oil from her spinach omelet with a napkin, "you showed him that you think of yourself as a joke."

"All right," Betsy said, "that's enough. Let's all agree the Dean is a prick and Anna is not a dime a dozen." She squeezed Anna's hand with genuine maternal warmth, which would normally have irritated Anna, but Betsy was a mom, and she couldn't help herself, and honestly, the gesture was comforting.

Betsy had once been in the trenches as an English adjunct herself. Now she was a stay-at-home mom raising an adorable preschooler named Katie. She organized neighborhood book clubs and tended a butterfly garden and was earnestly considering forays into urban beekeeping and a backyard chicken coop made up of Rhode Island Reds.

"Except," Anna said, "I am kind of redundant."

"Great, now you've internalized it." Nikki set her fork down as if Anna had ruined her appetite. Nikki's parents had emigrated from Nigeria when she was a toddler, hoping to give her more opportunities for advancement in the U.S. They must have high-fived each other daily since Nikki had sailed through university, where she met Anna and Betsy, and graduated summa cum laude. After receiving her doctorate in bioengineering, Nikki now worked for the government in a job she couldn't discuss, *highly classified, etc., etc.,* but which paid enough for a two-story condo in the poshest section of the city.

"Just hear me out," Anna said. "I swear I'm not putting myself down."

Nikki drummed her manicured nails on the Formica and Betsy's eyes were a little glazed from slurping up the dregs of her tomato juice and vodka, but they offered Anna their undivided attention.

"I've taught at a dozen universities," Anna said, "so I know this is the truth. I've seen it first-hand. We're all over the place, English adjuncts. There are literally thousands of us. We even look alike. Short, thirty-something brunettes. In fact, I bet any of us could take the other's place and no one in any English Department would know the difference. It's like we're clones."

"Maybe that's the answer," Nikki said.

"To what?"

"To your employment problems." Nikki lowered her voice and gestured for Anna and Betsy to huddle closer.

"Here's another truth," Nikki said. "First off, Anna, you'll get the job. You always do. But it's a crappy job. It's one class that pays three thousand dollars, tops, with no benefits or job security. So, you end up working at two other schools to make ends meet. That's three universities, teaching five to six classes. You spend all your time working and you never get ahead. And apparently you never will because no prick of a Dean is going to hire you for a full-time job since there are thousands of you. So many, in fact, you can swing a dead cat and hit a dozen."

"Nikki," Betsy chided, "let sleeping cats lie. Dead ones, too."

"Am I wrong?" Nikki looked at Anna, who wanted to either crawl under the booth or slap her friend in the face. Instead, she speared half of Nikki's omelet and stuffed it in her mouth.

"But you said you had an answer," Anna managed through a mouthful of Nikki's eggs and cheese.

"No, *you* had an answer," Nikki said. "Clones."

When the waiter came to clear the table, the women fell silent. Then, when he was out of earshot, Anna leaned forward. "Are you fucking with me?"

"No, you should definitely clone yourself. Then you can send the clones to teach your classes. You wouldn't even have to worry about scheduling conflicts."

"That would be brilliant!" Betsy said, snapping open her vintage Kate Spade purse and readying to pay the bill before it even arrived. "Oh Anna, you could finally finish your novel."

Anna had been working on a neo-Victorian remake of *Jane Eyre* for six years now. In it, Jane was an adjunct English instructor, the modern-day governess, and Rochester was the wild and unconventional university provost, lavishing the liberal arts with cash to the consternation of the administration. The administration, an overpaid assortment of deans and directors and provosts and advisors and presidents and vice presidents, served as Rochester's entitled and inbred family, who had made their fortune on the backs of Caribbean slave labor. And Rochester's first wife, the crazy woman in the attic, was a tenured professor who went mad during a paid sabbatical when she tried to publish her dissertation and realized she was completely devoid of original ideas.

"You can't clone people," Anna said. "That's speculative fiction."

"Academia's speculative fiction," Nikki shot back. "Cloning is science."

"Well," Betsy said, "there was Dolly."

"We're beyond Dolly now," Nikki said. "Besides, I think Anna might need something a little more advanced than a sheep to teach her English classes."

"Not much," Anna said.

"How many clones would you need?" Nikki asked.

"I guess, if I were to teach at three schools, I would need three clones."

"Great, three it is," said Nikki.

"Would they all look like her?" Betsy asked.

"Of course, they'll look like her. They'll come from her DNA." Nikki neatly picked up the fork that Anna used to steal her omelet and placed it in a doggy bag to preserve the saliva cells.

"But will they be like her?" Betsy asked. "You know, personality-wise?"

"You mean spineless drudges?" Nikki said.

"I'm right here," Anna reminded them.

"Could be," Nikki said. "It's hard to say."

"Would they have her memories?" Betsy took her credit card back from the waiter and signed off on a generous tip.

"You mean like learning to ride a bike or experiencing her first kiss?" Nikki turned to Anna. "Have you had that yet, Anna? Your first kiss?"

Anna glared at Nikki as she stuffed half a leftover cinnamon bun into the second doggy bag.

"The clones will be blank slates," Nikki continued. "Each one a tabula rasa."

Anna considered the three clones, three versions of herself, lecturing classes, commenting on rough drafts, holding office hours, attending faculty meetings — meetings where she was not considered faculty and had to leave before lunch was served. She always snuck back afterwards to cram leftover cookies and chips into her backpack, rodent-like in her settling of scores.

"Do clones eat?" Anna said.

"Yes, they eat," Nikki said. "They're not robots."

"I hope they like ramen."

"I can start them on a ramen diet in the lab, if you want."

"And what about clothes?" Anna said. "With three more mouths to feed, I won't be able to keep them in gloves and stockings."

"Oh, leave that to me!" Betsy squealed. "Katie's going through her Barbie phase. It would be like having three life-size dolls. We could even make up a story for each clone. This one loves horseback riding. This one loves cupcakes. This one's favorite color is pink."

"How long would it take?" Anna asked.

"I could do it over the summer," Nikki said. "Before the fall semester starts."

"But will they be ready?" Anna said. "I mean, can we pass them off as English professors?"

"I can't go from petri dish to PhD in three months if that's what you mean. I can probably get them to read. As far as an education, will Wikipedia work?"

"Absolutely!"

The clones arrived during a heatwave in the last week of August. Each carried a suitcase and was given instructions to speak to strangers politely but briefly and to always obey Anna. Meanwhile, Anna had prepared for their arrival by telling the other tenants in her apartment complex that she was a quadruplet, and that her sisters would be visiting for a spell in the autumn. She installed a three-tiered bunk bed in the living room and purchased three extra toothbrushes, color-coded, with matching cups.

It was strange, at first, looking at the clones, kind of like catching your reflection in a mirror when you're not prepared. Creepy, then relieved, then creeped out again because you were you, but you were also the stranger that scared you. Ultimately, Anna was glad she had never been particularly vain because, seeing her face again and again, she realized just how plain she was and that one eye was slightly lower than the other and her front teeth stuck out when her mouth was resting, kind of like a rabbit or a prairie dog. If she were vain, she might have become depressed by those buck teeth or even angry that her parents had never fixed them. Instead, she felt like they belonged to somebody else, and they did, to the clones.

The first morning with the clones was rocky. Everyone was hot. There had been a misunderstanding about peeing in the bathtub when the toilet was occupied. By breakfast, the clones were cranky and distracted.

"I don't like tea," one of the Annas said. She pulled a face and placed her mug in the sink. "I want coffee."

"I like tea," another Anna said, grubbing for favorite, although who would know since they all looked alike?

Then everyone turned to the silent clone.

"Don't you have an opinion?" the tea-hating clone asked.

The silent clone's eyes flicked from Anna to Anna to Anna before taking a big gulp from her mug that must have scalded her mouth severely. "I want orange juice," she said.

After the incident with the breakfast beverages, Anna learned three important things. First, the clones were not guests. She did not have to cater to their inconveniently individual palates. Second, she needed to tell them apart. She grabbed a permanent marker and wrote **1, 2,** and **3** on their left forearms. Third, a mutiny had to be quashed, then punished.

"Fine," Anna said. "Drink the tea or don't drink the tea. But no Pop-Tarts for anyone."

On the first day of work, even though the heatwave had broken, Anna was sweating as if she were trekking up the Rocky Mountains. The clones were edgy, hiding or pacing or primping somewhere inside the small apartment. Betsy and Katie had been brilliant with the outfits, sending clothes that matched the university where each clone worked, designating every outfit in the crowded closet with a number taped to the hanger.

Anna #1, the hater of tea, stood before Anna and Nikki for inspection. Did she look conventional and banal enough to teach effective business writing to a bunch of accounting majors? Nikki had brought the clone a cappuccino, and she sipped from it slyly, cutting her eyes at Anna whenever Nikki wasn't looking, like *see, people who fly first class and never shop at dented can stores, drink espresso*. The clone wore a grey pencil skirt with a satiny white blouse and black high heels. Her brown hair was done up in a chignon and she had on rose-colored lipstick and understated blush. Anna, in her flannel pajamas and bedhead hair, felt more than a little judged.

"She looks good," Nikki said.

"My feet are killing me," the clone said.

Nikki bent to examine the clone's feet.

"Don't coddle her," Anna said. "She's a complainer and a trouble-maker."

"Complaining makes her human." Nikki stood back up. "Besides, I think her feet really are killing her. Those heels are too small. After work, be sure to check for blisters."

"What are blisters?" Anna #2 asked from somewhere behind the sofa, where she had created a fort in the dusty darkness, just for herself and Anna's cat, Tipsy.

"That's not good," Anna said. "She should know what a blister is."

"They'll learn later," Nikki said, "when this one takes her heels off. Now let's keep it moving."

As Anna faced her fashionable clone for parting words, it was less like looking in a mirror than at the "after" picture in a makeover show. "You look very professional," Anna said, hoping to encourage Anna #1 without fueling her seditious nature. "These kids won't be as smart as they think they are, but your job is to make them believe they're even smarter. That's what business school is for. And if they grumble about reading Kafka, tell them it has nothing to do with Marxism. Kafka can be a conversation starter at a job interview."

"Franz Kafka was a German-speaking Bohemian Jewish novelist born in 1883." It was Anna #2 again from behind the sofa, trying to redeem herself after blister gaff.

"Is this going to work?" Anna said. She was sweating through her pajama top.

"I'm impressed," Nikki said.

"But," Anna grasped for words to express her sudden panic, "but I didn't show them how to use a copy machine."

"Look," Nikki placed a firm hand on each of Anna's dampened and narrow shoulders, "no one's going to Xerox their butt." Then she turned to the clone. "Time to get in the car."

Anna #1 obediently picked up her leather satchel and bag lunch and left the apartment. Nikki was dropping them off on the first day, with mass transit to follow, driving her government-issued SUV with tinted windows and a sunroof.

"Next," Nikki said.

Anna #3 strolled in from the kitchen, still munching on a Pop-Tart. They were her favorite food, in both Betsy and Katie's brief bio and in real life. They were also cheap, so Anna let her have as many as she wanted, although she now worried that if the clone kept it up, she might not fit into her new clothing.

"She looks perfect," Nikki said.

The clone did a flashy twirl in her jeggings and flannel, her face shining and free of makeup, her hair loose and curly. Anna #3 had the tricky job of teaching at the community college where the swing-a-dead-cat Dean worked. Anna had warned her to steer clear of him, to only bestow a friendly wave from afar, and to maintain a hip and youthful manner so as to be relatable to the diverse student population.

"Remember," Anna advised, "if you're at a loss for what to say, just mention white privilege or the patriarchy."

Anna #3 ran a hand down her curvy backside. Why didn't Anna have an ass like that? Then the clone flashed a kittenish smile. "Will there be lots of patriarchs around?"

"What?" Anna frowned.

Nikki pulled Anna aside and spoke in a whisper. "Keep an eye on this one. Last week I caught her making out with Artjom. He's from Estonia. He works as a janitor at the lab."

"Is he hot?"

"He's eighty-three."

Anna watched the clone as she applied glittered lip gloss and smacked her mouth seductively. "So, she's got a thing for older men."

"I think there's more to it," Nikki said. "On the drive over here, I had to stop for gas. While the other clones were getting snacks, this one was climbing into the cab of a truck. When I opened the door, she was locking lips with the trucker."

"Another Estonian?" Anna said.

"It was a lady truck driver."

"I see."

Anna returned to the clone and handed her a bag lunch, which consisted of two frosted Pop-Tarts. "You know what men want," Anna started, then felt she must add, "and women, too. They want a girl who plays hard to get. No, they want a girl who *is* hard to get." She felt guilty using propaganda, but it had to be done. "Don't just give it away. That will make you seem cheap and easy."

Anna #3's body sagged in disappointment. "Cheap?" she said. "Easy?"

"What Anna means," Nikki said, giving her friend the hairy eyeball, "is that you're one hot chick, on the inside and out, and you have to respect yourself and make sure everyone else respects you too."

This perked up the clone and she left the apartment at a jaunty trot for Nikki's SUV.

Then Anna addressed the sofa, where Anna #2 remained inside her fort, clutching Tipsy, the ancient and rotund orange tabby cat, and getting fur all over her turtleneck. "It's time to go."

"I don't want to," the clone said. "I'm scared."

"That's normal," Anna said as Nikki tapped her watch. "It's just first-day jitters. I always get them. As soon as you're in the classroom, they'll disappear. I promise, you're going to have a great day."

"Tipsy wants me to stay," insisted the clone. "He said so."

"All Tipsy wants is cheesy crave treats and maybe a few slow mice."

"What if I throw up in front of all the students and faculty?" Anna's #2's voice rose in alarm, and Tipsy licked her cheek. He never did that with Anna. "What if I faint?"

"Nothing like that will happen," Anna assured her. "Now let's see your pretty skirt."

The clone emerged from the fort in a long beige-colored skirt that looked as if it had been hand-stitched for a Civil War re-enactment.

"That's damn clever of Betsy." Anna rubbed the rough fabric between her fingers. "Half the staff at this freak show are wearing homemade clothes just like this."

"Ix-nay on the eak-fray," Nikki said, noting the clone's widening eyes.

"Oh no," Anna backtracked. "They're not freaks. They're nice people. They just pray a lot." Anna could not remember what evangelical synod the college actually belonged to, but she did know that it was a Christian denomination and that she had signed away her academic freedom in a document that also made her acknowledge Jesus as her Lord and Savior.

"Don't use any swear words," Anna said, "and steer clear of politics. Stick to Shakespeare. Not *Romeo and Juliet*, loads of jokes about VD in that play, but *Macbeth*. Christians love blood. It reminds them of the Passion of Christ."

The clone pulled at the cross around her neck until it tightened like a garrote. "They like blood?"

"Maybe I should give her a Xanax?" Nikki said.

"She's fine." Anna clapped her hands at the clone as if she were a spaniel. "Aren't you?

The clone nodded uncertainly, and Nikki ushered her into the hallway, where Anna handed her a bag lunch.

"It's PB&J," Anna said. "And maybe a special treat." There was no special treat.

Anna went to the window and waved at the SUV filled with her clones until it disappeared down the street. Then she turned to her desk. "Time to write a masterpiece," she said to Tipsy, who had not left the fort and wouldn't until Anna #2 returned.

At noon, just as Rochester was about to bestow a hefty travel grant to an English adjunct whilst the associate vice president of professional development suffered a stroke, the apartment buzzer went off. Anna hit save, scampered to the window, and peered outside. Nikki and one of the clones were waiting at the wrought-iron door. She buzzed them inside.

Anna glanced at her watch. It wasn't even two o'clock yet. The clones weren't expected home until dinnertime. Something must have gone wrong. Standing in the open doorway, Anna's hands tingled with anxiety, and she couldn't take a deep breath. She wanted to rush down the stairs to meet them, but instead she put her head between her knees and puffed into her cupped hands as a school nurse once taught her to do when she had an anxiety attack during second grade recess that had turned out to be an asthma attack.

Nikki was the designated emergency contact for all the clones since she could better respond to any health concerns, while also keeping too-inquisitive doctors at bay, but so far, the clones had been healthy. They played disc golf at a local park and went for walks in the neighborhood. They abstained from hard liquor and slept eight hours a night. They hydrated properly, bathed regularly, and were on a daily calcium supplement to prevent osteoporosis.

Anna's hyperventilating was somewhat under control when Anna #2 appeared with Nikki's arm encircling her waist, holding her up and pulling her forward. The clone's face was so red and swollen that her eyes looked like tiny pieces of basalt in molten lava.

"She threw up in front of all the students and faculty," Nikki said. "Then she fainted."

"How did that happen?" Anna helped them inside.

The clone listed to the couch, where she collapsed in a heap. Her khaki skirt, flecked with dried vomit, billowed up around her waist like a deflating hot air balloon. Soon Tipsy emerged from behind the sofa and started licking the inflamed skin on her face with fierce tenderness.

"Anaphylactic shock," Nikki said. "Turns out she's allergic to peanut butter."

"But I'm not allergic to peanut butter," Anna said.

"It's DNA we're monkeying with." Nikki sounded more than a little defensive. "There's bound to be a few hiccups. You should be happy. She finished teaching all her classes before her throat closed up and she nearly died."

"I guess so." Anna shrugged.

Nikki dug in her purse and pulled out a prescription bag. "Here's an epi pen. I'd ditch all the peanut butter and peanut-related snacks if I were you."

The clone groaned miserably on the sofa. Tipsy had stationed himself on her head like a massive orange shapka. To Anna, she looked like a sick kid sent home from school with a fever. All she needed was a juice box and a jar of Vicks to fully recreate Anna's own childhood.

"Go change," Anna said. The acidic smell of vomit with its nutty undertones was making her own stomach churn. "Then you can rest for the afternoon. Maybe you can get some reading done."

"For God's sake," Nikki said, "let her watch TV. It's been a rough day. The doctor was pretty sure she had a seizure."

"Fine," Anna said, "but it has to be something educational."

After Anna disposed of all the peanut-related products in the kitchen, she and the clone compromised on the Shakespearean rom-com, *Much Ado about Nothing*. The clone watched intently, stroking Tipsy, who rested his paw on her forehead as if testing her temperature. Anna continued writing at her desk in the corner of the living room.

"What are you writing?" Anna #2 asked when the film was finished. Her words were a little slurred through her still-swollen tongue.

Anna stopped typing and twisted around in her chair. "My novel."

"What's it about?"

It's hard to distill a novel in a few sentences, but since Anna's novel was so derivative, it was easy. "An impoverished English adjunct falls in love with a rich provost. But the tension isn't simply over class difference. He's married. Only she doesn't know he's married. He's lying to her, but he's lying to protect her. Anyway, it's more about Jane discovering her self-worth than a romance with Rochester."

"What's happening now?"

Anna turned back to the screen. "The provost's pyromaniac wife lit a fire in his bedroom, and Jane saved him. He's driving her back to her inner-city hovel in his BMW convertible."

"Does he kiss her?" asked the clone.

"No," Anna said, "that doesn't happen until chapter one hundred and eighty-six."

The clone went back to staring at the television screen.

Half an hour later, Nikki buzzed in with the other clones in tow. Everyone, including Nikki, looked beat, and Anna felt ashamed that she had been home all day and never even changed out of her pajamas.

"Do you want a glass of wine?" Anna asked Nikki.

"Thanks, but I'm heading straight back to work. I'm in the middle of a project for the Department of Defense."

"Top secret?" Anna said.

"I'd have to kill you if I told you," Nikki said.

Nikki faced the clones and gave each one a rough but affectionate punch on the shoulder. "Great work today, girls. I'm really proud of you."

The clones glowed under Nikki's praise, like softball players with their coach, and they waved fondly as she left.

"I'm proud too," Anna said, but it was a lame echo, and the clones were already too savvy for those tricks.

Once the door was closed, Anna #1 kicked off her shoes fiercely, each hitting the wall like a small cannonball and leaving a black scuff mark. Her heels were covered with red and yellow blisters threatening to erupt. She stripped down to her bra and underwear, tossed the work clothes on the floor, and hunted for her comfy T-shirt and yoga pants on the highest bunk bed. "I want some wine," she called over her bare shoulder.

"Let's put dirty clothes in the hamper." Anna gathered the clone's wadded-up blouse and skirt, which Anna thought the clone could have worn for a second day if she hadn't squashed them into a wrinkled ball. However, she did not remonstrate with the clone in light of her nasty blisters. Instead, she poured the clone a generous glass of wine, crossing her fingers that she would not be a mean drunk.

"How was your day?" Anna asked Anna #3, who had acquired a stylish peach-colored scarf, knitted with softly fraying yarn.

"It was good," she said.

"Where did you get the scarf?" Anna asked.

The clone paused and considered. "It was a gift."

"From whom?" In Anna's opinion, the clone took much longer than necessary to answer a simple question.

"A student?" the clone said.

Before Anna could ask another follow-up question, the clone snatched the wine bottle from Anna's hand and took a swig. She was about to pass it to the clone recovering from anaphylactic shock, but Anna intercepted.

"I don't think you should drink," Anna said to the swollen clone. "You nearly died today."

Anna #2's devastated expression left Anna in a total panic for the third time today. She had seen that look once before when she helped Betsy with Katie's second birthday party, and someone's bratty toddler ripped Katie's new plush penguin from her arms. The shock, the outrage, the gathering of air before the piercing scream. It had all terrified Anna. She knew she needed a distraction fast as tears were already gathering in the clone's eyes. She grabbed her phone and asked the clone, "What do you want on your pizza?"

The clone's face cleared instantly. "Pineapple and pepperoni," she sniffed.

"Done and done!"

Nikki had ordered pizza regularly for the clones, but due to low funds, Anna had not indulged their pizza cravings. Until now.

After she took the clones' orders, Anna left them to drink and discuss their respective days while she waited outside for the pizza delivery person. The air was finally beginning to feel like autumn. The acorns that had dropped over a month ago were almost crushed to dust beneath her fuzzy bunny slippers. Somewhere down the block, people were having a bonfire, and Anna thought it was strange how wood smoke could be both soothing and choking.

When she got back inside with the pizzas, the clones had bypassed the parental controls and were watching hard-core pornography. A woman on the screen was moaning tremulously as she serviced two men.

"I want to do that," Anna #3 said.

"No, you don't," Anna said, taking away the remote control. "She's only pretending to have a good time. In reality, she's living a sad and lonely life, unfulfilled by her career, and probably suffering from a VD, or several VDs, as a result of her poor lifestyle choices."

"What's a VD?" the clone asked.

"It's like one of Anna's blisters, except on your crotch," Anna said. "Trust me, she's not a happy person."

The clones looked doubtful, but they soon forgot the orgy in favor of dinner. Anna put on another rom-com, with weddings and mistaken emails and thematic messages about women being happy with themselves that were later undercut when all the women found the perfect man to make them happy.

Anna never had sisters. She was an only child, who liked to collect bugs with her imaginary friends, but the warmth of her new quadruplets as they scarfed down pizza and made catty remarks about the actresses' hairstyles, pressed against each other on the couch like a pack of wolf pups, almost made her wish she had. Sure, they were clones and not her actual sisters. And yes, she was exploiting their labor to save her own sanity and finish her novel, but still, the affection felt genuine. And Anna was relaxed. Super relaxed. As relaxed as she had been before she started teaching. She had no lesson plans or papers to grade. She was not getting bald patches or suffering from canker sores. Outside, she had enjoyed the crisp autumn air on her rash-free skin.

When the film was over, the clones lounged on the couch and discussed pedagogy while Anna cleaned up the dinner leftovers.

"Students need discipline," Anna #1 said, through wine-soured breath.

"A student cleared my air passage," Anna #2 said.

"My students are fun," Anna #3 hiccupped. "I can't wait to see them again." She finally unwrapped her scarf, exposing a large purple stain on her neck.

"What happened to you?" Anna #2 cried. She licked her thumb and tried to remove the stain. Anna #3 pushed her away.

"Did a student hurt you?" Anna #1 balled up her fists. "I will kill them."

The clone instinctively covered the mark as Anna marched over to inspect it. "That better not be a tattoo," Anna said. "Those things are expensive and permanent."

Reluctantly, the clone allowed Anna to lift her hand and inspect the skin, which was purplish, unevenly colored, and completely flat.

"It's a hickey," Anna declared.

The clone's cheeks turned deep pink and she sheepishly hid the hickey under her scarf.

"What's a hickey?" Anna #1 asked.

"A skin blemish caused by a lover sucking or biting the skin," Anna #2 said.

The first quarter of the semester was fairly uneventful. Anna worked on her novel, finding corrections and suggestions left daily by Anna #2, which annoyed her until she read them and realized the clone was a good editor, then she fumed silently and made the corrections.

Anna also did a lot of laundry. She built up her thigh muscles making countless trips to the basement laundry room, where she battled the other tenants for use of the washing machine. While sorting clothes, Anna often found blood on Anna #1's blouses, and when she confronted her about it, the clone said she got bloody noses from the dry air in her classroom. The clone then pointed out that perhaps if she didn't have to spend so much time in the classroom, she would not suffer from bloody noses, and Anna had backed off, determined to keep her mouth shut from now on and purchasing a large bottle of bleach.

There were discussions with Nikki when Anna #2 wanted to go to church on Sundays with campus ministry in a rusty minivan with a Jesus fish on the back. They decided to let her. Anna #2's desire to sing in the choir and praise the Lord seemed harmless enough, but Anna did not like the clone's pointed questions about her faith. There was a more heated debate when Anna #3 requested permission to go on dates, which irked Anna since she had not been on a date in over a year, but after Nikki bequeathed the clone with a large supply of condoms, Anna had to admit it was nice to have so many dinners paid for, not to mention the leftovers for lunches.

But there were still wrinkles to iron out.

For example, one night Anna #1 came into Anna's room and yanked her hair so hard she woke up with a scream. Then she blinked and blinked until her own face, a doppelgänger wearing a particularly vicious countenance, came into focus. Anna nearly jumped out of her skin.

"What the hell are you doing in here?" she cried.

"That slut is going to break the bed," Anna #1 said.

Anna got up and fumbled with her robe, eventually following the clone into the living room where the bunks beds were indeed swaying in a most disconcerting fashion. At first, Anna thought it was an earthquake, then she realized the floor beneath her feet was solid and still. The rocking movement originated from the center bunk, where two shadows grunted ardently, impervious to their audience. Anna #2 remained frozen on the bottom bunk while the bed above her bucked and bounced. She held on tightly to Tipsy, her face like one besieged in a bunker undergoing heavy artillery fire.

"Come on," Anna motioned for her to get out, fearing a total bunk bed collapse. "You can sleep in my bed."

Anna #2 dashed away from the leaping, tilting structure with Tipsy lodged safely under her arm. "They're going to kill each other," she said.

"No, they're not," Anna said, somewhat enviously.

"If the bunks collapse, they'll probably both die," Anna #1 offered. "Or at least be grievously injured."

Tipsy wheezed as the clone shifted him to the other arm.

"I'm sure it will all be over soon," Anna assured the clones.

But it wasn't. They stood for another five minutes in the glow of Anna #2's miniature magnetic reading light, but neither the beds nor the lovers showed any signs of letting up.

"He has a lot of stamina," Anna #1 said.

"That he does," Anna agreed.

From somewhere in the quaking darkness, a muddled voice said, "I want to try a new position."

"Nope," Anna said. "No new positions. You're all done. It's time to leave."

Anna used her sternest "teacher voice," which instantly halted all gyrations. Then a man's head popped out from between the bunks, sweaty and sex stupefied. When he saw three women glaring at him, all looking exactly like sleep-deprived variations of the woman now straddling him, he squeaked long and loud and shot out of the sheets.

As the man scrambled to the door, stumbling and plucking up clothes as he went, Anna #1 reached over and tugged Anna's sash from her robe, winding it firmly around her forearm. When she released it in one swift movement, a graceful psycho cowgirl, it unfurled like a bullwhip and hit the naked stranger in his inflamed junk. His screams were much more strident and distressed this time. When he raced out into the brightly lit hallway, Anna caught a glimpse of youthful buttocks.

"That better not be a student," Anna said.

After that night, there were rules about not bringing dates home and not sleeping with students.

In addition to laundry duty and lessons on moral turpitude, Anna fielded emails. She couldn't afford a cell phone plan that included all the clones, nor could she afford the actual phones. It was easiest for her to troubleshoot emails from all the universities herself, only flagging the most important missives. At first, she'd get a spasm in her chest whenever she opened a correspondence, asthma or anxiety, she wasn't sure which and couldn't afford a doctor's visit to find out, but the symptom soon abated when, day after day, no one questioned the legitimacy of the clones. Not their credentials, not their capabilities, not their humanity. As long as the clones said *wish it were Friday* or *almost Friday* or *so happy it's Friday*, and didn't break the copy machine, no one in any English Department suspected a thing.

Most of the emails were crap. Not spam or junk, just crap. First, there were the students:

Hey prof,

I've been throwing up all night. I won't be in class

Dear Professor Anna,

I need a recommendation for a scholarship. Can I get it today? Can you not mention I got a D in your class?

Hi Professor,

Have you heard of spoon theory? Anyway, I don't have enough spoons left to write my essay. I used up all my spoons just getting to Starbucks. I am hoping for a better supply of spoons tomorrow so maybe I can do some homework. Thank you for understanding.

Dr. Anna,

I did not do the reading today. I had a calculous test that was more important than reading Kafka. I had to prioritize and exercise my time management skills. Thank you for understanding.

Wow Professor

I know I plagiarized the last assignment, my bad, but can you bump my grade up a letter? My dad says that's your job.

Then, there was the administration:

Interdepartmental Memo:

Have you seen (place name of student here)? If so, express to them that our university cares deeply about all our students. Please let them know how much you care, too. Also, let them know there is a hold on their account in financial aid.

Interdepartmental Memo:

The unfortunate graffiti has been removed. The university does not condone racism of any kind. Please share our anti-racism beliefs and policies with your students. There will be mandatory training on cultural sensitivity for all faculty and staff. There will be no stipends for adjuncts.

Interdepartmental Memo:

This university does not condone sexual harassment. Whether the harassment happens to an attractive or unattractive student makes no difference at all to the university. Nor should it to you. Harassment is harassment. There will be mandatory training on sexual harassment for all faculty and staff. There will be no stipend for adjuncts.

Interdepartmental Memo:

Exciting news! The university will offer training for all faculty and staff on how to handle a mass shooting. Renowned FBI Agent Donald Smithfield will demonstrate the best way to subdue an active shooter. Cookies provided! Adjuncts will receive no stipend.

Then there were union updates:

Union Update 9/ 10/19

Contract negotiations continue to be contentious. We have asked the administration to provide us with dry-erase markers for our classrooms. The university is taking the next three months to consider our request.

Union Update 9/10/19

The dry-erase marker amendment was rejected.

Union Update 9/10/19

We pushed hard today. We requested that a chair be placed in our collective office so that we will no longer have to stand up or lean against each other. The Dean crunched up our request and threw it at our lawyer, who has since suffered a migraine. He will pursue his lawsuit separately. We will not be asking for any pay raises or stipends at this time.

Then there were the ones Anna flagged. The serious ones that needed private discussion. She waited until Anna #3 returned from her date, flushed and clutching a bouquet of tulips, before calling her to the computer.

"You've been receiving quite a few emails lately," Anna said.

"I'm a popular teacher," the clone answered.

"They're all from the same student," Anna said.

The clone picked at the waxy pink petals of her tulips. "I should get these in water."

"You can do that later," Anna said. "First, we need to put out this fire."

"Okay," the clone mumbled.

"I'm going to read the emails out loud," Anna said. "I'm not doing this to shame you, although shame might not be a wrong feeling here. I just want you to pay attention. To think about the consequences to your actions."

The clone sighed. "I only slept with him once. It was before the rule about not having sex with students."

"Be that as it may," Anna said. Then she read the student's emails one by one.

"Anna, I love you. I think about you all the time. Why did you give me the number to a Dunkin' Donuts?"

"I didn't have a phone," the clone said. "Plus, I thought donuts would make him feel better. They always make me feel better."

"Anna, I wrote you a poem. Can I read it to you? Meet me by the dumpster behind the cafeteria. Please come. I miss you. I've been thinking about you all through remedial algebra."

"He's a terrible poet," the clone said. "And that dumpster really stinks."

"Anna, you bitch! I threw your poem in the dumpster! I hope your heart shatters into a gazillion pieces!"

The clone laid her tulips on the desk, followed by her head.

"Anna, I didn't mean that about your heart shattering into a gazillion pieces. I still love you. We can work things out."

The clone lifted her head from the desk. There was a tan smudge where her matte finish foundation pressed on the wood. "You were right," she said. "About the porn lady. She was not happy."

Anna thought about patting her shoulder, about comforting her with a maternal squeeze, like Betsy would, but she really wanted the gravity of the situation to sink in.

"You were right about VDs, too," the clone said. "They suck. They suck the worst."

"You need to do something about this situation," Anna said.

The clone nodded. "I'll talk to Anna #1 tonight."

"Leave her out of this," Anna said. "She'll probably beat him to death."

The clone lifted her eyebrows, not with alarm but with a question.

"And that would be wrong," Anna said.

"Of course," the clone agreed.

"Let him down easy," Anna advised. "Lie about becoming transgender or having a contagious skin disease. It doesn't matter what you say. Just make sure he doesn't go to the administration. I don't want to end up on a sex offender list."

"Yes, I understand."

"And don't leave the tulips where Tipsy can get them," Anna said. "If he eats them, he'll get sick."

The clone nodded, then the computer pinged as another email arrived.

"Is that him again?" the clone asked.

Anna squinted at the screen. "No, it's an evite."

"What's an evite?"

Anna adjusted the screen so the clone could watch her open the online invitation. Inside the "envelope" was a hefty green cabbage sitting in the middle of a garden patch. The tinny electronic *wa-wa* of a baby carried through the laptop speakers. When Anna clicked on the cabbage, it began to rock back and forth, gently at first like a cradle, then faster and faster until it burst with a loud pop. The detonated cabbage leaves fell like confetti around a diapered, red-cheeked baby wearing a big blue bow on his head. The *wa-wa* stopped as the baby reached out, pulled a carrot from the ground, and sucked it like a bottle, smearing dirt all over his face. Beneath him appeared the words, *Frogs and snails and puppy dog's tails. It's a boy! You are cordially invited to Kristin's baby shower.*

"That's adorable!" the clone exclaimed.

"My cousin is a prolific breeder," Anna sighed.

"Congratulations!"

"You're not supposed to congratulate me. You congratulate the expectant mommy. It's her seventh."

When, Anna wondered, did popping out babies cross the line from *big family* to *litter*?

"Are you going?" the clone asked.

Anna would rather detonate herself, like that cabbage, than sit through another afternoon discussing breast pumps with women who felt comfortable exposing their breasts, not just to nurse newbies but to whip out like mammary juice boxes to kids that could walk right up to them. Even armed with non-alcoholic champagne and a Merry Munchkin gift basket, Anna was the specter of bareness at these events. If she got knocked up now, as her mother frequently reminded her, she would have a geriatric pregnancy. Chromosomal predators lurked like mutants in her aged yolks.

"No," Anna said.

"Can I go?" the clone said.

"Oh, you want to sit around for hours wearing a tight party hat and playing infant-themed games?" Anna added, "Sober?"

The clone nodded emphatically. "I love hats and games."

"Perfect, my mom will love you." As soon as the words were out of her mouth, Anna knew they were true. Her mother would like this cloned version of herself. Finally, the bouncy and convivial daughter she had always wanted, maybe even deserved. A girl who sang along to the radio and applied nail polish without huffing it, who received flowers from gentlemen callers. Sure, also a girl who had a VD, but a girl who might one day make her a grandmother.

"I'll buy my own gift," the clone said.

"Those are the magic words," Anna said.

A few days after her cousin's baby shower, Anna's mother called. Instead of working on her novel, Anna was playing *Call of Duty* with Anna #1 since it was an educational game that provided historical background on WWII. She paused the game just as she was about to throw a grenade into enemy territory. Anna #1 cussed savagely, then headed to the kitchen for another breakfast beer. Anna agreed it was better than tea. She covered the receiver and told the clone to grab her one, too.

"Hello, sweetheart," her mother said.

"Hello, mom," Anna said.

Anna #3 shuffled past the couch eating a Pop-Tart, and Anna swatted at her leg to get her attention. Then she put her mother on speaker phone.

"It was so nice of you to come to Krissy's baby shower." Her mother's garbled voice filled the room. "It meant a lot to her."

Anna #3 reached out to take the phone, but Anna held it away.

"It meant a lot to me, too," her mother said. "You did so well with the baby food game. Everyone was so impressed. You guessed the right baby food each time, even though you were blindfolded. You got liver and peas when no one else did. I was so proud."

"It was fun," the clone said, projecting her answer towards the phone. "My favorite was the apple avocado."

Her mother laughed. "Yup," she said. "You sure ate that all up. You picked the best one."

"Did it ever occur to you, mom," Anna said, reasserting her presence on the phone, "that I was hungry? Like stomach-growling hungry? Like food bubble coming out of my head that says, *hungry, hungry*? That maybe I wanted, or dare I say, needed, a free meal after purchasing yet another baby shower gift for my cousin's warren of offspring?"

The clone dove for the phone just as Anna jerked her arm to keep it away. The two wrestled for the device, Anna smacking the clone's face, and the clone smacking Anna's face right back, until the clone came away victorious, clutching the device protectively as Anna's mother bleated questions about baby food and serotonin reuptake inhibitors.

"Mom? Are you still there?" asked the clone.

"Yes, sweetheart. Do you need me and your dad to reinstate your allowance? I don't like the idea of you going to baby showers just to eat baby food."

"No, mom, I'm fine. That was just a podcast. It's about this sad woman who says stupid, hurtful things because she can't help herself. It's like Tourette's, but only for this one sad lady." She flicked her eyes at Anna, who was fuming on the couch.

"That doesn't sound like it'd be a very popular podcast," her mother said.

"It's not," the clone said. "It was cancelled, or maybe the lady jumped off a bridge. I don't remember. Probably the first thing."

"What a tragic story," her mother said. "It reminds me of that book you're writing. How is that going?"

"I stopped writing," the clone said. "It was a waste of time."

She stared pointedly at Anna again, who made a fruitless lunge for the phone.

"I think that's a wise choice," her mother said. "I never understood why you wanted to rewrite a story when Jane Austen did it so well the first time."

Anna's ears were starting to ring, a hive-like buzzing sound that still, unfortunately, allowed her to hear the fawning warmth in the clone's voice and the reciprocal cloying approval in her mother's.

"Anyway, the reason I called was to invite you and your new boyfriend to Thanksgiving. He sounds so successful and well-travelled. I can't wait for everyone to meet him."

Anna flashed on the youthful backside running out of her apartment in the dead of night. She figured the clone must have found a new boyfriend, traded up, hopefully not another student. *Successful and well-travelled.* It had to be an older man, a patriarch, probably one whose weightier wallet compensated for his saggier backside.

"I'm in love," the clone chirped.

All the clones, even Anna #2, who was cleaning Tipsy's water dish and adding ice cubes, paused when they heard Anna's mother exclaim with pure joy, "I'm so happy for you! I've been waiting so long for you to come out of your cocoon and start living your life."

"It's the new me," the clone confirmed. "I love you, mom."

"I love you, too," her mother burbled.

Anna turned the game back on and blew up Berlin.

On Thanksgiving Day, Anna #2 left early to volunteer at a soup kitchen, where she and her fellow Christians would serve three hundred turkey dinners to local bums. She gave Tipsy a pat on the head before departing and promised to return with giblets and gravy. Anna #3 prepped for her Thanksgiving meal, where she would play the "real" Anna and introduce her new boyfriend to Anna's family.

It had been five years since Anna brought a boyfriend home for Thanksgiving. Doug had been a pre-med student, who made killer artichoke dip that her family still talked about to this day. He was charming and solicitous with her aunts and grandmother and *hail fellow well met* with her uncles and grandfather. An all-around winner, everyone agreed. They held hands off and on throughout dinner, with occasional squeezes from his end when her mom described Anna's series of imaginary friends, and squeezes from her end when someone complimented his moustache or manners or asked a question about an ailment they were suffering from. They rode the high all the way home that night, and when Doug wanted to join Anna in her tiny shower, she let him, and when, instead of having awkward, slippery sex, he asked if he could pee on her, she consented.

From the sofa, Anna could smell the lavender bath bomb the clone had dropped in the tub. She soaked for over an hour while Anna and Anna #1 sprawled on the couch passing a bag of potato chips back and forth. When Anna #3 finally emerged from the bathroom, she borrowed, without asking, Anna's beloved crushed velvet frock and garnet earrings, then danced spritely into the room, a princess amongst her crumb-encrusted stepsisters.

Anna had been giving Anna #3 the silent treatment since the three-way phone conversation with her mother. When the clone asked what she should bring to the Thanksgiving meal, or if Anna could provide her with at least one childhood anecdote, or possibly a family tree, Anna had muttered darkly, "Why don't you hang yourself from the family tree?"

It bothered her more than she expected, the way her mother had taken to the clone. Her mother was now teaching the clone how to knit and, apparently, had even given her some advice about sex, such as *don't share your magic number* and *hold out for a ring*. Where had that advice been all those years ago when Anna began her slippery slope of water sports with Doug?

Anna stared into the kitchen where Anna #3 was lifting her tulips down from the top of the fridge and inhaling the blooms. She tried not to notice how her special-occasion dress, the one she hadn't worn in years, enticingly hugged the frame of her shapelier clone, who looked like she belonged on the cover of *Better Homes & Gardens*. The clone had been a tabula rasa, as Nikki said, except now her blank slate had a boyfriend and a mother who was proud of her.

Anna #3 hooked a purse over her shoulder and picked up the tray of crudités. Before she closed the door, she said airily, "You're both a couple of losers."

Anna wanted to hurl a snappy rejoinder at the closed door, but nothing came to mind. Anna #1 heaved herself off the couch.

"Well, she's right about one of us," she said. "It's time for me to head out."

Anna #1 had originally asked to go to the shooting range on Thanksgiving, but it turned out the gun emporium was closed, so she opted to go pheasant hunting at the local park. She had borrowed a crossbow from the university archives, modelled after one used at the Battle of Hastings, and she had been pointing it at all of them for days now, jumping from out from behind doors and furniture, stalking Tipsy on his way to the litterbox.

As Anna watched the clone fill her backpack with short arrows, beef jerky, and sports drinks, she suddenly did not want to be alone on the holiday. It seemed a dreary prospect, sitting on the sofa, smelling her neighbors' dinners, possibly replacing Anna #3's shampoo with Nair, and waiting, like Tipsy, for someone to come home with treats.

"It's kind of cold for hunting," Anna said.

"It's November." The clone pushed a sheathed bowie knife deep into the pocket of her military-style coat.

"Wouldn't you rather stay inside where it's warm and cozy?"

"If you've got pheasants hiding somewhere in the apartment that I can kill, then sure, I'll stay inside where it's warm and cozy."

"We can order pizza and get drunk," Anna said.

"We do that every weekend," the clone said.

"What about a zombie-movie marathon?"

The clone's eyes gleamed, and Anna knew she had finally hit pay dirt. Anna #1 was always outvoted when it came to television viewing. She loved horror films, especially anything with zombies, but for everyone else, zombies were scary and icky, and Anna #2 opposed them on religious grounds because it was evil to show resurrection without God signing off on it.

"*The Walking Dead* or *World War Z*?" the clone demanded.

"Your choice."

The clone held up the crossbow, which Anna checked was not loaded, and flexed her bicep, squinting icily like her favorite character, Daryl Dixon, from *The Walking Dead*. Anna queued up an episode.

The zombie marathon continued all afternoon in a haze of fermented grapes and greasy cheese and brains, brains, brains.

"Why are the biters' heads so easy to crush?" Anna asked as another biter was juicily decapitated in a basement cellar.

The clone shushed her.

It was strange, Anna thought, that you could step on their skulls, and they would burst like rotten fruit. She supposed that, though re-animated, the biters were still decaying, their skin falling off their bones, their bones becoming brittle, transitioning to dust. It was both sickening and satisfying to watch the biters' heads explode, like popping a zit, the kind that made a cracking noise and splattered the mirror.

During the carnage, Anna and the clone polished off three pepperoni pizzas and four bottles of wine. Sated, inebriated, and pacified by extreme violence, they didn't hear the voice until one of those reflective moments in the show, when a character looks sadly at a biter, recognizing someone they once knew who is now undead and whose mouth is stuffed boorishly with lasagna-like entrails. In the ensuing silence, Anna and the clone heard someone shouting outside the building. While Anna hit the pause button, the clone strode to the window.

"There's a girl in the garden," the clone said.

Anna rose woozily to a sitting position. "What?"

"She's not really in the garden, more like the lawn, and she's yelling at the building."

Anna stiffly joined the clone at the window, and they both gazed down at a woman in a green parka jumping up and down on the lawn, crushing the border of chrysanthemums near the walkway. She shouted obscenities into the frosty air, her warm breath creating clouds around words like *cunt* and *hussy* and *slut*.

"Maybe she's selling Girl Scout cookies," Anna said drunkenly.

"It's not the best pitch," the clone said, "but I'd still buy them."

"I know," Anna said. "I wish I'd thought of dessert. Maybe one of the others will bring home pumpkin pie."

"I've never had pumpkin pie."

"It's really good."

The woman's voice interrupted them with a torrent of slurs, followed by what Anna thought was her own name.

"Did she just say *Anna*?" Anna asked.

"That or banana." The clone retrieved her crossbow from the couch and returned to Anna's side. "Should I take her out?" The clone loaded the crossbow, careful to keep her right hand on the stock, then motioned for Anna to open the window.

Anna pushed the crossbow in the opposite direction. "You're not shooting anyone. On Monday, you're taking that damn thing back to archives."

"Fine," the clone sulked.

The woman in the green parka fell silent as an old woman in a pair of pink earmuffs started up the sidewalk to the apartment complex. Anna and the clone watched the old woman speed up to pass the woman in the green parka, who fell silent, her head tilting this way and that, following the old woman's progress along the path. The old woman carried a heavy stoneware pot with the lid taped shut. Once she got to the front door, she balanced the pot on her hip and pressed the button to the apartment where she would bestow what was likely a massive casserole.

The other woman hung back but paid close attention. She looked vaguely familiar to Anna. Maybe a professor or administrator from one of the colleges? A parent? But what would she be doing here? In her wine fugue, Anna's memory failed her, but she had a bad feeling that only increased the more she observed the woman. It wasn't just her potty mouth or strange familiarity; it was the intensity with which she glared at the old woman and her casserole. She was waiting, tensed, like a hawk hunting a vole.

Once the buzzer sounded, the old woman opened the door. At the same instant, the woman in the green parka shot forward, charging the door and hurling the old woman aside. The casserole fell to the ground, the stoneware breaking into big shards and spilling creamy green beans that steamed on the frigid front steps.

"Where do you think she's going?" The clone ran swiftly across the apartment and opened the door. "Is she coming here?"

"I don't know," Anna said. "Close the door."

They both heard shouting from the stairwell, then a burst of fresh expletives at the end of the hallway. "You!" The voice rang out clear and moving closer. "You're dead!"

Anna yanked the clone back into the apartment and slammed the door shut. Her hands shook as she fumbled with the chain.

The woman yelled only a few inches from Anna's head on the other side of the door. "I know you're in there. I saw your face! You little slut!"

Anna's fingers turned to mozzarella sticks, rubbery, unable to secure the chain. "I don't know you," she told the woman through the door. "You must have made a mistake. I've already called the police. You should leave now."

"Is he in there? Is he with you? I swear I'll kill you both!"

Anna was about to make good on her threat and call the police, but the next series of events happened very quickly. First, the woman kicked the door in, knocking Anna #1 to the ground and sending her medieval crossbow shuttling across the room. Then Anna, who had somehow avoided the flying door, ran for her phone, hurrying to the couch and thrusting aside empty pizza boxes in search of the device.

The intruder paused and stared at the dingy apartment. The soiled napkins and spilled parmesan packets, the empty wine bottles and a biter frozen on the television screen, a live rat in his mouth. Then she went straight for Anna.

Both hands closed around Anna's throat, cutting off her air supply. Anna flailed at the woman whose grip only tightened. When Anna #1 got to her feet and tried to attack the woman from behind, to pull her off Anna, the woman kicked out a long leg and sent the clone spinning through the air until she hit the coffee table. As the clone crashed to the floor, her head smacked against the wood with an icky thud, and Anna was glad that the clone was not a biter, or her head would have burst like a water balloon.

"You little bitch," the woman hissed. "You ruined my life."

Up close, Anna took in the woman's long, broad face, her big, squared teeth and flared nostrils, and suddenly she remembered where she had seen her. It was the horsey blonde, the Dean's wife, from the photo in his office. But why would the Dean's wife be choking her and wrecking her zombie-movie marathon?

She tried to pry the woman's fingers from her windpipe, snagging and scratching, but the woman would not let go. Anna twisted left, then right, but she couldn't gain any leverage. The Dean's wife was tall and strong, a Nordic Valkyrie, probably a cross-country skier and possibly an Olympic rope-climber. So, Anna gave up. She stopped fighting and went limp. The sudden dead weight surprised the Dean's wife, and she released Anna, letting her tumble to the floor.

Anna took in a few ragged breaths before making her move, the only move she could make against a Valkyrie, a low blow. She punched the woman beneath her parka, her fist a tiny stone jammed directly into the woman's groin. It wasn't as successful as it would have been with a man, but the woman still grunted in pain and doubled over. Anna took her advantage. She grabbed a fistful of the woman's hair and dragged the Dean's wife to the door. The plan, which was only now forming in Anna's mind, was to throw Dean's wife out in the hall, secure the door, then call the police.

As Anna grasped the doorknob, the Dean's wife wrenched her head away, leaving Anna with a fistful of white-blonde hair. The pain must have enraged her further because she lunged at Anna with renewed fury. She shoved Anna away from the door, then landed a sharp blow on Anna's left ear. Then she hit the right side twice as hard. Anna's ears went numb. Everything became muffled, like she was underwater. She felt the Dean's wife take a chunk of her hair and pull her head back, no doubt returning the favor, but instead of ripping Anna's hair out, she used it to hold Anna's head in place.

Then the Dean's wife swung hard with her fist, connecting with Anna's cheekbone. The pain was so intense, Anna felt wine and red sauce sluice back up her throat, but she swallowed it. Damn it! She should have projectile vomited, like one of those Amazonian frogs or tiny dinosaurs, then she could have blinded or incapacitated her attacker. Now it was too late. The Dean's wife tightened her hold on

Anna's scalp before jabbing again and again, aiming and connecting with Anna's nose. There was a wet crunch and Anna's mouth filled blood. Her eyes were squeezed shut, and what she saw when she peeked out at the world—the world consisting entirely of the Dean's wife's fist—was murky and misshapen and tinted scarlet. She closed her eyes again as the Dean's wife continued to pummel her with quick, severe punches.

Anna seemed to have forgotten her hands, her legs, her voice. How to use them. How to defend herself. She and Nikki had taken a Krav Maga class years ago, and now all Anna could remember was an old man in boxing shorts telling her that she walked like someone afraid of confrontation. She hadn't argued with him.

Between blows, Anna tried to speak, but it was unlikely the Dean's wife heard much less understood her, so she was surprised when the woman stopped to answer a question.

"Why?" the Dean's wife panted. "You want to know why? Because you slept with my husband."

When Anna attempted to explain that she would never sleep with a man so repulsive, such an entitled asshole, the words that came from her brain were jumbled and her mouth was unwilling to form them, so she just shook head back and forth, its heavy weight made it feel as if she was wearing a mascot's head over her own.

The Dean's wife pointed angrily at the tulips on the kitchen table. "Don't lie. I saw him give you those."

Then she released Anna's head and stalked to the kitchen. Anna stumbled to the door. She couldn't get her fingers to close around the handle. Then suddenly there were two door handles. No, three. And they were moving, rotating slowly in halo of light. She threw up onto her slippered feet.

When the vase of tulips came down on the back of her head, two things occurred to Anna before her knees buckled and she blacked out. The first was that her phone was in her pocket. It had been there since she ordered pizza. The second was that someone had let Daryl Dixon into her apartment because he was taking out his bowie knife and plunging it through the top of a biter's head. No, it was the Dean's wife's head. The bottom of the blade jutted out just beneath her chin, blood stippling the wallpaper.

Anna returned to consciousness in a puddle of her own sick and a scattering of flower petals. The Dean's wife was trying to open her mouth and scream but couldn't because a bowie knife had skewered her mouth shut.

"Oh shit," Anna said thickly, or thought she said, or tried to say. "We have to call 911."

She pulled the phone from her pocket and stared at the numbers requesting her private code. They were doubled and dancing, like the doorknob, and when she tried to hit the number seven, her finger missed the phone by several inches. Fuck it, she couldn't remember the rest of the code anyway.

"Give me that." Anna #1 took the phone from Anna and pocketed it in her army jacket. "Nobody's calling 911."

The Dean's wife whimpered, and Anna saw that while one of her eyes was closed, the other was wide open and darting wildly around the room, like a hornet looking for something to bite.

The clone took the handle of the bowie knife and pulled, but the blade was stuck in the woman's head.

"Damn it," the clone said. "I need to work my brachialis muscles. I've been spending too much time on biceps."

"I think we're supposed to leave it there," Anna gasped. "For the doctors to remove."

The clone ignored her and placed her foot on the Dean's wife's head, then used the leverage to pull the knife out. Blood bubbled from the woman's mouth as the blade heaved its way out, emerging from the top of her head with a popping sound like a champagne cork. The clone held the knife aloft for a moment, as triumphant as Arthur pulling the Sword from the Stone, then wiped pinkish brain matter from the blade onto the woman's green parka. Anna vomited again, though there really wasn't anything left in her stomach.

The Dean's wife's single open eye blinked erratically. Then her left leg shot out while the right remained inert, half of her wanting to run, the other half dead. Blood seeped from the hole in her head, and a small pool of urine grew beneath her parka.

"911." Anna stood up shakily, her hand braced against the couch for balance, just as the clone reappeared with her crossbow.

"911," Anna gasped again, relieved she could finally hear herself, though everything sounded like after a concert, as if her ears were in a different room.

"And what will we tell them?" the clone asked, loading the cross-bow. "That Thanksgiving festivities got out of hand?"

Anna blinked. It hurt like hell. "It was self-defense. She attacked me. You stopped her. I'll back you up."

"Which *I* do you mean, *you* or *me*?" the clone said.

"I mean..." Anna paused. "That is..." The clone had a point. She would have to explain her double to the police. But maybe, with her face so busted up and swollen, she and Anna #1 would no longer look alike. Although there were the other clones to consider. How would she explain them? Anna's brain hurt. There was a logic somewhere that didn't involve killing the Dean's wife with a crossbow, but she couldn't find it.

Anna #1 stared down at the Dean's wife in an appraising manner. The woman looked like roadkill. The clone lifted the crossbow and took aim. The Dean's wife tried to put up a hand to shield her face, but her brain misfired again, and the hand landed defensively on a slice of pepperoni pizza.

"She's not a pheasant," Anna screamed.

The arrow released like a bullet, piercing the Dean's wife through her wide forehead, the tip burying itself deep in the anterior of her skull. It wasn't like shooting a biter on *The Walking Dead*. There was less gore, but more horror. The Dean's wife trembled all over, her arms and legs thrashing around, foam spraying from her lips as she tried to scream, but only opened and closed her mouth soundlessly like a fish thrown onto a dock.

When it was finally over, the thrashing and foaming replaced by total stillness, Anna and the clone were holding hands tightly.

"Should we check?" Anna whispered. "To be sure?"

The clone knelt and carefully put her fingers on the carotid artery. "Gone."

When the clone left the room, Anna covered the Dean's wife's face with a paper napkin from the pizzeria. She could hear the clone digging in the hallway closet, but she didn't join her. Anna's nose throbbed, and her tongue kept finding an empty place where a molar had been. Had she swallowed it?

The clone returned with a two-person pop-up tent. She unfurled the polyester frame and spread it across the living room floor.

"Come on, help me," the clone said in a hard voice.

Anna forced her legs to move, then squatted next to the clone.

"Is this like a tortilla?" Anna asked.

"Just help me roll the bitch up," the clone said.

Anna helped the clone secure the Dean's wife snugly inside the fabric with duct tape.

"How do we get her out of here?" Anna said. "We can't just drag her through the door."

"We're not dragging her."

The clone motioned impatiently for Anna to come closer so they could lift the body together. The clone got down on one knee, and Anna mirrored her, wincing as the weight of her knee touched the floor. Anna's muscles wailed and she thought she might vomit again, but somehow, she braced herself to lift. Anna and the clone raised the body awkwardly, then each propped the dead weight onto one shoulder and leaned in to distributed it evenly between them. Anna stifled a cry of pain as they both rose to their feet.

They began the vertiginous shuffle into the hall, then paused in the doorway.

"I can't," Anna hissed. "Someone's going to see us."

"It's dark," the clone said.

"This is a body," Anna said.

"Stop overthinking this," the clone said.

When the clone forged ahead, Anna had no choice but to follow her or else let the body drop. For the first time since she moved to the apartment complex, Anna was grateful for the grimy shag rug in the hallway because it muffled their footsteps. Hefting the Dean's wife between them, they made it to the end of the hall without running into anyone. But when they opened the door to the stairwell, the old woman whose casserole pot had broken earlier was coming down the staircase, gripping the handrail in one hand and a single foil-covered plate in the other.

"What's that?" she said, pointing at the body. "Leftovers?"

"Yes," the clone said, "lots of leftovers."

"Your friend's nose is bleeding," the old woman said.

Anna checked her nose, but the blood was coming from a gap in the tarp. She tried to close it with her hand.

"I'm sorry about your dinnerware," the clone said to the old woman.

"Some people have no manners." The old woman held the front door open, and Anna and the clone two-stepped the body into the November night.

"No ma'am, they don't," the clone said.

"You young ladies have a happy holiday." The old woman secured her pink earmuffs onto her head and disappeared down the sidewalk.

In the brisk air, Anna's head felt clearer, even if the pounding in her temples hadn't stopped. She looked up at the night sky and thought she saw Orion's Belt. She couldn't remember if Orion was the archer, or if the archer was the centaur, but she was certain she saw some hunter pointing an arrow into a galaxy of stars. She remembered the clone positioning the crossbow and swallowed hard.

The clone took a small device from her pocket and pressed it. A nearby pair of headlights flashed, and car doors beeped as they unlocked.

"Awesome," the clone said. "She has a hatchback."

"Had," Anna whispered.

The clone ignored her and popped opened the back. She leaned the body against Anna while she put down the backseats to create more space. After they rolled the Dean's wife in, her head bouncing twice against the bumper, Anna and the clone tucked the tarp around the body. Then the clone placed a blanket over her, an ancient quilt found in the corner of the trunk and covered with white dog hair.

"She had a dog," Anna said sadly.

"Too bad she didn't think to bring it with her." The clone headed for the driver's side and settled in behind the wheel. "She might have stood a chance."

"You don't know how to drive," Anna said.

The clone scowled. "I can do a lot of things you don't know about."

"You don't have a license," Anna protested. "And you're drunk. And there's a body in the backseat."

"I'll let you pick the music."

Anna and the clone listened to Blondie as they drove down the quiet streets on Thanksgiving night. Anna was surprised by how many people had already put up holiday displays. Every street had houses with blinking icicle lights, illuminated wreaths, inflatable Frosties and Santa Clauses, and glowing nativity scenes, where the Baby Jesus outshone the rest of the manger crowd, radiant in his extra voltage.

As the clone sang along to "Hanging on the Telephone," Anna bent forward, flinching when the seatbelt pulled at her neck, and opened the glove compartment. The Dean's wife had a first-aid kit, a flashlight, toothpaste, a granola bar, and several packets of sauce from Chipotle. Anna thought of the Dean and his stupid burrito bowl.

"What did she see in him?" Anna asked.

The clone turned down the music, then tore open the granola bar. "Which one?"

It's true, Anna thought, two women had found something attractive in the swing-a-dead-cat Dean, had seen someone besides an insensitive jerk with cheap taste in food. "I can't believe Anna is introducing him to my family."

"You could have gone yourself," the clone said. "It's your house, your family, your holiday tradition."

"My mom likes Anna #3 better."

The clone stopped short at a red light and the body pitched forward, hitting the back of Anna's passenger seat.

The clone turned and looked at Anna. "Jesus Christ, your face."

Anna touched her hugely swollen cheek. She didn't need to ask to know how bad it must look.

"Family isn't about liking people," the clone said, a little hoarsely. "It's about blood. Why do you think I haven't killed you and assumed your identity?"

"You were going to kill me?" Anna said.

"It'd be easy enough," the clone said. "Easier than this one." She tipped her head towards the Dean's wife. "The point is, I could've done it ten times over by now, but I didn't. Why do you think that is?"

The light turned green, and the clone accelerated.

"Because," Anna said, "murder is morally reprehensible and illegal?"

The clone flicked Anna's swollen cheek.

"Ouch."

"Because," the clone said, "you're my blood. It's thicker than water."

Anna thought about her mother and Anna #3. She imagined the two of them adding pecans and celery and stale chunks of seasoned bread to her mother's signature turkey stuffing. It made her want to punch something.

The clone eased down on the brake, and Anna peered out the passenger window. They were at the business college, parked outside a brick building in an empty lot. Anna suspected it was the admissions building. Before she could ask, the clone had the hatchback open and was unloading the Dean's wife onto the asphalt.

"What are we doing here?" Anna said. "We can't leave her here. This isn't even her husband's college."

"I have a plan. Will you trust me?"

"Trust you? You were planning on killing me and taking my identity."

"I sure as shit don't want it now," the clone said, grappling with the body. A curled and waxy hand popped out of the tarp. Anna jumped back as if it were a tarantula. The clone stuffed it back inside.

"Your identity," the clone spun around, "is murderer. Your fingerprints are all over the crime scene. And the weapon. I wouldn't want to be you for all the money in the world."

"They're your fingerprints," Anna said. "You killed her."

"No, they're yours, dummy. You killed her."

Defiantly, Anna searched her concussed brain for a riposte. "Well, uh, then you could just as easily end up in prison for the crime as me. No one would know the difference."

"That would never happen," the clone said darkly, looking right at Anna. "Get out and help me. She's heavy, and she's getting stiff."

Trembling, Anna got of the car and helped the clone hoist the body back up between them. They walked like that for a while, like two huntsmen readying to field dress a carcass. Anna wondered what the clone had in mind for ditching the body. Leaving it on a bench? Adding a cadaver to the science lab? Placing it in the cafeteria freezer next to the tater tots? She trundled after the clone in the darkness, her aching feet faltering over rocky pavement with her armload of corpse.

Skirting the edge of campus, near the chapel, the clone veered left, ducking into a small forested area Anna hadn't noticed before. The seclusion of the woods, the way the branches and trunks and saplings enveloped Anna and the clone and the body, made her feel instantly safer. The stars were visible through the night-time canopy of bare maple and birch branches. The last of the autumn crickets chirped a requiem, the sturdy ones who survived the first frost and understood mortality enough to eat their frozen comrades.

"What do we do now?" Anna asked.

"The comparative lit majors created a peace garden before the school cut funding." The clone halted beneath a crab-apple tree, and

Anna could see past her to shadows of lilac bushes and hydrangeas. "It's gone wild since. Not many business and marketing majors want to pull weeds."

Anna reached out to touch a bloom now transformed into a rose-hip, tight and shiny in the starlight. She closed her eyes, let her head thrum. She wanted the weight of Dean's wife off her shoulders, off her conscience.

"When I first came here, it was completely overgrown, but I put it back in order," the clone said. "Now it serves a purpose."

Anna was surprised by the pride she heard in the clone's voice. Was this clone the same one who decapitated characters in video games and shot pheasants, and now humans, with a crossbow?

"What are those?" Anna pointed to several mounds of dirt. "Daffodils or tulips?"

"Truants," the clone said.

"I haven't heard of those," Anna said. "Are they in the same genus as tulips?"

"They're in the delinquent genus."

The clone crouched to set the body on the ground, and Anna followed suit. They laid the Dean's wife onto the damp earth and the clone picked up a shovel. Anna hadn't noticed that beside the mound of dirt where they were standing, there was a deep hole, which she almost fell into.

"Careful." The clone grabbed her arm and steadied her. "That one's not for you."

Anna stared into the hole. It looked very much like an open grave. "This is too deep for perennials," she said.

"I was going to bury Cody on Tuesday," the clone said.

"What did you say?"

"But I haven't got around to killing him yet, so we've got this space all ready for us."

Anna turned in a circle, once, twice, taking in the length of each mound, the number of them. Five in total. A chill that had nothing to do with the dropping air temperature crept down her spine. "You've been killing students?" she said. "For being truants?"

"Hey, it's his seventh absence. He still blames it on stomach issues. He doesn't even offer a doctor's note. Not even a fake one."

"So, you killed him?" Anna said.

"*Will* kill him. And now I'll have to dig another grave."

Anna thought her head couldn't hurt any worse, but now the pain made her skull feel cramped and screwed on wrong, ready to explode into shards all over the shriveled marigolds and tombless graves.

"Why don't you just fail him?"

The clone sighed. "The provost told us not to fail students. It hurts college retention rates."

Anna looked at the graves. Five students dead. Five students who weren't going home for Thanksgiving break, who wouldn't get to turn down cranberry sauce and sleep past noon and ignore homework and let their mother do all their laundry. If there was a moment for cloner's remorse, this was it.

"If it makes you feel any better," the clone offered, "Cody also texts in class beneath the table when he thinks I can't see him."

"I hate that," Anna said.

She couldn't bring herself to help the clone push the Dean's wife into the hole, though she heard the body hit the bottom with a conclusive thump. Then the clone covered the Dean's wife with dirt, shoveling with gusto, and soon the grave was filled.

"Should we say a few words?" Anna asked.

But the clone was already walking back to the car.

The apartment was dark when they got back. Anna reached for the lamp, but then changed her mind. She didn't want to see the broken glass or the crossbow or the blood or the empty bottles of wine. She knew everything would have to be cleaned up, the evidence removed, the car abandoned. The clone had told her as much on the drive home. But right now, all Anna wanted was to wade through the cluttered darkness and climb into her bed and press the less-bloodied side of her face to the pillow and sleep forever.

"Shouldn't the other two be back by now?" the clone asked. She didn't move to turn on a lamp either.

Anna imagined Anna #2 still serving slices of pie to the last round of hobos, while Anna #3, the one responsible for the mess they would soon be scrubbing from the vinyl wood-textured flooring panels, was likely enjoying a post-dinner *digestif* with her family.

"Anyway, it's better like this," the clone said. "The less they know."

Anna nodded, though the clone probably couldn't see her in the dark. They breathed together in silence for a moment. Then they both heard faint sobbing.

Anna froze. "Who's there?"

When the answer was simply an increase in sobbing, Anna finally switched on a lamp. They found Anna #2 curled on the sofa, her back to them, weeping uncontrollably into her knees.

"What's wrong?" Anna #1 rushed to her fellow clone. "I told you it would be depressing to work with a bunch of homeless people. Some of them probably had kids. Or lice. You should have stayed here with us."

"Is that his blood?" Anna #2 turned her blotchy, tear-stained face to them. "How could you let it happen?" She gulped for air in between sobs. "How could you?"

Anna and Anna #1 exchanged a long, worried look.

"The blood came from pheasant hunting," Anna said quickly. "I'm sorry we didn't clean it up before you came home." She trotted into the kitchen and returned with a rag rug that she tossed over the blood and piss and vomit. It covered the mess better than she expected.

"Liars!" Anna #2 uncurled her body to reveal what she had been wrapped around so protectively. It was Tipsy. His orange fur was mussed and matted from the snug embrace.

"He ate the tulips," Anna #2 yelled. "Why were they on the floor? The tulips were supposed to stay on top of the fridge so he couldn't get them. He's dead! You killed him! You're both murderers!"

Anna fought the urge to cover the clone's mouth. All she needed was more attention from the neighbors, who had already heard thuds and screams and loud allegations of adultery and now felicide.

"We didn't kill him." Anna swallowed hard, swallowed tears. She loved Tipsy, too. They had been together since she left college, through two moves, and the break-up with Doug. In fact, she loved Tipsy so much that she didn't mind when he loved her clone more than her. If anyone was to blame for Tipsy's death, it was the Dean's wife, who had clocked her on the back of the head with the vase, or else Anna #3 for accepting tulips from the deceitful Dean. But she had not killed her cat. She was not a monster.

"I brought him giblets and gravy," Anna #2 wailed. "Now he'll never know I kept my promise."

Anna #1 patted the grieving clone gently on the back as Anna removed Tipsy from Anna #2's lap with a quilt that she pulled off the back of the sofa. Anna wrapped the old cat up and held him like a baby. Tulip petals were caught in his whiskers. She plucked them out.

"At least he died doing something he loved," Anna #1 said.

"Eating poisonous flowers?" Anna #2 cried.

"There are worse ways to go," Anna #1 replied. "Believe me."

Anna #2 rubbed the tears from her eyes. "I called Nikki from the neighbor's phone. She's coming over with her equipment so she can clone him. She said I can have him back just the way he was. As good as new."

Anna shivered. Not at the thought of Nikki coming over and seeing the crime scene. In fact, Nikki would probably have excellent advice about removing evidence, but she couldn't let Nikki create another clone. She sat down next to Anna #2 and pressed her shoulder to her clone's shoulder.

"It doesn't work that way," she said. "He won't be the same cat."

"Yes, he will," Anna #2 said. "Nikki told me he'd be identical. Same color, same snaggle tooth, same everything."

"Sure, he'll look like Tipsy," Anna admitted, "but he won't be Tipsy. Like you and me. You look like me, but does that mean you're exactly like me?"

Anna #2 stroked Tipsy through the quilt in Anna's arms. "Maybe he'll be even b-better than b-b-before," she sniffled.

"Maybe," Anna said. "You're a better version of me. You're a better cat owner. You put ice cubes in his water. You groomed him every day. You remembered his giblets."

Anna #2 bent her head and wept into her hands.

"And you feed homeless people," Anna continued. "And you're a better writer. I never would have thought of that ending, with the university president taking bribes from rich parents to admit their slow-witted children. So much corruption and hypocrisy. It was a real page-turner." She did not hide the envy in her voice.

The door opened. All six eyes jumped to Anna #3 as she trundled inside, carrying several Tupperware containers and another bouquet of tulips.

Anna #2 pointed in horror at the flowers. "Murderer," she mouthed.

Anna #3 swirled to the kitchen and dropped her purse and bouquet and Tupperware on the table. "The front door is broken," she chirped over her shoulder. "I was able to just walk into the apartment building. You should probably call the landlord…" Her voice trailed off when she got a good look at the living room: three Annas huddled on the couch, delicately caressing a bundle of quilt. "What happened?"

"Tipsy died from eating tulips," Anna said.

"Your tulips," Anna #1 added.

"That's not possible. I was careful. I left them on the table."

"They were supposed to be on top of the fridge," Anna #2 screeched.

"Oh shit." Anna #3 sprinted to the couch and put her arms around Anna #2. "I'm so sorry," she said, stroking Anna #2's hair and kissing her head repeatedly before squeezing herself in between Anna and Anna #2 on the couch. Anna realized they had not been this close since that awkward first week, when they ate pizza and watched their first rom-com. This time, instead of feeling their closeness, their sameness, Anna felt their separateness, their individuality. No longer was each clone a tabula rasa.

"You can't clone Tipsy," Anna said.

"Why not?" Anna #2 said.

"You may get the new and improved Tipsy," Anna said. "Maybe this time he won't try to eat bees or pee in corners or become morbidly obese. But it won't be him that you love, because Tipsy's gone, and you can't clone him back into existence."

Anna #2 nodded sadly and relaxed her hand on the quilt. Then she recited the "Hail Mary" over Tipsy's body. To Anna's surprise, the other clones joined in the prayer and in Anna #2's subsequent tears. Then Anna cried, too, because Tipsy's death, preventable and private and final, was somehow much sadder than any of the bloody business that afternoon. And by the time there was a knock on the door, Anna and the clones had decided they would tell Nikki not to take a DNA sample from Tipsy, but instead invite her to the burial.

Anna set Tipsy down on the sofa between the clones and carefully dabbed tears from her bruised face. She was looking forward to seeing Nikki. She craved a friendly and familiar face, particularly one that was not her own. As Anna opened the door, someone on the other side pushed hard, causing the door to slam into her raised arms. She fell back into the apartment.

"Where is she?" a tall figure demanded. He stepped inside and closed the door behind him.

Anna's heart squeezed. It's the police, she thought. But when the figure moved into the lamplight, he was wearing an ill-fitting brown suit, not a uniform. She might not have recognized him as the Dean straight away except for his ponytail that couldn't decide between *founding father* or *aging rocker*.

"Sweetheart!" Anna #3 leapt off the couch to embrace him, but he elbowed her away.

"I got a text from my wife," he said, shaking his phone at Anna #3. "It must have been delayed. Your family's stupid fucking wi-fi. It was sent hours ago. She said she was coming here. Have you seen her?"

Anna stayed on the floor. She wanted to crawl away. Instead, she kept her head down, only risking a quick glance at the couch. Thankfully, Anna #1 had the good sense to disappear and Anna #2 buried her face in the quilt.

"No," Anna #3 said. "I haven't seen her. You only dropped me off ten minutes ago." She rubbed his arm up and down in a soothing manner. "I know you wanted to wait until after the holidays to ask for a divorce."

The Dean snorted. "There's not going to be any divorce. My wife can't find out about us. She'd kill me. She'd probably kill you too."

"But you promised," Anna #3 said.

"Listen," the Dean said. "It was a fling. It's over."

"You just met my family." Anna #3's body shook. "You spent Thanksgiving with them. You pulled the wishbone with Aunt Tattie."

The Dean smirked. "Yeah, I made a wish that Aunt Tattie was dead."

His gaze shifted to the couch. Anna #2 lifted her head and stared at him full on. The Dean took a step back.

"Who the hell is that?"

Anna tried to keep her face averted. "We're sisters," she said, praying he would not come any closer.

He crouched down to where Anna sat in the floor and lifted her chin up sharply. "Who the fuck are you? Who the fuck are all of you?"

Anna #1 stepped out of the shadows. "We're Anna," she said, lifting the crossbow and taking aim at the Dean, "multiplied."

"Stay away from me." The Dean jumped back, then snatched Anna #3 by the arm, twisting it up behind her. "I'll break her arm."

"Happy Thanksgiving!" Nikki's cheerful voice trilled in from the hallway as she pushed open the door. The Dean moved hurriedly behind it, covering Anna #3's mouth with his hand. Nikki was wearing a stylish burgundy trench coat and lifting a pie tin triumphantly. "I brought you all slices of my mom's pecan—"

The Dean shoved Anna #3 away from him. She slammed against the wall, her head knocking hard against it. Anna #1 moved closer, the crossbow loaded and ready to fire. Then the Dean reached around the door and clutched Nikki by the hair. She screamed and the pie fell. He swung Nikki into Anna #1, and the two women smashed into each other. The sound of a crossbow releasing made Anna scramble to her feet as both Anna #1 and Nikki crumpled to a heap on the floor.

"You monster!" Anna #2 shouted. She charged at the Dean, her fists extended to fight, but he slapped them away and punched her hard in the face. She dropped like a stunned bird against glass.

Then it was just Anna and the Dean, as it had been months ago in his office. He lunged at her. Anna leapt away.

"You stupid bitch," he said. "You're fired."

Anna backed up all the way to the couch. She looked down at the quilted form of Tipsy. Then she tore the blanket off her dead cat. Weeping, she grabbed him firmly by the striped tail. She lifted Tipsy into the air, his body much heavier and less rigid than she thought it would be, so that she had to swing him around and around her head before the momentum made him straighten out. She moved toward the Dean, and he took several steps back, his eyes never leaving the whirling cat.

She swung Tipsy faster and faster above her head until he was a helicopter, a blur of orange and white fur cutting through the air. Then Anna released him. The dead cat went sailing with formidable speed at the Dean's head before emitting an ear-splitting yowl that reverberated around the apartment. Then Tipsy hit the Dean with such force that he flew backwards into the kitchen, skimming across the tiles, and hurtling into the bottom of the refrigerator.

Anna #2 rushed past Anna to where the Dean lay unconscious on the kitchen floor. Tipsy, his heart now galvanized back into a living rhythm, had extended his claws to grasp the dean's ponytail, tearing into his scalp, and biting down hard on the man's large, bony nose.

"My little love," Anna #2 crowed. "It's a miracle!"

She lifted Tipsy from the Dean, but not before the cat emptied his stomach of tulip petals onto the Dean's face. Anna #2 hugged Tipsy to her chest, and he hugged her back, strands of the Dean's long gray hair interwoven in his claws.

Soon, Anna and Anna #2 were joined by Anna #3, rubbing her sore head, and then eventually Nikki, who had an arrow sticking out of the top of her shoulder, though she insisted it was no big deal. Then Anna #1 appeared with her crossbow. They all stared down at the Dean.

"I'll do it," Anna said. She reached for the crossbow.

Shannon Scott is an adjunct Professor of English at Hamline University, Augsburg University, and the University of St. Thomas. She has published essays, stories, and book reviews in various academic publications and popular journals. Her essays, "Imperial Pets: Monkey-Girls, Man-Cubs, and Dog-Faced Boys on Exhibition in Victorian Britain" and "Wild Sanctuary: Running into the Forest in Russian Fairy Tales" were recently published by Routledge and Manchester University Press. In 2013, she co-edited the collection, Terrifying Transformations: An Anthology of Victorian Werewolf Fiction, 1838-1896. In 2019, her story "American House Spider" was published in the anthology Nightscript.

 # ABOUT THE EDITOR

A S A MILITARY JOURNALIST, RACHEL A. BRUNE WROTE AND photographed the Army and its soldiers for five years. When she moved on, she didn't quit writing stories with soldiers in them, just added werewolves, sorcerers, a couple evil mad scientists, and a Fae or two. Now a full-time author and writing coach living in California, Rachel enjoys poking around former military installations and listening for the ghosts of old soldiers … or writing them into her latest short story. As the founder and chief editor of Crone Girls Press, her goal is to publish the best of dark speculative fiction and horror. In addition, she is a contributing editor to the **Writerpunk Press** anthology series, which benefits the PAWS no-kill animal shelter in Lynnwood, WA. She lives with her spouse, two daughters, one reticent cat, and two flatulent rescue dogs.